THE LOST TREASURE OF DRAKON

ALSO BY NELLIE H. STEELE

Cate Kensie Mysteries
Shadow Slayers Stories
Lily & Cassie by the Sea Mysteries
Pearl Party Mysteries
Middle Age is Murder Cozy Mysteries
Duchess of Blackmoore Mysteries
Maggie Edwards Adventures
Clif & Ri on the Sea Adventures

THE LOST TREASURE OF DRAKON

A MAGGIE EDWARDS ADVENTURE

MAGGIE EDWARDS ADVENTURES
BOOK THREE

NELLIE H. STEELE

A Novel Idea Publishing

This is a work of fiction. Names, characters, places, and incidents either are the product of the author's imagination or are used fictitiously. Any resemblance to actual persons, living or dead, events, or locales is entirely coincidental.

Copyright © 2022 by Nellie H. Steele

All rights reserved.

No part of this book may be reproduced in any form or by any electronic or mechanical means, including information storage and retrieval systems, without written permission from the author, except for the use of brief quotations in a book review.

Cover design by Stephanie A. Sovak.

❦ Created with Vellum

For anyone who's had a vacation mishap

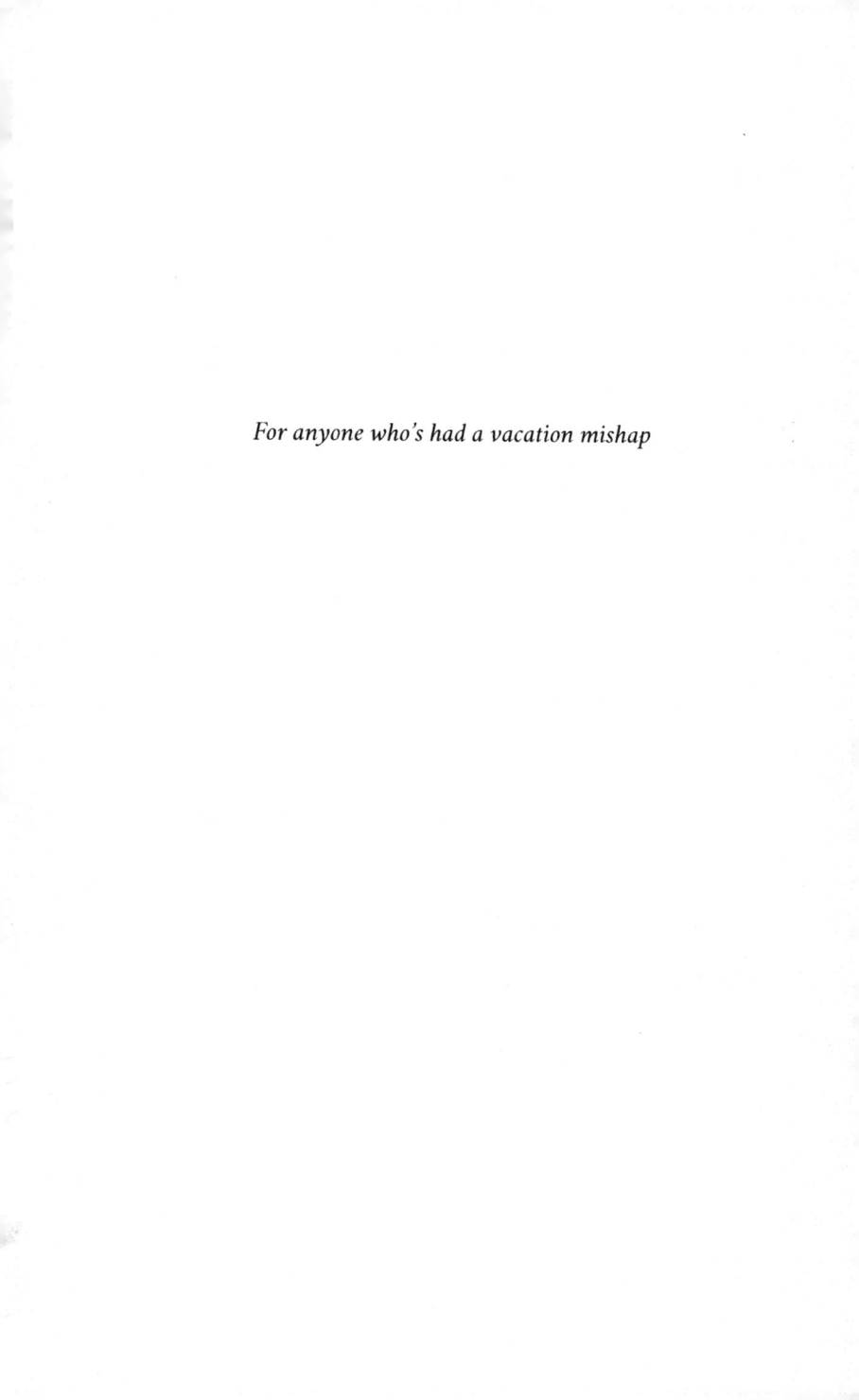

ACKNOWLEDGMENTS

A HUGE thank you to everyone who helped get this book published! Special shout outs to: Stephanie Sovak, Paul Sovak, Michelle Cheplic, Mark D'Angelo and Lori D'Angelo.

Finally, a HUGE thank you to you, the reader!

CHAPTER 1

"Maggie, we're going to be late," Henry shouted into the bedroom.

"We are NOT going to be late," Maggie called back. "I know exactly how long it takes to get to the airport from here. We have plenty of time."

"Buy whatever it is you're looking for when we get there. We're going to be late."

Maggie rolled her eyes and huffed.

"I saw that," Henry said, leaning against the door jamb and staring at her. He glanced at his watch before running his hand through his dirty blonde hair. "What are you doing, anyway?"

"Which pair?" Maggie asked. "These?" She slipped on a pair of large, cat-eye-shaped sunglasses with rhinestone embellishments. "Or these?" She pulled the cat-eye sunglasses off and switched them with a large, square, tortoiseshell pair.

Henry raised his open palm to the ceiling, waving it in front of him, and cringed. "Ummm," he stammered.

Maggie switched them again, directing her attention to

her mirror. She struck a pose, puckering her lips and arching an eyebrow.

"It's Scotland, princess," Henry said, "you may not even need them."

Maggie snapped her eyes toward him from behind the tortoiseshell frames. "Maybe I'll take them both."

"I hope the plane can get off the ground."

"Henry!" she exclaimed. "I didn't pack *that* much."

"Okay, okay, throw them both in. Let's just get going."

Maggie nodded and smiled as she tossed both pairs into her oversized tote carry-on. "It's so nice to be going on a trip I've actually planned with clothes I actually *want* to wear!" she said, as they strode into the living room of Maggie's apartment.

Henry proceeded toward the door, grinding to a halt when Maggie said, "Henry, can you grab this suitcase?"

"What?" he inquired, spinning to face her.

Maggie pointed toward a baby pink rolling hard-shell suitcase standing at her feet. Henry screwed up his face as he stared at it. "Another one?"

Maggie's jaw dropped open at the comment.

"I already took two down to the car!" he exclaimed, as he hurried across the room and grabbed hold of the handle.

"You said you were only taking a carry-on," she said, as Henry poked at the elevator button frantically.

"What's that have to do with anything?"

"If you aren't using your checked luggage space, someone should," Maggie said with a shrug.

She glanced around, her lips puckering as she stared down the hall. Henry noted her expression. "What?"

"Wonder who's moving in next door to me? I see painters in there. The last tenant was the sweetest little old lady. Quiet as a mouse. I hope it's someone like her."

Henry sighed as the elevator doors swooshed open.

THE LOST TREASURE OF DRAKON

"Finally!" He tugged Maggie into the elevator car and poked at the button for the ground floor.

"It won't go faster if you keep poking it," Maggie warned.

"It might," Henry shot back.

As the elevator eased to a stop, Henry ushered Maggie into and through the lobby of her apartment building. He tossed the last suitcase into the trunk of his car, parked just outside the main entrance.

Maggie hopped into the passenger's seat and buckled in. "Don't drive like a maniac," she cautioned, as Henry slid in behind the wheel. "We're not late."

"We are late, and I have never..."

"Driven like a maniac," they both finished.

"Yes, I know," Maggie said. "Yet we've been in two high-speed chases, and in both, you were the driver."

"I have no comment," Henry said, as he eased the car from the parking spot and onto the road. He accelerated in an attempt to make up for lost time. Maggie sighed from the passenger seat.

They arrived at the airport thirty minutes later. Henry dropped Maggie and her myriad of luggage at curbside check-in before he disappeared to park the car. He joined her within ten minutes.

They made it through security and to the gate with thirty minutes to spare before boarding began.

"See, I told you we had plenty of time," Maggie said, as they found the waiting area.

Maggie stopped short as the chairs came into view. Her eyes widened and her jaw gaped open.

"Oh, please don't tell me you forgot something," Henry said with a sigh.

"Why is *she* here?"

"Who?" Henry inquired as he scanned the seats. "Ohhhh."

He groaned as Maggie grabbed his arm and dragged him toward a strawberry blonde with her back to them.

"Emma?!" Maggie said, shock apparent in her voice.

"Maggie?!" Emma answered, as Maggie rounded the row of chairs and approached her.

"What are you doing here?" they asked at the same time.

Maggie frowned. "I am going on vacation to Scotland. What are *you* doing here?" She poked her finger toward Emma.

"Hi, Maggie," Ollie said from behind her.

"Ollie?" Henry questioned.

Ollie offered them a mock salute. "Fancy meeting you two here!" he jested.

"Uncle Ollie? What are you doing here?"

"We," he said, motioning to himself and Emma, "are heading to Scotland on some museum business."

"Really?" Maggie questioned, as she sank into one of the hard seats. "So soon after you started?" Maggie eyed Emma. Emma had recently accepted an assistant director position with the Rosemont Museum.

"When an opportunity comes up, you go," Emma said, her usual snarky attitude on display.

"I didn't think you'd take a flight this early for your vacation," Ollie said, as he sat across from Emma.

"We almost didn't," Henry replied, easing into the chair next to Ollie.

"We were *not* late," Maggie said. "And we didn't have much other choice. *Someone*–" She focused her gaze on Henry. "– *insisted* we fly early in the day, so we can get settled in, get a good night's sleep, and enjoy our first full day there."

Ollie nodded in response.

"Well, I'm glad to see you two on this flight," Henry said. "Will you have any free time when we're there? Maybe we could schedule something together."

Maggie widened her eyes and gave him the kill sign, until Emma glanced her way. She smiled sweetly at her. "Yeah, that'd be great. Why don't you all discuss it? I think I'll go grab a coffee. Anyone else?"

Everyone declined the offer and Maggie stalked off to find the nearest airport coffee shop. As she waited for her special order, a hand slipped around her waist and lips kissed her cheek. "You alright?" Henry asked.

"Yeah, I'm fine."

"You sure?"

"I just didn't expect Emma to be here. I just wanted a nice, relaxing vacation in the Scottish countryside. No bad guys, no guns, no car chases, no danger, no work. Just a relaxing time in a huge castle with an old friend."

"She's not going to Dunhaven, Maggie."

Maggie sighed. "I know. Although maybe she should."

Henry offered her a confused glance.

"I'm sure Uncle Ollie would love to see Cate. They used to work together at Aberdeen College."

"Oh, really?"

"Yeah, I told you. You must have been asleep when I was talking again." The barista handed Maggie her coffee, and they strolled back to the waiting area.

"Feel better?" Emma questioned, nodding to the coffee in her hands.

"Much. Hey, I was thinking, if you two have any time in your schedule, maybe you could head up to Dunhaven. I bet Cate would love to see you!"

"I don't know…" Emma hedged.

"Look, sorry about my reaction before," Maggie responded. "I was just surprised to see you, and Henry rushed me out the door this morning…"

"I did not," Henry objected.

"And I didn't get my coffee. And you know how I get when I don't have my coffee."

Emma winced, before puckering her lips and nodding. "Miserable."

"Right. Anyway, I'm sure there's a lovely B&B there. The town looks so cute. Come on, carve a little time out and come visit Cate!"

Ollie chuckled and began to answer, when the arrival of another person interrupted him.

Leo, sunglasses still on and leather travel bag clutched in his hand, slumped into a seat next to Ollie.

"Are you kidding me?" Maggie muttered. "What are you doing here?"

"Duty calls," Leo answered.

"Duty?" Maggie questioned, wrinkling her brows.

"Company business," Leo answered as he swiped at his phone, sliding his sunglasses up on his head. "Looking at a couple of potential products to bring into the lineup."

"Oh, I didn't realize you'd be leaving today!" Emma exclaimed, a bright smile on her face. "What a happy coincidence! Maybe we can carve some time out to do something together. Maggie suggested visiting Dunhaven, Scotland. An old professor of ours just moved into a castle there. Maybe we could check it out."

Maggie blinked her eyes at Emma and wrinkled her brow. Who was this cheery woman? Apparently, her relationship with Leo had blossomed after Maggie re-introduced them when she moved to Rosemont.

Leo raised his gaze from his phone screen, and a smile spread across his face. "I think I'd like that."

Maggie switched her gaze to Leo, a surprised expression forming on her face. She narrowed her eyes at him. Apparently, Leo was enjoying the relationship, too. She'd never known him to "carve out time" when "duty called" in the past. Maggie glanced across the aisle at Henry. With his eyes narrowed and a frown on his face, he stared at Leo.

"You know what," he said, leaping from the chair, "I think I need a coffee, too." He stalked from the waiting area. Maggie followed his departing form for a few seconds, before she hurried after him.

"You alright?" she questioned.

"Just fine, princess," he huffed.

With a coy expression, Maggie said, "He's not going to Dunhaven, Henry."

"Don't gloat," Henry answered, as he ordered a black coffee.

"What?" she questioned innocently. "I'm just pointing out the same thing you pointed out earlier."

"He might be going to Dunhaven. After you invited Emma, and then Emma invited him."

Maggie wrinkled her nose. "Sorry. But Cate says the castle is huge, so we can probably avoid them when they visit!"

Henry grumbled something unintelligible under his breath before taking another sip of his coffee.

"Come on, it won't be that bad. Let's head back," Maggie suggested.

They threaded through other travelers on their way back to the waiting area of their gate. As they approached it for the third time, Maggie froze. Her eyes went wide, and her jaw gaped open. The almost empty coffee cup slipped from her hand and thudded to the floor.

Henry gave her a questioning glance. "You okay?"

"Are you kidding me?" she questioned, staring straight ahead.

"What?" Henry asked, following the direction of her stare. "Oooooh."

In the seat Maggie had occupied moments ago, a head of

rainbow hair bobbed up and down in conversation. Next to her, a lanky, fair-haired Brit slouched in his chair with his arm draped around Piper's shoulders.

"What is going on here? Is all of Rosemont going to Scotland on this flight?"

Henry began to answer, when Maggie rushed toward their group.

"Piper?! Charlie?!" she exclaimed as she approached them. "What are you two doing here?"

"Hey, boss lady," Piper said. "Fancy seeing you here."

"Piper! That didn't answer my question. Are you going to Scotland?"

"We are, chicky," Charlie said, wiggling his eyebrows at her.

"When did you decide this? The last I heard, you were just hanging out on your week off and letting the newbies deal with the shop!"

"Rather a last-minute decision," Charlie answered.

Maggie raised her eyebrows at them, prodding for an explanation. "Last minute decision to travel to Scotland?" she questioned.

"Well," Piper said with a coy smile, "it *is* for our honeymoon."

Maggie offered an unimpressed glance, sticking her hand on her hip. "Honeymoon? Those typically occur *after* a wedding, not before."

Piper raised her eyebrows and shrugged. Charlie jumped from his seat and placed his hands on Maggie's arms. He guided her to a chair and eased her into it. He knelt in front of her. "Now, chicky, I realize this will come as a shock to you but… I am off the market."

Maggie pursed her lips and shook her head at him. "Yes, I know you and Piper are dating and–"

"No, no, chicky, not dating." He flashed his left hand. "Married."

Maggie's eyes went wide. "YOU GOT MARRIED?!" she shouted. Other conversations ground to a halt, and all eyes turned to Maggie. She offered an apologetic wave and a "sorry," before lowering her voice. "WHEN? WHERE? PIPER!"

"Last night," Piper said.

"Oh, wow! Best wishes, Piper!" Emma said. Ollie, Leo and Henry joined in to offer their best wishes to the happy couple.

Maggie, still wide-eyed, shook her head in response.

Piper shrugged. "When you know, you know."

Maggie still sat stunned, but after a moment, she stood and wrapped Charlie in a hug. "I know it's a terrible blow, chicky."

"I'll live," she said, as she kissed him on the cheek and offered her congratulations.

"Ugh," Piper mumbled as Maggie pulled her into an embrace. Maggie wiped a tear away that had trickled down her cheek.

"I just wish I'd have known. I could have…"

"Rented a ginormous hall and worn a killer dress. Yeah, I know. Thing is, we didn't want that. We just… wanted to get married, and we did. At the JOP last night."

"And then we scored some cheap seats on this last-minute flight, and we've got a honeymoon," Charlie added.

"Wow," Maggie murmured, still parsing through the latest events.

Charlie grinned at her. "And this isn't even the most exciting news, chicky," he said, wiggling his eyebrows again.

Maggie's jaw dropped. She attempted to formulate words to inquire when the announcement to board came over the PA system.

"That's us," Henry said.

"Figures you'd fly first class," Emma said.

Maggie pulled her lips into a thin line and rolled her eyes. "I have been on enough cargo planes in the last year to warrant a first-class seat across the pond."

Henry grabbed Maggie's bag and hand.

"Wait… their news…" She stumbled as Henry dragged her to the gate.

"We'll hear it later."

"Can't wait to tell you, chicky! We'll talk at the layover!" Charlie called after her.

CHAPTER 2

Maggie fidgeted in her seat, her arms crossed tightly over her chest. With her right leg slung over her left, her foot bobbed up and down as she stared with narrowed eyes at the seat in front of her.

"Need a pillow or something?" Henry inquired.

Maggie did not respond. She shook her head and pursed her lips. "She's pregnant. That has to be it! What else could it be? What news is bigger than getting married? Which… okay, can we just talk about that for a second? Who gets married like that? They've been dating for what? Three months? And BAM!" Maggie slammed her hand on the armrest, startling a few passengers around them.

Henry smiled and nodded, waving away the concern of the flight attendant.

"I guess we'll find out in New York," Henry offered.

Maggie craned her neck, searching the plane seats behind her. "I see them," she reported. She climbed up higher, kneeling on the seat. She narrowed her eyes at the couple, each with earbuds in, staring at Charlie's iPad. "Do her cheeks look puffy to you? Like maybe she gained a little baby weight?"

"No? Maybe. I don't know?"

"Sit down, Mags," Leo retorted from behind her. Maggie lowered her gaze.

She frowned at him. "How did you get into first class?"

"They needed someone to switch seats." He thrust his arms out to his sides and grinned. "And here I am. Selfless as always."

Maggie rolled her eyes at him and slumped back down in her seat. She crossed her arms again.

"Why don't you try to relax?" Henry asked. He slid his arm around her shoulders and pulled her close, kissing her cheek. "It's supposed to be the start of our vacation."

"Yes, and Charlie dropped a bombshell on us five seconds before we boarded. How can I relax?! And everyone we know is also going to Scotland." She sighed and pressed her fingers against her temples, massaging them. "This vacation is really starting off with a bang."

Henry rubbed her shoulders. "Relax, Maggie. We're finally going to have that nice, quiet trip you've always wanted. And listen, I promise I'll let you shop for more than yoga pants and black hoodies."

"No car chases?"

"Nope."

"No breaking into museums?"

"Nothing but a relaxing vacation in the Scottish countryside. No treasure hunts, no mysteries...just you, me and Scotland."

"And a castle."

"And a castle, just like my princess deserves."

Maggie offered him a slight smile as she eased against him, letting her head drop onto his shoulder.

"All right," she agreed. "Although I still think she's pregnant."

Henry let his head drop back onto the seat behind him and closed his eyes. "Same old Maggie," he murmured.

"Huh?" Maggie asked.

"Nothing."

* * *

Their flight landed safely at JFK, however, due to a delay in their landing schedule, their one-hour layover dissolved into a race between gates to make their flight to London. As a result, Maggie's curiosity was not satisfied.

"I can't believe this," she grumbled, as they settled in for the long flight over the Atlantic.

"At least we made the flight," Henry offered.

"Yes, but we don't know anything else about the big news! It's got to be a baby. That's why they got married so fast!"

"Let it go, Maggie. Relax, take a nap. Let's get ready to enjoy our vacation, huh?"

Maggie glanced back through the cabin. Piper and Charlie leaned across the aisle to speak to Emma and Ollie, who were seated near them. Emma's eyebrows shot upward, and her jaw unhinged. She glanced up toward the first-class area.

Maggie scrunched her face in frustration as she slouched in her seat. She threaded her arms across her chest again, a sour expression on her face.

"Cheer up, Mags," a voice said over their seats. Leo grinned and winked at her. "You're on vacation."

"Oh, shut up and sit in your comped seat, Leo," Maggie snapped.

Henry eyed her.

"Don't," she said.

He held his hands up in mock defeat. "I didn't say anything."

"Can you believe this?" Maggie exclaimed a moment later.

Henry glanced around as though trying to determine what he shouldn't believe.

"She is back there telling Emma alllllll her secrets. I bet Emma knows the baby names they picked out already. Piper probably asked her to be the godmother! How could she do this to me?" Maggie flung her hands in the air.

"Maggie, relax. We don't even know if she's pregnant. She'll tell you when she's ready."

Maggie frowned and glanced backward again. "But why would she tell Emma first?" she whined.

"We don't know she told Emma. Look, Maggie, we're supposed to be on vacation. Remember? No bad guys, no car chases, just a relaxing time in a Scottish castle."

Maggie sighed. "You're right. You're right. We made our flight despite the delay. Next stop: London! And then on to Scotland." She grinned at him. "I am officially relaxed." She flicked her hair and slid down in her seat, stretching her legs.

* * *

Maggie's lips formed an unimpressed frown, and she crossed her arms with a huff. "What do you mean 'canceled?'" she questioned.

She tapped her designer shoe on the tile floor in front of the desk. The airline employee offered a conciliatory smile, then returned her attention to tapping furiously at her keyboard.

"We can get you on standby for a flight in two days," she said after a few moments.

Maggie's eyes went wide. "TWO DAYS?!" she shouted.

"Standby in two days is the best you can do? Are you kidding me?"

"I'm very sorry, ma'am," her crisp British accent answered. "But all flights to Edinburgh have been canceled, not just yours. The weather there is too bad for the planes to land safely. Air traffic is backed up for several days." The crease between the woman's brow deepened as she offered Maggie another consoling glance and hoped it would be enough.

Maggie sighed, visibly attempting to compose herself. "Okay, I understand that this is a weather-related cancelation, but isn't this going to clear up in a few hours? I can't believe there are no flights before two days from now."

"Unfortunately, most of our flights were already booked, and with all the cancelations, we are struggling to get everyone accommodated." She waved her hand around toward the myriad of disgruntled people waiting in line to rebook a flight.

Maggie sighed again. "Well, what am I supposed to do here for two days? I have no hotel room booked, nowhere to stay."

"Well, London is a very nice city. I am sure you can find something interesting to do. And as for accommodations, here is a list of hotels. We can offer you a voucher for any of these locations courtesy of the airline." The woman produced a list of hotels and slid the paper toward Maggie.

With another frown, Maggie slapped her hand against the counter and snatched the paper. She narrowed her eyes at the woman and grumbled, "Fine," as she stalked over to a group of seats and slumped into one.

"Unbelievable," Maggie groaned, tossing her hands in the air. "Worst vacation ever."

"We're all stuck, Maggie," Emma replied.

Maggie squinted at her, unimpressed. "Yes, Emma, I know that. Thank you for pointing out the obvious."

Emma rolled her eyes.

"Don't worry, chicky," Charlie said, "I've still got friends in the area. You can always stay with the newly wed Mr. and Mrs. Rivers."

"Ah, just a sec," Piper said, holding up a finger. "Mr. and Mrs. is far enough, I'll stay Piper Brooks, thanks."

"You could hyphenate," Charlie suggested. "Piper Brooks-Rivers."

"Dude, that's... I sound like a tributary system."

"You may be better off sticking with just Brooks," Emma agreed with a chuckle.

Piper laughed and nodded. Maggie narrowed her eyes at the exchange. "Maybe Emma can stay with you two," she said. "You all seem to be best buds."

"Chill out, boss lady," Piper said, "I'm sure Indiana Jones will get you to Scotland."

Maggie continued to pout. "I saw you both talking on the plane. Did you spill your big news to her?"

"That we did, chicky," Charlie said with a grin. "We couldn't hold it in any longer. We had to tell someone."

"I think I'll go check on Ollie... or Leo... or anyone," Emma said, excusing herself and stalking off with her cell phone in her hand.

Maggie puckered her lips and shook her head. "I cannot believe you told Emma first!"

"Well..." Piper began.

"I thought we were friends, Piper!" Maggie moaned.

"But..." Piper tried again.

"And now I find out Emma knew all about the baby before I did. I'm crushed, quite frankly."

"Baby?" Piper said, her brow wrinkling. "What baby?"

"Yeah, chicky, I missed a link in the chain on that one."

Piper's eyes grew wide, and her jaw dropped open. "OMG! MAGGIE! Are you pregnant?"

Maggie's features expressed incredulousness. "Me? No! You are!"

"Huh?" Piper replied.

Maggie frowned for the umpteenth time. "Your big news. You're pregnant, right?"

Piper and Charlie shared a confused glance, before bursting into laughter. Tears streamed down Piper's face as she tried to compose herself. She waved a hand in front of her at Maggie.

"What? What else could the big news be? Why did you slink off and get married so quick?"

Piper wiped at the tears. "First off, boss lady, no one did any slinking. We wanted to get married, so we did. We didn't need anyone's permission."

Maggie waited. After a moment, she said, "And second?"

"Huh?"

"You said first of all, which implies there is a second of all. And also, you still haven't told me the big news. Nor, may I point out, have you said you aren't pregnant."

Maggie cocked her head and narrowed her eyes, pursing her lips.

"I am not pregnant. We did not get married because I'm pregnant."

"Okay, okay," Maggie said, holding her hands up in defeat. "So, what's the big news then?"

"It's about where we're going to live…" Piper began.

Maggie's face fell and her heart dropped. Tears filled her eyes. "You're moving to London, aren't you? That's why you came over here."

"Wow, you're super terrible at this, boss lady. How do you solve all those puzzles when you're this bad at inference?"

"Yeah, I'd tend to agree. You are failing miserably here. Though you did get one bit right. We are moving."

"To?" Maggie asked, her voice a squeak.

Charlie leaned back in his seat and grinned at her. "123 Westerfield Street."

"But that's…"

"Your address?! That's correct! One hundred points for the smart chicky! We're going to be your neighbors!"

Piper nodded and smiled. "We bought apartment 4B. We're literally your next-door neighbors!"

Maggie's eyes widened and her lower lip bobbed up and down, but no sound came out.

"That's exactly the reaction I hoped for," Charlie said. "We've left you speechless."

"How? Why?" Maggie finally choked out.

"It's prime real estate, chicky," Charlie answered. "When the previous tenant kicked the bucket, we made an offer posthaste. It has all the right ingredients. Perfect spot in town, lovely view and the best neighbor money can buy." He winked and wiggled his eyebrows.

"We can commute to work together!" Piper added with a coy expression.

Maggie sat in stunned silence for another minute, until Emma rejoined them. "Judging by the look on her face, I'd say you told her?" she questioned.

"We did," Charlie confirmed. "Stunned her into silence. She's so thrilled, she can't speak."

"Thrilled, yeah, that's it," Emma said.

"All right," Henry said as he approached the group, juggling a few items in his hands. He glanced up and ceased talking. "Everything okay?"

"Piper and Charlie just told Maggie the big news."

"Oh," Henry said, as he glanced at each of them in an attempt to read the situation.

"Maggie is stunned into silence over the fact that they are moving next door to her," Emma reported.

"That's the big news?" Henry inquired.

"That's it! We're neighbors!" Charlie confirmed, pointing between him and Maggie. He leaned forward toward Henry. "And maybe soon *we* will be neighbors, eh, mate?" He offered a knowing glance.

"Uh, well, that's a discussion for another time," Henry hedged, prompting an annoyed glance from Maggie. "We're on vacation, and... in crisis mode."

"Please tell me you found a cargo plane going to Edinburgh," Maggie said with a sigh.

"Never thought I'd see the day you'd ask for a cargo plane, Maggie," Ollie said, rejoining the group.

"No cargo planes, princess. But I did get us a car. And not just any car!" He paused for dramatic effect. "The *last* car they had."

"Oh, yay!" Maggie exclaimed, leaping from her seat and throwing her arms around Henry's neck! "Scotland here we come!"

"Wait," Emma interjected, "did you say the *last* car?"

Henry winced. "Yeah. With all the cancelations, accommodations and cars are really in short supply."

"So are hotel rooms," Leo announced, as he clicked off his phone's display. "This weather has really put a damper on everything."

"So, we're stuck here in the airport?" Piper asked.

"Too bad I didn't keep my flat here," Charlie lamented. "We could have nipped over there for the night."

Henry piped in, "I did manage to get us some accommodations for the night. They had room for everyone. It's just outside of Glasgow. I booked us for the entire weekend since I also heard a few of the roads are washed out heading to Dunhaven."

"Oh, great job, babe!" Maggie said, patting his chest.

"Yeah, that's wonderful," Leo complained. "If only we were in Glasgow."

"Maybe a cab?" Maggie suggested.

"Mags, it's like seven hours from here. I'm not taking a cab."

"It's a seven-hour drive?" Maggie inquired, sinking into her seat.

Henry nodded at Maggie's question. "Seven and three quarters to be exact, and if we leave now, we can make it by nine."

"Nine seems optimistic," Ollie added.

"Not with him driving," Maggie said, shaking her head. "We'll make it before nine, trust me."

"Well, looks like you two are set. I guess we'll be stretching out here in the airport lobby," Emma retorted, her chin set in her palm as she stared dejectedly at the floor.

"Well..." Henry said, hesitating for a moment before he continued.

"What?" Maggie asked.

"There's seven of us," Henry said. "And the only car they had left was a seven-passenger. So, technically we have room if everyone doesn't mind squeezing in together. Assuming everyone's plans suit a weekend in Glasgow?"

Piper's eyes lit up as Henry made his statement. Charlie grinned and reached for a high five from Henry. Ollie smirked at him. Emma's downcast expression changed to a hopeful one. Leo rolled his eyes.

"Of course, you did," Leo said. "Indiana Jones to the rescue."

"Do you want the ride or not, Leo?" Maggie asked.

He shrugged. "Yeah, I'll take it. Beats sleeping on the floor here."

"I agree," Emma said, already shouldering her luggage.

"We don't have anything scheduled until Monday, so there's no issue there. Everyone in then?" Ollie inquired.

"We are," Charlie announced.

"Lead the way!" Ollie said, motioning to Henry.

"Wait!" Maggie said.

"What is it?" Henry asked.

She bit her lower lip. "This isn't a cargo van, is it? We're not going to be sitting on the floor for over seven hours, are we?"

Henry chuckled. "Not even close, princess."

CHAPTER 3

Henry led them to the shuttle bus heading to the car park. They arrived in a nearly empty lot. Maggie scoured it searching for their vehicle. The shuttle bus eased to a stop near a boxy brown minivan. Maggie wrinkled her nose at it. It looked uncomfortable for a nearly eight-hour trip. It also looked small. She worried they'd be cramped, particularly in the back seat where three people would need to squeeze together into one bench seat. Hopefully, it ran well, she thought.

They piled out of the shuttle with all their luggage. As the bus pulled away, Maggie stared at the nearby minivan.

"Looks kind of tight," she muttered to Piper.

"What's tight?" Henry questioned, as he began to drag her suitcases toward it.

"That van. It's a tight seven-passenger," she said with a grimace. "I can squeeze in the back, though, for part of the trip."

"That's not our car," Henry shouted over his shoulder, as he continued through the near-empty lot.

THE LOST TREASURE OF DRAKON

"It's not?" Maggie glanced around at the limited choices, finding a handful of smaller vehicles, but no other vans.

"Nope," Henry said, spinning around to flash her a grin.

In the distance, Maggie spotted a large white cargo-style van. She winced as she caught sight of it. She'd rather take the minivan than that thing on a seven-plus hour drive. Henry aimed toward the large white van.

Maggie's apprehension grew with every step. As they came within feet of the vehicle, Maggie shouted, "I thought you said you *didn't* get a cargo van, babe."

"I didn't."

"Well, then..." Maggie paused as she searched.

Henry thumbed toward the white van. "This isn't our car." He crooked his finger and pointed to indicate behind the van. Maggie took a few steps and leaned to peer around the large vehicle. "*That's* our car."

Maggie's eyes widened and a smile spread across her face. "Please tell me you're not kidding."

"Not kidding. It was the only one left."

Maggie clapped her hands and bounced on her toes as she stared at the massive blue Lincoln Navigator.

"OMG! A Blue Diamond Metallic Lincoln Navigator!"

"Ugh," Emma groaned, "of course you'd know the color."

"Happy, princess?" Henry asked, as he kissed her cheek.

"Very. I could do over seven hours in this easily!"

"Perfect, chicky," Charlie said, as he tossed his bag into the trunk then loaded Piper's luggage. "We three can share the back seat." He grinned.

"Shotgun," Ollie called.

"Calling a captain's chair in the second row!" Leo shouted.

"Same!" Emma said.

Henry slid his eyes toward Maggie with a wince. She shook her head. "I'm so thrilled with this car, I don't care!"

She climbed into the car through the back door and waddled between the second-row seats to the third row. She settled in, pulling her seatbelt on and snapping it in place.

"I can't believe you're not whining about giving up the shotgun seat," Piper said, following Charlie to the backseat.

"Look, this trip has been a disaster so far," Maggie said. "First, Henry rushed me out the door. Then the whole 'big news' debacle had me on edge for the first flight. Then the canceled flight. This car is the first thing that's gone right! I don't care. I just want a nice, relaxing vacation in a lovely castle in the Highlands."

Henry climbed in behind the wheel. "On that note, princess, you'll be happy to hear our lodging for the weekend is also in a castle."

"Really?" Maggie asked.

"Really! It's not Dunhaven Castle, but it'll do."

"Which castle is it?" Ollie inquired.

"Clydescolm Castle," Henry answered.

"Ohhhh," Ollie said with a knowing nod. "Home of the Phantom Piper."

"The what?" Maggie questioned.

"Phantom Piper," Ollie repeated.

"That sounds ominous," Maggie said with a gulp.

"Don't tell me you believe in ghosts, boss lady," Piper teased.

Maggie shrugged. "I don't. Not completely. But it sounds very ominous, and I'd like to hear more."

"Perhaps I should save the tale for when we arrive at the castle," Ollie suggested. "Might be a nice bedtime story." He turned to face them and held his cell phone's flashlight under his chin. "Or not." He offered a spooky laugh.

"Always so dramatic, Ollie," Emma said with a laugh.

"Your stories were the best in class," Piper chimed in. "I can't wait to hear it."

Maggie gave another hard swallow. This vacation was not beginning the way she'd hoped. While she didn't believe in ghosts, it was yet another bad omen.

The group spent several hours driving north toward Scotland, then west toward the coast. With limited stops, and Henry's enthusiastic driving, they made it to the town just outside of Clydescolm Castle by nightfall. The small hamlet sat in a valley below the castle.

Henry parked the large SUV, and they walked to a local pub for a meal, before heading to their accommodations for the night. With a warm breeze off the water, the night was nice enough to spend on the patio. They squeezed in seats around a table together.

Maggie stared up at the castle on the hill, overlooking the water. Its grey facade looked formidable, even centuries after its completion. She scanned the green hillside for any specters sporting bagpipes.

"Looks very imposing," Maggie noted, as they perused the menu.

"The food or the castle?" Emma questioned.

"The castle," Maggie clarified. "I can't wait to see what Cate's looks like. I saw a few pictures, but I can't wait to see it in person."

"Hopefully Monday," Henry said.

"Oh, speaking of," Maggie replied, "I got a text from Cate. A few of the roads to Dunhaven were affected by the heavy rains. She'll keep us updated on progress. She also said everyone is welcome at Dunhaven Castle." Maggie tapped at her phone before reading the message from Cate Kensie. *"I've got plenty of room for everyone. Please let them know they are welcome to stay here. It'll be nice to see Ollie again, and yes, I remember Emma, Leo and Piper."*

"Awww, that's a really sweet invitation," Piper said. "She was always really nice."

"And this lady was one of your professors?" Henry asked.

"Yeah," Piper confirmed. "I had her for American History. I think it was during her last semester there."

"That's really something that she inherited a castle and just up and moved to Scotland," Emma said.

"Any weird legends about Cate's castle, Uncle Ollie?" Maggie inquired.

Ollie chuckled. "Several, actually. Ranging from devil worship to ghosts."

"Devil worship?" Piper questioned, her brow scrunching. "Seriously?"

"Dunhaven Castle's got quite a reputation. Maybe don't mention it to Cate. I've no idea if she's sensitive about it," Ollie suggested.

"I'd love to hear the story about the Phantom Piper," Maggie said, changing the subject after they all placed their orders.

"Me too!" Piper agreed.

Ollie offered a coy smile. "All right. The story really begins centuries ago, when the Vikings sailed from Scandinavia. Those of you who paid attention to my lectures will recall the violent attacks along the coastline and Scotland's islands."

"Over looting of metals and objects, right?" Piper asked.

"Correct," Ollie said, waving his finger at her with a smile. "You paid attention! The looting would eventually turn into settlements. Now, all the spoils from the attacks had to go somewhere, right?"

"Back to Scandinavia?" Maggie suggested.

"Some of it, likely yes. Some of it was hidden."

"Wasn't some of it recently found?" Henry asked.

"Oh, yes, several Viking caches have been found over the years," Ollie confirmed. "The most recent find was earlier in the year on the Isle of Man."

"Wow! That's fascinating," Maggie said.

"And some of it has never been found, including the famed Clydescolm Cache."

"Or fabled," Emma interjected.

"Depends on what you believe. Is the treasure real or is it a myth? No one knows. Well, except maybe for one person," Ollie teased.

"Who?" Charlie asked.

"The Phantom Piper," Ollie announced, leaning back in his seat and folding his hands across his stomach.

"The ghost guy?" Maggie responded.

"He wasn't always a ghost guy," Ollie replied. "He was once a living, breathing Scotsman. A lord, in fact!"

"Did he live in the castle?" Piper asked.

"That he did," Ollie confirmed. "Lord Kendrick MacClyde."

"Did he build the castle?" Maggie asked, as the waitress returned with trays loaded with food.

"Nay," the waitress answered before Ollie could. "He didnae build the castle, only lived there. I assume you're telling the tale of our ghost piper?"

"Yes," Ollie confirmed. "We're staying at the castle for the weekend, and my esteemed colleagues wanted to hear it."

She nodded as she set his fish and chips in front of him. "Well, best tell them so they can be on the lookout. He roams the entire estate there."

"Have you ever seen him?" Maggie asked her.

"Aye, I certainly have," she confirmed.

"Really?"

"Aye," the girl repeated. "Roaming on a moonlit night. Heard the pipes playing and saw a mist floating along the hillside. And I knew that was him."

Maggie raised her eyebrows at the girl's statement. She

told them to enjoy their meal as she topped off water glasses and disappeared into the pub.

"Now who still believes it's all fake?" Maggie questioned, an eyebrow arched. "A close encounter from a local."

"They're probably told to play up the whole ghost thing for tourists," Emma contended.

"Or she saw a ghost," Maggie replied with a shrug, digging into her salad.

"Is there more to the story, Ollie?" Charlie inquired.

"Yes, though the details are slim," Ollie answered. "The rumor is Kendrick stumbled upon a Viking treasure hoard. It contained gold, silver, and gemstones.

"The treasure hoard had quite the impact on him. He became anxious, paranoid and secretive. He hid the treasure, secreting it away with a series of clues and protective measures designed to keep people away. And even after his death, he continues to patrol the estate to ensure the safety of the treasure. Kendrick was an avid bagpiper, so if you hear the sound of bagpipes and can't find the source, chances are… Kendrick MacClyde is near."

Thunder rumbled in the distance as the breeze turned cooler.

"Did anyone ever find it?" Piper asked.

Ollie shook his head. "No."

"That could be because it's not real," Emma chimed in.

"It could be," Ollie admitted.

"Then what caused his paranoia and all that?" Maggie asked.

"Landowning families were often inbred to the point that it caused problems with some of the generations," Emma answered.

"Ah," Maggie said, snapping her mouth closed as she processed it. "Well, I guess we'll find out when we're all alone in the castle tonight." She gave a fake shiver.

"I'd bet we'll all sleep just fine," Emma contended.

"Maybe we'll find a treasure!" Maggie exclaimed.

"I thought this wasn't a working trip?" Henry asked.

"The last time I checked, the government didn't task us with finding Viking treasure," Maggie countered.

"No one did, princess," Henry whispered, as he stole a kiss from her.

Thunder boomed in the distance, sounding closer than it had before.

"Better eat up," Ollie said. "Storm's blowing in."

Piper grimaced at the growing black clouds on the horizon, and everyone dug into their meals. They piled back into the SUV for the climb up the hill to the castle, just as large drops of rain pelted the windshield.

"Whew, just made it!" Maggie exclaimed, as Henry fired the engine. She studied the impressive facade of the castle as they wound up the road toward it.

Henry eased the vehicle to a halt just outside the front door. A gusty, wet wind blew Maggie's hair across her face as she stepped onto the gravel and raised her eyes to take in the entire castle. Another boom of thunder sent everyone scurrying into the foyer, while Charlie, Henry and Leo wrangled the suitcases from the back.

"Welcome to Clydescolm Castle," a man with a Scottish brogue greeted them. "Home of the Phantom Piper!" A booming clap of thunder punctuated his last statement.

CHAPTER 4

"Hi," Maggie said, as she scanned the large foyer. The space had been converted to accommodate a check-in desk. A stone floor covered in a large area rug greeted incoming guests as they entered through the massive wooden doors. Stone walls rose from the floor with various archways leading to other spaces. A fire roared in a gigantic fireplace across from the ornate wooden check-in desk. Several armchairs were grouped around its warm glow. A coat of arms hung above it, painted on a shield, with two swords crossed behind it.

"Lovely place you've got here," she continued. "My boyfriend called earlier and made arrangements for us to stay the weekend. The reservation is probably under Henry Taylor."

"Oh, Americans, are you?" the man asked, as he shuffled through papers.

"Well, most of us," Maggie said, closing the gap between the front door and the desk.

"Here we are," the man said, as he pulled several sheets of

paper from the pile. "Aye, four rooms under Henry Taylor. He called in the nick of time. You got our last four!"

"Lucky us!" Maggie said. She dug in her purse and passed a credit card to the man. "Just put them all on there, we can sort it out between us."

"Easy enough," he said with a nod. Henry, Charlie and Leo pushed through the doors while Maggie waited for her card to be processed. They were soaked from the heavy rain that now fell.

"Uh-oh. You're soaked!" the man said, as he shot them a glance. "Best get you to your rooms so you can change into something dry and warm. You may want to enjoy our fire here or in the sitting room through those doors to warm up."

"Thanks," Maggie said. The man passed along their keys and explained how to navigate to their rooms. He also informed them of breakfast arrangements.

"Any questions?" he asked when he concluded.

"So, ah, where can one find this Phantom Piper?" Maggie inquired. Emma gave a tsk with her tongue and rolled her eyes.

"Oh, lassie, all over the grounds. By the caves over yonder." He motioned with his arm. "Near the old stables just that way." He leaned over the desk and lowered his voice. "And sometimes even roaming about the halls of the castle itself."

Maggie lifted her chin and her eyebrows, then gave him a coy nod. "I'll keep my eyes peeled."

The man offered her a teasing smile and a wink. Maggie rejoined the others, huddled near the fire.

"Okay, Henry got us their last four rooms, so we'll have to pair off."

Piper snatched a key from Maggie. "Obviously, Charlie and I are paired. It *is* our honeymoon."

Henry began, "And I figured Ollie could room alone since he is the…"

"Don't say oldest," Ollie warned jokingly.

"Wisest," Maggie added, handing him a key.

"That leaves us four," Maggie said, gesturing to herself, Emma, Henry and Leo. "Looks like we split girls and guys."

"Wonderful," Leo said, with a roll of his eyes.

"Ugh," Emma groaned. "The last time we shared a room, I got kidnapped at gunpoint."

"That wasn't a room, it was a tent. Totally different," Maggie argued, as they dragged their luggage across the thick carpet toward the stairs.

"Okay, fine," Emma countered. "The *last* time we shared a room, I got food poisoning, and *then* we got shot at while trying to escape into the desert."

"Oh, come on, we're on vacation, Emma!" Maggie answered. "What's the worst that can happen on this trip? We see that ghost piper, that's about it."

"We'll see," Emma said as they lumbered up the steps. "And *you're* on vacation. I'm on a business trip."

Ollie found his room two doors away from the stairs. Piper and Charlie continued down the hall, disappearing into their bedroom a few doors down. Maggie, Emma, Leo and Henry found their rooms at the end of the hall, across from each other.

Rain continued to pelt the window at the hall's end, and lightning streaked through the sky. Maggie spotted the guys' room as Leo pushed through the door.

"Thank GOD there are two beds," he exclaimed, as he tugged his suitcase through the door.

Henry rolled his eyes. "Feel about the same way, mate."

"You going to make it through the weekend?" Maggie inquired.

"Yeah. I'll probably fall asleep right away with all that driving. How about you?"

Maggie stretched. "Yeah, I'm exhausted. I can't wait to stretch out in bed. Maybe after a nice relaxing bath."

"Enjoy," Henry said. He stole a kiss before flashing his dimples at her with a grin, and heading through the open door to his room.

"Hey, what makes you think you get–" Maggie overheard him ask before the door closed. With a sigh, she turned and maneuvered her two suitcases and carry-on bag through the door to her and Emma's room.

Emma had tossed her single duffel bag onto the luggage stand. Maggie glanced around the well-appointed room. Rich, dark woods with intricate carvings paneled the room. Thick, blue and green tartan curtains framed the windows. A matching quilt lay on the large four-poster bed. A few heavy pieces of furniture rounded out the space.

"Is there another one or two of those around?" Maggie inquired, nodding at the luggage stand.

"Maybe in the closet," Emma answered. "I can't believe you brought two suitcases in for the weekend."

"At least I didn't bring *all* of them."

Emma rolled her eyes. "I can't believe you brought three suitcases *and* a carry-on."

"I like to be prepared."

"Prepared for what?"

"Anything and everything." Maggie abandoned her luggage in the middle of the room and wandered to the window. She pulled back the sheer curtain behind the tartan drapes and glanced out. "Oh, pretty! We have a view of the sea."

"Technically that's the Firth of Clyde," Emma said.

"Whatever. You know what I meant." Maggie scanned the green countryside extending to the side. The land sloped sharply away toward the water just a few yards from their window.

"Are you going to just leave your suitcases in the middle of the room?"

"No, I'm going to move them in a minute. I just wanted to see the view!"

Emma tried to shove the suitcase from the walkway, issuing a yelp as she struggled to push the heavy luggage around. "What is in this thing?"

Maggie shook her head and dragged the luggage toward the wall. "If we're going to survive the weekend, you need to chill out."

"I'm going to get ready for bed. I'm exhausted," Emma said sharply. Maggie tipped her luggage over and rummaged through it for her nightclothes.

"Is there a nice tub? Maybe old-fashioned and clawfooted or something?" she shouted.

Emma emerged from the bathroom moments later. "There's a plain tub," she announced. "Bathroom's all yours."

In her pajamas, Emma climbed into bed and squeezed her eyes shut.

Maggie shrugged and wandered into the bathroom, indulging in a warm bath before she completed her nightly routine. She emerged into the room, turned off the rest of the lights, and slid between the sheets under the tartan quilt.

Wind whistled past the window, and the blowing tree limbs cast spooky shadows across the floor of the bedroom. Maggie turned on her side away from the shadowy images. After a few moments, she slipped from between the sheets and wandered to the window.

The rain had stopped, and the clouds were breaking up. A sliver of the quarter moon peeked from behind a dark cloud as it sailed past. Maggie scanned the grounds for any ghostly presence. She strained her ears for the sounds of music. All that reached her was the howling of the wind.

After a few moments, she wandered back to the bed and perched on the edge. She swiped her phone from the nightstand and sent a text to Henry. As she waited to determine if he was awake, she drummed her fingers against her leg.

No answer came and, after five minutes of waiting, Maggie dumped her phone on the night table. With a sigh, she collapsed onto her pillow. Clouds raced through the night sky outside their window. Maggie squeezed her eyes shut. They popped open moments later, and she blew out a long breath.

She flopped over onto her other side and whispered, "Hey, Emma, you awake?"

She received no answer. "Emma?" she asked again, this time raising her voice slightly.

"Ugh, what?" Emma groaned, her back still facing Maggie.

"Oh, good, you're awake."

Emma twisted to face Maggie; her face wrinkled into a mask of confusion. "What? I wasn't. Why did you wake me up?"

"I can't sleep."

"Okay, so?"

"Let's go exploring!" Maggie said with a grin.

"Maggie, it's the middle of the night. Go to sleep," Emma grumbled and collapsed into her pillow. She wrangled the sheets over her shoulder and clutched them tightly to her chest.

"Are you sure? The rain stopped. We could look at the ocean in the moonlight!"

"It's not the ocean."

"Whatever, the water. You know what I mean. Maybe we'll see the ghost! Or find a treasure!"

"Will you quit with that treasure stuff? I'm on a business trip, and you are on vacation. Just relax."

"Come on. If you don't want to go outside, we can poke around in here! It's a big old castle. There's probably tons of interesting stuff!"

"Go to sleep, Maggie."

"Fine," Maggie grumbled as she settled back into her pillow. She fidgeted around a few times and adjusted her covers. With a huff, she closed her eyes again.

"Okay, all right, fine. Let's go look around," Emma agreed.

Maggie popped her eyes open, a grin spreading across her face. "Really?"

"Yeah. Now that you woke me up and we had a ten-minute conversation, I can't sleep either. So, why not?"

Maggie bounded from the bed, flicked on the light and pulled on her robe.

"Did you buy that just for this trip?" Emma asked, as she tied the string on her fluffy pink bathrobe.

"Maybe," Maggie answered. "Why?"

"Just didn't expect you of all people to have a tartan robe," she answered, narrowing her eyes at Maggie's blue and green plaid.

"When in Rome," Maggie said, as she adjusted the robe in the mirror.

The two women stepped into the hallway and Emma eased the door closed. She opened her mouth to inquire about where to go, but Maggie was already darting down the hall. Emma rushed to catch up to her.

"Did you know I'm part Scottish?" Maggie asked. "I did one of those DNA tests, and they said I'm Scottish."

"Fascinating," Emma grumbled.

"You should try one. Maybe you're also Scottish."

"Then I can buy a tartan robe, too. Really get in touch with my roots."

"Very funny, Emma."

They padded down the hallway. Thick red carpeting stretched the length of it. Stone archways sectioned off areas or led to other halls. Maggie pranced down the hall, turning corners and ducking into other hallways randomly.

"Hey, maybe we shouldn't be wandering around everywhere," Emma suggested.

"Why?"

"Well, maybe we're not supposed to be in certain areas."

"Then they should have roped them off."

"Or maybe they just trust their guests won't traipse through the halls at all hours of the night."

"Where's your sense of adventure?" Maggie asked, as they ascended a circular set of stone steps.

"I left it in Egypt when we got trapped in Cleopatra's tomb," Emma replied.

Maggie rolled her eyes. "We got out. So, it was fine." Maggie led her through a large stone archway into a circular room.

Emma began to reply, when Maggie cut her off.

"Oooooh!" Maggie cooed in awe. "Look at this!"

An open-mouth smile lit her face as they stared at a medium-sized room filled with books. "This must be the library."

"Mmm, I would think they'd have a larger library on the main floor."

"So, what's this then?" Maggie inquired, as she ran her fingers along a row of books.

"Smaller, private library, maybe," Emma suggested, bending to read some of the titles. "Perhaps one of the former dukes was an avid reader or enthusiast on some particular topic and he collected books on it."

"Earl," Maggie answered.

"Huh?"

"They aren't dukes, they are earls. That's why he's Lord."

"Oh, of course, you'd know their station."

"It's not like that. I looked them up on Wikipedia on the drive here. I was curious."

They spent a few moments perusing the stacks. The scent of leather-bound books filled their nostrils. Maggie pulled a few books from the shelf and leafed through them.

"Maybe we shouldn't be pawing through their private library," Emma said.

"It's not like it was closed off, Emma. For all we know, this is a library for guests to use!"

"Somehow I don't think so," Emma replied, as Maggie snapped a book shut, sending a cloud of dust into the air.

Maggie waved the dust away and coughed. She pulled another volume from the shelves and perused it, before returning it to the shelf. A few books later, she murmured, "These are all about Vikings."

"Yes, and early Scotland," Emma added.

Maggie slid the book back into its spot and tilted her head to read more titles. She reached for another book. Hooking her finger on the top, she pulled. Her brow furrowed as she gave it another tug. With a grunt, she tried again.

"Hmm, stuck," Maggie said.

"Just leave it alone," Emma said.

"I wanted to see it. It's titled *Viking Treasure.*"

Emma clicked her tongue. "You and your treasure."

Maggie scrunched her lips and grasped the book with both hands and yanked. It gave way, tilting at a forty-five-degree angle. A clang sounded and the bookshelf popped toward her with a creak.

CHAPTER 5

Maggie stumbled backward several steps, bumping into Emma and nearly knocking her over.

"Ouch, watch it!" Emma said, as Maggie crashed into her.

"The bookcase opened!" Maggie said with a shaky voice.

Emma's eyes widened. "Again? How do you constantly stumble upon things like this?"

"Come on, let's check it out!" Maggie answered, recovering from her surprise and grasping the shelf and pulling it open further.

"No," Emma objected, pushing against her efforts. "We shouldn't be running around someone else's castle."

"It's a secret passage! We can't pass this up! Maybe the treasure is up there! The book that triggered it was called *Viking Treasure*."

Emma rolled her eyes. "Yes, I'm sure the treasure is just sitting behind this secret panel and managed to remain hidden for centuries."

"Let's find out."

Maggie shoved Emma's hands away and pulled the bookcase open more. She glanced inside.

"Well?" Emma asked.

"It's a staircase leading down." Maggie pulled her phone from her pocket and toggled on her flashlight. She raised her eyebrows and widened her eyes, a grin crossing her face as she glanced at Emma. "Come on!"

"What? No!"

Maggie took a step toward the circular stone steps. She craned her neck to try to glance as far around as she could. "Oh, come on, Emma! We found a secret passage!"

"Did you learn nothing in Egypt?"

"What does Egypt have to do with a secret passage in a Scottish castle?" Maggie asked.

Emma huffed and crossed her arms. "The last time we descended a set of stairs in a passage you mistakenly opened, we got stuck. Then we nearly got smashed by a giant ball, bitten by a scorpion, and crushed under a collapsing ceiling."

Maggie stared at her, an unimpressed expression on her face. "That was totally different. That was a tomb. This isn't a tomb, it's just a secret passage. Come on, have a little fun."

Maggie grasped Emma's hand and pulled her toward the staircase. Emma, unprepared for the sudden yank, stumbled forward and onto the stone landing inside the bookcase.

Giddy with excitement, Maggie hurried down the first steps with her cell phone's flashlight bouncing off the stone walls surrounding them.

"Maggie, wait!" Emma called as she hurried after her.

"Oh, now you're excited, huh?"

"Not really. I just don't want you to get stuck by yourself. You'd never survive, and I'd never hear the end of it."

Maggie rolled her eyes. "I would survive."

The two argued back and forth over the odds of Maggie's

survival before she stumbled into a cobweb. She shrieked and swatted at the air.

"Ewwww, is it off me? Make sure there are no spiders on me!"

"See what I mean?" Emma answered.

"Oh, stop. Lots of people are afraid of spiders. Just make sure there are no spiders in my hair." She handed Emma the phone. Emma shined it at Maggie, who squinted against the beam.

"I can't see when you're holding your hands up like that."

"Well, stop shining the light in my face!"

"How can I see your hair if I don't? Just put your hands down."

"Well?" Maggie asked, her eyes squeezed shut.

"Ohhhh..." Emma mumbled. "Hold still."

"What? Why?"

"Just don't move."

"Okay," Maggie said, her voice trembling.

"Oh, I'm not sure I can do this," Emma said. "It's so big."

"What is? A spider?!"

"Yeah, huge, black, hairy and..."

Emma's subsequent words were cut off by the screeching Maggie emitted. She danced in a circle, swiping at her hair and shrieking an unintelligible set of words which sounded like, "Get it off me!"

Emma burst into laughter as Maggie came to a halt, asking if she was safe. "Yes," Emma answered, handing her phone back to Maggie.

"What?" Maggie asked. "What's so funny?"

"There was no spider," Emma said between chuckles. She waved her hand in front of her as she continued to giggle.

Maggie narrowed her eyes. "That was NOT funny!" she said, stamping her foot on the ground.

"I thought it was."

"Oh, really?" Maggie began, crossing her arms and cocking her hip. "I'll have you know…"

"Shh," Emma said, holding her hand up. "What was that?"

"What was what?" Maggie said, lowering her voice.

"Turn off your flashlight."

"Why?"

"Just turn it off," Emma said, cocking her head in annoyance.

Maggie toggled off the flashlight. The stairway plunged into darkness. Emma stared behind them.

"I don't see any light."

"Me either. But we're in a hidden stairway."

"But there should be light filtering from the bookcase we opened. We're not that far from it." Emma retreated a few stairs back toward the entrance. "Uhhhh," she mumbled, her voice taking a panicked edge. "Maggie, come up here."

Maggie followed after her, flicking her flashlight on again. "I can't see a thing."

"Yeah, that's because there's *no* light from up there." Emma waved her arm toward the opening.

"Oh, come on," Maggie said. "We must just be too far away." She pushed past Emma and hurried up several steps.

They reached the landing, and Maggie glided the beam over all the surfaces. Her brows scrunched, and she dropped her arms at her sides as she swiveled her head around. "This must be…" She paused, still searching. "Maybe we came too far and missed the opening."

"Doubt it. Plus, there were no stairs leading up when we opened the passage. This is it, Maggie. We're trapped. Again."

"We're not trapped," Maggie argued. She swiped at her phone. "I just need to…" She pulled her lips into a grimace. "I have no signal. Okay, okay, it's fine." She pushed against the back of the bookcase. "Help me," she grunted.

"It's not going to work, Maggie. It's closed! We're stuck!" Emma huffed, crossing her arms over her chest.

"There *has* to be a trigger on this side," Maggie said. "For situations just like this."

"Situations like when two idiots wander into a passage they shouldn't even be in and get stuck?"

"Yes, just like that," Maggie said with a groan. "Help! Help!"

She pounded against the bookcase, then groaned and slumped against it. "We're stuck," she whined.

"Like I told you," Emma said. "Someone locked us in here."

"Maybe they just closed it by mistake," Maggie suggested.

"Whatever. The end result is we're stuck."

"There has to be a trigger." Maggie climbed to her feet. "Let's look for it."

She shined the flashlight at the back of the bookcase. Together, they searched for a mechanism to open the passage. Maggie followed the edge of the opening, hoping to find a trigger there.

"Great," Emma said, slapping her hands on her thighs. "Nothing."

"Nothing I can see so far," Maggie answered.

Emma slid to the floor, resting her head in her hands. "Why do I listen to you, Maggie Edwards?"

"Because I'm fun?" Maggie suggested. She collapsed to the floor next to Emma. "Oh, come on, someone will find us."

"Who will find us, Maggie? They have no idea we went lurking around the halls, found a secret passage, opened it, and then went inside."

Maggie attempted to come up with a response but found none. She sighed and squeezed her lips together in a thin line.

"Turn off the light. We should conserve the battery,"

Emma said, letting her head rest against the central column behind her. "Cleopatra's tomb all over again."

Maggie frowned and fiddled with her phone.

"Turn it off!" Emma repeated.

"I'm trying! I can't get it!" The light bobbled wildly as Maggie tried to swipe at her phone to toggle off the light.

"Wait!" Emma shouted, grasping Maggie's arm.

"I said I'm trying! The stupid thing is stuck!"

"No, leave it on."

"Huh?"

Emma scrambled to her feet and raced to the bookcase. "Shine it here!" She waved her pointed finger wildly at a stone near the bookcase's edge.

Maggie climbed to her feet and approached with the flashlight. Emma dug her fingernail into a crevice.

"What are you doing? Trying to claw your way out?"

"No," Emma answered. "The stone is smoother here. See?" She grabbed Maggie's hand and shoved it against the stone's face near where she pried.

"Ohhh," Maggie said, her eyebrows raising as she felt the smooth stone. "Yeah. You think it's a trigger?"

"I hope so." Emma continued working at it while Maggie held the flashlight. She hopped from foot to foot in nervous anticipation.

"Let me try," Maggie suggested after a moment. Emma waved her away, dismissing her without a word.

Maggie rolled her brown eyes.

After another moment, she grunted, "Almost there."

The stone shimmied in its space. "There!" Maggie exclaimed.

Emma hooked a finger behind the stone and grunted with effort as she struggled to inch it out of its spot. Maggie bounced up and down as the stone slid toward them. After another moment, Emma had it freed. Her arm fell as the heavy stone slipped from its perch.

She placed it on the floor and dusted her hands off on her robe. Maggie aimed the flashlight's beam at the open space, bending over to get a better look.

She screwed up her face. She expected to find a mechanism to unlatch the bookcase and shove it open. Instead, five brass cylinders stared back at them.

Stacked on top of one another, the cylinders each had the letter "A" on them.

"What is this?" Maggie questioned.

"Looks like a lock."

"Lock for what?"

"Probably the bookcase." Emma spun the top cylinder. She groaned.

"What?"

"It has all twenty-six letters of the alphabet." She tried the second. "Same thing here. I'm sure all the rest are the same."

Maggie's eyes fell to the floor, and she bit her lower lip as she tapped around on her phone.

"So that means we need a five-letter keyword to open this," Emma said.

"Yeah," Maggie said. "And there are…" she tapped on her phone and her eyes widened, "over eleven million random possibilities, so we probably can't just try every combination."

"Well, we could," Emma countered, "if we want to spend the rest of our lives in here."

"Maybe we can deduce it?" Maggie suggested.

"Got any guesses?"

"Ummm," Maggie murmured. "Enter."

Emma wiggled her eyebrows. "It's not a half-bad guess." She twisted the cylinders to spell the word. Nothing happened. "Nope."

Maggie bit her lower lip in thought. "The book that led inside was called Viking Treasure. Can we get anything from that?"

"Jewel?" Emma offered. Maggie nodded, encouraging her to try it. Nothing happened.

They spent another twenty minutes trying any five-letter word which came to mind. None of them worked. Eventually, Emma collapsed back onto the floor, and Maggie joined her soon after, toggling off her flashlight. The space plunged into darkness again.

"I can't believe you got us stuck again," Emma said, sighing into the blackness.

"I'm sorry!" Maggie exclaimed. "I just thought it would be fun to try to find the treasure."

Emma huffed again.

"I saw that," Maggie claimed.

"It's pitch black, so I doubt it."

"So, you admit you did something I could have seen if there was light."

"Just be quiet, Maggie. I can't hear myself slowly dying in this passageway."

Maggie climbed to her feet and dusted her robe off. "Come on," she said, flicking on the flashlight and aiming it at Emma.

"Ah, stop shining that at me. Turn it off."

"No, we need it to get out of here."

"How do you propose we do that? Try all eleven million combos?"

"No, we never made it to the end of the stairs. Let's keep going. There must be a way out of here."

"How do you figure that? There's no guarantee."

"No, there's no guarantee, but it's probable."

"Oh, really? And how do you figure that? It could lead to a dead-end chamber."

THE LOST TREASURE OF DRAKON

"Well," Maggie explained, pacing the small landing in front of Emma, "let's suppose it leads to a dead-end as you proposed. That implies no one could get into that chamber except through the bookcase." Maggie pointed to the closed bookcase behind her.

"Right," Emma said.

"So, then why have a keyword tumbler lock on *this* side of the door? That implies they do not want people sneaking into the castle from wherever this leads. Which means someone can get inside from this passage."

Emma mulled it over. "Or they kept someone down here in a dungeon and they didn't want them to escape."

"Or that," Maggie acknowledged. "But I doubt it."

Emma rose to her feet. "I guess we'll find out when we find a torture chamber at the bottom."

Maggie offered her a wry, narrow-eyed glance. Together, they proceeded down the stone circular steps.

When they reached the end, they were met with a long corridor ending in a rectangular opening.

"You think that's the torture chamber?" Maggie whispered with a gulp.

"There's only one way to find out."

They inched forward until they reached the doorway.

"At least there are no scorpions in Scotland for us to run into," Maggie said. "There are none, right?"

"No," Emma confirmed.

Maggie shined the light into the space, finding it did little to beat back the darkness in the cavernous area.

"We're going to have to go in," Maggie said with a sharp nod.

"You first," Emma said.

"Fine," Maggie groaned.

She pressed her lips together, before inhaling deeply and stepping over the threshold. Maggie shined her light around the space. On the wall next to her, she found a handle.

"What's this?" she questioned, focusing her light on the object.

"Don't touch it," Emma said. She placed her hand against the wall, using it as a guide to wander further into the room.

Maggie held her hands up in defeat but continued to study it. Attached to a large rectangular box, a thin metal channel led upward. Maggie followed the metal upward toward the ceiling. She squinted at the darkness above.

Maggie puckered her lips as she reached for the handle. Emma's warning rang in her mind. The last time she'd touched something she shouldn't, they'd been trapped inside a tomb for hours. And she did get them into their current predicament.

Still, she thought, as her fingers caressed the cool metal handle, perhaps this could get them out of it. With her mind made up, Maggie closed her hand around the handle and cranked it. It made a clacking noise as she spun it.

CHAPTER 6

The clacking noise echoed throughout the chamber.

"Maggie!" Emma shouted, spinning to face her. "You didn't!"

Maggie continued to spin it. Lights flickered overhead, blinking on and off until they finally glowed to life. The cavern illuminated with weak light from the bare bulbs strung overhead.

"Let there be light!" Maggie exclaimed. She shoved her phone into her robe pocket.

Her eyes roamed around the space. It appeared to be a large cave. Several crevices were hidden behind large stalagmites.

"Wow," Emma said, her voice echoing.

"Yeah, no kidding."

They wandered around the area. Maggie let her fingers caress the rough stone walls.

"Do you think this was manmade or natural?"

"It looks natural," Emma said, "though some of it may have been altered. Obviously, the doorway leading to the stairs."

Maggie's fingers rubbed against something rough, and she stopped to peer at it. Emma continued further into the chamber.

Maggie bent to study the rough spot. She brushed the dirt and dust away before blowing on it.

"Hey, Maggie!" Emma shouted.

"Yeah?" Maggie called, her eyes never leaving the spot.

"I feel air!"

Maggie swung her head toward Emma. "Really? Do you think it's a way out?"

"I hope so."

Maggie returned her attention to brushing dirt away from the protrusion in the stone. As she worked, the lights overhead dimmed, then died.

"Ugh," Maggie groaned. She pulled her phone from her pocket and flicked on her flashlight, before trudging back to the entrance and giving the handle several cranks to restore the lights.

Emma breathed a sigh of relief. "Thanks."

Maggie hurried across the chamber, searching for the spot she'd just left. After a few minutes, she located it and knelt down to study it.

"Maggie!" Emma called.

"What?"

"Come help me search for a way out!"

"Just a second."

"No, not just a second," Emma countered. "Now!"

"But I found something here."

Emma stormed across the chamber and pulled Maggie upward. "We can look at it later, now come on!"

"Okay, okay," Maggie huffed.

They crossed to the far side of the cavern. A breeze tickled Maggie's cheek and rustled her hair. She stopped short. "I feel the air!"

"Yes, this is where I felt it too, but I don't see any openings."

"Come on, let's search, there must be something."

"Let's hope it's not a tiny hole in the wall and is large enough to climb through."

Maggie nodded. They parted ways, searching the crevices for some crack from which they could escape. Maggie wandered to the corner opposite Emma. The breeze felt stronger there. The sound of rolling water reached her ears.

"Emma!" she yelled excitedly. She waved her over to her location.

"Did you find something?"

"Nothing conclusive," Maggie admitted, "but shh. Listen." She held her finger in the air to silence Emma and cocked her head.

Emma's eyes widened. "Water!"

Maggie grinned and nodded. "There's got to be an opening around here somewhere!"

"Let's find it and get the heck out of here."

They hurried to the wall, searching for any opening.

"Here!" Emma shouted from behind an outcropping. Maggie followed the sound of her voice and located her. Emma gave her a broad smile as she pointed toward a large hole in the wall.

"We're saved!" Maggie exclaimed, pumping her fist in the air.

"You were right! There was an exterior entrance," Emma said. "After you!"

"Wait!" Maggie said. "Come look at this thing I found."

Emma screwed up her face and sagged her shoulders. "Really? Now? I want to get out of here and go back to sleep! I'm cold and tired."

"But…"

"Can't we just go? We'll look at it tomorrow."

"Promise?"

Emma rolled her eyes. "Yes, I promise."

Maggie nodded and squeezed through the opening and into the brisk night air. Her slippered feet trod across the spring's green grass. The sliver of moon glowed in the now-clear night sky. It glistened off the water lapping at the sheer cliff side.

Emma emerged behind her. She blew out a sigh of relief. Emma craned her neck to glance up at the castle behind them. "What's the fastest way to the front door? I hope it's not locked."

"I'm not sure." Maggie glanced left and right before she pointed in one direction. "This way, I think. Looks like town is down there, and the front faces town."

"Right, let's go."

Emma grabbed Maggie's hands and tugged her along. Maggie pulled back, grinding to a halt.

"Now what?" Emma asked, exasperated.

"Listen!" she whispered.

"To what?"

"Shh," Maggie hissed. She turned her head to listen. Her eyebrows shot up and she glanced sharply at Emma. "Hear that?"

Emma's brow furrowed. "Yeah," she breathed. "What is it?"

"Sounds like…"

"Music."

Maggie's eyes grew to the size of saucers. "Bagpipes."

Maggie wrapped her arms around her midriff as she her eyes darted around. A chill raced up her spine and she shivered.

"Where is it coming from?" Emma questioned.

"A ghost," Maggie groaned, biting her lower lip.

"It's not a ghost. Ghosts aren't real."

THE LOST TREASURE OF DRAKON

"Says you," Maggie shot back.

"Sounds like it's coming from back this way," Emma said, taking a few steps toward their previous location.

"Come on, let's get out of here."

"Oh, *now* you want to go, huh?"

"Yep," Maggie confirmed.

Emma turned back to face the direction from which the music floated. She flung her arms out and shrugged. "It's gone." She spun back to face Maggie. "Okay, let's go."

Maggie nodded and hurried around the castle's side. They reached the large front doors. Maggie pressed the depressor on the large iron handle. The door didn't budge.

Maggie pouted at it. She pressed the button again and jiggled the door. It wobbled in its frame, but did not give way.

"Are you kidding me?" Emma cried.

Maggie huffed, cocking her hip as she pulled her phone from her pocket. She tapped angrily at it before holding it against her ear. "At least this time we have reception."

After a few rings, Henry's sleepy voice answered. "Maggie?" he questioned.

"Yeah. Hi, babe. Umm, would mind doing me a huge favor?"

"Favor? Now? It's the middle of the night."

"Well, it's kind of important."

The covers rustled and Maggie heard a yawn on the other end of the line. "Okay, sure. What is it?"

"Emma and I kinda got locked out. Can you swing down and open the front door and let us in."

"What?" Henry questioned.

"Henry! This is no time for questions. Come on, hurry up! It's cold out here!" Maggie poked at the phone to end the call.

"Is he coming?" Emma inquired.

"He'd better be."

53

They waited a few more moments, shivering in the chilly night air, before the sound of a lock disengaging rang through the air. The large front door creaked open on its hinges.

"Ah, finally, thank you!" Maggie exclaimed, as she pushed past Henry and into the warmth of the castle. She rubbed her arms.

Henry stared at them as they passed him. "I want to ask, but I don't even know where to begin."

Emma rolled her eyes and shook her head. "Your girlfriend couldn't sleep. And ended up getting us in trouble as usual."

He turned his gaze to Maggie.

She shrugged, still rubbing at her arms. "I tried texting you, but you were asleep."

"So, what? You went out for a nightcap in your pajamas?"

"Not exactly," Maggie answered.

Emma sighed. "After dragging us through the castle halls, Maggie managed to stumble upon a secret passage. And, like typical bull-headed Maggie, she ran right into it to explore. And, of course, someone shut us in there. And we got stuck."

"Whoa, wait, back up," Henry said. "You found a secret passage?"

Maggie smiled and nodded, excited by her find. "Yes! Hidden behind a book called Viking Treasure in a small, private library upstairs!"

"And then you went into the passage and got stuck?"

"Not got stuck," Emma corrected. "We were locked in."

"Oh, stop being so dramatic. You act like someone did it on purpose," Maggie said.

"Maybe they did," Emma argued.

"Somehow, the bookcase we used to access the passage got closed, and we were stuck. We couldn't open it, so we had to find another way out. We came out on the other side

THE LOST TREASURE OF DRAKON

of the castle." Maggie motioned to the side facing the water. "But then the door was locked!"

"Maybe you shouldn't go roaming around at night," Henry suggested.

"I already tried that suggestion. All I got for it was locked in a cold, musty stairwell."

"You two are no fun. We haven't even told you the best part yet."

Henry stood speechless for a moment as Maggie offered a coy glance. "Do I want to know?"

Emma crossed her arms. "It's stupid."

"No, it isn't," Maggie argued, swatting at her. "We heard the ghost piper!" She raised her eyebrows and offered a cat-who-caught-the-canary grin.

Henry's features twisted into an amused expression. "You aren't serious."

The smile vanished from Maggie's face, and she replaced it with an angry frown. Henry chuckled.

"She is," Emma said.

Henry's facial muscles tensed as he attempted to hold back his laughter. Maggie's expression soured further.

"Sorry," he choked out amidst giggles. He sobered and cleared his throat. "You were saying?"

"I wasn't. I'm not going to tell you so you can make fun of me."

Maggie tightened her robe's tie and stormed up the stairs.

Henry winced. "Maggie, wait," he said, as he raced up the stairs after her. "Come on. I didn't say I didn't believe you. And I didn't mean to laugh. I just... it took me by surprise, that's all."

Maggie offered him an unimpressed glance, her arms crossing tightly over her chest.

"Look, why don't we talk about this in the morning?"

She didn't budge.

"Come on, Maggie," Henry urged. "We're supposed to be on vacation."

After a few moments, Maggie relented. "Fine," she said, grasping his hand. "We'll talk about it in the morning. Besides, I want to go back to the cave we found. There's something in there I want to look at."

"Deal. We're here for the weekend. Let's make the most of it."

She smiled and gave him a peck on the lips before skipping up the remaining stairs.

"Nice moves," Emma whispered, as she trailed behind Maggie.

CHAPTER 7

Despite returning to bed, Maggie found herself preoccupied with the secret chamber and the ghostly music. She tossed and turned for most of the night. Light soon filtered in through their north-facing window. Maggie wandered to it and peered out, but could not see the sun rising.

She opted to head for the shower while Emma still slept. When she emerged from their ensuite bathroom, Emma was rummaging through her duffel.

"Good morning," Maggie greeted her.

Emma answered with a yawn and a sluggish, "Morning. You owe me a new robe."

Maggie arched an eyebrow. Emma flashed her back to Maggie and pointed a finger to her rear end. A large smudge of dirt covered it. Maggie spotted several other dirty marks on the sleeves and front of the robe.

"Yikes!" Maggie said, with a wince. "Sorry. I'll go into town and get you a new one."

"Don't worry about it, I was only joking," Emma said, before disappearing into the bathroom.

Maggie sauntered to the night table and snatched her phone. After snapping a few pictures from her window, she sent a text to Henry and made plans to meet for breakfast.

Minutes later, she stepped into the hall as Henry emerged from his room. They said their good mornings and strolled out of the castle into the fresh morning air. With the plan of walking to town, they started their descent, following the winding drive.

"Did you sleep when you went back to your room?" Henry asked.

"Eh, more or less. Hey, while we're in town, I need to look for a new robe for Emma. I kinda ruined hers. It got all dirty while we were traipsing around the castle last night."

"I can't believe you found a secret passage."

Maggie shrugged as her shoes slapped against the road. "It's not *that* much of a stretch. I bet the whole place is full of them. The more interesting thing is the cavern we found. I want to go back there and look at the spot on the wall I saw last night."

"Spot on the wall?"

"Yeah," Maggie explained. "There was something rough on the wall, like a carving. I'm not sure what it was, but I'd like to find out."

"How could you see anything? Wasn't it dark?"

"No. There was a crank on the wall which powered overhead lights, so we had enough to see while we searched for a way out. Emma found an exit before I could really get a good look at it."

They reached the small town below and found a cafe serving breakfast. After a leisurely meal, Maggie and Henry strolled through the quaint town, perusing the shops.

"It's so nice to do real shopping," Maggie said, buying souvenir after souvenir.

THE LOST TREASURE OF DRAKON

Henry hauled the bags for her, seeming less than enthused. "Yeah, it's a real blast."

"Oh, be quiet. Oh! A clothing store. Let me just pop in and see if I can find a robe."

Maggie spent another hour perusing the shop, finding not only a robe, but a new sweater and several pieces of Celtic jewelry.

They wandered back up the hill to the castle. Henry dropped all the packages at Maggie and Emma's door. They agreed to meet in fifteen minutes to explore the castle and Maggie's latest find.

Maggie pushed through the door, dragging her bags with her. Emma sat on the bed with pillows propped behind her. She stared down at a book.

"Did you get that from the library we found last night?"

"No," Emma answered curtly. "I'm never touching another book in that library."

"You're no fun." Maggie rummaged around in the bags. "I bought you something."

Maggie pulled the robe from the shopping bag. She shook it out and held it up. "What do you think? To replace the one I ruined."

Emma eyed the robe Maggie held. Sherpa fleece trimmed red and blue plaid fabric.

"You didn't have to do that. I was only kidding."

"Yes, I did. Besides," Maggie said, glancing to Emma's ratty robe tossed over an armchair, "that robe has seen better days."

"I like that robe," Emma protested.

"Apparently. Looks like you've worn it for one hundred years, and then some."

Emma rolled her eyes as she hopped off the bed and snatched the robe from Maggie's hands. She held it out and studied the item.

"Try it on, make sure it fits!"

Emma slipped the robe around her. "Good job on the size."

"Fits like a glove!"

"Wow. I don't think I've ever had a robe this nice," Emma admitted. She ran her hands up and down the fabric. "Thanks."

"You're welcome. And please, retire this thing." Maggie picked up the thin pink fabric and waved it in the air.

Emma snatched it back and folded it, placing it in her suitcase. "I'll keep it for when I'm sick."

"Henry and I are going to go exploring. Want to come?"

"Ummm," Emma hesitated.

"Book's that interesting, huh?"

"Not really. I just..."

Maggie grabbed her hand. "You're not butting in, and you're not a third wheel. Besides, we'll get Leo to come with us."

"I wasn't going to say that."

"Yes, you were." Maggie pulled her toward the door, and they exited into the hallway, finding Henry waiting.

"Where's Leo?" Maggie inquired.

Henry wrinkled his nose. He thumbed toward their room. "In there. Why?"

"Well, go get him," Maggie said.

"Why?" Henry asked again.

"For Emma," Maggie whispered, through clenched teeth.

"I can hear you," Emma said with a huff.

With understanding dawning, Henry offered a nod and disappeared into his room. The two men emerged a few minutes later, arguing.

"Well, here I am, as demanded," Leo said, flinging his arms out.

THE LOST TREASURE OF DRAKON

"We're going exploring. I thought you might like to join us," Maggie said. She tilted her head toward Emma.

"Am I going to get dirty?"

"Probably with Maggie in the lead," Emma answered.

"Speaking of, I heard you had quite an adventure last night," Leo said, directing the statement to Emma.

"We did," Emma answered. "My robe paid the price for it, too."

"It wasn't a big loss," Maggie retorted. "Come on, let's go!"

The party of four paraded down the hall, with Maggie detailing plans for an outdoor walk while the weather held, and an inside exploration when the predicted rain began to fall. As they rounded the bend, they bumped into Piper and Charlie.

Everyone exchanged their good mornings, despite the noon hour approaching. "Looks like a nice day so far. Want to join us on our little excursion?"

The couple exchanged a glance, then agreed.

"But only, chicky, if we can head to the pub for a spot of lunch."

"Deal. We'll take a walk around the grounds, head to town for lunch, then back here. While we eat, I can tell you about what we found last night!"

"Found last night? Huh?" Piper questioned, as Charlie draped his arm around her, and they followed Maggie down the hall.

"Yep!" Maggie exclaimed. "Come on! Lunch is on me!"

The group spent the remainder of the morning wandering the gravel paths which wound around the castle's grounds. The lush green grass and rolling hills gave them several picturesque photo opportunities.

After their walk, the group descended the hill into town for a pub lunch.

"Back again, eh?" the waitress asked.

"Yes," Maggie answered, "and with a bigger appetite. I'll have the fish and chips." She offered a broad grin. "I've always wanted to order that at a real pub."

"Haven't run into our Phantom Piper, have you?" she joked, as she jotted down Maggie's drink order.

"Ummm," Maggie said, biting her lower lip.

"Not me," Leo said. "All I ran into was my bed."

"Yeah, I bet all that passive riding in the car was probably exhausting," Henry retorted.

"I was tense. Your driving is horrendous."

"Told you," Maggie chimed in.

"I was trying to make good time."

"I thought the driving was fine, mate," Charlie said.

"Thank you, Charlie. At least someone appreciates that I got us here in record time."

"I didn't say I didn't appreciate it," Maggie countered. "Just that you drive like a madman sometimes."

"But he *did* get us here in record time," a new voice said.

"Uncle Ollie!" Maggie exclaimed. "I was wondering where you were! Would you like to join us for lunch?"

"Popped into town for some sightseeing," he said, as he dragged a chair to join them. They flagged down the waitress and added Ollie's order to her list.

"Find any interesting sights in town, Ollie?" Emma inquired.

"Mmm, yes. I visited the cross statue on the hill. Beautiful handiwork and even more beautiful views. And I toured the small church. A lovely woman showed me around. Great stained-glass windows and some really old graves! If you have a chance before the rain, check it out."

"Maybe we can head over there after lunch," Piper said. "I'd like to get a few more pictures of the view."

Everyone agreed to sightseeing.

THE LOST TREASURE OF DRAKON

"So, boss lady," Piper said, after they finalized their plans, "what was it that you found last night?"

"Yeah, chicky, and where? Weren't you in bed?"

"No," Emma said with a groan. "*We* were not in bed."

Ollie's eyes widened. "You two were up roaming the castle last night?"

"Indeed we were. And Maggie got us into hot water as usual," Emma lamented.

"It was only warm water, not hot," Maggie argued. "Tepid really."

"Do tell," Ollie said.

"Well, I couldn't sleep. So, I suggested we take a walk around the castle and explore. Actually, I wanted to go outside, but Emma was a spoilsport."

"You got your wish anyway," Emma retorted, after sticking her tongue out.

"Well, anyway, we found a little library upstairs. It had lots of books on Vikings. And I found one called *Viking Treasure*. I figured I'd leaf through it, maybe borrow it for some light reading to fall asleep.

"Except when I pulled it, it triggered a mechanism. Turns out the bookshelf hid a secret passage!"

"You found a secret passage in the castle?" Piper inquired.

Maggie nodded with an excited grin.

"Yep," Emma answered, folding her arms over her chest. "Got stuck in it, too."

"You got stuck in it?" Leo asked.

Emma nodded.

"Wow, you really know how to get into the thick of things, chicky," Charlie said.

Emma continued her nodding, pursuing her lips, as Maggie explained further.

"There was a spooky spiral stone staircase leading down.

To where..." Maggie paused dramatically as she leaned in toward the table. "Who knows?"

"So, we crept inside..."

"Wait, stop," Leo said, waving his hands in front of him. "Who the hell creeps inside a secret passage in a castle with no idea where it goes?"

"Maggie," Emma retorted.

"Will you just listen?" Maggie snapped.

"Fine, fine, continue. I was just wondering."

"Anyway," Maggie began again, narrowing her eyes and leaning toward the table. "We crept inside, and started circling down the staircase."

"What was at the bottom?" Piper asked.

"And why'd you close the bookcase behind you?" Charlie added.

"We didn't," Maggie answered.

"But you said you got stuck inside," Charlie said.

"Someone closed us in," Emma answered.

"What?"

"We don't know if it was deliberate, but yeah, we got locked in. Someone closed the bookcase while we were going down the stairs."

"Wow! So, how did you get out?" Piper asked.

"We found a different way out."

"There was no trigger to open the bookcase from the other side?" Ollie questioned.

"There was," Emma explained. "But it was locked with a five-letter code."

"We tried a few words but couldn't get it open." Maggie lowered her voice and arched an eyebrow. Her voice turned gravelly. "So, cold, scared, and desperate, we were forced to find another way out."

Emma rolled her eyes at Maggie's dramatic account.

"We descended into the depths of the passage," Maggie

continued, her voice still low in pitch. "At the bottom, we found a huge cavern. Pitch black.

"Armed with only my cell phone flashlight, we thought we'd never find a way out."

"Did you see light from the outside? Is that how you found your way out?" Piper asked.

Maggie shook her head. "No light. But I did find a crank on the wall."

"And like usual, Maggie touched it."

"Did it open a doorway into the castle?" Charlie inquired.

"No, it was a power source. I cranked it and lightbulbs lit overhead. Which made it so much easier to explore."

"Why would there be power in a cave under the castle?" Leo asked.

Maggie shrugged. "That's the question. *And* I found something else."

CHAPTER 8

Maggie shot the group a coy glance following her statement.

"What was it?" Ollie asked.

"Some kind of carving in the wall. I didn't get to explore it thoroughly because Emma found a way out and insisted that we leave. I want to go back today and get a better look at it."

"Well, as you noted, I was cold, scared, and desperate, so it's no wonder I insisted we leave when we had the chance," Emma said.

"Where'd you come out?" Piper asked.

"On the side of the castle overlooking the Firth," Emma answered.

"Wow," Piper replied.

"Oh, but that's not the whole story," Emma said. "Continue, Maggie. Tell them what happened next."

"Nothing much. We found out that we were locked out of the castle, and I had to call Henry to let us in."

"No, not that. The other part. Between escaping the creepy cavern and the locked door."

Maggie glanced down at her napkin and traced the outline. "I…"

"We heard bagpipes, and Maggie thinks it was the ghost."

"What else could it have been? We were standing outside and suddenly there was music. We couldn't figure out from where, and no one was around."

"Not a ghost," Leo said. "There are no such things as ghosts."

"Then where did the music come from?" Maggie questioned.

"Maybe somebody was practicing their bagpipes in the castle."

Maggie looked unconvinced.

"That could be it," Emma answered. The group went silent for a moment while their food was delivered.

Henry scrunched his eyebrows. "What I don't understand is why you went back up to the bookcase when you found a way out."

"Oh, we went back up before we found the cavern."

"Why did you decide not to see what was at the bottom?" Piper asked, as she stabbed a few pieces of her salad.

"Maggie ran into a cobweb and thought there was a spider on her."

"You *told* me there was a spider on me," Maggie shot back.

Emma shrugged as she picked at her food. "Anyway, I noticed while we were checking for spiders that the passage had gone darker, so we went back up to check."

"That must have been scary!" Piper said.

"It was. Especially when we couldn't find a way to open the bookcase, and then when we did, it was password protected."

"I'm curious to know what the symbol carved into the cavern's wall looked like," Ollie said.

"I didn't get a great look. It was covered in dirt and dust. It kind of looked like a snake or a serpent type of creature."

"Loch Ness monster?" Ollie said, with a chuckle.

"You know, it kind of did look like that, yeah," Maggie answered.

"Oh, don't tell me you believe in that, too?" Emma said.

"They saw *something*, Emma," Maggie countered. "They have a picture for Pete's sake."

"Would you mind if I tagged along with you to take a peek at this carving?" Ollie inquired, directing the conversation back to the subject at hand.

"Not at all. In fact, I'd like for you to see it!" Maggie said. "Anyone is welcome to join us."

"If it's all the same to you, I'll stay on the outside. I'm not taking any chances getting stuck in some creepy cave," Piper said.

"You are such a fraidy-cat, Piper," Maggie said.

"And I'm still alive because of it," Piper claimed.

"Okay, okay. You can be our lookout for the Phantom Piper," Maggie said.

Piper wrinkled her nose but agreed. With their plans set, they finished their lunch while discussing the sights in the area. Following lunch, they wandered around the town, with Ollie in the lead.

As the clouds began to accumulate in the blue sky, they climbed the hill toward Clydescolm Castle. Maggie led the group around the castle's corner. She scoured the area for the opening she and Emma had emerged from the previous night.

Her brow furrowed as she propped her hands on her hips, scanning for the opening. "It was right here!" she exclaimed, flinging her hand toward the rocks sitting below the castle.

"Sure it was," Leo taunted.

"She's correct," Emma said. "I was with her, and we came

THE LOST TREASURE OF DRAKON

out somewhere around here. But I can't find the opening now. It must be difficult to see."

Piper stood with crossed arms staring at the rock face. "Maybe for the best, boss lady," she said.

"Oh, here, found it!" Emma called. Barely visible behind an outcropping, Emma peeked out and waved her hand.

"Told you it was here," Maggie said to Leo, before stalking over.

"How fascinating," Ollie said, as they slipped out of the increasing wind and into the confines of the cave. Charlie stayed behind with Piper while everyone else followed Maggie and Emma.

Cell phone flashlights sprang to life as they entered the cavernous space. Maggie made a beeline across the cave's length toward the opposite side. The cranking noise echoed off the stone walls as Maggie turned the crank on the wall.

Bulbs flickered to life, illuminating the space.

"It's interesting that someone rigged up these lights," Ollie said, as he scanned the lightbulbs hanging from the ceiling.

"Yeah, makes me wonder why," Henry chimed in. "There's got to be a reason."

Ollie scanned the room. "And this is the stairway leading to the castle?" he asked, as his gaze fell on the curved stone stairs disappearing from the cave.

"Yeah. Come on," Maggie offered, "I'll show you."

Maggie illuminated her cell phone's flashlight again, and darted up the stairs with Ollie and Henry.

Maggie pounded her fist against the back of the bookcase when they reached the top. "This is the bookcase we came through last night."

She shined her flashlight onto the brass cylinders. "And here is the lock thingy."

"Ah, yes," Ollie said as he adjusted his glasses and peered at the cylinders. They read "DOUBT."

"We tried every word we could think of," Maggie said with a shrug.

Ollie chuckled as he fiddled with the tumblers. "Well, it isn't queen, visit or admit," he announced as he straightened up.

"Good guesses," Maggie said. "Should we join the others?"

"Yes, I'd like to see this carving you found," Ollie answered.

They descended the curved stairway, reaching the cavern below. Emma stooped near the wall halfway across the chamber. She brushed at a specific spot.

"Did you find it?" Maggie asked, while she gave the crank a few more turns to keep the lights on overhead.

"Yeah," Emma said, her face set with concentration as she worked flicking dirt away with her finger.

Ollie joined her, plopping onto his backside next to Emma and adjusting his glasses. He leaned closer to the wall. "Very interesting," he murmured.

"Yes," Emma agreed. "I can't make out the whole thing yet, but it appears to be some kind of dragon."

"Correct," Ollie said, as Maggie leaned over his shoulder. "And by the looks of the stylization, it's Viking."

Maggie studied the dirt-caked carving. A large head protruded from a curved body. A horn jutted from the back of its head, and its tongue curled from its snub-nosed snout. The body was formed by a crisscross of braided lines. The carving seemed to continue further to the right, but the dust covering it made it impossible to view.

"Yes, Viking, I'd agree," Emma answered. She made a few more swipes with her fingertip. "This is slow-going. A brush would make this easier."

All eyes turned to Maggie.

Maggie stood and frowned. With a wrinkled nose and puckered lips, she dug in her purse and pulled a makeup brush from her bag. She handed it to Emma. "Someone owes me another brush."

"Might be able to hit up the government if you stumble upon another discovery," Ollie joked.

Emma worked on brushing dust and dirt away from the body portion of the dragon. Its neck curved back while its belly jutted forward.

"Try a bit over here," Ollie suggested, pointing to the area behind the arch of the dragon's back.

Emma moved her focus to the right of the dragon's body. "I'm not seeing anything here," she said as she worked.

"I'm guessing something is there, because it looks like there is a second dragon here." Ollie pointed to an area caked with grime directly to the right of the other dragon's head.

Emma lifted her eyebrows. "I see it," she said, moving the brush to swipe on the new area. With careful work, Emma unearthed the head of a second dragon.

Ollie joined in, working with his fingers to uncover as much of the body as he could. Emma returned the brush to the first dragon. She unearthed the bottom and began working toward the emerging body of the second dragon.

After fifteen more minutes of work, and another crank on the power supply, they had uncovered the rough outline of two dragons connected by a Celtic knot.

"Now," Ollie said, as they both pulled back to study the carving, "I propose there is something in the middle here."

He tapped his finger in the space between the dragons' bellies.

"It's a safe bet," Emma answered. "But it must be something more subtle than the illustrated dragons."

"Mmm, yes, it's likely it is. May I?" he inquired, reaching for the brush.

Emma relinquished it and allowed Ollie to take the lead

on uncovering anything underneath the layers of dirt between the two dragons.

"See anything?" Henry questioned.

"Nothing yet. Can someone shine a stronger light at the area?" Ollie asked.

Henry flicked on his flashlight and shined it on the spot.

"Looks like something right here," Emma exclaimed, pointing toward a dark spot.

"Indeed," Ollie said, as he worked quickly but carefully to brush dirt away.

A symbol slowly began to take shape as Ollie flicked the brush around. A centralized circle with eight equidistant spokes pointing toward runic symbols filled the space between the two dragons.

With the rough work complete, Ollie leaned back again.

"Interesting," he noted as he studied it.

"Definitely Viking. Both the stylization of the dragons and these runes suggested that," Emma said.

"Yes. But why is it here?" Ollie questioned.

"Maybe somebody liked carving," Leo suggested. He sat across the room, his back leaning against a rock as he scrolled on his phone.

"You think it has some meaning, Ollie?" Henry inquired.

"I don't think it was placed here for kicks and giggles," Ollie answered.

"Or because someone liked carving," Maggie said with a roll of her eyes.

"Listen," Leo said climbing to his feet, "I hate to be a real buzzkill over your misplaced enthusiasm, but perhaps we should talk about what's going to happen tomorrow rather than fangirling over the snake carving."

Emma wrinkled her nose at Leo's comment.

"It's a dragon carving," Maggie retorted. "And no. We're all having a nice time fangirling here."

"While it is a neat archeological discovery, he may have a point," Emma said with a sigh.

"I don't mean to take away from it," Leo added. "I'm sure it is, but we're leaving tomorrow and I, for one, would like to know what's going to happen, since we're all stuck in one car together."

Maggie wandered to the opening of the cave and tapped a few times on her phone before she answered. "Has anyone checked if their meetings have been canceled or the conditions of the roads to their destination? I just got a text from Cate that says we likely won't be able to get to Dunhaven until mid-week. So, Henry and I have no plans until about Wednesday."

"Good point, Maggie," Ollie said. "I, for one, have not, but before we make any decisions, we should check. We may very well have no plans."

Emma had already risen and joined Maggie near the cave's mouth. She waved her phone around in the air. "How are you getting reception in here?"

"I've got like one bar," Maggie said. "Here, switch places with me."

"Ah, there we go." Emma's thumbs flew across her display. As she typed, she updated them. "They would like to change our meeting from Monday to Tuesday afternoon. I'm responding with an affirmative, unless you object, Ollie."

"No objections here."

"Okay," Emma said, as she fired off her email. "So, we'd need to be in Aberdeen by Tuesday at two."

Leo waved his phone in the air triumphantly. "*My* meeting was *not* canceled. Which means I need to be in Inverness by tomorrow night for a 9 a.m. on Monday morning."

"How are you getting signal over there?" Emma questioned.

"I have an iPhone, which beats your Android any day. I told you to get an iPhone when you upgraded."

"I like my Android," Emma mumbled.

Maggie rolled her eyes and crossed her arms. "Okay, okay, back to the topic at hand. We drive to Inverness tomorrow. Leo can go to his meeting, we'll do some sightseeing, and then Tuesday morning, we'll drive to Aberdeen. Then we can all head to Dunhaven to finish out the week. How's that sound?"

"I could just take the car and go to Inverness myself, and let you stay here with your carvings," Leo suggested.

"No, no way," Henry countered. "You're not stranding us here with no car."

"I'm hardly stranding you. I'll be back Monday night. It's only three and a half hours from here. If I leave right after my meeting, I'll be back by the afternoon."

"No way," Henry repeated. "It's our car, mate."

"Which you don't need, *mate*. Just stay here another night!" Leo argued. "Maggie loves the castle, and maybe you can find some more carvings to play with."

"I, for one, would like to see Inverness," Emma said with a shrug. "I can't speak for Piper and Charlie, but they are honeymooning, so they'd probably like to sightsee, too."

"Ohhh!" Maggie exclaimed. "It's near Loch Ness. Oh, can we go? Say we can go!"

"This is stupid," Leo retorted, crossing his arms. "There's no point in dragging everyone to Inverness."

"There is a point. I want to go to Loch Ness!" Maggie shot back.

"And, I'll point out again, it's our car, mate."

"Fine, fine," Leo acquiesced, flinging his arms in the air. "We'll *all* pile into the car and drive three and a half hours to Inverness and hope we can find a hotel, just so Maggie can see Loch Ness."

"Well, I'd like to see it, too," Emma chimed in.

Leo bit his lower lip and raised his eyebrows. "I guess it would be something to see. Anyone mind waiting for my meeting to finish before we visit?"

Maggie wrinkled her forehead and scrunched up her face. "Who are you?"

"Sounds like we have our plan then," Ollie said, as he rose to stand and brushed dirt off his clothing. He glanced back toward the carving. "I am sorry to leave this behind."

"We should tell someone," Emma said. "Get it documented."

"Definitely." Ollie pulled his phone from his pocket and snapped several pictures of the crudely uncovered carving. Emma did the same as did Maggie.

"What?" she asked when Emma shot her a look. "I found it. I want to put it in my scrapbook."

Thunder rumbled in the distance outside the cave.

"Sounds like the rain's coming," Emma said.

"Yep, I'm heading inside before I get caught in the rain," Leo answered. He strolled to the opening and disappeared from the cave.

The lights overhead flickered. "Well, I guess that's our cue," Maggie said.

CHAPTER 9

They filed from the cave into the cool breeze outside. The skies had darkened considerably, with ominous gray clouds moving up the coast. Maggie scanned the area in search of Piper and Charlie.

"Hmm, they must have gone in," she said to Henry.

"Odd they didn't call in to tell someone," Ollie said.

"Yeah," Maggie agreed, "Piper would have warned us about the weather if they were retreating into the castle."

"Should we head in? Looks like the skies are about to let loose," Henry said.

"Yeah. I just want to get one last picture from up top here," Maggie said as she hiked a bit further up the hill.

Rounding the corner, she almost ran into Piper and Charlie.

"*There* you are!" she exclaimed. She spun to face the rest of her group. "Found 'em! What are you doing up here?"

"We heard something, and we were following up on it."

"Heard something?"

"Yeah, chicky, we heard… "

"Maggie! Hurry up, it's starting to rain!" Henry shouted, as large drops of rain began to fall.

"Okay, okay. Hold that thought, Charlie," she said, as she hurried up the hill and snapped a few pictures.

Maggie hustled down the grassy hill to rejoin Henry. The others had already started their return to the castle. Rain fell more freely as they rounded the corner, and Maggie and Henry dashed to the front door, slipping inside just as a downpour began.

Thunder rumbled overhead and lightning lit the sky.

"Wow, sounds like another bad storm," Maggie said, wrapping her arms around her midriff.

Henry slipped his arm around Maggie's shoulders and gave her a kiss on the cheek. "You afraid of storms, princess?"

"No," Maggie said, glancing around the foyer, "though in a castle like this it may be creepy. Especially with that Phantom Piper around."

"Ghosts aren't real, babe," Henry assured her.

"I wouldn't be so sure about that, mate," Charlie interjected.

Henry scrunched his eyebrows together.

"Come on, then, we'll tell you all about it. Piper's in the sitting room. They've got lots of board games we can play."

Piper knelt in front of an open cupboard perusing the selection of games. "They've got tons of classics!" Piper exclaimed.

"Did you pick one, fair maiden?"

Piper narrowed her eyes and reached into the cupboard. She shimmied a game box out from between the others. "Yep!"

"Ollie, you in, mate?" Charlie asked, as he dragged another armchair to the round table across the room.

"No, thanks. I'd like to do a bit of research," Ollie

confirmed. "They've got hot chocolate in the library." He raised a mug clutched in his right hand.

"Ohhh," Maggie exclaimed. "I'm grabbing one. Anyone else?"

With everyone interested, Maggie disappeared from the room to retrieve the warm comfort food. She returned with a tray full of mugs loaded with marshmallows, peppermint stirs and drizzled with chocolate sauce. A plate of shortbread cookies rounded out the selection.

Charlie had arranged the chairs in close proximity around the table. Maggie eased the tray onto a nearby low cabinet. "Hot chocolate for everyone!"

"Did you sprinkle cinnamon on mine?" Leo asked.

"Yes, actually, I did." Maggie lifted a mug from the back of the tray and passed it to Leo. She passed the others out before she settled into a chair next to Henry.

After a sip of her hot chocolate, she asked, "What game are we playing?"

"Clue!" Piper exclaimed. "It's a special Clydescolm Castle edition, complete with rooms from this castle!"

Maggie grimaced at the choice. "Clue? You want to play a murder mystery game in a creepy castle?" Thunder boomed overhead, and she winced and slouched in her seat.

"What better place to play a murder mystery game set in a creepy castle than in a creepy castle during a storm?"

"She's got a point," Henry said.

"I guess so," Maggie agreed with a shrug.

"Scared?" Emma inquired.

A bolt of lightning streaked through the sky and a loud clap of thunder boomed, just as the room plunged into darkness.

"Now I am," Maggie answered, as blackness surrounded them.

Lightning shot across the sky, illuminating the room with

spooky shadows. Charlie and Henry toggled on their cell phone flashlights.

The doors to the sitting room opened and a man stepped inside. He carried a candelabra with him. The glowing flames lit his face from beneath his chin, casting eerie shadows across his features.

"Sorry for the trouble," he said. "I hope the power won't be out for long, but in the meantime, we've got plenty of candles."

He transported several unlit candelabras into the room along with battery-powered hurricane lamps. With them all lit, and a promise to restore the power as quickly as possible, he disappeared from the room again.

"Clue by candlelight," Piper said, with an arched eyebrow. She high-fived Charlie as the flickering flames glowed against the game board.

Ollie settled into his chair with a fresh hot chocolate, a shortbread cookie, and his stack of books.

"Choose your characters!" Charlie said. "I shall be Professor Plum."

He snatched the purple game piece from the center of the board and placed it on its starting square.

"I'll take Colonel Mustard," Henry said.

Leo puckered his lips. "I guess that leaves me with Mr. Green." He rolled his eyes and stuck the game piece on the board.

"Calling Mrs. Peacock," Piper said. "Because I'm digging her hat on the picture."

"I'll take Miss Scarlet," Maggie said.

"Of course you will," Emma said, with a roll of her eyes. "Looks like I'm Mrs. White."

With the character selection out of the way, three cards placed in the clue envelope, and the others distributed with game sheets, they handed the die to Maggie.

"Miss Scarlet always goes first," Piper said.

"Of course she does," Emma groaned.

"Oh, pipe down, Emma," Maggie retorted. "It's just a game."

She rolled the die and made her move, passing the die on to Henry.

"So," he said, as he tossed the die and clacked his character three spaces along the game board, "what's this about ghosts being real?"

Charlie raised his eyebrows and grinned, the candlelight flickering off his features eerily. Piper leaned forward as Emma made her move. She pulled a single candle toward her, holding it under her chin. With one eyebrow arched, she began her story in a gravelly voice.

"We were standing outside the cave waiting for you. Suddenly, from seemingly nowhere, a strange sound on the breeze." She whispered the next word. "Music."

Piper tilted her head, raising both eyebrows and puckering her lips in a coy smile.

"Bagpipes, to be exact," Charlie added.

Maggie winced, her skin turning to gooseflesh. "Really?" she asked with wide eyes.

Piper nodded. "The strains of bagpipes floated on the wind. We scanned the horizon in all directions, but we couldn't find the source. Then, as suddenly as it began, it was gone.

"*But*," Piper said, raising her voice and banging her hand against the table, rattling the game board and its pieces, "then, the skies darkened, and thunder rumbled in the distance. An icy wind gusted past us. And there it was again. The sound of bagpipes playing a forlorn song."

Maggie held her mug close to her chest as she clutched at her collar. A shiver passed through her.

"We heard it once more just before you came out of the

cave. We searched every time we heard it, but we never found anything. Just a cold icy wind, and the haunting sounds of a bagpiper not of this world."

Piper raised her chin and narrowed her eyes, before she blew out her candle and plunged her face into darkness.

Maggie jumped in her seat. Piper relit the candle and put it down next to her. Maggie frowned, pulling her legs up onto the chair as she curled into a ball, considering the story.

"Earth to Maggie, it's your turn," Emma said.

"Oh, sorry," Maggie mumbled, grabbing the die to roll it.

Henry rubbed her arm. "Come on, Maggie, don't get so upset. It's just a story. They're just teasing."

"Uh, actually, mate," Charlie corrected, "we're not."

"Yeah, we really heard the bagpipes three times."

"And we really couldn't find out where they were coming from."

"The second time we heard them, it almost sounded like it was coming from everywhere all at once. It was pretty creepy."

Emma made a face. "Are you guys being serious or just trying to razz Maggie?"

"No, a thousand percent serious," Piper said. "I'd never torment her that much. I'd never hear the end of it."

Emma's brows scrunched together.

"Really?" Henry inquired.

"You can't seriously think you heard a ghost playing bagpipes," Leo chimed in.

Piper shrugged as she moved her game piece into the library. "I heard what I heard. Believe what you want, dude."

"And I heard it, too. So, you can believe us, or call us both liars," Charlie answered.

"There has to be some reasonable explanation," Leo retorted.

"I can't believe I'm saying this, but I agree with Leo," Henry said.

"Yeah, there is," Piper answered. "Some bagpiper bit it and now he's roaming around the countryside playing his pipes as a ghost. Miss Scarlet in the library with the revolver."

Leo offered a card to Piper in response to her accusation. She jotted something on her investigation sheet and play moved on.

"It's not a dead bagpiper," Leo replied.

"There is a Phantom Piper," a new voice said. "And he guards a treasure."

Everyone jumped in their seats and spun to face the entrance. The man who had brought the candles in earlier stood framed by flickering orange light.

"And," the man continued, "he's not just anyone. He's the former Lord MacClyde. You can check out his portrait in the portrait gallery located just beyond the library." He motioned towards it. "If you dare." He offered a ghoulish laugh, before his demeanor changed completely. "Anything I can get you folks? We're still working on the power. We hope to have it restored soon."

With everyone's needs tended to, the man disappeared from the room again.

"I bet you he tells that story a hundred times a day," Leo said.

"Probably to every tourist that comes here," Henry added.

"When the lights are back on, I'm going to that portrait gallery to take a gander at this guy," Maggie said.

"You think you'll recognize him, huh?" Emma inquired.

"No, I don't. I never saw him, remember? I only heard him."

"So, what's the point?"

"I just want to see him. Then I'll know if I come across him."

"Oh, come on, Mags," Leo cried. "You can't seriously believe in ghosts."

Maggie pouted but didn't respond.

"Then how do you explain what we heard, mate?" Charlie asked.

"I don't know about ghosts, but I do believe something is going on here to cause that music," Emma said.

"Probably a button behind the front desk that the guy hits every so often so he can drive tourism," Leo spat out.

"He wasn't behind the desk last night when Emma and I heard it."

"Oh, right, while you were roaming around the property in the middle of the night. Remind me again why you were doing that."

"I couldn't sleep."

"There's always some truth in every fable," Ollie said.

Leo rolled his eyes. Maggie slumped further in her seat. Emma offered a nod, and Charlie wrapped his arm around Piper, who frowned.

"Either way, we're out of here tomorrow, so the mystery will remain unsolved," Leo said.

"Speaking of, I got us all set at the hotel in Inverness for the next two nights," Henry added.

Maggie smiled and squeezed his arm, but offered nothing else.

CHAPTER 10

They continued with their game, playing several rounds, until they ordered dinner from a local eatery. The lights flickered to life in the middle of their meal.

As the group broke up in the early evening. Maggie wandered toward the library, joined by Emma, Henry and Ollie. They wound their way past it to find the portrait gallery. Large paintings lined the long hall. The floorboards creaked as the quartet made their way into the darkened space. Dull light filtered in through the windows on the far side.

Maggie felt around on the wall, finding a switch and flicking it. A large chandelier hanging in the middle of the room blared to life.

Maggie shielded her eyes as they adjusted before focusing on the row of portraits across from the windows. She scanned the line of them. Lord MacClydes, ranging from the 1600s to the present, stood in a row.

They began with the oldest, working their way toward the current Lord MacClyde. Maggie studied face after face of the MacClyde family, until she found a portrait near the middle of the room with the nameplate Lord Kendrick MacClyde.

"Here he is!" Maggie exclaimed. She stared up at the nineteenth-century man in his finery. He posed with the infamous bagpipes he was rumored to play even in death. With narrowed eyes, she stared at his painted face. "What is your story, Kendrick?"

"I think we've heard it from a few different people," Emma answered. "He found some treasure, then hid it. Then he returned as a ghost to protect it."

"Where'd he put it? And why did he hide it? And is he really a ghost?" Maggie asked.

"I don't think he's talking," Henry said.

Maggie gave him a final glance, before continuing down the line of portraits. They reached the end where the portrait displayed the current Lord MacClyde. Maggie's jaw dropped.

"Is that the guy from the lobby?" Maggie asked. "The one who gave us the candles when the power went out?"

"Looks like it," Emma answered.

"Really? *He's* Lord MacClyde? Wow! Why didn't he say anything?"

"A lot of them are quite different from the lords and ladies of yore," Ollie said. "Most of them have to work at keeping these old places up. He probably turned it into a hotel to keep the place running."

"And he probably tells all the tourists about the Phantom Piper to keep the tourism going strong," Henry added.

"Likely," Ollie said.

Maggie wandered down the row of portraits again. She stopped at a portrait of the Earl in the early 1900s. She studied the portrait for a minute, before returning to Kendrick MacClyde. She stared up at it for a few moments.

"He's *not* a ghost roaming the property, Maggie," Emma said as she passed her.

"I know!" Maggie insisted. Her gaze flitted to Kendrick again before she followed Emma from the room.

"At least I think," she muttered under her breath, as she stalked away.

The four of them retreated upstairs to their rooms to turn in for the night. Maggie lay awake staring at the ceiling or watching the clouds roll by outside. Something about the portraits nagged at her, but she couldn't place it.

"Emma," she whispered into the dark. She received no answer. "Emma?"

A soft snore from Emma's direction indicated she was asleep. Maggie sat up and grabbed her phone from the night table. Her thumbs flew across her keyboard to send a "You awake?" message to Henry.

She tapped her foot under the covers as she waited for a response. None came. With a sigh, Maggie pressed the phone icon and stared at Henry's number for a moment. Her thumb hovered over the call button before clicking off her display.

She set the phone on the table and flung herself back in the pillows. With a sigh, she stared out the window. She squeezed her eyes shut and concentrated on sleep. After a few moments, she blew out a long breath and opened them.

Maggie swung her legs over the side of the bed and slipped into her slippers. She tied her robe around her and paced around the floor. She settled at the window, leaning against the woodwork as she stared out at the night sky. Her eyes surveyed the ground below.

Maggie grasped the handle and inched the window open. The sound of water reached her ears. Maggie leaned out, feeling the cool wind on her cheeks. She strained for any other sound. With her eyes closed, she listened, in particular, for the distinctive sound of bagpipes.

With no telltale sounds on the wind, Maggie eased the window shut. She returned to pacing around the room. After a stint in the armchair where she passed the time by tracing the pattern formed by the plaid on her robe, Maggie leapt up and grabbed her phone and key.

She quietly pulled the door open and crept out, easing it shut behind her. She wandered down the dimly lit hallway.

Maggie strolled through the halls, ending up at the private library. She stared at the book entitled *Viking Treasure*, before she reached out toward it. She tugged on the book, triggering the bookshelf to open. Maggie toggled on her flashlight and hovered inside the open bookcase.

She stared down into the musty stairwell. Cool, damp air filtered from below. Maggie lifted her foot to step inside the passage, before she changed her mind. With a shake of her head, she returned to the library and pushed the bookcase shut.

"Don't do anything stupid, Maggie," she muttered to herself.

She returned to roaming the halls of the castle. She perused the selection in the downstairs library. The large space was lined with floor-to-ceiling bookshelves. Heavy navy draperies framed the two window seats in the room.

Maggie parked herself on one and stared out the window again. The change in scenery held her interest for a quarter of an hour before the restlessness crept back into her limbs. She rose and gave another look through the shelves, before she shuffled from the room.

Maggie entered the hall and glanced in the direction of the stairway leading to her room. She spun on her heel in the opposite direction and headed further away.

In a few steps, she found herself hovering outside the portrait gallery. Maggie twisted the knobs on the doors and pushed them open. She wandered into the space. Moonlight filtered from the windows. Long shadows were cast across the floor from the grilles in the windows.

Maggie's eyes scanned the portraits with their eerie moonlit shadows. She flicked on her cell phone's flashlight rather than turn on the overhead lights. She waved the light over the portraits as she strode down the room's length.

She stopped, her light hovering over the portrait of Kendrick MacClyde. What was it about this portrait that had kept her up, she pondered? She tilted her head as she continued to study his features. She stared at the bagpipes he clutched in his hands.

Something about them caught her eye. She leaned forward to get a closer view, when a noise startled her. Maggie jumped, the phone flying from her hand and clattering to the floor. The light bounced around wildly, before the phone landed face down with the light pointing toward the ceiling.

A figure appeared at the far end of the room. Limned in light from the hallway, the man wore a kilt and clutched something at his side.

Maggie swallowed hard, her throat going dry and her heart thudding in her chest. Goosebumps pocked her flesh as she wondered if she was encountering the ghost of Kendrick MacClyde.

CHAPTER 11

The man took a step toward her.

"Stay back!" Maggie warned, holding a shaky hand out in front of her. Maggie sidestepped toward her phone on the floor.

The figure took another step. Maggie dashed for the phone, swiping it from the floor and shining it at the man.

He held up a hand in front of his face as he squinted against the light. "Ms. Edwards?" he inquired, as he attempted to peer at her.

"Wh-who are you?" Maggie asked.

"William MacClyde, your host. Will you lower that light?"

Maggie blew out a long breath and dropped her arm at her side, pressing the other against her chest. "Oh, Lord MacClyde, you scared me half to death."

"Scared you?" he questioned.

Maggie studied him, realizing he held a lantern at his side, not bagpipes. He must have been retrieving them from whenever they were after the power outage earlier.

"Yes. I thought you were someone else. Maybe a ghost."

"The ghost of Kendrick MacClyde?"

"Something like that," Maggie answered.

"No, sorry to say, I'm a regular human being, so there'll be no tales for you to tell when you return to America about your encounter with the Phantom Piper."

"That may be for the best," Maggie answered.

"What are you doing down here, anyway?"

"I couldn't sleep. We came in here earlier to look at the portraits and something was bothering me about them. I wanted to take another look."

"Bothering you about them?"

"Yeah, just something niggling at me. I'm not sure what. It's probably nothing. Just my imagination running wild over those ghost stories everyone keeps telling around here."

"Oh," he said with a chuckle, lighting the lantern and joining her in the middle of the room. "There he is. Old Kendrick himself." They stood in front of the nineteenth-century earl's portrait, both gazing up at it.

"Yes, with his bagpipes, no less."

"Aye. Those bagpipes that will haunt the countryside."

Maggie remained silent for a moment as she studied the portrait. "That's it!" she exclaimed after a moment.

"That's what, lass?" William inquired.

"The bagpipes. *That's* what I noticed earlier."

"Aye? They're very prominent. Hard to miss."

"No, no, no," Maggie said, as she hustled across the room and flicked on the light. She rejoined him and pointed to an outline painted onto the bag.

William squinted at it. "Looks like a wrinkle in the fabric."

"That's what I thought, too, but look closer."

He leaned in and gazed at it. Maggie snapped a picture on her phone and then flicked at it to enlarge one area.

"It's a symbol!" she said triumphantly.

"Aye, so it is. Some kind of serpent, by the looks of it."

Maggie shook her head. "That's a dragon. A Norse one, too."

"Oh?" William raised his eyebrows. "You sound quite knowledgeable."

"The thing is," Maggie admitted, "we just found one of these carved in a cave under the castle."

"What?"

Maggie nodded. "Come on, I'll show you."

Maggie led him through the castle halls and to the front door. "Oh, is this unlocked?" She toyed with the handle. "Last time we got locked out."

"Lucky for you, I've got the keys. And when did you get locked out?"

Maggie arched an eyebrow. "It's a long story."

"Unless you've suddenly grown tired, I'm all ears."

Maggie led him around the side of the castle and toward the cave. She toggled on her flashlight in search of the opening. "It's around here somewhere."

The man scrunched his eyebrows as he eyed Maggie searching the rock.

"Ugh, forget it. It's hard to see even in the daylight."

"Too bad. I'd have loved to have seen this symbol. And you still haven't told me about getting locked out."

"There's another way in. Come on, I'll show you and I'll explain on the way."

They traipsed back into the castle and Maggie led him to the small library.

"We came here the other night when I couldn't sleep the first time. I was looking through the books and found this one." She pointed to the book entitled *Viking Treasure*. "I thought this sounded interesting, so I tried to take it." She tugged on the book and the mechanism to open the bookcase disengaged with a click.

Maggie tugged the bookcase open further. "And voila! A secret passage."

William wrinkled his nose. "I never knew about this."

"Really?"

"No. No one ever told me."

Maggie lit her flashlight and stepped inside. "This leads down to the cave. The last time we came in this way, we got locked inside."

"Who closed you in?"

"If it wasn't you, I have no idea."

"It wasn't me, lass."

Maggie narrowed her eyes at him. Who else could it have been, she wondered?

"I cross my heart!" he added, when she didn't speak again.

Maggie took a deep breath. "Well, anyway, if we follow these down, we'll find the carving."

Maggie led him down the circular stone steps and into the large cavern. She cranked the crank on the wall and the lights sprang to life.

"Wow," William said, his voice echoing in the chamber.

"Yeah, that was kind of neat," Maggie said, as she crossed the room. "Here's the carving."

"Ah, so it is. Let me see the picture again." Maggie held her phone next to the stone wall. "Aye, they do look similar."

"Yes. Which suggests Kendrick MacClyde was aware of this."

"A safe bet. Though I'm not sure what it means."

"This is a Viking symbol, according to my uncle."

"Viking?"

"Yes, like the treasure Kendrick supposedly stumbled upon and still guards."

William pursed his lips and glanced around the cave. "Well, looks like we missed out on it. This place is empty."

Maggie nodded.

"A bloody shame, too. I could have used that money."

"Really?" Maggie asked, as they retreated up the stairs, this time finding the passage still open.

"Aye. Running a castle is expensive." They roamed the halls as they discussed the financial difficulty facing William MacClyde.

"Don't you make good money on the hotel bit and tourism?"

William clasped his hands behind his back and shrugged. "Enough to keep me afloat. And I try to drum up interest with the haunting story, but that's all a bunch of bunk. There are no such things as ghosts. And this old girl's falling apart. I don't know how much longer I'll be able to keep her going."

"That's so sad. What will happen to Clydescolm Castle if you leave?"

"Oh, she'll sell to someone for peanuts. And that will be the end of the MacClydes at Clydescolm. After fourteen generations, I'll be the one who lets the family down." He offered a disgusted sigh.

"You can't look at it that way. Times are different now."

"Aye, they are, lass. Though, no offense, but as an American, you may view things quite differently."

Maggie wiggled her eyebrows and nodded. "I suppose so."

"Well, here we are back where we started," William said, as they arrived in the portrait gallery. "And none the richer for it."

Maggie offered a consoling smile.

"Can I get you anything, lass? Perhaps a glass of warm milk to help you sleep?"

"No, I'm okay. I'll just wander back to my room. Hopefully, the stretch of my legs and fresh air will make me sleepy."

"Well, good luck then. I'll leave you to it."

"Thanks," Maggie said, as he wandered to the door.

"Oh, lass, if you wouldn't mind, please shut the lights off when you leave. Expenses and all that."

"Will do," Maggie promised.

She shook her head as she watched the man amble away.

"What a shame," she mumbled, as she returned her attention to the portrait of Kendrick MacClyde. Her mind rambled through the possibilities of finding a large Viking treasure and William saving his castle with it. Too bad, as he pointed out, the cavern was empty. Had the treasure been there before, Maggie wondered?

She studied the picture of Kendrick with his Viking dragon carefully hidden in the folds of the bagpipes. The conversation with William replayed in her mind. Was he really unaware of the cave? Had that secret not been passed down through the generations?

Someone had to know after Kendrick. He couldn't have wired the lights, could he? Maggie pondered when lights were invented, and after a quick Google search, confirmed it was after Kendrick's time.

Her forehead wrinkled and she hurried to the earliest portrait. She studied them all carefully, finding nothing of interest. When she reached Kendrick's again, her eyes fell to the dragon immediately.

She continued down the line. Nothing else of note until she came to a portrait of William's grandfather. As she studied it, something caught her attention. The man stood in a kilt, his hands clasped behind him, and his head held high. A set of bagpipes sat near his feet. Hidden in the folds of the bag was the symbol of the dragon.

It couldn't be a coincidence. Maggie snapped a picture of it. Perhaps they were the same bagpipes, handed down through the generations. Maggie swiped between the two pictures on her phone. No, the design was entirely different. So, then why did they both contain an image of the dragon?

None of the other pictures contained any dragon imagery. With a sigh, Maggie flicked off the lights and wandered back to her room. She crept inside. Emma slept soundly, undisturbed by Maggie's entrance.

Maggie disrobed, tossing the plaid garment over the armchair before she slipped between the sheets. She felt as awake as she did when she'd left the room earlier. With a sigh, Maggie grabbed her phone and toggled open her photo gallery. She swiped between the two pictures she'd taken of the portraits. Why did they both have dragon symbols?

After twenty minutes and no new solutions, Maggie placed the phone on the charger and rolled over, finally falling asleep.

CHAPTER 12

Bright light streamed through the window the next morning. Maggie groaned as the light filtered through her still closed eyes.

She rolled onto her back and covered her face with her hands. A moan escaped her lips.

"Good morning," Emma said.

Maggie glanced at her through slits. "Ugh," she groaned.

Emma folded her pajamas and tucked them into her suitcase. "I'm finished in the bathroom, so it's all yours."

Maggie sighed as she perched on the edge of the bed. "Oh, I'm really regretting last night," she moaned, as she staggered to the bathroom.

"What happened last night?" Emma called into the bathroom, as Maggie turned on the shower and adjusted the water.

She wandered into the bedroom and pulled clothes from her suitcase. "I couldn't sleep, so I got up and wandered around all over the place again."

"Seriously?"

"Yeah, seriously." Maggie retreated into the bathroom and closed the door. "Tell you about it after my shower!"

She emerged from the bathroom forty-five minutes later.

"There," she said as she tossed her pajamas into her suitcase. "That helped a little. But I am in serious need of some coffee."

"So, what's up with you wandering around the castle again?" Emma asked, as she zipped her duffel bag shut and dragged it to the door.

Maggie sighed. "Well, I couldn't sleep. You were asleep, Henry was asleep, so I just decided to explore on my own."

"Wait," Emma interrupted. "You didn't wake me up?"

"I tried. But you were totally out."

Emma shook her head. "Of course, you tried."

"Anyway," Maggie continued, as they stepped into the hall. "I went to the bookcase and…"

"You didn't go in it, did you?" Emma burst.

"No. Will you stop interrupting me?"

"Sorry!" Emma said. Maggie knocked on Henry's door. The door swung open immediately. Leo stood with his sunglasses on, luggage at the ready.

"Breakfast?" Maggie asked.

"Make it quick, I'm ready to roll."

Maggie scrunched up her face. "Ready to roll? We have plenty of time. Relax."

"I'll relax when we make it to Inverness," Leo said. "Good morning, Emma. Sleep well?"

"Amazingly, I did, despite Maggie wandering in and out of the room."

Henry appeared at the door. "What? You went roaming around again?"

"She did," Emma confirmed.

Maggie nodded and recounted the tale as they wandered down to the lobby for a continental breakfast.

"I went to the private library and opened the bookcase. I did *not* go in. Instead, I went to the other library, then I went to the portrait gallery, and I found something strange."

"Strange?" Emma inquired, as Maggie sipped her coffee.

"Mmm, yeah," Maggie said with a nod. She pulled up the pictures she snapped. "Both these portraits have that dragon thing on them." Maggie pointed it out.

"Huh," Emma said as she swiped back and forth. "That's odd. We should show this to Ollie."

Maggie nodded in agreement. "Anyway, while I was in the portrait gallery, Lord MacClyde himself showed up. We had a discussion about the symbol, and I showed him the carving in the cave…"

"Wait, stop," Henry said. "You took the earl into the cave?"

"I did. Don't say it. Not everyone's a bad guy, Henry." Maggie shot him a glance ceasing any lecture he may be about to launch into. He held up his hands in defeat as he took a bite of his pastry. "And he's got a really sad story. He says without more tourism, he's not going to be able to keep the castle going much longer."

"Not surprising given the size of this place," Leo said, glancing around. "The bills in this thing have got to be astronomical."

"Yeah, he said as much. It'll go out of his family after something like fourteen generations or whatever."

"That's sad," Emma said.

"Yeah," Maggie agreed. "Too bad that treasure isn't real."

They finished their breakfast and Henry began to load the luggage in the car's trunk. Maggie wandered back to the portrait gallery for one last look at the paintings. "Where did you hide that treasure, Kendrick?" she questioned aloud.

"Talking to yourself?" Emma inquired.

"No, I'm talking to him," Maggie said, flicking a finger

toward the painted image of Kendrick. "He's got that dragon on his bagpipes. It's got to mean something."

"That he was really into Viking lore, maybe," Emma suggested.

"And then his great-great... whatever, his descendent, was too?"

"Maybe." Emma shrugged as she glanced at the pictures. Maggie puckered her lips and stared at the enigmatic earl. "Anyway, I was sent here to collect you."

Maggie's facial expression changed in an instant. With her eyes wide, she crossed her arms over her chest and said, "Collect me? Henry sent you to collect me?"

"No," Emma said. "Leo did. Henry warned him not to do it. He said you'll just deliberately take longer."

"He's right," Maggie said, flipping her hair over her shoulder and returning her gaze to the portrait. "Just for that, I'll stand here for another two minutes and stare at this guy."

"Are you sure you're not standing there for another two minutes to stare at him because he's not bad looking?"

"That's not hurting," Maggie admitted.

Emma shook her head and chuckled. She looped her arm through Maggie's. "Come on."

"All right," Maggie acquiesced. "We have to stop by the front desk first, though. I'd like to say goodbye to William."

"Oh, William, huh?" Emma said, as they threaded through the halls. "First name basis."

Maggie shrugged. "I guess I could say Lord MacClyde, but do people really use that anymore?"

"Uh, I think they do," Emma informed her.

Maggie lifted her eyebrows. "Well, then I guess he should be calling me Lady Edwards."

"Lady Edwards? When did you get a title?"

"Last night," Maggie claimed.

Emma's eyes went wide, and she slid them sideways to

stare at Maggie. "Is there something you want to share about what happened between you and Lord MacClyde?"

"No."

"Then how did you end up with a title?"

"Oh, I bought one on one of those sites. You know, they plant a tree, and you own like a patch of grass here. For fifty bucks, you can be a lady too, Emma. And it's for a good cause."

Emma chuckled again at Maggie. "I'm not sure yours is as real as his."

"Either way, a title's a title."

They swept into the foyer and Maggie spotted the kilt-clad man shuffling through papers at the makeshift front desk.

"Hi!" Maggie said, as she approached and leaned against it.

"Well, Ms. Edwards," he grinned. "Did you manage to get any sleep?"

"I did. But not before I bought a title, so you can call me Lady Edwards now." She winked at him.

"Oh, well, milady," he said, with a bow.

Maggie giggled at his over-the-top display. She drummed her palms on the desk and said, "I just wanted to thank you for our stay. We really enjoyed it."

"I hope you'll return."

"I'd love to," Maggie said. "I'll have to plan for it."

"Where are you headed now?"

"First to Inverness, then to Aberdeen, and then to Dunhaven."

"Dunhaven? What kind of business is taking you to a small town like Dunhaven?"

"Personal. I'm visiting a friend there."

"I see. Well, I hope you'll have a lovely time. Maybe your

friend can even get you in to see the castle there. I hear it's haunted, too." He winked at her.

Maggie laughed. "My friend owns the castle, and she swears it's not haunted."

"Your friend owns it? I didnae realize you were friends with Lady Cate Kensie."

"Do you know her?"

"No, I only know of her. I've never had the chance to meet her. Though I understand some of my ancestors were good friends with some of her ancestors."

"Maybe one day your families can reconnect!"

"You never know. Well, safe journeys to you."

"Thank you!" Maggie called, as she strolled to the front door. She stepped out into the bright sunshine. "Figures it's sunny as all heck when we're leaving."

"*There* you are," Leo exclaimed, leaping from his lean against the car.

"I told you if you rushed her, she'd take longer," Henry said.

"Whatever, just get in."

"We have plenty of time!" Maggie exclaimed. "Where are Piper and Charlie?"

"Already in the back," Henry said, thumbing toward the backseat.

"And Uncle Ollie?"

"That I don't know. I sent him a text, no response. But he knows we're leaving at eleven, so he should be here." Henry leaned back against the car's frame and crossed his arms.

"Seriously? Perhaps someone should call him," Leo groused.

"He'll be here. Never known Ollie to be late," Henry said.

"We've got plenty of time, Leo," Emma called from inside the car.

"I guess so," he said with a sigh, drumming his fingers on the car's door.

Maggie climbed into the backseat and plopped down next to Piper.

"Hiya, boss lady, sleep well?"

"Not at all," Maggie said. "I may doze off. I apologize ahead of time."

"No worries, chicky. I'd offer my arm, but it's already spoken for," Charlie teased, giving Piper a kiss on the cheek.

"I'll survive," Maggie said, as she balled her hoodie and shoved it against the back window.

Leo joined them inside, and Henry slid behind the wheel.

"Where's Uncle Ollie?" Maggie asked, as Henry fired the engine.

The passenger door swung open, and Ollie climbed inside the car. "Where've you been?" Emma inquired, noting the smudge of dirt on Ollie's jacket.

"Exploring," Ollie answered. "And I found something very interesting!"

"What's that?" Maggie called up to the front.

Ollie swiped at this phone and pulled up an image. He passed it to Emma. "Give it to Maggie when you're finished."

Emma studied the image, enlarging it and dragging the picture around, before returning it to its normal size. Maggie tried to view it from her seat in the back.

"Switch with me," she asked Leo.

"What? No way. I'm not cramming myself back there. I need room for my legs."

Maggie rolled her eyes. "Fine," she grumbled, as she reached for the phone.

She looked at the picture, recognizing the dragon carving. She stared at it, zooming in and out as Emma had, not certain what her untrained eyes should be finding. "Is there something I should be seeing here?"

Emma grabbed the phone from her and enlarged the image. She handed it back, pointing to a specific area. "See anything here?"

Maggie squinted at it. "Looks like metal or something."

Ollie nodded. "Yes, metal. I took the opportunity to remove more of the dirt. I didn't get very far in the time I had, but I managed to unearth that."

"Is it stuck in there?"

"It almost looks like it forms a keyhole of sorts. I'd have loved to explore further, but Inverness calls," Ollie said.

"Any research on this to back up your keyhole theory?" Emma asked.

"I have my grad assistant checking on that now. It's far easier for her to research it than me while we're traveling!" Ollie swiped at his phone when he got it back. "No report yet."

With no new information, Maggie leaned her head against the balled-up jacket and closed her eyes. The lack of sleep the night before was taking its toll. She hoped to nap before they stopped for lunch.

CHAPTER 13

Maggie jumped as her body shook. "Huh? What?"

"Lunchtime, sleepyhead," Piper said.

"Oh, okay," Maggie said, as she stifled a yawn and stretched.

She climbed from the car and stretched again. "Ohh!" she exclaimed. "This looks nice!"

Rolling green hills overlooked a small pond. The restaurant, a rambling white building which also housed a ballroom for special events, and an inn, perched over top of the still waters.

"Nothing but the best for you, princess," Henry said. Maggie grinned at him. "Did you have a nice nap?"

"I can't complain. At least I got some sleep. Maybe I'll get another hour on the next leg of the trip. For now, though, let's eat!"

The group traipsed into the eatery and was seated on the patio overlooking the water. Bright sunshine shone overhead, and white clouds dotted the azure sky.

THE LOST TREASURE OF DRAKON

Maggie pulled her hoodie on over her short-sleeve top as a cool breeze blew past them. "What a beautiful day!" she said.

"It really is pretty here," Piper agreed. She tapped on her phone and took a selfie with Charlie, before snapping a picture of Henry and Maggie, then Emma and Leo, and finally leaning in for another selfie with Ollie.

With another few taps, she sent the picture to everyone before she stared at something else on the phone.

"Oooh, look!" she exclaimed, flashing the phone's screen toward the table's center. "Our living room is painted."

"I can't believe you bought the apartment next door to me. There's a waitlist for the building, I thought!" Maggie said.

"I can be very convincing, chicky," Charlie told her. "Also, a little extra jingle can go a long way."

"Yeah, that place was crazy expensive, but I couldn't think of a better place to live than next to my favorite boss."

Maggie scrunched up her face. "I'm your only boss."

"I guess you win by default then," Piper said with a shrug.

"What she means to say is, we couldn't think of a better person to borrow a cup of sugar from," Charlie added.

"Maggie's always out of food," Henry warned.

"I am not. I always have sugar," she said, glancing at Piper and Charlie. "It goes with my coffee, which I also always have."

"Any answers from your GA yet, Ollie?" Emma inquired, as the conversation lulled.

Ollie checked his phone. "Nothing yet. It may take her a while to search for anything similar to the dragon we found."

"So, what are you heading to Inverness for, Leo?" Emma said, turning the conversation to him.

"New product. The boss got a hold of some perfume

that's only made here and wanted to ask about partnering. His wife can't get over the scent and he's sure it's going to be a hit."

"Must be some perfume!" Maggie said.

"Really," Emma agreed.

"Can you get us a sample?" Maggie questioned.

"I'll see what I can do," Leo said, offering a nod to Emma.

"Thanks," Emma said with a sweet smile.

After a lovely lunch, they all climbed back into the car to continue the trip. Maggie balled her sweatshirt and placed it against the back window for another quick nap. She closed her eyes and nestled her head against it when the car swayed without warning.

Her eyes shot open, and she glanced around, wide-eyed. "What's going on?"

"Some jackass is riding my tail," Henry said through gritted teeth.

"Slow down and let him pass," Maggie grumbled, as she buried her head in the balled sweatshirt.

The car swayed again. "Henry!" Maggie shouted.

"It's not me! I slowed down; he won't pass!"

Maggie craned her neck to glance out the back window. A dark black sports car with darkly tinted windows followed at a close distance; close enough that Maggie could practically make out the time on the driver's ostentatious wristwatch.

She waved her hand in the back window. "Go around, jerk!"

"Don't think he can hear you, boss lady," Piper said.

Maggie scrunched her face at the car. "What is he doing? GO AROUND!"

She flailed her arm wildly.

Maggie turned around and flopped back into the seat.

THE LOST TREASURE OF DRAKON

After a moment, she twisted to face him again. "Seriously?" The car nosed toward the center of the road before it shot into the opposite lane. "Finally!"

She felt their car decelerate as Henry slowed for the other car to pass. With narrowed eyes, he glared out the driver's window, throwing his hand in the air. The other car swung into the lane in front of them, then jammed on its brakes.

The passengers in the Navigator were tossed forward as Henry jammed on the brakes, the tires squealing.

"You've GOT to be kidding," Emma shouted.

"Yeah, what's with this guy?" Leo cried.

Henry pulled over on the shoulder, letting the car ahead of them continue until it was out of sight.

"What a complete jerk!" Maggie shouted, as they crawled to a stop.

"Let him get ahead," Ollie said. "Give him a few minutes."

They waited a few moments before Henry eased back onto the road. "So much for my nap. I'll never sleep now," Maggie grumbled. She rummaged through her tote bag in search of some reading material. She spotted a few guidebooks in Emma's bag.

"Hey, Emma, do you mind if I look at your books?"

"Not at all," Emma said. She grabbed the literature and passed it back to Maggie.

"Can I see one?" Piper inquired.

"Sure," Maggie said, handing one of the books to her before she settled in with the other. She leafed through the book, scanning a few of the pages before she searched for things near the Inverness area. She landed on the Loch Ness page.

"Did you know Loch Ness is black?" Maggie said.

No one answered.

"And it contains two hundred and sixty-three billion

cubic feet of water, but is not the deepest or largest loch in Scotland?"

"Thank you, guidebook Maggie," Leo retorted. Maggie shoved the back of his seat.

"Did you know the first reported sighting of the Loch Ness monster was by an Irish priest?" Ollie asked.

"Really?" Maggie asked.

"Yes, Saint Columba," Ollie answered. "He supposedly compelled the monster not to attack one of his followers."

"Did it work?" Emma asked.

"Yep. According to the tale, a man was swimming when he was attacked by the beast. The priest sent one of his followers to rescue the mauled man. When Nessie approached Columba's follower, the man made the sign of the cross and told the beast to leave him alone. The monster stopped immediately and swam away."

"No way, Ollie. Really?" Charlie inquired.

"That's the story," Ollie said with a shrug.

"That's not in the guidebook," Maggie complained, as she flipped pages.

"Good thing we brought the prof along," Piper said. "He's full of fun stories."

Ollie offered her a salute from his front seat perch. "Any other cool stories?" Charlie asked.

"Oh, there are always interesting stories in Scotland," Ollie answered.

Maggie shuffled through a few more pages, before becoming engrossed in another entry. "Here's one," she replied. "Blackmoore Castle. Can we go here? It's not that far from Inverness."

"What's special about it?" Piper asked.

Maggie flashed her a picture as she detailed the entry aloud. "First, the blackened stones. It says here some kind of fungus grew on the stones and no one knew why. It created a network of blackened squiggles that resemble veins in the human body. In the early to mid-1800s, superstitious villagers believed the blackening represented some sort of issue with the castle.

"They believed the tragedies that befell the Fletcher family– that's the people who own it – were the result of the castle's black veins, assuming some kind of demonic possession of the building materials existed. Others argued the castle's bricks blackened as a direct result of the strange on-goings, which included the tragic death of Anne Fletcher, Duchess of Blackmoore.

"Fuel was further added to the fire when Robert Fletcher, the seventh Duke of Blackmoore and Anne's husband, remarried an orphan girl who claimed to be able to communicate with the dead.

"Lenora Fletcher, nee Hastings, was often shunned by both her high society counterparts as well as those below her station, though no one ever disproved her claim as she often provided information that only the deceased could provide."

Maggie glanced up at the car's other occupants, her eyebrows raised high. "Wow, what a weird story!" she said.

"Yeah, talking to the dead? That's super creepy, dude." Piper shivered.

"She probably made it up," Leo said.

"Why would she make that up?" Emma questioned.

"To marry the guy. He probably married her because of that story," Leo answered.

"So, you're saying she was a gold-digger?" Maggie inquired.

"If the shoe fits," Leo said with a shrug.

"Can we go here?" Maggie asked. "It's not far, and the castle looks really cool!"

"I'm up for it," Piper said. "I want to see those black veins."

"Fine with me," Emma agreed.

"Whatever," Leo grumbled.

"What do you say, babe?" Maggie asked Henry. He glared at his side mirror, his hands gripping the steering wheel until his knuckles turned white. "Henry?"

"That jackass is back," Henry growled.

"What?" Maggie questioned, her eyebrows squashing together as she whipped around to search the road behind them.

She didn't have far to look, the dark car with its tinted windows practically rode on their bumper.

"Seriously?" she asked, as she flung her arms in the air.

The black car inched into the opposite lane again. "He's going to pass, mate," Charlie said.

The other car swerved into the oncoming lane and sped up.

"I can't get the license," Maggie announced. "The plate's all muddy."

"Yep, in both locations," Henry said, as he tromped on the accelerator. Everyone pitched backward, pinned to their seats. Henry layed on the horn as the car pulled even with him. "Come on, you want to race?"

"Stop it!" Maggie shouted. "Let him pass!"

"He obviously doesn't want to pass. Every time I slow down, so does he," Henry said.

He slammed on the brakes, sending the car's occupants flying forward at the sudden change in speed. Henry slowed enough to pull in behind the other car. It shot into the lane they occupied formerly, matching their pace.

Henry's face scrunched as he pressed the accelerator down. Their SUV shot forward, pulling ahead of the sports car.

"Omigod, omigod, omigod," Piper exclaimed. "There's a car coming straight for us!"

"Yeah, I see it," Henry said, his eyes on the side mirror.

The oncoming car blew its horn as they continued to barrel toward it. The sports car showed no sign of giving up its pursuit to allow them to reenter the proper lane.

With traffic ahead of them, the oncoming car inched toward the side of the road, hesitant to pull over further and risk driving into the deep trough that ran along it. The horn screamed at them as they careened closer to the traffic ahead.

Henry urged more speed from their car, swerving into the appropriate lane and cutting off the threatening sports car. The black car wiggled in the lane as the driver fought to maintain control without wrecking. The oncoming vehicle, horn still blaring, passed them.

They approached the car in front of them at too fast a pace, and Henry darted into the opposite lane again before swinging around it. The sports car followed in pursuit, veering into the lane behind them, as Henry pressed their SUV to maintain its lead.

Within seconds, the sports car caught up and lurched into the opposite lane. It began to inch closer to them.

"Whoa!" Leo exclaimed. "He's going to side-swipe us."

Henry flattened the pedal to the floor. The SUV gunned forward, its hood leaping in the air. The other car swerved away, before it too sped up, matching their speed and inching closer.

"Come on!" Maggie yelled.

"Hope you got the insurance, mate," Charlie said. "This joker's going to hit us."

"What is he doing? Are all Scottish drivers crazy?" Maggie asked.

Emma braced her arm against the roof as Henry urged

more speed from the engine. He glanced at the other car with narrowed eyes before he studied the road ahead.

"Hang on, everyone," he said.

"I don't like the sound of that," Piper said, as she clung to both Maggie and Charlie, squeezing her eyes shut as tightly as she could.

"Remember we're in an SUV with a high rollover rate," Maggie said.

Henry stared daggers at her through the rearview mirror.

"Just sayin'," Maggie shrugged.

"High rollover rate?" Emma questioned, as her eyes grew wide. Her foot pressed an imaginary brake on the floor as though she could somehow control the car. "Why would you say that?"

"He loves the emergency brake trick to spin us in a circle," Maggie explained, as the cars continued to careen down the road at breakneck speeds.

"Oh God," Emma groaned, as her face turned ashy.

"Please don't kill us," Leo groaned.

"I have everything under control," Henry promised.

Maggie noticed Ollie hanging on to the pull bar calmly as though they were moseying along. He'd make a good driver's ed instructor, Maggie mused.

Together they sped down the road, approaching a crossroads. Maggie swallowed hard, praying no one was about to dart across the road.

As the crossroads sped toward them, the other car inched closer again. Feet from the intersection, Henry jumped on the brakes. Smoke poured from the tires as the car fought to slow from their high speed.

The dark car continued forward as Henry maneuvered the car onto the side road. He stepped on the accelerator again, sending the car flying down the road.

Maggie spotted the other car swing around as they pulled off the road.

"He's on to you, and turning around to follow," Maggie called.

"Damn it," Henry grumbled. "Hang on."

Henry eked more speed out of the engine as he sped down the road, searching for an offshoot. He found one several yards ahead and took the turn on two wheels.

"Oh, I'm going to be sick," Emma groaned.

"What is with this guy?" Charlie lamented, craning his neck to stare behind them. He patted Piper's hand. "Don't fret, fair maiden, you're in the hands of a pro. Henry's never lost a car chase."

"Let's hope there's not a first time for everything," Leo said.

Henry used the next few side roads to create as nonlinear of a path as he could between him and the pursuing vehicle. After a series of quick turns, he suddenly swerved into the field. The car slowed and bounced along the grass, shooting for another road as the crow flies. He urged as much speed as he could, given the uneven terrain.

The sports car proved unwilling or unable to follow them across the difficult topography and was forced to continue along the road.

Within minutes, they pulled back onto pavement and Henry shot forward. Maggie scanned the road behind them.

"Clear, for now," she reported.

"We need to find a place to pull over that's safe to regroup."

"Look!" Maggie exclaimed. "Signs for Blackmoore Castle. Follow those. That'll be safe. There's bound to be tons of tourists there."

"Good idea, Maggie," Ollie said.

Henry eased the car onto another roadway, following the

signs pointing toward the castle. They continued along, searching for signs, when Piper groaned.

"Uh-oh," she said.

"What?" Emma questioned, glancing backward at her. "Ohhhh."

"Henry," Maggie said, her eyes fixed on the road behind them. "He's back."

CHAPTER 14

*H*enry tensed his jaw, flipping his eyes between the castle rising in front of them and their pursuer to their rear. The blackened stones of Blackmoore Castle rose high on the moor above them.

"Take the next right," Ollie shouted, as he clung to the assist bar.

Henry skidded off the road onto the other street, with the black sports car following in hot pursuit.

"On the left!" Emma shouted, as a large sign announcing the entrance to Blackmoore Castle beckoned.

Henry swung into the marked entryway. A short distance away, a parking lot yawned. Cars were parked in various spots and people milled around, some returning from the castle above, some meandering through the gardens, and others heading up to the large domicile high above.

He eased into a parking space near several other vehicles. Seatbelts were removed with haste, and the doors popped open as the occupants of the Navigator spilled out, pleased to be out of the vehicle.

Maggie climbed from the car and glanced around the

parking lot. The dark sports car hovered near the egress of the parking lot several feet from them. Maggie scrunched up her face and straightened her posture. She stormed toward the waiting car.

"Maggie," Henry warned.

"Hey! Who do you think you are, you jerk?" Maggie shouted, as she thundered toward the car.

In response, the car's engine revved. Before she could comment further, Henry grasped her arm and tugged her away.

"Leave him," Henry warned. "There's something very wrong here."

Maggie shot another irritated glance toward the car, but allowed Henry to lead her away. As they retraced their steps back to the Navigator, the sports car sped around a corner and charged back toward the road.

"That was some extreme road rage," Leo said.

Henry shook his head. "That seemed odd."

"What could be the reason?" Emma said.

Henry shrugged. "I'm not sure, but it looks like he's gone now."

Maggie sighed. "Well, at least we got to the castle. Should we go up?"

"Yeah, I want to see those stones up close," Piper said.

"They do look eerie," Charlie admitted.

"I'd like to take a walk through these gardens," Emma said.

"They are beautiful," Maggie agreed. "It will be a nice way to end the trip before we climb back in the car and head to the hotel."

With their plan in place, the group headed up the steep walk to the castle hovering above them. The gigantic castle loomed high above, casting long shadows over them as they proceeded up.

Maggie snapped several pictures of the castle. Piper and Charlie stopped for a selfie, using the massive structure as a backdrop. With multiple pictures taken, they walked the last leg and arrived at the entrance to the castle.

They pushed through the large wooden doors and into the impressive foyer. Marble floors stretched throughout the cavernous space. A grand curving staircase swept upward.

Maggie's eyes floated up as she took in the entire space and snapped a few pictures. A letterboard announced the day's tours. With one beginning in ten minutes, the group bought their tickets, and spent the remaining time before the tour commenced snapping pictures.

A tour guide named Melanie gathered a group of about thirty people in the foyer to begin the tour. In a speech that she'd likely given hundreds of times before, she explained the rules to them, reminding everyone that photography was permitted, to stay with the tour group, and not to touch anything.

"Do you think we'll see a ghost?" Maggie asked Emma as the tour set off, wandering from the foyer into the large sitting room to the left.

"No," Emma answered flatly.

Several tour-goers snapped photographs of the generous room as they shuffled inside. Melanie pointed out various aspects of the architecture, as pictures continued to be snapped.

Maggie raised her hand as Melanie's speech wound down.

"Yes?" she inquired.

"Can you tell us about…" Maggie paused as she consulted the guidebook she'd shoved in her tote. "Lenora Fletcher?"

The green-eyed guide offered a coy smirk at Maggie's question. "Aye, I can," she answered, flicking her auburn hair over her shoulder. "In fact, it was in this very room that the

Duke of Blackmoore, then Robert Fletcher, proposed to then Miss Hastings."

Maggie's eyebrows shot skyward as she glanced around the space, as though she expected the see the scene play out.

"He had his estate agent collect her in Glasgow straight from the orphanage and bring her to the castle. And in this very room, he asked her to marry him. But he had a condition attached to his offer.

"He requested she determine why his beloved first wife threw herself from one of the turrets."

Maggie arched an eyebrow, shoving her hands into her back pockets. "That'd be the day I'd marry someone still hung up on his first wife," she murmured to Emma.

"She was an orphan. The offer probably was astounding."

"Okay, good point," Maggie said. She raised her voice and addressed the guide again. "So, did she?"

"What?" Melanie questioned.

"Did she find out why the first wife killed herself? Could she really see dead people?"

"More on that later," the guide said with a wink. "Any other questions?" She searched the crowd, before she said, "Okay! Let's keep moving then!"

They passed through the sitting room, viewing a large dining room with an exquisitely set table, a library, and a tearoom on the main level. Other areas remained roped off.

They used a rear set of stairs to climb to the second level, where they viewed a variety of bedrooms, before they climbed a circular set of stairs to a turret.

The group crammed into the smaller room, standing shoulder to shoulder. A hush fell over the room as Melanie stood on a small stool near one of the windows. She clasped her hands in front of her, an amused smile on her face.

After she caught the group's attention, she proceeded with her tale. "This is the very tower from which Anne

Fletcher, the Duchess of Blackmoore, fell to her death. And where the duke's second wife asserts the first Mrs. Fletcher appeared on several occasions."

People gaped around the room as though they expected to see the ghost wandering through the crowd or hovering near the ceiling. Maggie shivered.

"Did it suddenly get cold in here?" she asked Henry. He slipped his arm around her shoulders and pulled her closer to him.

"So, did she find out why she killed herself?" Piper inquired.

"That is where the tale turns more sordid," the guide explained. "You see, the second Mrs. Fletcher claimed the first did not, in fact, throw herself from the tower, but rather that she was thrown from it."

"You mean she was murdered?" Maggie asked.

Melanie offered a slow nod. "Who murdered her?" Charlie shouted.

"An associate of the duke."

"Wait," Leo said, waving his hands in the air. "Did the guy actually murder her, or did this Lenora person just say that?"

"The story was confirmed by the duke's own brother."

"Did he go to jail?" Maggie asked.

Melanie shook her head. "After he attacked the current Mrs. Fletcher, Duke Blackmoore fought him in a duel..." She paused dramatically. "And killed him!"

"Wow, this place has some history!" Maggie said with a whistle.

"Yeah, no wonder they think it's haunted," Piper added.

A few others in the group asked questions before the group moved on. They descended to the second level, ending up on the opposite side of the castle from where they started.

Melanie led them into a long hall-like room. Large portraits lined both sides of the room. The group wandered down the massive corridor, following their backward-walking guide.

She stopped in the middle of the room near the interior wall. Her hand motioned to a massive painting hanging above them.

"And here is the duchess herself," Melanie said. "If you're interested in learning more about her, she wrote a series of memoirs. They were recently found among a friend of the family's things. Her descendants are in the process of publishing them. One of the first lines in the manuscript is 'My name is Lenora Fletcher. I am the Duchess of Blackmoore. And I can communicate with the dead.'"

The guide offered the coy smile again, before she wound down the tour, suggesting participants take more photos or ask her any additional questions.

Maggie glanced up at the painting and swallowed hard. Two adults stood behind three children in the large portrait. A tall man with dark curls stood straight as a rail in his nineteenth-century finery, his head topped with a top hat. His hand rested on a small girl's shoulder.

Next to him, a woman with piercing blue eyes stood. Her hair was pulled up into an upswept style and she was wearing a light blue floor-length dress. She held two boys' hands.

"She totally looks like she could talk to the dead," Maggie said.

"What's that supposed to mean?" Emma asked.

"It means she kind of looks creepy. Like she's hiding a secret behind those eyes."

"Wow, that's judgy, boss lady," Piper said.

"Yeah, I think you're just jealous, chicky."

"Jealous? What?"

"Maybe that she married a Duke and you're stuck with him," Leo said, tossing his thumb in Henry's direction.

"Hey!" Henry groused.

"I think she's kind of pretty," Piper said.

"Yeah, she's V.P.," Charlie said.

"V.P?" Maggie questioned.

"Very pretty," Piper and Charlie explained together.

"I didn't say... oh, never mind," Maggie said, as she returned her gaze to the portrait.

The others milled around, taking in all the portraits. A few guests spoke with Melanie as the tour came to a close. Henry and Ollie wandered the room, commenting on several of the portraits. Piper and Charlie took selfies with the portrait of Robert and Lenora Fletcher as their backdrop. Leo scrolled through his phone.

Maggie studied the portrait before movement through the open archway leading to the hall caught her eye.

"Hey! Who's that?" Maggie whispered, grasping Emma's arm.

"Huh?"

"That lady!" Maggie said, pointing into the hall. "She looked just like her!"

"The duchess?"

"Yes! Do you think it was her ghost?" Maggie dragged Emma a few steps closer to the doorway. "Come on, let's go look around."

"What? No!"

"Oh, come on," Maggie said.

"The tour's over."

"So? No one will miss us. Come on! Live a little." Maggie grasped her arm and tugged her into the hall, escaping the group.

"Maggie!" Emma breathed.

Maggie kept a firm hold of Emma's arm as they entered the hall. She glanced up and down, before selecting a direction to go. She pulled Emma along, darting up the hall to their left. A massive red runner in the center of the hall's floor dampened their footfalls.

Maggie wound around a corner and into another hall. They paraded past an alcove with a large secretary desk tucked into it. Maggie glanced into the open rooms as they passed. She found no one.

As they rounded another corner, a woman wandered down the hall in front of them.

"There!" Maggie hissed. She raised her voice. "Excuse me, miss?"

The woman stopped and twisted to face them. "Yes?" she said, in a British accent. Her dark brown hair fell around her shoulders, curling on the ends. Her large blue eyes were as piercing as the woman in the portrait. In fact, Maggie figured she could be a dead ringer for Lenora Fletcher.

Maggie approached her cautiously, with her eyes narrowed.

"Have you gotten separated from the tour group?" the woman inquired, in a crisp British accent.

"Ah, well," Maggie hedged, as she closed the gap between them. She bit her lower lip, tilting her head and reaching out toward the woman. She clamped a hand down on her arm. "Aha!"

"What do you think you're doing?" the woman cried, wrenching her arm from Maggie's grasp.

"She's real. Not a ghost!"

"Certainly not!" the woman retorted. "Just who do you think you are, and what do you think you're doing?

She stuck her hand out. "Hi, I'm Maggie Edwards and this is my friend Emma. Maybe you've heard of us?"

"I have not," the woman said.

"Oh, well, we're famous, sort of. We found Cleopatra's tomb and the Library of Alexandria." Maggie gave a knowing smile and a nod. "And now we're here in Scotland on vacation."

"Ah, how lovely. Did you need directions back to the tour?"

"Yes," Emma said. "If you could…"

Maggie interrupted her. "Wow! You really look like her! So, are you part of the tour?"

"Excuse me?" the woman said.

"You look like the lady. What's her name?" Maggie flitted her hand in the air as she tried to recall the duchess's name. "Lenora! That's it! You look like her!"

The woman's eyes widened as Maggie continued. "So, what do you do? Appear during the tour and scare the heck out of everyone? Do you do like a skit?" She glanced down at the woman's attire. "Oh, you probably shouldn't wear those clothes though. No one will believe you're a ghost in that outfit."

The woman crossed her arms and narrowed her eyes. "No," she said in an unimpressed tone.

Maggie crinkled her nose and stared at her. "So, then what do you do here?" she asked.

"I live here."

"Oh. Oh! Oh my gosh, you own this place?"

"Yes," the woman answered. "My name is Lenora Fletcher. I am the Duchess of Blackmoore."

CHAPTER 15

Maggie guffawed at the woman's words. "No way," she said. "Are you kidding?"

"No, I certainly am not!" Lenora said, her tone incredulous.

"Maggie–" Emma tried.

"Can you communicate with the dead?" Maggie asked in a teasing voice.

Lenora's full lips formed a frown. "If you honestly think I haven't heard that before…"

"Sorry. It's just that the tour guide just said those words. She said it's in a new memoir coming out about the first Lenora. The one in the portrait."

"Yes, that Lenora was my great-great-great-grandmother."

"Well, there's no doubt about that. You really look like her."

"I was named after her."

"Good choice on your parents' part. Anyway, we were just looking around." Maggie swung her eyes around the place.

"Would you mind doing that elsewhere? People live here,

you know? How would you feel if someone went poking around your house?"

Maggie recalled the moment she'd entered her apartment after someone had more than poked around in search of the Golden Scarab of Cleopatra.

"We didn't touch anything..." Maggie began. She sighed. "But I understand. When my uncle was kidnapped, someone trashed my apartment and I felt so wronged by it. I can't imagine having people traipsing around your home on a daily basis."

"Yet, here you are," Lenora said.

Maggie winced. "Yeah, sorry. I just wanted to look around."

"I was dragged," Emma said.

Emma's comment earned a half-smile from the current owner.

"And apologize for violating your privacy profusely," Emma added.

Lenora drew in a deep breath and exhaled. "It's all right. I understand how tempting it may be. Though, please, think before you act next time."

"I promise," Maggie said.

Lenora gave them a nod and turned to depart.

"Oh, um," Maggie said, halting her progress. "Could you tell us the way back? It's like a maze in here."

Lenora puckered her lips and nodded. "Make a left at the end of this hall, make another left at the end of that hall. Go halfway down and duck into the upstairs parlor and go out the doors on the opposite side. You'll find yourself in the hall near the portrait gallery."

"Thanks."

Lenora nodded again and left them.

"Nice meeting you," Maggie called after her.

She waved a hand in the air without turning back.

"Nice going, Maggie," Emma spat.

"What?"

"Oh, are you part of the act? Can you talk to the dead? Hahahaha, so funny! You totally insulted the current duchess."

Maggie cocked her head, and puckered her lips with a roll of her eyes. "Oh, come on. She's a dead ringer for the other duchess. Who wouldn't think that?"

"Any normal and polite person," Emma contended.

"Yeah, right. Tell me you were not thinking it. Especially when she said, and I'm quoting here, 'My name is Lenora Fletcher. I am the Duchess of Blackmoore.' It's like she *knew* we'd just heard that and was totally playing it up."

"Even if she was," Emma said, as they hung a left into the next hall, "it's *her* castle to play it up in."

They turned into the next hall as Emma sighed. "I can't believe you got us caught. You're *always* getting me in trouble."

"Yeah, well, thanks for throwing me under the bus. 'I was dragged.'" Maggie mimicked.

"I wasn't taking the rap for roaming around her house!"

They ducked into the upstairs parlor as instructed. "Wait, is this right?" Maggie inquired a few steps in, furrowing her brow. "There's no door across the room."

"There's one there," Emma said, pointing to the wall adjacent to them.

"Maybe that's the one she meant," Maggie said with a shrug. She stepped toward it, when her eye was drawn to two large portraits on the wall from which they had just entered. Maggie's eyes widened.

"Look!" she exclaimed, swinging her arm up to point at the portraits.

A life-sized portrait of the original Lenora Fletcher hung on the wall next to a portrait of her husband Robert. She held an open book in her hands as she stared out with her dazzling blue eyes. Robert stood next to her, clutching the silver head of a cane. He held something in his other hand, though Maggie could not make out what it was.

Something on the portrait caught her eye and she stepped closer.

"Maggie, let's go before we get caught again."

"Just a second," Maggie said, flitting her hand in Emma's direction to dismiss her concern.

Maggie stared at the portrait of Robert Fletcher. In his back hand, he held an envelope. A symbol graced the red wax seal. Maggie's eyes widened as she recognized the image.

"Emma!" she said, waving her over to the portrait. "Look! The symbol of the dragon!"

"Where?" Emma asked, her voice betraying her disbelief as she stepped closer.

"On his letter. In the wax. It's the dragon! The SAME dragon we saw on the portraits at Clydescolm."

Emma's jaw dropped open. "Oh, wow, it is!"

Maggie pulled her cell phone from her pocket and snapped several pictures. "We've got to tell Uncle Ollie." She glanced back in the direction they'd come. "Do you think Lenora knows anything about this?"

"I think we've bothered that poor woman enough," Emma said. "I'm not going to wander around her house again."

"Okay, fine, Uncle Ollie it is!" Maggie said.

Emma's brows scrunched together as she gave one last look at the symbol. Maggie pulled her from the room and they emerged in the hallway.

Maggie recognized the entrance to the portrait gallery across the hall. They hurried into the space where a few people still milled around.

"Hey, where have you been?" Henry said, as she approached.

"You're not going to believe this!" Maggie exclaimed. "Where's Uncle Ollie?"

The man wandered up to them from behind. "Where did you two sneak off to?" he asked.

"We just stepped out to look around. And guess what - the lady who owns this place is named Lenora, and she looks *just* like that Lenora!"

Maggie motioned to the large portrait hanging on the wall as Piper and Charlie joined them, along with Leo.

"Really?" Piper inquired.

"Yeah!" Maggie responded.

"Like a passing resemblance, or eerily similar?"

"Eerily similar; as in, did Lenora Fletcher also live for hundreds of years and it's the same person? And then she said, "My name is Lenora Fletcher". I couldn't believe it. I almost passed out. I thought she was joking!"

"Maggie, will you get to the point?" Emma asked.

"Oh, right." Maggie's voice sped up, betraying her excitement. "Anyway, she told us how to get back to this room. And we had to go through another room to get here. And in that room, there were two giant portraits."

"Get to the point, Mags," Leo groaned.

Maggie frowned at him before she continued. "The portraits were of Lenora and Robert." She waved a pointed finger toward the family portrait across the room. "But in this one, Robert was holding an envelope with a wax seal. And there was a symbol in the wax seal." Maggie swiped at her phone with a shaky finger. "Wait 'til you see it." Her words mixed with a laugh.

Maggie bit her lower lip and flashed the phone in the group's direction.

"Is that…" Piper asked, uncrossing her arms and letting her words hang in the air.

"Uh-huh," Maggie said, her voice rife with enthusiasm. She grinned as her eyes darted to each person in the group.

Ollie took hold of her phone. "Amazing! And you say this is an envelope in the duke's hand?"

"Yes!"

"An odd coincidence, wouldn't you say, Ollie?" Emma said.

"I'd say it's more than coincidence. These depictions are identical!"

Ollie held a picture of his phone next to Maggie's. It displayed the image from the cave under Clydescolm Castle. The dragon on the wax seal matched the symbol from the cave's wall.

"That is odd," Henry agreed. "You think they're connected?"

"I should imagine so," Ollie said. "I'd like to see this in person."

"Sure," Maggie answered. "It's just across the hall."

She pointed toward the room as she walked toward the hallway. The group followed, about to exit, when Melanie called, "Excuse me! That area is off-limits to guests. I'm sorry."

"Drat," Ollie said, as Melanie herded them down to the foyer.

"Should we at least visit the gift shop?" Maggie asked.

"You go ahead. I'm going to email my assistant with this bit of information and see if she can find anything."

The group perused the selection at the small souvenir shop before making a few purchases. As they stepped into the bright sunshine, Ollie pocketed his phone.

"Anything from her yet?" Emma asked.

"Nothing definitive. I've included the detail about Blackmoore Castle, and Duke Blackmoore being connected to the symbol. Let's see if that additional piece of information helps us at all."

After meandering through the gardens below the castle, the group piled into the car. As they headed for their hotel, the sun hung low in the sky. With no new information, they all turned in early.

CHAPTER 16

The following morning, the group wandered through the streets of Inverness as they waited for Leo.

"I'm in favor of leaving that bloke behind," Charlie muttered, as they window shopped.

"I'm right with you, Charlie," Henry agreed.

"He's not that bad," Emma contended.

"Speak for yourself, brainy," Charlie retorted. "He was a bear this morning. He nearly took my head off when I asked him if he wanted a to-go cup of tea."

"He's always like that before a big meeting," Maggie informed them.

"He's always like that, period," Piper said. "He's goofy."

"He's not," Emma countered.

"Ooooh, somebody has the hots for Leo," Piper teased.

"No I do not," Emma spat back.

Maggie arched an eyebrow.

"Stop looking at me like that," Emma warned, pointing a finger at Maggie.

Maggie rolled her eyes. "It's okay if you like him. He's a great-looking guy with a good job. And he's nice to you."

Emma gave Maggie an unimpressed glance.

"What? He's nicer to you than I've ever seen him be to anyone. I think he likes you."

It was Emma's turn to roll her eyes. "I'm sure he doesn't. He dated you, so I'm not the type of girl he's looking for. And besides, that would seem weird after you two broke up."

"There's no weirdness here. Leo and I were not well-suited. Obviously, he dated me, and obviously, it didn't work out. It might work much better between you two."

Emma chewed her lower lip.

"You have my blessing," Maggie assured her.

"Lucky you," Piper teased. "You can date the bear."

Emma shook her head at the collective group, but offered no further response.

"Maggie," Henry warned, "if you keep buying stuff, we're not going to fit it in the car."

"I'll find room," she assured him, as she handed another bag off to him.

"Don't forget to leave room for the Loch Ness souvenirs," Ollie said with a chuckle.

"We'll never get the return flight off the ground," Emma groaned.

"Hey, any word from your grad assistant?" Maggie asked, as they stopped for a late morning snack.

"Nothing yet."

Maggie crinkled her nose. "She's not a very good assistant."

"This information may be very difficult to track down," Ollie explained.

"Did she find anything when she ran the image through the database?" Emma asked.

"She only confirmed what we know already. It's Norse."

Maggie's shoulders slumped. "Why is it always so hard to get information?"

"It's old," Emma said.

"Yeah, princess, this stuff's been buried for centuries in some cases."

"Nothing worthwhile..." Ollie began.

"Is ever easy," Maggie finished. "I know, I know. That doesn't mean I can't complain about it."

"What I can complain about," Charlie said, "is going to pick up that bloke from his meeting."

"Maybe we can push him off the boat and into the loch," Henry suggested, as they stood from their sidewalk table.

"And let the Loch Ness monster eat him," Piper said.

"Wow, that was dark," Emma said, her nose wrinkled.

"Don't fret, brainy," Charlie said, "I doubt even the Loch Ness monster would want him."

Emma rolled her eyes. "He's not *that* bad," she contended, as they wandered to the parked car a block away.

They climbed into the vehicle, and after picking up Leo, a brief stop at the hotel for him to change, and a reshuffle of seats, they continued on to the nearby loch. Leo supplied each of the ladies with a perfume sample from his latest business venture.

"Ugh," Piper moaned, as they piled into the car again. She sneezed. "Did you use the whole bottle?"

"No," Maggie answered. "I did not. Just a spray here and there."

Piper sneezed again.

"I think it smells nice," Emma said. "Thanks for the sample, Leo."

"You're welcome. I'm glad you like it."

"If you like it so much, how about you sit back here squished next to her after she drowned herself in perfume?" Piper said, after another two sneezes.

"I'll switch if you'd like," Emma answered.

"Switch after the gift shop," Henry called, "I'm not stopping again."

"Honeymoon's over already, huh?" Maggie teased.

"I'll move up with Piper," Charlie said. "Switch with Leo."

"No way, uh-uh," Leo retorted. "I need room for my legs."

"I fit," Charlie responded.

"I'm taller than you."

"By a smidge," Charlie answered.

"Why don't I move?" Maggie suggested. "Then I'll be on my own, and no one can complain about my smell."

"Fine," Emma said.

They stopped at a local gift shop. After a few purchases, they continued on to the parking area near the loch. Emma took the backseat for the short trip, swapping with Maggie.

"I can still smell you," Piper said.

Emma fidgeted next to her.

"And she," Piper said, thumbing at Emma, "won't sit still."

"Careful what you wish for," Maggie said, with a wink.

"It's a little tight back here," Emma complained.

"I didn't have any trouble fitting," Maggie said.

"We'll swap back after the loch."

"No," Piper disagreed, "no way. I can still smell you, but it's way less."

Henry eased the car into a parking spot, and everyone piled out.

"Remind me never to get trapped on a vacation with you all again," Leo said.

"No one asked you to get trapped on this one, mate," Charlie countered.

"We could leave you here," Henry added.

"Very funny," Leo answered.

Emma climbed from the car, a frown on her face. "I'm not looking forward to the return trip."

THE LOST TREASURE OF DRAKON

"Maybe the perfume will blow off me and I can sit back there without giving Piper any sneezing fits." She glanced around, shielding her eyes from the bright afternoon sun. "Where's the loch?"

"We've got to walk a bit," Henry said. He motioned for them to follow. They exited the parking lot and crossed a small stone bridge, before Henry turned left.

"Cruise Loch Ness," Maggie read from a nearby sign. "Is this the boat you rented?"

"No," Henry answered. "I chartered my own."

They continued past the sign touting a cruise and further down to a small dock area. Smaller boats lined it. Henry gazed up and down the row, until he caught sight of a man milling around near one of the crafts.

Using a set of access stairs, he led them to the floating dock and approached the man.

"You Henry?" the man inquired.

"Yep," Henry answered. "Angus?" He stuck his hand out to shake the man's hand. "Good to meet you. This her?"

"Aye," the man answered, waving his hand to the boat.

"She looks great," Henry said with a nod.

"Will you be needing a hand with her?"

"No," Henry answered. "I am an experienced sailor. We'll be just fine."

Angus studied Henry up and down, before he nodded.

"Okay, she's all yours then. If you have any trouble, you've got my number."

The man handed the keys over, and with another nod, he strolled away.

"You should have let him captain the ship, babe. We're on vacation."

"Nope, I prefer to handle it myself. Don't worry, there'll still be plenty of time for selfies."

With a smile, Maggie climbed aboard along with the rest

of their group. She settled into a seat near Emma. "Wow! Loch Ness! I wonder if we'll see the monster."

Emma rolled her eyes.

"Hey," Maggie warned, as she held her phone up, "I saw that. Come on, take a selfie with me."

"You and your selfies," Emma complained.

"I'm going to take it whether you're ready or not."

Emma leaned closer to Maggie and smiled.

"Too bad you can't take one with Indiana Jones, there," Leo taunted. "He's too busy skippering the ship."

"I think it's captaining," Maggie answered, as the boat's engine growled to life.

In short order, they were cruising up the short distance into the wider waters of the loch. Maggie scanned the water, glistening under the bright sun as they trolled along. She snapped pictures of the rolling green hills surrounding them.

Ollie offered more history involving the loch as they cruised along. As the subject turned to the infamous Loch Ness monster, Maggie narrowed her eyes, staring at the water.

"I don't know how anybody could see anything in this water," she said.

"It's when it comes out of the water," Leo said.

"Don't encourage her. She already believes in the thing," Emma told him.

"I'm pretty sure I'm not the only one," Maggie said. "Tons of people have seen this thing."

Emma puckered her lips at Maggie's statement, but refrained from comment.

They continued through the water. Maggie stared at the ripples created as their boat passed. In the background, Ollie continued his discussion. He pointed something out, drawing everyone's attention to the left side of the boat, but Maggie's gaze remained fixed on the water, mesmerized by the glistening ripples. As she stared, the ripples seemed to change. Maggie narrowed her eyes as the water swirled in a new direction.

She swallowed hard, leaning over the side of the boat.

"Guys," she said.

No one heard as Maggie leaned further over, her eyes growing wide. A form swam under the water. The ripples parted as a small portion of the unidentified creature peeked from below the water.

"Guys!" Maggie said again, her voice growing with excitement.

Another swish of the water and a portion of a black scaly body flicked out of the loch, disappearing as quickly as it appeared.

Maggie pulled her phone from her pocket. With shaky hands, she toggled on her camera app. She pointed the camera toward the water and pressed record. She waited a few moments, but nothing appeared. With a furrowed brow, Maggie toggled off the video and leaned over the boat again.

Something dark floated just under the surface. Her eyes lit up and she snapped a picture. On the screen, it was impossible to make anything out. Maggie squeezed her lips together in frustration.

She flicked her gaze back to the water. A black hump crested before slipping beneath the surface again.

Maggie's eyes widened and she positioned her camera facing the water again. "There you are," she whispered. "Come on, come on."

She held her breath and chewed her lower lip as she waited. Two black humps slid up and down again. Maggie snapped a picture but missed the creature.

"Shoot!" she hissed.

She pursed her lips and flicked her hair over her shoulder, aiming the camera at the water again.

Seconds later, a sleek black head poked from the water. Two black steely eyes gazed at Maggie. Two humps projected from the water behind it.

Maggie's jaw dropped open. "The Loch Ness monster," she breathed. She centered the creature in her phone's camera. A smile spread across her face. She'd be famous after this picture hit the media. She licked her lips and pressed the button to snap a picture.

CHAPTER 17

Just as her thumb touched the red button, the boat rocked violently. Maggie swayed and struggled to keep to her feet, her arms flailing wildly.

"Hey! What the heck!" she shouted. She glanced over the side of the boat. The creature was gone. Her shoulders slumped as the boat slowed its swaying.

"That maniac just zipped past us," Henry shouted.

"He nearly hit us, mate," Charlie said.

"Yeah, and he got me soaked," Piper said, stripping off her drenched hoodie.

"Ugh, me too," Emma complained, wringing out her shirt.

Maggie stared in front of them. Another boat sped away, leaving them in its wake.

"It doesn't matter," Maggie said.

"Umm, I think it does, boss lady," Piper disagreed.

Maggie shook her head. "No," she said, her voice giddy with excitement. "While you all were gawking on that side of the boat, you'll never guess what I saw!"

"As usual, you lucked out and didn't get soaked because you weren't with us?" Emma asked.

"Nope," Maggie announced, squaring her shoulders and holding her chin high. She arched an eyebrow at them.

"Well, are you gonna tell us, Mags, or just stand there and gloat?" Leo asked.

"I saw the Loch Ness monster," Maggie announced.

Emma guffawed. Piper rolled her eyes. Charlie furrowed his brows. Leo burst into laughter, doubling over. Ollie narrowed his eyes at Maggie.

"Laugh all you want. I have proof!" Maggie waved her phone in the air. "He was tricky, but I got him!"

"Him, huh?" Emma said with a chuckle. "Did he introduce himself?"

"No," Maggie said, with an unimpressed glance. "You know what I mean." She continued, her voice rising in pitch with excitement. "I saw something swirling under the water. Then a black scaly thing breached it. Then two black scaly humps. I tried to get a video, but it didn't work. The humps came out of the water again, and I tried to snap a picture, but I missed it." Maggie frowned.

"Get to the point, Mags," Leo said.

"Yeah, boss lady, do you have the proof or not?"

"I do! I looked in the water again and I saw it just below the surface." Maggie waved her hand in the air and narrowed her eyes in a dramatic display. "So, I readied the camera. And I waited."

Maggie glanced from face to face, ensuring she had everyone's full attention. Satisfied that everyone, including Henry who had emerged from behind the steering wheel to listen, hung on her every word, Maggie proceeded.

"And then, a black head poked out of the water with two beady black eyes. And behind it, two big black humps. This thing must have been like thirty or forty feet long!" She swiped at her phone. "And it was then that I snapped the picture that will make me more famous than Jennifer

Aniston when she was married to Brad Pitt." Maggie flipped the phone to face them and raised both her eyebrows, a triumphant expression on her face.

Piper wrinkled her nose. Emma's eyebrows raised, before she set her jaw and crossed her arms, shaking her head. Charlie winced. Leo rolled his eyes. Ollie pursed his lips.

"Ah, babe," Henry said.

"Yes?" Maggie inquired.

"The picture's all blurry."

"What?!" Maggie exclaimed. She spun the phone to view the picture. Her eyes widened and her jaw dropped open. "No!" She stamped her foot on the boat's bottom. "Oh, no, no, no!"

Maggie pressed her palm to her forehead as she stared at the blurry photo on her phone. A large black blob was visible, but the picture was so blurred, it couldn't be made out as anything else.

"That idiot who sped past us ruined my picture! Ohhh," she lamented. She glanced at the others on the boat. "I saw it. I did!"

"Mmm-hmm," Piper said. "Sure you did."

"Yeah, Mags, it could have been anything."

"It was the Loch Ness monster. Black, scaly, huge. I *saw* it."

The others avoided making eye contact with her.

"Doesn't anybody believe me?" she squeaked. She glanced at Ollie. "Uncle Ollie?" She flicked her gaze to Henry. "Henry?"

"I believe you saw something..." Henry began.

"Unbelievable!" Maggie fumed.

Any further ranting was cut off by a boat speeding toward them. The whine of the engine drowned out any conversation.

"Is that the same guy?" Charlie shouted, as the other craft aimed toward them.

"What the hell is he trying to do?" Henry shouted, as he dove behind the wheel and pushed their own engine faster, making a hard turn.

Maggie swung her head in the direction of the other boat. It raced toward them. Henry's quick maneuvering, coupled with the force of the other boat passing them, caused their craft to rock violently. Maggie lost her footing, stumbling backward with her arms flailing overhead. The cell phone flew from her hands and skittered across the boat's bottom.

As she struggled to maintain her footing, the back of her knee smacked into the bench seat behind her. She failed to remain standing, and toppled over the boat's side into the icy waters. Despite the warmer month, the shock of the cold water hit her like a multitude of knives stabbing at her body.

She flailed as she treaded water, attempting to keep her head above the waves. Water sloshed over her face, and she spiraled to find the boat. Only Henry, Leo and Ollie had remained aboard. She turned again, searching the horizon. Piper, Charlie and Emma bobbed several yards from her.

Henry scanned the waters for his displaced passengers. Maggie grimaced as she realized she was now swimming in the same water as the creature who'd poked its head out at her only moments ago. Her lower lip began to tremble, not only from the cold and the monster, but as she spotted the other boat swing around and line up for another run on their craft.

"Henry! Look out!" she screamed, pointing at the other boat. The skipper of that ship wore a ball cap low, making it impossible to see his features.

Henry, who aimed the boat toward Maggie, reversed course as quickly as he could. Maggie glanced to the other boat. Her eyes widened as she realized she was now the target. She gulped in a breath and disappeared into the icy waters.

With her eyes squeezed shut, she thrashed around blindly. Her hand smacked a large scaly object. A bubble of air burst from her mouth as she offered a silent underwater exclamation.

Maggie shot back to the surface, gasping for air. Her eyes darted around searching for her boat, the second craft, and the creature she'd just tapped underwater.

After avoiding the other boat's trajectory, Henry had ended up near the others who fell overboard. Leo and Ollie hauled Emma aboard. An already rescued Piper shivered with her arms clutched around her midriff.

Maggie spotted the other boat across the loch. It swung in a circle with water spraying in a wide arc. The craft lined up for another run on their boat.

"Ugh!" Maggie groaned. She waved her arms in the air and shouted. "Hey, here! Over here!"

The boat continued to aim at her former conveyance. Henry hurried to the wheel to maneuver their craft away. Leo and Ollie struggled to haul Charlie aboard.

He'd never move their boat in time, Maggie figured. She kicked her legs and surged out of the water, arms waving overhead. "Hey you! Yeah, you, you jerk! Over here! Come and get me!"

The boat's skipper took notice and adjusted his path. Maggie grimaced and her eyes grew wide as the boat approached at a fast clip. She'd need to time her breath right, and she began to worry she'd not make it far enough under the water to not be struck.

Maggie attempted to swim out of the boat's path, finding the freezing water and speed of the craft difficult to outrun. She inhaled a deep breath and plunged under the water. Something rushed past her, but with her eyes shut, she couldn't see it. In an instant, something smacked into her square in the back. The force caused her to release air from her lungs. Whatever struck her pushed her further underwater and propelled her across the loch.

The force on her back released, and she clawed at the water, searching for the surface. Maggie emerged from the depths of the loch. She coughed and panted for air. She rubbed her eyes and scanned the area. She'd surfaced near their boat.

"Hey!" she shouted, waving her arms. Henry, who scanned the water, pointed and shouted to the others aboard. He aimed the boat at her and Maggie began to paddle toward them.

She stopped mid-stroke and returned to treading water. She motioned toward the other craft. It swung around and aimed again at their location. "Go, you'll never make it!"

"It's too late," Henry called, as they pulled up next to her.

Charlie and Leo reached over and yanked Maggie over the side of the boat. She climbed aboard, soaked and freezing. She snapped her head in the direction of the other craft. It barreled toward them. Henry hurried to urge their boat to move, but it wouldn't be fast enough. He'd hit them, or at least swipe them hard enough to do damage, or knock them overboard again.

"Hang on," Henry warned. Maggie clamped a hand on the side rail as she braced for impact.

She eyed the other craft, a grimace on her face. Charlie scrambled to find a flare gun and load it, in a last-ditch effort to stop the impending impact.

Before he could aim, the water in front of the other boat swirled. The boat wobbled for a moment as though something had tapped it. Another few seconds passed before the water swirled again. This time the impact against the other craft boomed. The craft listed hard before giving in to the roll. It flipped over, dumping its skipper into the icy waters. The boat glided to a stop, its wet bottom glistening in the overhead sun.

Maggie scanned the waters for a survivor. She found none.

"What the hell was that?" Charlie asked, as he lowered the flare.

"No idea, but I'm getting us the hell out of here," Henry said, as he pushed the boat away from the other disabled craft.

"The better question is, what was he trying to do?" Maggie asked. "He was trying to run into us. Multiple times! Was he crazy?"

"Or on a mission to kill us," Piper said.

"Why would he want to kill us?" Maggie questioned.

"I'm not certain, but we should remain cautious. That's the second time someone has come after us. I can only imagine it's a result of our recent discoveries," Ollie said.

Maggie's shoulders slumped. She inhaled deeply and glanced around the boat, as Henry high-tailed it away from the other craft. "Is everyone okay?"

Slow nods met her gaze. Emma and Piper tried to wring their clothes out, shivering from the cold water and wet clothes.

"I'm okay," Emma reported, "but I'd really like to be on dry land."

"Me too," Leo said. "That was crazy."

"Says the guy who's completely dry," Maggie retorted.

"That's because I played by the rules. Remain seated and keep your hands inside the ride at all times." Leo waved his hands in the air, wiggling his fingers.

Maggie finger-combed her soaked hair as she shook her head at him.

"I hope that's the end of the excitement, and we scared off

whoever was after us," she said before sighing. "I just want to go to Aberdeen, get your meeting over with, then head up to Cate's for a relaxing long weekend at the castle."

"It certainly scared me off," Piper said. "What hit that boat?"

"And with enough force to capsize it?" Charlie added.

"And," Henry called, "how did you get so close to our boat so fast? Were you a champion swimmer?"

Maggie shook her head. "No. Something pushed me there."

"What?" Emma said, her face pinching with confusion.

Maggie shrugged as she peeled off her hoodie and wrung it out. "Something pushed me there. Hit me right in the back and shoved me."

"Ew," Piper grimaced. "Some nasty sea creature was rubbing all over you."

"That nasty sea creature probably saved my life," Maggie admitted. "I really need to find a towel."

"Yeah, no sitting in the rental until you are dry," Leo said.

Emma frowned.

"What? You'll ruin the seats!"

"What sea creature exists in a loch like this large enough to do that?" Charlie asked.

Ollie rubbed his chin, saying, "The only thing big enough to flip a boat like that is…"

"Don't say it," Emma groaned, holding a hand up to stop him. "I do not want to hear that our lives were just saved by the Loch Ness monster."

Maggie lifted a shoulder and let it drop. "I told you I saw it. Speaking of, where's my phone?"

She found it wedged under a seat as they trolled back to the dock. Henry moored the boat, and they began to disembark. Angus wandered down the dock toward them. He eyed them with a furrowed brow. "You went swimming?"

"Not by choice," Emma said, as she pushed past him.

He raised his eyebrows, following her retreat.

Henry climbed to the dock last. He handed the keys over to Angus. "She handles like a dream. Some jackass jetted past us a little too close and a few people fell out."

"Oh," Angus said, his mouth forming a wide "o." "I bet they weren't pleased."

Henry shook his head. Maggie smiled at him. "Still, we had a lovely time. Thank you for renting the boat out." She extended her hand out to him for a handshake. Her sleeve dripped onto the docks below.

Angus offered a hesitant smile, before he lightly grasped her fingers and moved them up and down. "Anytime, lassie," he said with a chuckle.

CHAPTER 18

The group retreated toward their car, stopping at the nearby gift shop along the way. They purchased new t-shirts, hoodies and towels, changing in the nearby gas station's bathroom.

"Ugh, I really never wanted to change in a gas station bathroom, but I am really glad to be dry," Piper said, as she settled into the backseat.

Maggie folded her towel, embroidered with the words, "I swam with Nessie," and tossed it onto her seat before she plopped into it.

Emma climbed in behind her, a frown still on her face as she took her seat. "I never wanted to change in a gas station bathroom either. And certainly not into this!"

"Oh, stop, you look great!" Maggie said.

"Really?" Emma shot back. She raised an eyebrow as she twisted to face the third row of seats. "I can't believe *this* is all they had in my size."

Maggie eyed the light blue t-shirt, emblazoned with a smiling "Nessie" popping out of the loch, peeking from under the fuchsia hoodie which read "Got Nessie?"

"The blue looks great on you, and the fuchsia really sets it off. Very on fleek."

Piper laughed. "Oh, yeah. It's on fleek all right. If you're a toddler from the 80s." She snorted.

Charlie joined in the chuckling. "Good one, fair maiden. She does resemble that."

Emma narrowed her eyes at them.

"You can change as soon as we get back to the hotel," Maggie said, with a wave of her hand.

"We have to eat first, remember?"

Maggie puckered her lips and lowered her eyes. "I'm sure no one will notice," she said with a shrug. "Besides, Nessie did save your life. The least you can do is advertise for him."

Emma spun, slamming her back into the seat, crossing her arms and shaking her head. "Worst trip ever."

"Isn't Nessie a her, boss lady?"

Maggie waved her hand in the air. "Whatever. Him. Her. It. Still saved our lives."

The group stopped for a meal before returning to their hotel. Maggie spent the evening indulging in a long soak in the tub. After her icy plunge into Loch Ness, she enjoyed the warm water surrounding her.

"Are you going to be in there all night?" Emma called from the bedroom.

"Probably," Maggie said, as she sank lower into the water. "Why? Did you want a soak?"

"No," Emma answered. "I hate baths."

"How can you hate baths?"

"They feel like a waste of time! Hey, what's your cell phone password?"

"Why?"

"No reason."

Maggie closed her eyes and adjusted her head against the tub.

"So, what is it?" Emma shouted a moment later.

Maggie's eyes shot open. "5187," she said. "Don't post anything stupid on my Instagram."

"I don't even know how to use Instagram," Emma answered.

Maggie scrunched up her nose at the comment. She spent another ten minutes lounging, before the water turned from pleasantly warm to tepid. Maggie pulled the plug, toweled off, dressed in her pajamas and robe, and shuffled out in fluffy slippers.

Emma still held her phone.

"I wonder if they have beautiful, huge claw-footed tubs at Dunhaven Castle? What did you need the phone for?" she asked as she plopped into the armchair near the window.

Emma tossed it aside. "Nothing."

"Come on, what were you doing?"

Maggie reached over and swiped the phone from the bed. She toggled it on and stared at the screen. Her blurry picture of the Loch Ness monster lit up the screen. She arched an eyebrow at Emma. "I thought maybe I could make something out."

"You can make something out. The giant black thing is the Loch Ness monster. You know, the thing that toppled a boat and saved our lives."

"Unfortunately, that picture isn't going to pass muster. I wondered if Charlie could clean it up, but it's beyond saving."

Maggie glanced ruefully at it. "Yeah, I'm afraid so. Just my luck that I see the Loch Ness monster and I can't prove it."

"I'm sure you'll survive."

"So, what's your meeting for tomorrow?"

"Oh, a private collector is considering giving us access to display their collection."

"Wow! What's all in it?"

Emma explained the details of the collection, and how she hoped it would draw people into the Rosemont Museum.

"My idea for increasing patronage is to bring these private collections in for brief display periods. That way we can appeal to a broader variety of people without needing to acquire pieces for permanent display. We can also do themed events around the different collections. And my hope is it will keep people coming in regularly to see new things."

Maggie nodded with a smile. "That sounds like a great way to drive traffic, yeah."

Emma smiled, squeezing her hands together in front of her. "Thanks. I think it could be exciting."

"Do you think you'll be able to work it out with the collector?"

"I hope so! He seems interested. Of course, some of that has to do with our notoriety."

"Use it to your advantage!"

"It just seems odd to me."

"Own it," Maggie said, flicking her hair over her shoulder and jutting her chin in the air. "You did awesome work finding Cleopatra's tomb and the Library of Alexandria."

Emma nodded at Maggie's suggestion. "Hey, thanks for giving up your vacation to help us with our business trip. I know this isn't what you imagined on your big trip to Scotland but..."

Maggie waved away her concern. "I'm having a blast! We've stayed in a castle, albeit not the original one I figured I'd be in. We went to that cool haunted castle. I saw the Loch Ness monster."

"You took a terrible photo of it," Emma said. Both women giggled over the ruined picture. "And the castle wasn't haunted. The duchess could talk to the dead."

"Whatever. The black veins were really cool to see, and I

enjoyed the gardens. It's been a great trip even with the weird issues. And we may be on to a fun mystery."

"You mean with the Norse dragon?"

Maggie nodded. "I can't believe Uncle Ollie's assistant hasn't found anything out yet. It's so frustrating."

"It's a lengthy process. We may not have information for years."

Maggie grimaced.

"You never were good at patience."

"Nope," Maggie agreed.

"So, what are your plans for tomorrow?"

"I found this museum that looks fun. The Gordon Highlanders Museum. I think we'll take a trip there while you and Uncle Ollie meet with your collector."

"I hope you enjoy it."

After a few more moments of conversation, they turned in for the night.

* * *

Gray skies met them the following morning. A light drizzle was falling as they climbed into the car. They'd spend the morning driving over to Aberdeen. In the afternoon, Emma and Ollie had a meeting with a private collector in the area, at his estate on the outskirts.

While they were at the meeting, Maggie and the rest of the group planned to visit a museum within the city's limits.

They spent the morning traveling west to east across the breadth of the country. Maggie enjoyed the scenery despite the overcast skies, appreciating the rolling green hills and quiet countryside.

They stopped for lunch just outside of Aberdeen, before continuing to the country estate and dropping Emma and Ollie at the doors to the large home.

THE LOST TREASURE OF DRAKON

"Wow, that's quite a place," Maggie said, as she hopped into the passenger's seat, replacing Ollie.

"Yeah. This guy must have quite a collection."

"I'll bet. I hope to see it in Aberdeen."

"Think they'll pull it off?"

"Uncle Ollie can be pretty persuasive."

Their SUV rumbled down the gravel drive and aimed for Aberdeen's museum. Within thirty minutes, they wound through the city's streets, arriving at the Gordon Highlanders Museum. Henry swung in through the open gates near the sign boasting of a tearoom, gift shop, garden and free parking.

"Oooooh! A duchess tearoom! That sounds so fun! Can we go?" Maggie asked.

"We just ate!" Leo replied.

"So? I can always eat," Maggie said.

"Maybe after we go through the museum," Henry suggested.

"And the gardens," Piper shouted from the back.

"I bet they're pretty. Aww, I kind of feel bad for Emma missing this. I bet she'd love it."

"Maybe next time," Henry said, as he eased the car into a parking spot.

They climbed out and strolled to the entrance.

"Oh! A gift shop," Maggie cooed, as they purchased their tickets.

"Oh, brother," Henry groaned.

"What?" Maggie said as she began eyeing the offerings.

"I hope you brought another suitcase," Henry teased.

"Don't worry, I always travel with an empty duffel for just such a need." She winked at him as she selected a few items.

After completing her purchases, she and Henry strolled hand-in-hand to the main gallery, the Grant Room. The others in their group had gone ahead of them and were already working their way through the displays in the room.

Maggie studied the replica of the battle of Waterloo. A red-coated soldier rode a white steed. The wide-eye horse rose on its hind legs as the soldier raised his sword in the air. Another solder squatted next to the mounted man, a frightened expression on his face.

They continued around the room, reading more history of the Gordon Highlanders. After working their way through the exhibits, they moved on to another gallery. Henry's interest perked as they entered The Armoury. Glass cases housed a variety of weaponry from Napoleonic times. Henry studied each of the guns displayed carefully. Maggie gave most a cursory glance, unimpressed by the display of firearms. She waited in the corner of the room.

"Not interested, princess?"

She raised her shoulders in a shrug. "I'm not terribly impressed."

"Want to go?"

"No, take your time," Maggie said. "You waited for me in the gift shop."

Henry flashed her his dimples in a wide grin as he returned to studying the firearms. When he finished, they moved on to the next gallery, the Hamilton Room. Housing temporary exhibits, the room's contents changed on a regular basis.

Maggie and Henry found the remaining three members of their group in the gallery. Piper stood in front of an exhibit with Leo and Charlie. She waved her arms emphatically and pointed at the display case in front of her.

"Wonder what's got Piper so fired up?" Maggie murmured, as they studied the first exhibit.

Henry glanced over his shoulder before returning his

gaze to the display. He shrugged. "Maybe they're into it with Leo again. He really is a pain in the arse."

Maggie chuckled. "Now you know what I've been living with for years."

"Hey, you almost willingly went back to living with that when you left me in Egypt."

"I was confused."

"Confused is an understatement."

Maggie smiled at Henry and grasped his chin between her thumb and forefinger. She planted a kiss on his lips. "Obviously. I must have been out of my mind."

"You must have been," he agreed, stealing another kiss, before wrapping his arm around her shoulders and pulling her toward the next display.

They took in another two exhibits as they neared the one where Piper, Charlie and Leo were stalled.

"...don't need to see the picture," Piper insisted. "That's it!"

"I'm not saying it isn't. I'm just saying we don't know," Leo contended.

"You're an idiot," Piper said, flinging her arms in the air.

"Ummm, not really," Leo answered.

"You kind of are, mate. That's definitely the symbol, and it has to be related. It says his name right there."

Maggie's brow wrinkled. "What are you three arguing about?" Maggie asked, as she sidled up to Piper.

"This!" Piper exclaimed. She waved her hand at the display case and accompanying plaque.

Maggie glanced at it. Her posture stiffened and her eyes went wide. "The dragon!"

CHAPTER 19

A drawing of the Nordic dragon headed the display's plaque. Maggie pulled her phone from her purse and swiped to the picture she'd taken at Clydescolm Castle. She held it next to the symbol on the label.

Piper tossed her hands in the air emphatically. "Thank you! That's what I said." She eyed the phone's image compared to the plaque. "Exact match."

"Oh, yeah," Leo mumbled.

"Was there any doubt?" Maggie asked.

"Apparently, there was," Piper said. "Genius over here thought it looked 'kinda similar,' but not exact."

"I didn't say that," Leo contended. "I said I wasn't sure and until I saw the picture, I couldn't say."

"Well, I was sure. Maggie's made a huge issue out of it every time we saw it. I recognized it right away."

"It's not like hubby dearest backed you up," Leo said.

"I didn't say she was wrong."

"And you didn't say she was right."

"Neither of you were very supportive. I'm not an idiot, you know."

Maggie tuned out the argument and studied the story on the plaque. She read aloud as she scanned the words with her eyes.

"The Lost Treasure of Drakon. Drakon was a ruthless Viking leader who launched devastating raids on Scotland in the early 900s. He amassed a fortune in gold and jewels, which he hid in an undisclosed location.

"The booty lay hidden for centuries before it was supposedly discovered by Lord Kendrick MacClyde. Lord MacClyde claims to have stumbled upon the fortune in a location he refused to disclose. Following the find, he worried he had been cursed. He ensconced the treasure in another secret location.

"To protect its location from marauders, treasure hunters, and curiosity seekers, as well as to safeguard his family from the supposed curse, Lord MacClyde formed a pact with fellow Scottish gentry, Duke Robert Blackmoore, Lord Randolph MacKenzie and Sir Frederick MacKenna. The aptly named 'Brotherhood of the Dragon' protected the Viking treasure in its new location with a series of four keys.

"Each man held one key, similar to the one depicted to the left belonging to Sir Frederick. To access the hidden treasure, all four keys must be combined."

Maggie glanced at the large, rusty brass key in the glass display case. With a decorative handle on one end and prongs on the other, the weighty item possessed an almost esoteric appearance.

Maggie leaned over to peer at the item at eye level. "Do you think..." her voice trailed off as she readied her camera for a picture. She snapped several at various angles.

She straightened and faced the group. "Uncle Ollie and Emma really should see this."

"It *has* to be related to what you found in the cave," Piper said, with a nod of her rainbow-colored head.

"Yeah, definitely. Remember Uncle Ollie said he thought he saw metal in the carving. I'd bet it's an elaborate keyhole. And these," she said, pointing at the glass-shielded key, "are the keys."

Piper gave another nod, staring at the item.

"We really need to get Emma and Uncle Ollie."

"Should we go?" Henry asked.

Maggie checked the time. "Do you think they'll be done?"

Henry glanced at his watch. "By the time we get there, maybe."

"I can't wait any longer, I'm too antsy. This is exciting! Let's go get them and come back!"

"Do we *all* have to go?" Leo asked.

"No, I'd be happy to leave you here," Henry said.

"I'm sure you would be," Leo shot back.

"Why don't we stay here," Piper suggested, "while you and Indiana Jones go get the prof and the brainiac?"

"We can visit the gardens," Charlie said, wrapping Piper's hand in his.

"Okay," Maggie said with a nod. "Take pictures for me."

"Did you want to stay? I can go get them," Henry offered.

Maggie pursed her lips in thought. She shook her head. "No, I'll come with you so I can explain everything on the way back."

Henry nodded. "All right, let's head out then."

They parted ways, with Piper, Charlie and Leo remaining behind, and Maggie and Henry heading to the parking lot.

"I can't believe we found that key!" Maggie exclaimed, as she climbed into the front passenger's seat.

"Yeah. Good call on coming to this museum," Henry said, firing the engine.

"Dumb luck, really," Maggie said, as she tapped around on her phone. "I sent a text to Emma and Uncle Ollie and asked if they were finished."

"Emma will love that. You blowing up her phone while she's in a work meeting."

"This is more important," Maggie said.

"I'm not sure she'd agree."

"Well, okay, it's more fun."

"Again..."

"Yeah, yeah, I get it."

"What did you say?" he asked, as he wound through the streets of Aberdeen.

"I said 'Are you done yet? You'll never guess what we found!'"

"Wow, cryptic."

They drove for a few more minutes, leaving the city limits behind. Maggie's phone chimed as the buildings thinned out around them.

"It's Uncle Ollie. He says they shouldn't be much longer, but don't start back just yet." Maggie's thumbs whipped across her virtual keyboard. She read her response as she typed it: *Too late. On our way. See you soon. Hurry up!*

"Mmm, Emma's going to love you," Henry said, with a shake of his head.

Maggie tossed the phone into the cupholder and sighed as she stared out the window at the passing scenery.

"Relax, princess, enjoy the scenery."

"I can enjoy the scenery *and* be anxious. I'm that talented," Maggie assured him.

The buildings fell away to rolling green hills and within fifteen minutes they arrived at the estate. Maggie glanced at her phone.

"Anything?" Henry questioned.

"Nothing." She frowned and tapped around on the screen. "I sent a message that said WELL?!?!"

Henry eased the car into the driveway and waited at the end. He killed the engine when Maggie received no response from either party. Maggie slid out of the car and paced the gravel drive.

She checked her phone with every spin. "Where are they?" she said, with a huff.

Henry leaned against the car's front. "They'll text when they're ready."

"Why aren't they ready now?!" Maggie exclaimed.

"Relax, Maggie, the key isn't going anywhere."

Maggie dropped her head between her shoulder blades and sighed. After another ten minutes, her phone chirped. She swiped at it and read the message.

"It's from Uncle Ollie," she reported. "He says they are wrapping up and should be ready in twenty minutes or so. He said they can take a car back to the museum if we don't want to leave. Don't want to leave? Did he even read my messages?" Maggie's thumbs pounded the screen. "We are already here. Pick you up in ten."

"Come on, let's go." Maggie skirted around the car's front and pulled the door open.

"He said twenty min…"

The expression on Maggie's face as she stood on the running board was enough to stop Henry's statement.

"Okay," he acquiesced, holding up his hands in surrender, before he slid behind the wheel.

They rumbled up the driveway to the front entrance. Maggie tapped her foot on the floor and drummed her fingers against her forearm. Ten minutes later, the front door swung open. A middle-aged man stepped out followed by Ollie and Emma. Maggie studied him as they spoke a few more words. The man's dark features gave him an almost sinister appearance.

After a few more moments of speaking, Emma smiled broadly and shook the man's hand, then Ollie followed. He motioned to the car and Maggie heard her name and Henry's spoken. Ollie gestured for them to join him.

"Ugh," Maggie groaned, as she popped her door open and slid to the ground. She plastered on her winning smile and circled around the car to join them.

Ollie had introduced Henry by the time Maggie rounded the car and approached the group. Ollie motioned toward her. "And this is my niece, Maggie." He beamed as he slid his arm around her shoulders. "Maggie, this is Sir William Thomson."

"Hi, Maggie Edwards," Maggie said, extending her hand.

"Lovely to meet you, Ms. Edwards. I'm so pleased to make your acquaintance. I'd hoped to have the chance when I heard Ollie was attending this meeting. I understand you were quite instrumental in several key archeological finds."

Maggie grinned. "Well, it was a team effort, but I'd certainly like to think I was a key part of the team."

"It seems like you were more than just a key part," Sir William said, his hands clutched behind his back.

"Well, will we be seeing some of your private collection gracing our little museum?" Maggie inquired.

"I am confident we can work out the details."

Maggie smiled and nodded. "That's excellent to hear."

"On that note, I'll pass along the details and have the museum director get in touch with your agent," Emma said.

Sir William nodded an affirmative to Emma, and Maggie took the opportunity to speed the goodbyes. "Well, we shouldn't keep you any longer."

"No trouble at all!" the man said.

"We left a few of our friends back at the museum, so we really should be getting back." Maggie tilted her head toward the car in a silent signal to her companions.

"Oh," Ollie said, with a raise of his eyebrows. "Oh, yes, of course. Well, I was so pleased to see your collection."

"Oh, please, come back any time," Sir William said with a nod.

They said their final goodbyes, and Maggie raced around the car, flinging the door open. She took her seat and strapped in before the others even began to climb into the car.

"Come on!" she encouraged, as Ollie and Emma slid into the captain's chairs in the middle row.

"Geez, Maggie," Emma complained, "relax. You're on vacation, remember?"

Maggie squashed her lips together and shook her head as she twisted in her seat to face Emma. Henry fired the engine and guided the car down the drive.

"Haven't you read any of my messages?"

"Ah, no, I was a little busy," Emma retorted.

Maggie rolled her eyes. "We found something at the museum!"

"Yes, I saw something in the messages, though I only glanced at them," Ollie said. "What did you find?"

Maggie swiped at her phone to bring up the pictures she had taken.

"Oh, please," Emma groaned, "this doesn't have to do with the Loch Ness monster again, does it?"

"No," Maggie assured her with a shake of her head. She spun the phone to face them. Ollie leaned forward, squinting at the object.

Maggie swiped to another picture.

"Is that the..." Emma began.

"Yes!" Maggie squealed triumphantly. "The dragon! They have an entire write-up at the museum. Here, I took a picture of it. You can read it."

Maggie passed the phone back to them. Ollie held it between them as they both studied the screen.

"Interesting. So, the metal I detected in the carving may well be a keyhole."

Maggie nodded enthusiastically. "Yes! Which means if we found the other three keys, we could theoretically open the chamber hidden by that carving and find a Viking treasure."

"A cursed Viking treasure," Emma said.

Maggie frowned at her. "Oh, come on, you don't really believe in that stuff, do you?"

"This coming from the woman who believes in ghosts and the Loch Ness monster?"

"That's different," Maggie said.

"Hmm," Ollie murmured, "yes, very interesting, I would like to see the key."

"Do you think you can persuade the museum to let us borrow it?" Maggie asked.

Ollie chuckled. "Let's not get ahead of ourselves."

"We'd still need three other keys," Emma pointed out.

"Which we may be able to find."

"How do you propose we do that?" Emma asked.

"Well, one of those keys has to be at Clydescolm Castle," Maggie said. "Surely, we could find it. The other must be at Blackmoore Castle. Maybe we can ask that Lenora girl about it."

"That Lenora girl, as you called her, doesn't really like us after we roamed around her castle. I doubt she's going to invite us in to tear apart her castle in search of a key."

"Don't be so negative," Maggie said.

"That still leaves one key," Ollie said.

Maggie smiled. "If I'm not mistaken," she said, "Randolph MacKenzie was Cate Kensie's ancestor. I'm certain she'll let us tear her castle apart to find the key."

"How do you know that?" Emma questioned.

"Cate said she was working on a book about the castle's previous owners. The last time I talked to her she was writing about Randolph MacKenzie, the owner in the mid-1800s. This has to be the same guy!"

"Mmm, that may be a good bet," Ollie said. "Let's go to the museum, take a look at the key, and go from there."

Maggie nodded as her phone rang. "Oh, it's Piper." She swiped to answer. "Hey, Piper, we're on our way back. I…" Piper's shrill voice cut her off. Maggie paused before she blurted, "WHAT?!"

"What is it?" Henry asked.

"Wait, I'm putting you on speaker." Maggie held the phone out and toggled on her speakerphone. "Okay, now say that again."

"The key is gone."

CHAPTER 20

"Wait, wait, slow down. What you do mean gone?" Maggie asked.

Henry's brow furrowed. "What's she talking about?"

"We went for a walk in the garden. When we came back in, I said we should take another stroll past the key to take a look at it. The glass case was empty. It's totally gone, dude."

"Maybe they took it for cleaning," Maggie suggested.

"Nope, don't think so."

"Why?"

"Because they just locked down the entire museum and the police are here."

Maggie closed her eyes as her shoulders sagged. "So, someone stole it," she assessed.

"Yep. And now we're stuck here waiting until they clear us of not being thieves." Piper sighed. "Worst honeymoon ever."

"Okay, look, sit tight and we'll be there soon."

"There's no sense in coming here. You won't get in."

"Well, I guess we'll find somewhere to wait," Maggie answered.

"Any chance Charlie's got his laptop on him?" Henry called.

"Uh," Piper said. They heard a scuffle as she asked Charlie.

Charlie's voice floated over the phone. "Of course, I've got my laptop, what kind of amateur do they think they're working with?"

Henry breathed a sigh of relief. "Put Charlie on."

"Yeah, mate, Charlie here."

"Can you tap into any security they have? Get this person on camera?"

"Mate, is the grass green?"

"Do it," Henry said.

"And then what? Tell the police?"

"No, let us know."

"Oh, right. All right, I'll have it in a jiffy."

The line disconnected as they overheard Leo's voice objecting to the scenario. Maggie flung herself back into the seat with a sigh. "Can you believe this?"

"At least it's a vote of confidence," Ollie said.

"What do you mean?" Maggie questioned.

"Someone didn't steal that key because they wanted a souvenir," Ollie said. "They stole it because they believe it leads to something."

"And now one-quarter of what we need to find is gone."

"If not more," Emma added.

"Thank you, Emma, you're always a ray of sunshine," Maggie groused.

"Well, we have no idea if they have other keys."

"Let's hope they don't," Maggie said.

"Does it matter if they don't?" Emma countered. "We're missing one of them now."

"And with any luck, Charlie can help us recover it."

"Ladies, please," Henry said.

Maggie's phone rang before any further conversation could ensue. "Charlie? Tell me you've got something," she said.

"Oh, chicky," Charlie answered her, "if you were here, you may incur the wrath of my fair maiden when you fling your arms around me and…"

"I'm going to stop you there and assume you found something," Maggie interrupted.

"That I did, chicky, that I did."

Maggie toggled on the speakerphone as Charlie continued. "There's no direct camera on the key, so I had to work backward to try to find a suspect. Several people left the parking lot just before the key was discovered to be missing. I ruled out the families and elderly couples and the like and ended up with three suspects.

"From those three, I believe I have fingered the correct thief. I'm sending the footage to your phone now."

Maggie furrowed her brow. "How did you…"

"Just watch the video, chicky."

Maggie swiped to an incoming message from Charlie and pulled up the video. Emma clicked off her seatbelt and climbed forward to view the supposed evidence.

An individual left the museum and crossed the parking lot. With a ball cap pulled low and a thick black hoodie, they clutched at the straps of a backpack strapped to their back.

Maggie was about to question why Charlie considered this the most likely culprit, when the video angle changed to another camera. The person wandered to a black sports car. The front license plate was smeared with mud.

Maggie's jaw dropped open as she recognized the car that had nearly run them off the road on their way from Clydescolm Castle to Inverness.

"That's the same car that came after us!" Maggie exclaimed.

"One hundred points to the smart chicky," Charlie answered.

Emma collapsed back into her seat. "So, they've been following us since Clydescolm."

"They probably figure we're here to investigate something," Ollie said.

"Yeah, that'd be my guess," Henry agreed. "Any chance we can identify the person of interest, make a run on getting that key back?"

"I'm fifty steps ahead of you, mate," Charlie answered. "While I can't get the license, which means I can't track the owner, who is likely a fake name anyway, I've followed them on any street cam I could find."

"And?" Henry asked.

"And they're heading your way, mate. Left on the same road you took to get Ollie and brainy."

"My name is Emma," Emma shouted.

Maggie waved her away. "But they could be anywhere now, right?"

"Or not," Henry said.

"What?" Maggie asked, glancing up at him. Henry's eyes remained on the road ahead of them, his grip tight on the steering wheel. Maggie followed the line of Henry's stare. Her eyes grew wide as she spotted the black sports car blazing a path toward them.

"Hang on," Henry warned, as the car flew past them in the opposite direction.

Emma squeezed her eyes shut as she grabbed on to anything she could. Maggie braced against the dash as Henry slammed on the brakes, making a hard turn on the two-lane road.

With the car facing the opposite direction, Henry slammed his foot on the accelerator. The hood of the car leapt in the air as the tires fought to find purchase on the road. With a squeal of the wheels, they rocketed toward the sports car.

As the distance between them narrowed, Henry showed no signs of slowing.

"Henry," Emma said. "Henry!" Her voice grew shrill as the car in front of them grew larger in the windshield.

Henry eased off the accelerator as they rode on the sports car's bumper. The car sped up, trying to lose them. Henry did not let up, increasing his speed to match.

"Where you going, buddy?" he murmured through gritted teeth.

The car slowed ahead, causing Henry to slam on his brakes. Everyone tumbled forward as their seatbelts strained to hold them against the seat. As the SUV's hood dove toward the road, the other car sped off, disappearing around a bend.

Henry floored it, flattening the SUV's passengers against their seats from the force. As they rounded the bend, the black sports car was nowhere in sight.

"Where'd he go?" Maggie asked, as she scanned for any sign of it.

Henry sped ahead as they all searched. He slowed as they approached the entrance to Sir William's country estate. "This is the only turn-off."

A small cloud of dust billowed from the gravel. "And I'd bet that's where he went," Maggie said.

"That dust isn't from us," Henry agreed.

"We can't follow him. The gates are closed," Maggie said.

"Maybe we should go back for Piper, Charlie and Leo," Ollie suggested. "It seems there's nothing to be done here."

Maggie sighed as Henry swung the car around and headed for Aberdeen. After five minutes of travel, Maggie spoke. "Why would that car disappear into Sir whatever-his-name-was's place?"

"Sir William," Ollie said. "And I'm curious about that myself. Though given his collection, I'm not surprised."

"Are you saying some of it was stolen?" Henry inquired.

"I'm not accusing him of anything, but I don't believe we saw his entire collection today."

Emma huffed. "I'm starting to think we only got the invite because of who we are."

"I wouldn't sell yourself that short," Maggie said. "He may very well want to do business with you. He may also be quite involved in the black-market business."

Emma wiggled her eyebrows. "Maybe. Though I'm not certain I want to do business with him if he's just stolen from a museum. Perhaps this is how he gets his in, and then robs the place."

"Oh, good point. I never thought of that," Maggie said, as she tapped on her phone with her thumbs.

"Anything from Piper?" Henry asked.

"I just sent her a message to ask how it's going. I also sent one to Cate asking her about Randolph."

Maggie's phone chimed. "It's Cate. She says yes, Randolph is her ancestor." Maggie typed a return message, tapping around on her phone to attach a picture. "I sent her a book, telling her why I asked."

"And here's a message from Piper." Maggie opened it then rolled her eyes. A picture of Piper wearing an annoyed expression, with her lips puckered and flashing a thumbs down, appeared on her screen.

"And?" Henry asked.

"Not good. Piper's annoyed." Her phone chimed again. "She says they're next in line to get cleared by the police." The phone chimed again. "And she says this is the worst honeymoon ever."

"The dunk in Loch Ness was really a low point," Emma said.

THE LOST TREASURE OF DRAKON

The country gave way as buildings filled in around them.

"Piper says we can't get near the museum," Maggie reported. "They have it cordoned off."

"Are they out?" Henry asked.

"No," Maggie reported. "Not yet. I guess they questioned Leo and are now moving on to Piper and Charlie."

"Tell them I'll get as close as I can and wait there."

Maggie passed the message along as Henry neared the museum. A flurry of activity surrounded it. Henry approached a uniformed officer who signaled for him to turn around. Henry lowered his window. "Hi. We're picking up people from inside the museum."

"Can't wait here, sir. No one will be going in or out for a while."

"They texted and said they are next in line to be cleared," Henry said.

"What are their names?"

"Piper Brooks - eh, Rivers, Piper Brooks-Rivers. No Brooks."

"Sir…" the officer began, as Henry bumbled through the name.

"Sorry," Henry cut him off, "she just got married. But she kept her last name. Piper Brooks. Charlie Rivers. Leo Hamilton."

With an unimpressed stare, the officer radioed to his colleagues. "Yeah, I've got a... What's your name, sir?"

"Henry Taylor."

"I've got a Henry Taylor here. Says he's picking up museum patrons that you've got inside. Names Brooks, Piper, Rivers, Charlie, Hamilton, Leo. Can you confirm?"

They waited a moment before his radio crackled. "Affirmative. Finishing with Ms. Brooks now. Still need to interview Mr. Rivers."

"They should be out soon. You'll need to find another place to wait."

"But..."

"I said, find another place to wait."

Maggie leaned over Henry, a broad smile on her face. "Hi, Officer, I'm sorry, I don't think I caught your name."

"Oh, here we go," Emma murmured from the backseat.

"It's Phillips, miss."

"Officer Phillips. I hate to be a pain but if they'll be out soon, would it hurt if we just waited here?"

"Well..."

"I mean, the entrance is right there. They'll come out and straight to the car, and we'll be on our way and out of your hair."

"We need to keep the street clear for additional emergency vehicles," he explained.

"Oh, we won't block the street. Henry can pull off to the side. Right, Henry?" Maggie inquired of him, batting her eyelashes and offering another smile.

The officer bobbed his head side to side a few times before the gesture turned into a nod. "Well, I suppose if you can get that boat off the road, it'll be all right."

"Thank you," Maggie said with a relieved smile. "We really appreciate it."

"You're welcome. And enjoy the rest of your stay."

Maggie offered her thanks again as Henry maneuvered the car as far off the road as he could manage.

"Nice job, Maggie."

"I can't believe that works every time for you," Emma said.

As they waited for the rest of their group, Maggie's phone chimed. "Okay, Cate says she hasn't heard of anything like this, but she's going to look into it. She said we are welcome to search Dunhaven for the key. She'll even help."

"Well, there's one we'll have access to find," Ollie said.

"Now, we'll have to work on the rest," Maggie said. "Including the one that was just stolen."

"Here they come," Henry said. He fired the engine.

The trio emerged into the bright sunshine. Leo, looking beleaguered, shaded his eyes against it with his hand as he dragged himself to the car.

Maggie hopped out of the front seat and climbed past the captain's chairs into the back. "Ollie said you can ride shotgun," she called to Leo, as she reentered the SUV.

"What? No," Henry protested.

Leo slid into the front seat as Piper and Charlie piled into the back.

"What a day," Leo moaned.

"I'll bet that was uncomfortable," Emma said.

"It was," Leo answered, as Henry waved to the officer manning the road and pulled away.

"They shoved us into that little theater. It was so stuffy," Piper said.

"At least you're out now."

Charlie pulled his laptop from his bag and set it on his lap as they drove. "What are you doing?" Maggie asked.

"Searching for that black car," he answered.

"Oh, we know where it went," she reported.

Maggie recounted the story about happening upon the sports car and its last known location. Charlie's fingers scrambled across the keyboard as he switched gears.

"What are you doing now?" Maggie asked.

"This Sir William guy's got to have some security system with all those collectibles. I'm going to tap it and see what we can see."

Maggie smiled at him, pleased with the plan.

"Maybe we should tell the police and refrain from doing

anything illegal. At least while I'm in the car. Just a suggestion," Leo shouted from the car's front.

"We can let you out if you're uncomfortable, and you can walk back to London," Maggie proposed.

"Okay, so even if we find something," Piper said, "how are we going to get it? And even if we did get it, that still leaves three more to find."

"Ah, one of those we have covered. Randolph MacKenzie is Cate's ancestor. So, it's likely that one is at Dunhaven Castle. Cate said we can search for it while we're there."

"Okay, that's one."

"The other one must be at Clydescolm, and I'm betting we can search that castle, since this could lead to a find that will salvage Lord MacClyde's financial situation."

"Two," Piper counted.

"The third is likely at Blackmoore Castle, and with my in there, we may be able to find that one."

"In?" Emma questioned. "Are you serious? The woman was *not* pleased with you. I doubt she's going to invite you to search her home."

"Don't be so negative. We can try!"

"That still begs the question: what are we going to do about the original key we just lost?" Emma said.

"That's simple," Henry said. "We'll steal it back."

CHAPTER 21

"Am I the only one uncomfortable with the illegal aspect of what we're planning?" Leo asked, as he paced the floor of one of their hotel suites.

"Yeah," Maggie said, studying the crude drawing on the tiny hotel's notepad.

Leo flung his arms out to the sides. "Seriously?" He ceased his pacing as he surveyed everyone else in the room.

"Yep," Henry confirmed from over Charlie's shoulder.

"Clearly, I have no issue, mate," Charlie added.

"I have a slight issue," Emma admitted.

"Thank you!" Leo said emphatically.

"But not enough to stop me from going along with the plan."

"I don't see that big of an issue," Piper answered. "We're stealing from thieves. Are they seriously going to call the police and be like, 'Oh hey, officer, these people stole the key we stole earlier'?"

"First of all, that's not the issue. And second, you bring up a very good point. I doubt they'll report us to the police.

They'll likely sic on us whoever has been trying to kill us already."

"They've already done that, so we may as well fight back," Maggie said.

Leo spun to face Ollie. "Please, Dr. Keene, talk some sense into them."

Ollie crossed his arms and leaned back in the armchair. "Piper has a point. In a way, we're righting a wrong."

"Unbelievable," Leo shouted with a roll of his eyes, his hands flying high in the air.

Ollie's phone rang as Leo resumed his pacing. He answered the call, and after a few seconds said, "I've actually got the entire group here. Let me put you on speakerphone."

"Hello team," Agent Thomas's voice said through the phone's tiny speaker.

"Hey, Frank," Maggie said. "How are you?"

"Doing well. And I apologize in advance for interrupting your vacation, but we have a situation, and you are nearby."

"Very," Ollie said.

"There's been an item stolen from a small museum in Scotland. We aren't certain of its worth, but if someone was willing to steal it, we'd like to know why."

Maggie chuckled.

"We know," Henry answered.

"And we're pretty sure we know its worth and why it was stolen," Emma added.

Frank paused. "Oh, you do?"

"We were there," Piper informed him.

"What?" Frank inquired.

Ollie chimed in. "Several team members were at the museum and saw the key, the stolen item. In fact, two of them were there when it was stolen."

"We're already on top of the situation," Maggie said. "We believe it is one of four keys that will lead to a Viking treasure trove known as the Lost Treasure of Drakon. We've tracked the missing key to an estate outside of Aberdeen, and we're working on asset retrieval now. We also believe we have leads on the other three keys and will work to gather them after we've retrieved this one."

"Well, it seems you have the situation well in hand. I suppose all I need to say is carry on," Frank answered.

"We'll let you know when we've made progress," Ollie said.

"Thanks, Ollie," Frank said, before signing off.

Ollie ended the call and glanced to Leo. "Well, there you have it. We're now sanctioned by the U.S. government, so you don't have to worry about doing something illegal."

Leo rolled his eyes. "It worries me that you were willing to do it with or without their blessing."

"All right, where are we on progress here?" Maggie asked.

"Well," Emma answered. "I'd say if he stole this key, he's keeping it here." She tapped her crude diagram of the halls. "We were here, in this gallery." She pointed to a square room with two sets of doors. "We entered through these doors. I'd wager the other set of doors leads to another gallery of sorts with heavier security, where he keeps items not viewable to most guests."

Emma pointed to the set of doors leading to a large question mark she'd drawn as a placeholder.

"And I'd bet he's keeping this item in the safe, which I'd guess is in that room," Charlie said.

"Guess? You're not in yet?" Maggie questioned.

"Oh, I'm in, chicky. I can see the gallery brainy mentioned. What I can't see is the question mark room. It's like a black box in there. I've got nothing."

"How do you know there's a safe?" Henry inquired.

"Well, what I did do is search for plans, specs and orders this guy has made since he purchased the property. I found a number of plans for a room like brainy mentioned. None of them share anything in common. We could be working with anything from pressure-sensitive flooring to laser beams, or both."

"Wonderful," Maggie groaned.

"You still never answered how you know there's a safe," Henry prompted.

"I found an order for a state-of-the-art safe. I don't see it in any of the other rooms. I'd bet it's in there. And if the key isn't laying around in his black box room, it's probably in the safe."

"Okay, so we've got to get into the house, into the room..."

"Which had a key-coded entry door," Ollie reported.

"And across the room with we don't know how many security components and into a safe."

"And not just any safe," Charlie said. "This safe has three levels of releases. The first is voice recognition."

"We may be able to fake that with recorded clips," Henry said.

"The second is facial recognition. Which I can also fake. And the third is fingerprint - specifically, thumbprint."

"Do you really think you can fake all this?" Leo asked.

"Yes," Charlie answered. He flashed an iPad at him. "If you have more than twelve pictures on the internet, I can fake your 3D image." Charlie raised the iPad with the outline of a human face and held it in front of his face. The image of Sir William Thomson appeared. When Charlie spoke, the man's voice emerged.

"Okay, so that takes care of the safe, outside of his thumbprint," Maggie said.

"And we'll need access to that, and the property in general," Henry pointed out.

Charlie raised a finger and tossed the iPad aside. "I've got that covered, sort of. The scuttlebutt on Twitter is all about his Great Gatsby Roaring Twenties party occurring tomorrow night."

"That's our in," Henry said.

"Except the problem is," Maggie said, "we can't waltz into the party and get his thumbprint. He'll recognize us."

"He'll also recognize me and Ollie," Emma said.

"So, that leaves…" Maggie began.

Henry flicked his gaze to the couple. "Piper and Charlie. Can you two infiltrate the party and retrieve his thumbprint? Pass it off to Maggie and me. We'll pose as waitstaff."

"No can do, mate," Charlie said. "As much as I'd love to infiltrate a Roaring Twenties party with my new spouse, old Charlie's got to provide tech support on the backend. Hiding you from the security cameras and the like. And second, you can't pose as waitstaff."

"Why?" Henry asked.

Charlie spun his laptop around, flashing a website from the catering company hired to staff the party.

Henry wrinkled his nose and scrunched his eyebrows together. "All women waitstaff?"

"It's their specialty, mate," Charlie answered.

Maggie's eyes wandered in the air as she parsed through their options. "That means, Emma and I have to pose as waitstaff, Henry and Charlie have to stay outside, leaving Piper and Leo to infiltrate the party."

"Are you kidding me?" Leo inquired. "This guy is probably the one trying to kill us, and we're going to waltz into his house uninvited, steal his thumbprint and then help you rob him?"

"I'll be fine on my own," Piper said. "I can do it."

Leo heaved a sigh. "No, I'll do it."

"Don't put yourself out, Oscar," Piper said.

"Oscar?" Leo asked.

"The grouch," Piper explained.

He narrowed his eyes at her. "I'm just vetting options. I'll do it. I'm not going to let a defenseless woman wander into this party alone."

Piper offered an unimpressed stare, crossing her arms. "I'm hardly defenseless, you dope."

"Whatever, you know what I mean."

"Okay, so Piper and Leo go to the party. They secure the thumbprint and pass it to Emma and me. We access the vault room and the safe, swipe the key, ditch the party, and move on to Dunhaven to find the second key."

"I'm not liking this plan," Henry said.

"You just don't like to be sidelined," Maggie answered. "But we have no choice. You can't go in."

"I don't see a way around it, no," Henry agreed. "So, are we all in agreement then?"

Nods met his question. "All right, then let's work on getting what we need to pull this off."

CHAPTER 22

The white van trundled down the drive.

"Caterer delivery," Maggie called from the window. The security guard waved her away from the main entrance and to the back of the house. Maggie parked the car on the other side of the two vans already there.

"Everybody ready?" she asked through the window, into the back.

"As ready as we can be," Piper announced.

Maggie slid the earpiece into her ear. "Testing," she said.

"Loud and clear, chicky," Charlie answered.

"Great," Maggie said, as she slid from the front seat and unzipped her hoodie. Emma joined her, still clinging to the hoodie wrapped around her. "Take that thing off."

"Do I have to?" Emma moaned.

"Yes," Maggie said.

Emma peeled the hoodie off, revealing her short, form-fitting gold flapper costume. "I feel ridiculous," she said.

"You look great," Maggie said, as Emma tugged at her hemline.

"Why did it have to be a flapper party?" Emma groaned.

181

Piper came online, crackling to life in their ears, her voice sounding odd as she channeled a new persona. "Everything's jake, don't get the heebie-jeebies now."

"What did you do, Piper," Leo asked, "swallow a 1920s slang dictionary?" He turned to Emma. "I think you look great."

Color rose in Emma's pale cheeks.

"Don't be goofy, fella, they'll think I'm the bee's knees."

She stepped from the back of the van with Leo's help. Emma eyed her outfit.

"Why couldn't I have been the mob moll?" she asked, staring longingly at the boxy men's style striped suit Piper wore, with a Fedora pulled low over her forehead.

"Don't be a dumb, Dora, you've got great gams."

"Okay, okay, we get it, Piper," Maggie said. "Just get in and let us know when you've got his thumbprint."

"Okay, I'll get the print from the big cheese and then skedaddle with the flat tire here, since I'm a gatecrasher." She angled her thumb toward Leo.

"Let's just get this over with," Leo said, as he adjusted his collar and donned his mobster-style hat.

Together, they hurried around the side of the house, disappearing from view.

"Here we go," Maggie said. "You got my camera feed?"

"Clear view. I see what you see, chicky," Charlie reported, as Maggie toggled on the camera hidden in a brooch.

"Okay, wish us luck."

Henry's voice crossed the airwaves. "Maggie, be smart and be careful."

"Will do, babe."

Maggie and Emma crossed the gravel parking area toward the kitchen door.

"Just relax and let me do the talking," Maggie said.

Emma blew out a slow breath and nodded. "Don't worry about that. My mouth is so dry, I'll choke on my words."

"Relax, Emma," Maggie said, squeezing her forearm. "We can do this."

"From your lips," Emma said.

They pushed in through the kitchen door to a bustle of activity. Flappers darted everywhere, and food preparers hurried to set out appetizers or fill trays with glasses of champagne.

"Sorry, we're late – heck of a story, don't ask," Maggie announced, as she grabbed a tray of champagne flutes and scampered away. Emma struggled to juggle one and darted after Maggie.

Leo's voice crackled in their ears as he gave their fake names to the security guard checking in guests. With Charlie's pre-laid groundwork, one Mr. and Mrs. Reginald Patterson now appeared on the electronic guest list.

"We're in," Piper whispered, as the din of the party sounded in their ears.

"We're on our way up to the main floor," Maggie reported.

Glasses were lifted from their trays as soon as they entered the large ballroom. Hundreds of people, dressed in their 1920s finery, milled around the ballroom and the garden, flitting to and from other rooms on the main floor. The chatter from partygoers created a constant drone of noise, punctuated by the occasional high-pitched giggle from a woman or boisterous laughter from a group of men.

Maggie scanned the room in search of Piper and their host. She did not want to run into him, since she could be recognized.

She skirted the room with Emma following close behind. Piper and Leo wandered across the open area.

"I've got eyes on Sir William," Piper said. She grabbed two

flutes of champagne from a nearby waitress and sauntered toward him with Leo in tow.

"Sir William," Leo said. "Lovely to see you again."

Maggie heard a momentary pause, before the man said, "I'm sorry, I seem to have forgotten your name."

"Reginald Patterson and my wife, Sophia," Leo lied. "We met at…"

"William, you old lounge lizard!" Piper gushed, leaning forward to kiss his cheek. "I hope you haven't forgotten me! We were at the Met gala together *years* ago."

"Oh, I…" he began, but Piper continued.

"Thanks so much for having us, fella, this really is the cat's pajamas."

"I'm so pleased you're adopting the spirit of the party."

"Well, I came with the flat tire over here, but don't you worry, once he gets a bit of the giggle juice, he'll be jake. Speaking of, looks like you could use another bevvy yourself." Piper giggled.

"Oh, thank you," he answered.

"Reg, be a doll and take this off the fella's hands. Well, I'm going to scram and mingle at this wingding."

Moments later, Piper reported, "We've got the glass."

"We're near the ladies' room," Maggie said.

"Meet you inside."

Maggie and Emma pushed through the door to the restroom near the ballroom. Maggie dumped her tray on the counter. Emma did the same. They both rolled their hemlines down from the shortened height the waitstaff wore. Piper pushed through the door moments later, holding the glass by its stem.

Maggie grabbed her purse and removed a pair of black satin gloves, pulling them on.

"Did Leo touch it?" Maggie questioned, as she accepted the glass.

"Nope," Piper reported, "grabbed the stem."

Maggie nodded. "Okay, get Leo and get out."

Piper bobbed her head up and down. "Get in and out quick, boss lady," she said. "Good luck."

"See you on the flip side," Maggie said.

Piper disappeared through the doorway, rejoining the party outside. A few seconds later, Maggie and Emma emerged. Without their trays, they blended in with the crowd, appearing to be guests.

They sauntered through the ballroom, exiting into the hallway and wandering down the hall toward a sitting room Emma recognized. "Can you make it from here?"

"Yeah," Emma said, with a tentative nod. Sweat beaded on her forehead.

"Relax, Emma, almost home," Maggie said.

She bobbed her head again as she swallowed hard. Emma led Maggie through the sitting room and into another hallway. They approached the gallery Emma had visited yesterday and slipped inside the double doors.

A massive room yawned in front of them. Glass display cases were placed at various locations, housing a variety of items, from swords to vases to jewelry.

"Wow, is this the collection coming to Rosemont?" Maggie inquired.

"Well, it might not be after we rob him," Emma answered.

"Either way, I can see why you were interested. It's fantastic."

"Stop gawking at the jewelry and focus, princess," Henry's voice cut in.

"I'm focused," she retorted as they crossed the room, heading for the double doors on the far side of the room. "We're at the vault room doors."

Maggie pulled a USB device from her evening bag and plugged it into the keypad. Numbers rushed past on the touchpad as the program worked to identify the code. Within a minute, they heard the lock disengage.

"We're in," Maggie whispered.

She and Emma slipped through the door after she pulled the USB drive from the keypad. They stopped inside to assess the space.

"Okay, we've got some kind of control pad to the left," Maggie said. She aimed the camera toward it. "See that?"

"Got it, can you get closer?"

Maggie stepped forward toward the blank screen. "Tapping into the system now," Charlie reported.

Emma scanned the rest of the room. "I see the safe!" She pointed toward a large structure across the room.

Emma took a step forward. Charlie shouted, "Don't move."

Both Emma and Maggie froze. "What is it?"

"Lasers. That control panel is connected to a web of cameras and lasers blanketing the room. We've got to find a way around them, or the next step brainy takes is going to set off the alarm."

Emma winced and backed up a step.

"Can they see us?" Maggie asked.

"No, I patched the feed to show a blank room."

Maggie chewed her lower lip while she waited for confirmation to proceed. "Can you disable the lasers?" she asked after a moment.

"I'm working on it, chicky."

"Can you work faster?" Emma asked.

"I'm going to ignore that," Charlie said.

Another minute passed before his voice crackled in their earpieces.

"All right, here's the sitch," he said. "I can disable the lasers, but only in a restart sequence. If I turn them off, it's going to draw attention. But I can cycle them to restart without calling too much attention."

"Okay, let's do that."

"There are a few things though. It's only going to be off for about two minutes. Then the grid will start to come back on one by one."

"Ugh," Maggie groaned.

"So, you're going to have to hustle."

"Okay, wait. We need to ready the face-voice app and thumbprint so we can open the safe right away."

"All right, lasers off on your go," Charlie answered.

Maggie pulled the glove from her right hand, tucking it into her dress. She removed the iPad and handed it to Emma, who toggled into the app they needed. Maggie pulled a rubber finger cone over her thumb.

She held the glass in her left still gloved hand and rolled the rubber cone across the thumbprint on the champagne glass. She set it on the floor and stood, blowing out a breath.

"You ready?"

Emma nodded, holding the iPad in both hands.

"Okay, we're good to go," Maggie reported.

"Okay, lasers cycling off in… 3…2…1… and you're good," Charlie said.

Maggie's heart thudded in her chest and her knees felt wobbly as they sprinted across the room, darting around the display items in the room. They reached the safe in twenty seconds. Maggie pressed her thumb against the print pad.

A beep sounded and a green light lit. A panel in the safe slid down, revealing a camera. "You're up," Maggie said, stepping aside.

"Ninety seconds," Charlie reported.

Emma held the iPad up to the camera.

"William Thomson," she said, as the image appeared. Sir William's voice sounded from the speaker, and his face appeared on the iPad's display. A red light flashed repeatedly. Three seconds passed before the blinking red light turned to steady red and a buzzer sounded.

Wide-eyed, Emma glanced to Maggie whose jaw hung open. "It didn't work."

"What?" Charlie asked.

"The app thing didn't work." Maggie glanced at the screen. "Oh, wait, I think the feather headband is interfering. It's poking out above the iPad, and I think the camera's getting it."

Maggie yanked the headband from Emma's head.

"Ouch," Emma protested.

"Just try again," Maggie said.

"Sixty seconds," Charlie said.

The camera still waited for the appropriate facial scan. Emma nodded and aimed the iPad screen at the camera. "William Thomson," she repeated.

The red light began to blink rapidly again. Within seconds, it turned to a steady green light, and the door released.

Both Emma and Maggie exhaled at the same time, realizing they'd been holding their breath.

"We're in."

"Forty-five seconds."

"Maggie, grab the key and get out of there," Henry said.

Maggie nodded despite Henry not being able to see them. She pulled the door open and stared inside. Several items were stacked on the three shelves inside. She pawed through them. Her heart skipped a beat.

"It's not here."

"What?" Henry asked.

"It's not here!" Maggie squealed.

CHAPTER 23

Maggie rifled through the items in the safe again.

"Move," Emma said, checking the safe. "She's right. Not here."

"Now what?"

"Now, get the hell out of there," Charlie said. "You've got less than thirty seconds."

Maggie swung the door on the safe shut, and they scrambled across the room.

"STOP!" Charlie called, as they came within ten feet of the door.

Both Maggie and Emma skidded to a halt.

"Do not move," Charlie said. "The lasers are back on."

Maggie's knees threatened to buckle. "What?" she whimpered.

"Grid's up," Charlie said.

"Well, turn it off, we aren't out yet!" Emma squealed, her voice shrill with panic.

"I can't," Charlie said.

"What do you mean you can't?" Maggie asked. "How are we going to get out of here?"

"I can't cycle them again; it'll be a red flag. You're going to have to navigate out through them."

"How?! We can't see them!"

"No, but I can see the layout in the security system. You'll have to navigate out with my instructions."

"Are you kidding me?" Emma asked.

"Okay, okay, just take a deep breath," Maggie said. "We can do this."

"Okay, way to step up, chicky. You're up first." Maggie blew out a long breath. "There is a beam one foot from the floor. Lift your foot and step forward over it then stop."

Maggie nodded and lifted her foot, hoping she judged one foot well enough. She swung her foot forward and placed it on the ground, lifting her back leg high before bringing it down next to her right leg.

"All right, now brainy. Do the same, step right next to Maggie over the laser."

Emma followed a similar set of actions to Maggie, ending up next to her.

"Okay, brainy again. There is a laser at your shoulder height. Bend over and slide under it, another foot forward."

"Okay," Emma said.

"Unless you'd like to limbo, then try that."

Emma rolled her eyes as she crouched and side-stepped under the invisible beam. She stood on the other side. "All right, hold there. Maggie..."

"Same as Emma?"

"No," Charlie said. "That beam actually slants diagonally, so Emma could get under it, you can't. Turn ninety degrees to your right and step forward to where Emma was. You'll need to follow her there."

Maggie followed the instructions.

THE LOST TREASURE OF DRAKON

"Okay, brainy, let's move you out of the way to the door. This one's going to be tricky."

"Oh, please don't say that," Emma said.

"There is a beam at chin height *and* at shin height."

"You're kidding."

"Sorry, brainy, I'm dead serious. Turn to the side. Lift your foot. Higher. Higher. A tad higher," Charlie said, as he watched her on-screen.

"Come on, it's practically waist high!"

"I want to be sure you clear it! All right, push your leg out toward the door while you bend at the waist."

Emma folded into her leg as she swung between the beams, then pulled her other leg between them.

"Okay, chicky. Your turn. Limbo forward, then thread the needle."

Maggie swallowed hard and crouched under the beam, taking a step forward. She straightened before she turned to the side. She raised her leg and folded forward. As she stuck her leg through and swung her top half, her balance faltered.

Emma braced her, allowing her to regain her balance without falling to her right side.

"Whew, thanks," Maggie said, as she steadied herself and pulled her left leg through.

"Okay, made it."

"You're clear to the door," Charlie said.

"That's great, but where is the key?" Maggie said.

"Doesn't matter. Get out of there and we'll regroup," Henry said.

"No, no way," Maggie argued. "We won't get another shot at this. Emma, anywhere else this could be?"

"Anywhere, it's a huge mansion!"

"Anywhere else we should look?"

Emma pursed her lips. "His office?"

"Good thinking, Emma," Ollie's voice said. "It may be there."

"We'll try there," Maggie said.

They retraced their steps through the outer gallery and into the hallway. Emma threaded through the halls toward the office she mentioned. They rounded the corner housing the room they sought.

"Shoot," Maggie mumbled, as she pulled Emma back around the corner. "We've got a problem."

"What is it, princess?" Henry answered.

"Armed guard outside the office door," Maggie reported.

"Well, the presence of the armed guard outside the office indicates something of value inside," Ollie reasoned aloud.

"Very true, but also useless to us if we can't get past him."

"I'm on it," Piper's voice said, joining the conversation.

"What? Piper! Where are you?"

"Still inside. Leo and I waited in case you needed an assist. Emma, where am I going?"

Emma talked Piper from the ballroom to the office, having her come toward them from the opposite side of the hall.

"Okay, get ready to make a dash for the office," Piper said.

Maggie peeked around the corner. Piper stalked toward the security guard. She wobbled on her feet, weaving from side to side in the hall. She sang at the top of her lungs.

"I'm gonna rouge my knees and roll my stockings down and... all... that... JAAAAZZZ. Oh, Excuse me, fella," she said, using her 1920s persona, "I seem to have lost my way."

"Ma'am, this area is off-limits."

"Whoops!" Piper said, throwing her arm in the air and nearly toppling over.

"Ma'am, you'll need to continue back to the ballroom. Down this hall, take a right. When you see the..."

"Blah, blah, blah," she said, her fingers and thumb forming a duck mouth that opened and closed. "Right, left, left, right."

"Ma'am, please."

The man attempted to contact another security guard, when Piper threw herself into his arms.

"Oh, I think I may be sick," she said, puffing her cheeks and making a retching noise.

The man ceased his attempt to contact someone and caught her. He dragged her in the direction she'd come as she threatened to toss her proverbial cookies all over his suit. Maggie and Emma raced down the hall and slipped into the office, securing the door behind them.

"We're in," Maggie said.

She hurried across the room to the desk and began rifling through drawers. Emma pulled drawers open at the bottom of a floor-to-ceiling bookcase.

"Heeeey, there you are," Leo said over their earpieces. "I wondered where you went. Thanks, pal, I've got it from here."

A rustling sounded and a few seconds passed before they heard Piper. "Okay, we're clear," Piper said. "Anything?"

"Nothing," Maggie reported.

"Me either," Emma said.

At the same time, their gaze fell onto a painting across the room. Maggie flicked her gaze to Emma. With a nod, they both raced to the painting. Emma reached it first and lifted the painting. She grunted with effort.

"Help me," she choked.

Maggie grabbed one side and together, they pulled the painting from the wall.

"There's a safe," Maggie reported.

"What are we working with?" Henry said.

"Can you see my feed, Charlie?" Maggie asked. "Looks like we've got thumbprint with a key code, four-digit."

"All right, any chance you..."

"I still have the print, it's in the purse."

"Let's hope it's clear enough. I'm finding potential four-digit codes to try."

Maggie nodded and donned the fake thumb.

"Ready when you are."

"Okay, try 1965."

Maggie pressed her thumb against the pad and input the code. "No."

"1986."

"Nope."

"1987."

Maggie shook her head as the red light lit again. "No."

"Are these random numbers?" Emma asked.

"No, brainy, I'm using life events. His birth, his marriage, birth of his first child. Give me a second." Silence filled the airwaves until Charlie's voice crackled to life. "2011."

Maggie pressed her thumb against the print pad, then tapped 2011 on the keypad. A chime sounded and the green light sprang to life. "Got it!" Maggie exclaimed. Emma pulled on the handle and hauled the heavy door open.

"And got the key!" she exclaimed as she withdrew the brass item. They slipped it into the purse.

"Good work, ladies," Henry said.

"And now for your next trick, you've got to disappear without using the hall," Charlie said. "Your security guard friend is back."

Maggie glanced to the desk. "We'll use the window. Henry, get ready to get us out of here. Piper, Leo head to the car."

"Copy that, boss lady. See you there."

Maggie and Emma hefted the large painting up to hide the safe before continuing across the room. They swung open the large window and stepped outside, squeezing between the house and a large bush.

"Ouch," Emma hissed, as they eased the window shut behind them. "This thing has thorns."

Maggie cursed under her breath as they shimmied around the thorny bush and onto the lawn. With their heels sinking into the soft soil, they hurried around the corner of the house and broke into a sprint toward the waiting van. Piper and Leo climbed. They slowed their pace, steadying their breathing as they hurried across the gravel parking area.

Maggie slipped into the passenger seat, and Emma climbed into the back as Henry pulled away from the other vehicles. With a salute, he drove past the guard and turned onto the road outside.

Maggie blew a long breath out as they left the estate safely behind.

"Fascinating," Ollie's voice sounded from the back of the van.

"If we can find the other three, it could lead to another amazing discovery," Emma answered.

"Great work, everyone," Maggie said through the grate leading to the back. "One down, three to go."

"Let's hope the next three are much easier," Henry said.

CHAPTER 24

"I texted Cate," Maggie said, as she climbed into the SUV the next morning. "She's looking into the location of the other key, but she hasn't found anything so far."

"Too bad," Emma answered. "At least it's not raining, though."

"Yeah," Maggie agreed. "I think we're supposed to have nice weather for the rest of the trip."

"Fingers crossed," Piper said.

"Hey, nice job last night," Maggie said. "You really saved us in a pinch."

"You're welcome, chicky," Charlie said, with a wiggle of his eyebrows.

"I was talking to Piper. Though I suppose you were a big part of getting us through the laser field."

"No problem. I don't mind helping out two broads like you," Piper said, in her 1920s persona.

"I think you actually enjoyed that role," Emma said.

"She did," Leo answered, his head resting against the headrest, sunglasses on.

"I think you actually enjoyed it, too," Maggie said.

"Meh," Leo answered.

Maggie offered a coy smile behind his back.

Henry fired the engine and, after a stop for to-go coffees, they aimed for Dunhaven. The buildings of Aberdeen fell away to the rolling green hills. The terrain roughened as they drove further from the larger cities and into the Highlands.

Maggie watched the passing scenery from the backseat. Eventually, a castle appeared on the horizon.

"Is this it?" she questioned.

"Wow, it looks huge!" Piper said, ducking her head to stare out the windshield.

"It does."

"If we have to search every inch of that place for the key, we'll be here through the summer," Leo groaned.

"I'm not sure I'd mind that," Maggie murmured, as she stared up at the rambling gray stone building with its turrets and towers.

They passed through the small town of Dunhaven, continuing toward the castle. Excitement built in Maggie as they pulled from the road onto a winding gravel drive. Gardens on both the left and right meandered through the property.

Maggie studied the massive structure in front of them. It rose high into the cloudless sky. A few people, looking tiny in comparison, stood near the entrance. Two tiny dogs frolicked in the grass nearby. Everyone gawked at the castle as they approached. Even Leo seemed interested.

"This place looks incredible!" Maggie blurted, as excitement overcame her.

"Yes," Ollie agreed. "We'll have a fantastic time touring it, I'd say. Unbelievable to know the person who owns it."

"And for her to invite *all* of us to stay with her," Emma said.

Henry eased the car to a stop. Maggie recognized Cate and Molly. An older couple stood nearby and a tall man, about Cate's age, cavorted with the two dogs.

Maggie bounced in her seat as she waited for the others to pile out of the car. Ollie strode to Cate before Maggie made it out of the car.

"Hi, Cate!" he said.

"Hi, Ollie," Cate answered, in her even-toned voice.

They shook hands and Ollie said, "Thank you so much for inviting the entire crew. We really appreciate it. This trip hasn't been at all what we expected."

"No problem. I'm happy to have you all. As you can see, I have plenty of space." She offered a clumsy chuckle as she waved her hand toward the castle.

Ollie moved on to greet Molly. Maggie squeezed out between the seats and hopped to the gravel driveway below. She hurried to Cate as the others still hung back.

"Cate!" she squealed, as she wrapped her in a hug. "It's so good to see you! And Molly!"

She moved on, pulling the strawberry-blonde woman into a hug. Molly, a former department administrative assistant, had been her boss when Maggie worked as a graduate assistant during her Master's degree.

"Oh, hi, honey!" Molly said, her voice rife with as much excitement as Maggie's. "It's great to see you again!"

"You, too!" Maggie pulled back, still clutching Molly's hands, and looked her up and down. "You look great! Scotland agrees with you!"

"So does living in a castle," Molly answered with a snicker.

Cate introduced the rest of the people with her.

"Hi, everyone," Cate said with a smile. "Welcome to Dunhaven Castle. Most of you know me and Molly. But you haven't met Jack, my estate manager." Cate motioned to the tall man in a flannel shirt who gave them a wave. "And Mr. and Mrs. Fraser, my head groundskeeper and housekeeper, and of course, my friends. And, last but not least, Riley and Bailey."

Cate motioned to the two small pups.

"Well," Maggie said, releasing Molly's hands and wrapping her arm around Henry's bicep, "this is Henry Taylor, my boyfriend. Henry, this is Molly and Cate. And you remember Emma, right? Leo. And Piper, I think she had you for a class. And then the only other person you don't know is Piper's husband, Charlie."

Piper bent down to pet Riley.

"I remember Riley," Piper said. "Sometimes I'd see you with him at the park. Hiya, buddy!"

"Husband?!" Molly blurted. "When did you get married, honey?"

"Last week," Piper said.

"Oh my goodness!" Everyone offered their congratulations to the couple. "I can't wait to see pictures."

"Oh, no pictures," Piper said, as she rose to stand and Charlie wrapped his arm around her shoulders. "We JOP'ed it, so nothing to see."

"No pictures?" Mrs. Fraser said with a harrumph. "No reception? No cake?"

Piper shook her head and shrugged.

"Well," the woman said with a wag of her finger. "We'll fix that. I'll get right on making a wedding cake for after tonight's supper when I get back to the kitchen."

"That's not..." Piper began.

"I insist," Mrs. Fraser interrupted. "No guests of Lady Cate's are going to not have a wedding cake on their honeymoon!"

Cate offered an amused grin and a shrug. "It's best not to argue with her. Mrs. Fraser knows best."

"You're darned right I do," Mrs. Fraser said with a nod.

"Oh my gosh, LADY CATE?! It sounds so posh! And you got another dog?" Maggie asked.

"I did," Cate replied.

"Actually, Riley did," Jack chimed in, his Scottish brogue apparent. "Little laddie kept running off, and eventually brought us to this little fellow." He stroked the gray and white dog's fur.

"Bailey's a bit shy," Cate explained. "But Riley loves attention."

The little black and white dog stood staring up at Emma, who hadn't said hello to him yet.

"They're so cute, Cate," Maggie said. Her eyes scanned the castle. "And this place looks amazing!"

"Wait 'til you see the inside!" Molly said.

"Shall we go in?" Cate asked.

"Yes!" Maggie answered.

"I'll grab our bags," Henry offered.

"I'll help," Jack said. "Just tell me what belongs to who and I'll see that it gets to the right room."

"Thanks," Henry said, with a nod.

"They'll get along well," Maggie murmured, as Molly threaded her arm through Maggie's and pulled her into the castle.

Cate walked with Emma, asking her about the latest developments in her career. Ollie, Leo, Piper and Charlie gathered their bags from Henry and wandered in behind them, while Cate's staff brought up the rear.

Maggie's eyes floated upward as she entered the massive foyer. Hallways jutted off at various places, and doorways framed both sides of the entrance, leading to other rooms. A large, rounded marble staircase with a thick red runner led up to another level, splitting several steps up into two staircases which led in opposite directions.

"Oh, wow!" Maggie exclaimed. "This is amazing! On the first leg of our trip, we stayed at Clydescolm Castle, and I thought it was really nice, but it's nothing compared to this!"

"The sitting room is here," Cate said, pointing to a door on the left. "The library is down the hall there. Everyone's bedrooms will be upstairs and to the left. That's where mine and Molly's are, too."

"I hope I don't get lost!" Maggie said, as Jack and Henry entered with several bags.

"Don't worry, I thought the same thing when I came," Cate said. "Why don't we get everyone settled in their bedrooms, then we can regroup and I'll show you around?"

"Sounds like a plan," Maggie agreed.

Cate led them up the grand staircase and through a series of halls. Maggie noticed they had lost the Frasers on the way upstairs, but Molly remained with them.

"Wait until you see your room, Maggie," she said, squeezing Maggie's hand.

Cate stopped outside a dark wooden door and turned the knob. The door swung in and revealed a large blue room. A four-poster bed stood in the center, with thick blue bed curtains hanging from the top. An ornate antique white ceiling rose from the blue walls. Two chandeliers hung to light the space. The bedroom was larger than Maggie's combined kitchen, living room and dining area. Her eyes bulged at the room.

"Ollie, I put you here," Cate said.

"Thanks!" Ollie said.

"This one's yours, right?" Jack asked, as he jiggled the bag slung over his shoulder.

"Yes, and thank you for carrying it."

"No problem, Dr. Keene."

"Oh, please, call me Ollie."

Jack dropped his bag from his shoulder and stalked into the room, setting it on the luggage rack.

"Mind if I continue with you?" Ollie inquired.

"Not at all," Cate said.

She shuffled down the hallway and opened a door across the way. Another large room greeted them, this one in gray.

"Leo," she announced.

"Boy, I could get used to this," Leo said, as he stalked inside with his bag and tossed it on the luggage rack.

Cate zigzagged across the hall to a room with rich red paint and gold trim.

"Newlyweds," she said with a smile.

Henry's room came next, equal in size to Ollie's, but done in a deep green plaid theme. Emma's room was catty-corner to Henry's and in a pleasant lilac and silver theme. Maggie's room sat next to Emma's. Cate opened the door to a gold room. A large bed stood in the middle and a chaise lounge was positioned next to a large fireplace.

"Oh, I love it!" Maggie said, as Henry dropped her bags in the room.

"Now, wait until you see MY SUITE," Molly said. "Everyone's welcome to begin the tour there!"

"Good idea, Molly," Cate said. "And then I can point out where my suite is, in case anyone needs anything."

They continued down the hall and took a left into another corridor. A set of wide double doors were positioned at the end. Halfway down the long hallway, Molly stopped and opened a door. "Here's my palace!"

Maggie stepped in with her mouth hanging open. The rose-colored sitting room had two armchairs, a settee, and a chaise grouped around a large fireplace. Beyond the sitting room was a large bedroom with a four-poster bed.

"Wow!" Maggie said.

"Told you it was nice. Way better than what I had in Aberdeen."

"And I'm just down the hall through those double doors," Cate said. "So, if anyone needs anything, you'll probably find me there or in the library. Jack and the Frasers are also staying while you're here, and they are in this hall as well."

"Can we see the rest of the castle?" Maggie asked.

"Sure," Cate said with a chuckle. "We'll start with the areas we still use."

The group gathered in the hallway as Cate explained further. "Several of the wings are closed off since we don't use the spaces. However, I understand you're on the hunt for a brass key which may have belonged to Randolph MacKenzie."

"We are," Ollie said. "It's one of four keys that we believe will open a Viking treasure horde. We'd like to find them all, if possible."

"Viking treasure?" Jack inquired.

"Yes," Ollie answered. "We found this symbol at Clydescolm Castle." He swiped at his phone and swung the picture toward Jack and Cate. "It's associated with the Brotherhood of the Dragon, which Randolph was supposedly a part of. He received one of the four keys distributed to safeguard the treasure."

"Wow, you Americans live a way more exciting life than I expected," Jack said. "Poor Lady Cate stuck with us boring Scots."

"Lady Cate is quite happy with the boring Scots. That's an interesting symbol," Cate said, as she studied Ollie's phone. "I don't have any knowledge of that, but maybe I haven't researched that far into Randolph's life yet. Do you know around what year this Brotherhood was formed?"

"I'd say sometime in the late 1860s," Ollie conjectured. "A crude estimate, but I'm using some of the others in the group and the few clues we have about their lives to come up with it."

"Ah, we didn't know Randolph then," Cate said, signaling to her and Jack. Jack stared at the floor as he shifted his weight from foot to foot. Maggie furrowed her brow at the statement. "Ah, that is, I focused on my research on his life at an earlier point in time."

Ollie nodded with a smile. "Well, we may get you some more information!"

"You already have," Cate said. "And you're certainly welcome to explore any areas for this key – no limits. Just let Jack know you need the keys, and he'll get you access."

"Thanks," Maggie said. "We really appreciate you letting us poke around in your home."

"No problem," Cate said. "I'm happy to help as much as I can, but you don't need my permission if you've got a hunch you want to follow!"

Cate began to move them down the hall, branching off into another hallway.

"And thanks for having all of us," Emma said. "We really appreciate it, especially given the short notice."

"Yeah, thanks a lot, Dr. Kensie," Piper said.

"You're welcome. I'm happy to have all of you. And please, call me Cate."

"Or Lady Cate," Maggie said with a wink.

"Or just Cate," Cate answered, as they entered a large gold and antique white room. Portraits filled it. "I figured we'd start in the portrait gallery."

Maggie wandered into the room, gazing at the various portraits. "Here is Randolph," Cate said, pointing to a portrait of a man with dark, unruly hair and thick eyebrows. Emma sidled next to Maggie to study it.

"No sign of the dragon," she murmured.

Ollie approached and narrowed his eyes at the portrait. He frowned and shook his head. "Nothing."

"Are there any other portraits of him?" Piper asked.

"Yes," Cate said. "I'll point them out as we come across them. Maybe one of them will contain the symbol you showed me."

Cate led the group downstairs and they threaded through several rooms. The two dogs trotted behind them as they made their tour.

"There's a picture of Randolph in the closed-off west wing," Cate said. "Before we head there, let me show you the kitchen, in case anyone needs to navigate there for a late-night snack."

After they traveled down to visit Mrs. Fraser, who had a plate of cookies ready for the guests, Cate led them back up the stairs to open the closed-off wing. The dogs chose to stay in the kitchen, stretching out under the table.

They wound through a series of halls, and Maggie wondered if she'd be able to find her way back here if they wanted to explore later. They arrived at a set of large double doors and Jack fiddled with a set of keys, fitting one into the lock. It clanked, and Jack twisted the knob and pushed the door open. It creaked on its hinges as it swung into the massive hallway.

CHAPTER 25

Maggie's eyes widened as she winced at the noise. "We're sure this place isn't haunted, right?" she whispered to Emma.

"Oh, stop," Emma hissed.

"No ghosts, I promise," Cate announced.

"Sorry," Maggie said, "I didn't mean to—"

"No worries," Cate said. "When I first came, I thought that, too. But I promise, no ghosts."

Maggie glanced at the massive hall as they stepped through the door. Window-shaped patterns of sun painted the parquet floors. Decorative panels and intricate trim work detailed the antique white walls. Five crystal chandeliers hung in a row from the ceiling. Cate flicked on a switch and warm light glowed. Paintings hung along the length of the hall between the windows on both sides of the space.

"There's a painting of Randolph here," Cate said, as she led the group halfway down the hall.

She gestured toward a massive painting on the wall.

"There!" Maggie shouted. "In his hand." She lined her camera up and snapped a picture.

Clutched in Randolph's hand, he held a missive. The dragon symbol marked the cream-colored envelope.

"Oh, I see it!" Cate said. "I never noticed that!"

"So, this is the evidence we needed to make the connection," Emma said. "This must be the Randolph MacKenzie mentioned in the Brotherhood."

Cate nodded. "From what I know of Randolph, I'd believe it. He seemed to be quite outgoing, and he'd love something like this."

"So, you think he could have hidden the key here?" Maggie inquired.

"I've never seen this symbol before, but he very well may have."

"Do you mind if we explore before dinner, maybe look around for this symbol?"

"Not at all!" Cate said.

Henry approached the painting, glancing up at it before tilting his head and peering behind it. He toggled on his flashlight and pressed his head against the wall next to the painting.

"Could it be that easy, mate?" Charlie asked.

"Doesn't hurt to try," Henry said. He glanced at Cate. "Mind if we take this down?"

"Ah," Cate said, biting her lower lip. She glanced at Jack, who winced as he shifted his weight.

"We'll be careful, I promise," Henry said, flashing his dimples.

Cate nodded and let out a chuckle. "Thanks for the reassurance. Though, not just with the painting."

"Aye, that's been on that wall for a long time. Moving it around may cause something to break, so please, be careful in case it lets loose," Jack added.

"Don't worry, Lady Cate," Ollie said. "Most of us are trained in antiquity handling."

Jack stepped forward to help Leo, Henry and Charlie lift the large painting from the wall. They eased it upward and away from the wall, slowly lowering it to the floor. It remained in one piece. An outline of dust layered the wall behind it.

"Don't let Mrs. Fraser see that," Jack said to Cate.

Cate nodded at him. "She'll have the cleaning crew's heads."

They studied the painting and the frame.

"Could it be hidden somewhere on the painting?"

"Doubtful," Ollie answered. "The key is larger than this could conceal. Perhaps in the frame, but I'm not seeing any compartments or triggers." Ollie ran his fingers along the edge, front and back.

Henry checked the dusty wall, running his fingers along it, searching for any hidden panels.

"Anything?" Ollie inquired.

"I'm not seeing anything," Henry answered.

"Darn," Maggie said, stamping her foot on the floor.

"Sorry," Cate said with a wince.

"No, it's not your fault," Maggie said. "But it would have been nice if it had been that easy."

"There are still a few hours before dinner. You're welcome to keep exploring," Cate said.

"If you don't mind, that would be great," Maggie said. "And we'll get this painting back on your wall."

"I don't mind at all," Cate said. "If you're okay on your own, I'm going to sort through a few things I know are Randolph's or from that era. Maybe I'll find a clue there."

"I can stay with you," Jack said.

"Oh, if you don't have anything better to do," Maggie said. "But if you're busy, we're happy to skulk around the castle ourselves."

"Oh, well–" Jack began.

"Actually, Jack, could I have a word with you?" Cate asked.

"Sure," Jack said. "Well, looks like you're on your own. If you find any locked areas, give me a shout. I'll be in the kitchen sneaking biscuits. Ah, that's cookies to you Americans." Jack offered them a wink and a smile, before he backed away and followed Cate.

"Well," Maggie said as they departed, "I guess we should get this painting back up on the wall and then move on."

Carefully, they reset the painting. Maggie stared at it.

"At least we know they're connected," Emma said.

"Yeah, but it's not doing us much good."

"Come on, let's move on."

"Maybe we should split up," Piper suggested.

"Okay, that sounds good. We'll cover more ground that way," Maggie answered. "I guess we'll pair off and…" She glanced to Ollie.

"And Ollie is going back to the portrait gallery to see if there are any other clues there," Ollie said with a chuckle.

Maggie offered him a smile. "You could come with Henry and me."

"I'll leave you two to wander around the spooky castle."

Maggie's smile dissolved into a grimace. "Why'd you have to say it like that? Now I've got the jitters."

Emma rolled her eyes and tugged on Maggie's arm. "Oh, come on, 'fraidy cat, you'll be fine."

They discussed a plan to meet in front of the portrait in two hours. Each pair selected a hallway in the large wing to explore further and set off.

Maggie and Henry wandered down the wide hallway on the right.

"This place is amazing," Maggie said, as her eyes lifted to the ornate trim work framing the ceiling. Sheets covered some of the items hanging on the wall.

"I wonder if there are any more paintings of this guy," she asked, as she peeked behind a sheet.

"Cate didn't say there was," Henry answered, opening the drawer on an ornate gold console table.

"There's got to be some clue as to where this might be."

"Like the dragon symbol."

"Exactly," Maggie said, sending another cloud of dust billowing in the air as she let a sheet drop against a large mirror.

"Maggie..." Henry began, stopping his search and turning to face her.

"Don't say it," she said, with a shake of her head.

He pressed his lips together and took a deep inhale. "In a castle this size..."

"I know, I know. We may not find this." Maggie crossed her arms. "At least not this weekend."

Henry offered a sly grin and a shake of his head.

"What? I'm not giving up. Even if it means I have to summer in Scotland."

"Oh, the lengths you'll go to for this job."

"I know," Maggie said, with a coy grin, "I really give until it hurts."

They swung around a corner and found several doors on either side. Starting with the first door on their right, they worked their way through the rooms. No paintings of Randolph MacKenzie were in any of them, and nothing else caught their eye to warrant further investigation.

"Maybe someone else found something," Maggie mused aloud, as they crossed the hall and tried a door there.

The ornate doorway swung into a large open room. Devoid of much of its furniture, the still shiny parquet floors were on full display. White walls trimmed with gold accents rose to meet a tray ceiling, detailed in gold.

Crystal and gold chandeliers hung in various locations. A

white sheet covered a large object across the room. Maggie wandered to it and lifted the sheet.

"Wow," she whispered, as she revealed the white and gold baby grand piano.

A few other sheets hung over busts and statues in the room.

"This must be a music hall," she said, her voice echoing in the space.

"Yeah," Henry agreed. He raised his eyebrows and shook his head as he studied the ceiling, the gold columns, and the crystal chandeliers. He wolf-whistled. "Can you imagine having enough money to build a concert hall in your home?"

"I wish I could," Maggie said. "This is amazing."

Maggie continued to gawk at the large room as Henry approached the fireplace. Framed in white marble, he toggled on his flashlight and ducked his head inside.

"Anything?"

"Doesn't look like it," he said. He stuck his hand inside and felt around. "Nothing but soot."

Maggie puckered her lips into a frown. "Maybe it's hidden inside the piano."

She pulled back the sheet and studied it for any sign of the dragon symbol. Henry slid underneath, checking the underside.

"Help me lift this up," Maggie said, as she struggled to heft the lid up.

Henry climbed to his feet and pushed it open, setting the stand to hold it open. They glanced inside. Henry hovered his hand over top to reach inside. Maggie slapped it back. "Don't put your dirty hand in there!"

"Sorry, princess," he said, holding his hand up in defeat.

"Here," Maggie said. She pulled a tissue from her pocket and handed it to him. "Wipe your hand off."

Satisfied with his cleaner fingers, Maggie let him sweep

the inside of the piano to search for any hidden items. He came up empty.

"Guess we can close it."

"Wait!" Maggie exclaimed.

"What is it? You see something?"

"No, but I have to try this out." Maggie rounded the piano and pulled the bench from under the keyboard. She eased herself onto it, her back straight and shoulders pressed back. She stretched and wiggled her fingers as she bit her lower lip. After a deep inhale and exhale, Maggie positioned her fingers over the black and white keys. With a raise of her eyebrows, her two index fingers tapped out "Chopsticks."

After her performance, she tilted her head to Henry, a tight-lipped grin on her lips.

He wrinkled his eyebrows. "Seriously?"

"It's all I know how to play," Maggie said.

He shook his head and chuckled at her. "I really thought you were a concert pianist."

"Sorry, I never took piano lessons. And apparently, my playing didn't jiggle loose any brass keys, so I guess we should move on."

Henry nodded in agreement. Before Maggie could stand, a noise sounded. Rustling from across the room drew both their attention.

"What was that?" Maggie whispered, wide-eyed.

Henry shrugged in a silent response. They remained quiet, straining to listen for any noises. Another shuffling sound. Maggie's eyebrows shot skyward. "There it is again!" she hissed.

"Probably disturbed a ghost who's upset with your terrible piano-playing."

Maggie frowned and shook her head at him.

"It came from over there."

She pointed toward a large window across the space.

Henry's eyes searched for the source of the sound. He tiptoed across the room and pulled back a heavy red drape, searching behind it. The noise sounded again.

Henry tapped his finger in the direction of a set of double doors across the room.

He crept to the door. Maggie sneaked over to him and hovered behind him as he grasped the handle. He twisted his neck to face her. She gave him a nod. He depressed the handle and swung the door open.

CHAPTER 26

Maggie stared through the open door into what lay beyond it in the hall. Her jaw dropped open. After a moment, she recovered and let her guard down, dropping her shoulders and breathing an audible sigh.

Henry did the same.

"You two," Maggie said, with a shake of her head.

"You two," Emma repeated. "We heard noise coming from this room."

"And you thought it was a ghost?"

Emma narrowed her eyes. "Thought it was something."

"Ha!" Maggie said, with a triumphant laugh. "You *did* think it was a ghost! You came to see if a ghost was in here playing the piano."

"We didn't think a ghost would play the piano that badly," Leo said, as he strolled into the room.

"Very funny," Maggie said with a wrinkle of her nose.

"Wow, this place is amazing!" Emma said, scanning the room.

"Isn't it? The entire castle is amazing, but this room is really beautiful."

Emma approached the piano and swiped her fingers up the keys as she continued to swivel her head, taking in the room.

"Let me show you how it's done," Leo said, plopping down on the bench with a smarmy smirk at Emma.

He placed his hands over the keys and cleared his throat.

Henry puckered his lips and crossed his arms, side-eyeing Maggie. "Another Chopsticks rendition?" he whispered.

Leo depressed one pedal as his fingers flew across the keys, pounding out a flawless arrangement of "Fur Elise" by Beethoven.

"Wow," Emma said.

"Did not expect that," Henry added.

"I took piano lessons for fifteen years," Leo said as he finished. "This room has great acoustics."

Clapping burst from the doors they'd opened moments ago.

"Great playing, Leo," Cate said.

Leo stood and bowed.

"Sorry," Maggie said. "We came across this room and had to test it out."

"No problem. I'm sure the space is happy to be filled with music again."

"I can't believe there's a music hall in here!" Emma said.

Cate nodded. "Finlay, the son of the man who built Dunhaven Castle, added it. He was a musician and so was his wife, Moira. They'd often give concerts. I thought maybe you'd stumbled upon something in here, since Moira and Finlay were Randolph's parents."

"Sadly, no," Maggie answered. "We just really liked the room."

Cate shrugged. "Well, that's okay, too."

"Did you find anything?" Maggie inquired.

"No," Cate answered with a shake of her head. "But I

figured I'd come check on you since it's getting close to dinner. Just in case you got lost."

"Thanks," Maggie said.

Piper and Charlie strolled through the door.

"Did we hear music?" Piper questioned.

"You did!" Maggie said. "Leo was entertaining us with his musical capabilities."

"And doing a fantastic job," Cate added.

"Aw, we missed the concert," Piper complained.

"Wow, this room is very Gucci," Charlie commented.

"Very Gucci, indeed," Piper agreed.

Jack entered a moment later. "Oh, we had the same idea, I see," he said to Cate.

"Yes," Cate answered, "I figured I'd better check in case they got lost."

"Play another song, Oscar," Piper called.

"I'm going to ignore that, but I will play another song," Leo said. "Since this is likely an opportunity I'll never have again."

"Know any waltzes?" Maggie asked. "It feels appropriate."

"Really?" Leo questioned. "Does anyone know how to waltz?"

"Actually," Jack said, "we do."

"One waltz coming up," Leo said. He wiggled his fingers and began a slow introduction to "The Blue Danube."

"Oh," Cate said, with a shake of her head. "No."

The group heckled her to participate.

"M'lady," Jack said to Cate, with a deep bow.

Cate held in a giggle and curtsied, as Leo readied to play the main piece of music. The couple came together in closed position. Cate offered a nervous chuckle as Jack swept her around the room with flawless form.

"You're better than you were last time we waltzed."

"I've been practicing, Lady Cate," Jack answered. "Can't

have Mrs. Campbell upset with my dancing skills at the next party."

Maggie stared longingly at the couple. She heaved a sigh. "Wow, that's so romantic. They're waltzing in a massive music room of a Scottish castle."

She stared over at Henry. He did a double-take and squashed his eyebrows together. "What?"

"We should take dancing lessons."

Henry frowned with a huff and crossed his arms. Across the room, Charlie bowed to Piper, before they mimicked Cate and Jack's form and tried to follow their steps.

"We're waltzing!" Piper exclaimed.

"In a castle, no less," Charlie said.

"Best honeymoon ever," Piper said, as Leo gave an emphatic ending to his playing. Both dancing couples and the onlookers applauded.

As Leo took his bow, Cate suggested they head back to the main castle to freshen up before dinner.

"Oh, where's Ollie?" she asked.

"Already back there in the portrait gallery," Maggie answered.

"Okay, we'll swing by there and let him know it's almost dinner time."

After collecting Ollie, Cate led the group to their rooms, before continuing down the hall to hers. Maggie stepped into her gold-themed room and tossed herself across her bed. She ran her hands along the gold satin duvet cover as she stared up at the detailed ceiling. "I'm going to enjoy sleeping here," she said to herself as she swept her hands over the decorative pillows. "But first, dinner!"

She pulled herself from her bed and rummaged through her luggage, searching for something nicer than her athletic leggings and t-shirt. She settled on jeggings and a tunic sweater with a pair of slouchy pull-on boots. After fiddling with her hair and makeup, she emerged into the hall. Henry already waited for her, still in his same clothes.

"You didn't change?"

"No," he said with a shrug.

"We're dining in a castle!"

"Forgot my tux," he said, with a flash of his dimples.

The others emerged from their rooms. Maggie stared in stunned silence. "I was the only one who came prepared for a dinner in a castle?! No one else changed?"

"Relax, chicky, I did," Charlie said. "I was wearing a blue hoodie earlier; now I've got my tuxedo hoodie on."

Maggie glanced at the printed picture of a tuxedo on Charlie's hoodie. Likewise, Piper had swept her hair into an updo and switched tops, the new one sporting the picture of a ball gown's top.

Emma shrugged. "I didn't think it mattered if we changed."

"It doesn't," Cate assured them, as she rounded the corner. "We're all very casual here."

They headed downstairs to the dining room. Maggie counted twelve place settings.

"I hope no one minds," Cate said. "I invited everyone to join us."

"Of course not," Maggie said.

"I thought Molly would enjoy catching up with you," Cate answered.

Maggie nodded as Cate told them to pick any seat they'd like. The scent of delicious food already filled the air with a lovely aroma. Mrs. Fraser and Molly appeared, carrying more steaming food items, and set them on the sideboard.

"Anything I can help with?" Cate asked.

"You know better than that, Lady Cate," Mrs. Fraser said, as she darted from the room.

"I'm starting to wonder who's really in charge here," Maggie whispered to Emma.

"Not Dr. Kensie."

Maggie shook her head in response as she settled into a seat. Molly and Mrs. Fraser bustled in with the last of the serving dishes, Mr. Fraser and Jack in tow. With the last pieces of food delivered, everyone helped themselves and settled at the table.

"So," Maggie said, "what's it like living in a castle?"

"Fantastic," Molly answered.

"How are your rooms?" Cate asked the group.

Everyone agreed they were more than comfortable, and talk turned to other facets of castle life. After a lull in the conversation, Ollie brought up his excursion to the portrait gallery.

"I had a lovely time gazing at your ancestors, Cate. Douglas MacKenzie seemed to be a very interesting man."

"He was," Cate answered. "Very forward-thinking."

"Anything you can tell us about Randolph that may inform our search?" Maggie questioned.

"He, too, was fairly forward-thinking. I imagine this brotherhood you mentioned would have intrigued him quite a bit. He was a good sport and very outgoing, so it seems just up his alley. Did you find any hint of it in the west wing?"

"No," Maggie admitted.

"There's another closed wing. You're welcome to check it out tomorrow."

"Are there any secret passages?" Piper asked.

"Yes," Cate said with a nod. "There's a secret lab under the library and a secret passage in the hall outside of the library."

"There's also another one from the portrait gallery that leads to the east wing," Mrs. Fraser said.

"And one from the tearoom to this room," Jack said.

"I'm sure there are others," Mr. Fraser chimed in, "but they've been lost over time."

"Or removed for updates," Jack said.

"Aye," Mr. Fraser answered.

Maggie raised her eyebrows. "Can we look in those?"

"Sure," Cate said.

"I'll open the east wing tomorrow," Jack said.

"And I can show you how to access the hidden passages," Cate added. "What were the names of the others in the Brotherhood? If I can find a reference to them, it may give us some clue as to where Randolph put his key."

"One of them was William MacClyde," Ollie said. "With the upset to our travel plans, we stayed at Clydescolm Castle last weekend. It's there where we discovered the dragon symbol.

"And when we went to Aberdeen for our meeting," Ollie continued, "Everyone else went to a museum, where they found a reference to the key and learned of the existence of the Brotherhood."

"And found one of the keys," Maggie said.

"Which was stolen while we were there," Piper added.

Cate's eyebrows shot up. "Stolen?"

"Yes," Ollie said.

"The museum exhibit said there were three other keys. One owned by Lord MacClyde, one given to Randolph MacKenzie, and the third given to Duke Blackmoore," Maggie added.

Cate nodded in understanding. "So, have you made any progress locating the other two? The Blackmoore key or the MacClyde key?"

"Not yet," Maggie said. "They are next on our list, after we find Lord MacKenzie's key."

"We're figuring you'd be the least resistant to us poking around for the key," Henry explained.

"Yeah," Emma added. "I doubt the current owner of Blackmoore Castle will be very cooperative. Maggie insisted on sneaking away from the tour group and parading around the castle when we visited. The owner caught us, and she was none too happy."

Cate winced.

"Yeah, exactly," Emma answered her expression.

"But that's how we even discovered their involvement. Duke Blackmoore also had a portrait with the dragon symbol."

"So, even if you retrieve the key from Dunhaven and the other two, you still can't find the treasure, right?" Molly inquired.

"We could," Maggie explained. "We believe we found the location at Clydescolm Castle. We just need the keys to open it."

"But you're missing the fourth key. The one that was stolen," Jack said.

"No," Ollie answered. "We recovered it."

Jack's brow furrowed. "How?" he asked.

"Creative methods," Henry said.

No one spoke for a few seconds.

"Wow, you Americans really do lead exciting lives," Jack said.

The conversation turned to other topics after they planned to scour the castle for clues the following day. After their meal, Mrs. Fraser, Molly and Jack disappeared downstairs for a few moments, after clearing a spot on the sideboard.

Mrs. Fraser pushed through the hidden door into the dining room and held it open. Jack shuffled into the room, and Mrs. Fraser warned him to be careful. He carried a three-tiered cake, covered with white icing; pink and red roses were formed from icing, cascading down the sides and sweeping onto the cake plate below. A bride and groom stood on top of the cake under a wedding arch.

"Awwww," Piper said, climbing to her feet.

"Wow!" Maggie exclaimed.

"Now, I dinnae know your favorite, so I made a raspberry-filled cake with buttercream icing."

"Where did you get the figures?" Emma asked.

"The bakery in town. Young Scottie owes me a favor or two," Mrs. Fraser answered with a wink.

"We should get pictures!" Maggie said. She snapped a few on her phone.

Molly held a silver set of cutlery, including a cake knife and a server. "And these are for you two. Don't worry, we have a real knife to cut and serve, these are just your keepsakes for pictures."

Piper offered a misty-eyed smile at them as she accepted the knife.

"Wait!" Maggie said. "Pictures."

"And we have a camera, too," Molly said, as she readied the DSLR for the snapshots.

Charlie and Piper each grabbed the cake knife and sliced into the cake. Maggie and Molly snapped pictures.

"I don't think I've ever seen Piper so emotional," Maggie whispered to Henry, as they made the second cut and removed the slice of cake.

After the traditional feeding of the cake, minus the smearing across the face after a warning from Piper, Mrs. Fraser and Molly cut the rest of the cake and served it.

"Mmmm," Emma exclaimed. "This is the best cake I've ever tasted."

Maggie snapped another picture of the happy couple before diving into her piece. "Ohhhhh," she moaned, "it really is."

"Yes," Cate agreed. "You've really outdone yourselves, Mrs. Fraser and Molly."

Piper wrapped her hand around Charlie's.

"Yes, thank you," she said. "This really was more than we ever expected."

"Aww, honey," Molly said, "we were happy to do it."

"Aye, you only get married once. At least, that's the way it used to be and the way it still should be," Mrs. Fraser said, with a curt nod.

"We're in it forever, me and my fair maiden," Charlie said.

"Yeah, we're old-fashioned like that," Piper said.

They finished their cake and chitchatted a bit more, moving to the sitting room with hot chocolate provided by Mrs. Fraser and Molly, before turning in for the night.

CHAPTER 27

Maggie changed into her pajamas and sat at the vanity brushing her hair. She imagined living in a castle all the time, as she slipped between the sheets and stared out the window at the moonlight. She turned onto her other side, away from the window. After a few moments, she flopped onto her back.

With an aggravated sigh, Maggie tossed the covers back and donned her robe. She paced around the floor of her room. It was large enough to entertain her for a few minutes, before she ducked into the hallway. She glanced up and down the hall. No lights glowed from under anyone's doors.

Maggie scrunched up her nose. She tiptoed to Henry's door and tapped against it. With no response, she pressed her ear against his door and knocked lightly again. Her shoulders slumped, and she shook her head at the large wooden object.

Maggie crossed the hall back toward her room. She stood for a moment with her hand on the doorknob, before she stalked down the hall and knocked at the next door.

The door swung open a few seconds later.

"Come in. I can't sleep either," Emma said.

Maggie stalked into the room and sank into the armchair near the fireplace. "Sorry, I tried Henry, but he must be asleep."

"Surprise," Emma said as she settled into the second chair. They sat in silence for a few minutes. "Want to go exploring?"

Emma offered an unimpressed glance Maggie's way. "The last time we did that, someone locked us in a secret passage."

"That's not going to happen here. Cate's not going to shut us into a secret passage. Come on, maybe there's some cake left."

"Should we eat Piper and Charlie's wedding cake?"

"What are they going to do with it? They can't take it with them."

"Good point. We're really doing them a favor."

"Yep," Maggie said. She rose and dragged Emma to her feet. They stepped into the hall. "Now, we just have to find the kitchen."

They wandered through the halls until they arrived at the main staircase and proceeded to the main level. After a bit of wandering, they found a stairway leading down and used it to navigate to the servants' area.

"Down this hall," Maggie whispered.

"Right," Emma agreed.

They hurried down the length of the hall and into the large kitchen. Maggie scanned the space before pointing to a cake saver. "There!"

Emma scoured the kitchen for utensils and plates while Maggie searched for a knife and server. In short order, they each had a slice of cake to enjoy. Maggie squeezed her eyes closed after the first bite.

"Mmmm, this is good."

"Yep," Emma said, her mouth still full of cake.

They helped themselves to another slice, before covering what remained of the sweet treat. Maggie stalked around the room as she ate the cake. "I think we should look around."

"That's the sugar talking."

"No, come on. We should at least check out the secret passages."

"If we can find them."

"I bet we can."

"No bet."

"Come on, Emma, live a little. Fifty bucks says we find at least one of the passages."

Emma finished the last of her cake and washed her dish. "Okay, fine," she said.

They restored the kitchen to the way they'd found it before they hurried upstairs and found the dining room. Maggie flicked on the lights. "Where to start?" she asked, as she scanned the walls.

Emma stepped toward the darkly paneled walls. She pressed against them in several areas.

"Often the panels were spring-loaded," she explained.

Maggie lifted her eyebrows and chose another wall to work on.

"Aha!" Emma exclaimed. Maggie twisted to face her. One of the wooden panels had popped open. Emma offered a coy grin.

"We found one!" Maggie said, clapping her hands. "You owe me fifty bucks. Let's go in."

She toggled on her cell phone's flashlight and shined it into the passage.

"Double or nothing, we can't find them all," Emma said.

"You're on. I think we can do it."

They stepped into the secret passage. Maggie shined her light along the walls, searching for any clues to the brass key. They wound around behind the other rooms in the castle before they reached a dead-end. After a bit of maneuvering, Emma found the trigger to open the panel. They stepped into the tearoom. Gray streaked through the white marble floors, accented with gold tiles and trim. A round table sat near a fireplace, under a large chandelier. Lace curtains covered floor-to-ceiling windows.

"Wow!" Maggie whispered. She spun in a circle as she crossed the room, gaping at everything. "So beautiful."

"This castle really is amazing," Emma agreed.

Maggie plopped into one of the chairs. "Tea?" she said in a posh voice.

"Of course," Emma said, matching her tone.

Maggie poured an invisible teapot into an imaginary teacup. "You must try the cucumber sandwiches," Maggie continued. "They are simply to die for."

"I hoped to sample the scones."

"Oh, yes, you must have the scones."

They raised invisible teacups from unseen saucers, before taking an imaginary sip. They both giggled.

"Oh, I can't imagine living somewhere like this," Emma said.

"Me either," Maggie said. "I was thinking about it while I got ready for bed. It's amazing here."

Emma leaned back in her chair. "Do you think we'll find the keys?"

"I know we will," Maggie said.

"Hi ladies," Cate said from the open entrance to the tearoom.

"Oh!" Maggie exclaimed. "You startled me."

"Sorry," Cate said, as she sauntered over to the table. "Trouble sleeping?"

"Probably too much excitement," Emma said. "It's not for lack of wonderful accommodations. The room is so nice, and the bed was very comfortable. And thank you again for taking all of us on such short notice."

"No problem. And it's okay," Cate said. "I understand. I couldn't sleep the first few nights here either."

"Who *wants* to sleep in a castle this great?"

Cate offered a shy smile. "I am rather partial to it," she said. "How about some real tea?"

"Sure!" Maggie said. She stood but Cate waved her back to the table.

"Stay here, I'll get it and bring it up. You can have tea in the tearoom."

"Oh, please, let us help," Emma said.

"Oh, no, it'll only take a minute."

Cate returned within fifteen minutes with an ornate tea tray set with beautiful china. A saucer of shortbread cookies sat in the middle.

"I have a confession," Maggie said, as Cate poured tea from the teapot into each cup.

"Oh?"

"We ate some of the wedding cake."

Cate's eyebrows raised at the admission.

"Actually," Emma said, "we ate a *lot* of the wedding cake."

Cate giggled. "It's okay. I'm sure no one will mind."

They sipped at their tea, while they confessed having found the tearoom by way of the secret passage.

"Couldn't wait to search them, huh?" Cate asked.

"We're on a mission to find them all," Maggie said.

"Do you want me to let you do it by trial and error, or just show you?"

"Maybe you could show us," Maggie said.

"What?" Emma exclaimed. "I thought you were sure we could find them?"

Maggie shrugged.

"Well, are you ready to pay up?" Emma asked.

"We made a bet," Maggie explained.

"Ohhhh," Cate said. "Well, far be it from me to interfere with a bet."

"Maybe you could remind us of where they are," Maggie said.

"Hallway near the library and portrait gallery and there's a secret lab under the library."

"Maybe we'll find the key in one of them," Maggie said, before biting into a shortbread cookie.

Cate lifted her eyebrows and sighed as she stared into her teacup. "I don't remember seeing it when I cataloged everything in the secret lab. I really hoped you'd find it in the west wing since the portrait of Randolph was there."

"Well, we found out that Randolph was a member of the Brotherhood," Emma answered. "So, that's half the battle."

"Randolph built the east wing, so perhaps you'll have more luck there."

"Are there plans for it?" Emma inquired.

"Yes, there should be. Jack can help you with that. Though I'll warn you, they are often not accurate."

"Do they show the secret passages?" Maggie said.

"They don't always. Douglas's lab was not marked. So, if Randolph was as secretive as Douglas, not everything may be marked."

Maggie pursed her lips and nodded.

"I'm going to continue to search for clues," Cate promised.

"It's okay. We're happy to explore on our own, too," Maggie said.

"And if Randolph built the east wing, I think that's a really promising lead," Emma added.

Everyone nodded.

"Well, I suppose we should get to it," Maggie said.

"Oh," Cate said, concern crossing her face, "now? You don't want to try to get some rest?"

"Nah, who needs to sleep? I'm way too excited! We'll get a few hours before sunrise. *After* we find the other secret passages. Only three more to go!" Maggie said, as she drained her teacup and grabbed another shortbread.

"Well, I'll leave you ladies to it," Cate said. "Oh, fair warning, the one near the library leads outside to the crypt. It's quite a walk to and from, so you may want to save traversing that one for the daylight hours."

"Thanks for the tip. Well, we just need to find it," Maggie said, "so as long as we do that, I can win."

Emma snagged another shortbread. "One for the road," she said.

"To the portrait gallery!" Maggie said, thrusting her fist in the air.

They wandered through the halls, locating the foyer and ascending the grand staircase to the second floor.

"Where the heck was this room?" Maggie inquired as they reached the next floor.

"Left?" Emma asked.

"Maybe."

They wandered to the left before Emma began shaking her head.

"No, wait," she said, "maybe the other way."

They retraced their steps and took another hallway. They arrived at an open space overlooking the floor below. Thick purple carpet ran down the center of several sets of stairs that met in the center to lead to the floor below.

"Now where?" Maggie asked.

"Ummm," Emma eyed the multiple doorways and hallways as she scratched her head. "There. Maybe."

She pointed toward a large set of double doors angled in the corner.

"Oh, yeah, maybe!"

They proceeded to the doors and pushed them open.

"Success!" Maggie grinned as rows of portraits greeted them in the large space.

"Now," she said, as they stepped inside, "if I were a hidden passage, where would I be?"

Emma puckered her lips as she took in the space.

"Oh!" Maggie said wide-eyed. "Behind the portrait of Randolph?!" She hurried to the life-sized painting and tugged on it.

The large art piece did not budge. "There goes that idea," Maggie said with a frown.

Emma's eyes continued to search the space. They focused on the red inset panels at the far end of the room. She strode across to them and pushed at them.

Maggie joined her, trying a few panels. "Do you think there'll be a spring-loaded panel here?"

After a few moments, they both gave up. "Apparently not."

Maggie wandered around the space, pushing on other panels. None of them triggered a secret doorway to pop open.

After another moment of scanning, Emma tilted her head. She stared at a gold inset near a red panel. Emma crossed to it and pushed on it. She narrowed her eyes when the piece did not budge.

"Find something?" Maggie asked as she joined her.

Emma remained silent. She curled her fingers around the golden flower and pulled. The piece inched away from the wall. Maggie's jaw dropped. "Emma! This must be the way to open the passage!"

Emma tugged more on the flower, but it wouldn't budge. It stuck two inches from the wall. "But it hasn't triggered anything."

"Maybe there's more than one," Maggie said, as she searched the area. "Here's one."

She stepped to the flower on the opposite side of the panel and yanked on it, but it didn't move.

"Shoot," she said, stamping her foot on the floor.

Emma pursed her lips and grabbed hold of the protruding golden flower. She twisted it to the right. Repeating clicks sounded as Emma turned the flower upside-down. A clank echoed in the large space, and the red panel popped open into the room.

CHAPTER 28

Maggie stared at the new opening in front of them. "Emma! You did it!"

Emma offered Maggie a proud smile.

"How did you know?" Maggie asked, as she pulled the panel open wider.

"This flower didn't sit flush like that one."

"Clever girl," Maggie said, striking a pose. She toggled on her flashlight and stepped into the passage. "East wing, here we come!"

Emma ducked in behind her, leaving the panel open behind them. They wandered through the darkened passage until they came to a dead-end. After fiddling with the panel, they managed to open it. It led into a darkened hallway. Moonlight filtered through the windows, giving the long space an eerie countenance.

Maggie grimaced. "Yeah, maybe we should have waited until daylight."

"Scared?" Emma asked.

"A little," Maggie admitted. "Come on, let's look around."

They crept down the hall with Maggie strafing it with her

flashlight. Maggie stopped, her shoulders hunched. "What is that?" she whispered.

A creaking noise echoed in the hallway. Both women spun around and faced the direction from which they'd just come.

"No!" Emma shouted, as she broke away from Maggie and raced down the hall. The panel they'd left open elicited a groan then a crack as it snapped shut.

Emma banged against it. "No!" she cried again.

Maggie rejoined her, tapping on the panel. She tried pushing and pulling decorative elements near it and even jimmied the sconce on the wall.

"Now we're stuck!" Emma cried.

"We can open it again when we need to."

"Oh really? We can't open it right now, *and* if we leave it, will we find it again?" Emma glanced up and down the long hallway. "What are the chances we find the exact spot again? Everything looks the same!"

"Oh, come on," Maggie said, as she poked around at another few elements, none of which opened the panel, "it's not that bad. We're stuck in a fantastic castle. Let's just search around and see if we find anything."

"I guess at least there are no traps or scorpions this time," Emma said with a shrug.

"That's the spirit!" Maggie said. "Plus, we have cell phones that *work*. We can text someone to open the doors to this wing tomorrow morning. Easy!"

"Sure," Emma said, as she slogged down the hall. "We'll just have to sleep over here on a hard floor."

"Maybe we'll find a bed!"

They wandered through the darkened halls, peeking into closed rooms as they went. A few covered furniture pieces dotted mostly empty rooms.

"We'll never find anything in these rooms. There are dozens of them and it's so dark," Emma said.

They reached the end of the hall. A staircase led to a door at the top.

"Where's that go?" Maggie questioned.

"Only one way to find out," Emma answered.

They mounted the stairs and proceeded up. The door swung into a neutral-colored turret room. Wooden floors graced the rounded space. A sheet covered a low chaise across the room. Unlit candles sat on a console table above a covered mirror, and two large French doors led to a stone balcony outside.

"Wow," Maggie said, as she swung the doors open. "What a view."

"Yeah," Emma agreed. "I bet it's even better in the daylight."

"We'll have to check it out tomorrow."

They closed the doors and crossed the room, exiting and descending to the hall below.

"May as well try this hall," Maggie said, as she swung her beam to the side.

They wound through the hall, exploring several of the rooms which included an upstairs sitting area decorated in gold and black and a bedroom suite in pale blue with pink accents.

"Makes you wonder who used these rooms," Maggie said, touching the decorative settee in the whimsical fabric.

"It's amazing they had this many rooms to use," Emma answered, as she stretched in the stick armchair. "They don't build 'em like they used to, as they say."

"That's for sure."

Maggie's phone chimed. Emma leapt from the chair. "Was that a text?"

"Yeah!" Maggie said.

"Oh, yay, someone's up!" Emma answered, hovering over Maggie's shoulder.

"It's Piper!" Maggie said, as she swiped into the message and read it aloud. "Hey, boss lady, where are you?"

Maggie talked as she typed. "East wing, a light blue bedroom. We're stuck over here. The panel snapped shut and we can't get it open."

Three dots popped across the screen, indicating Piper typing. "*Sit tight, we're coming to you*," Maggie read.

She clicked off her phone and pressed it under her chin. "What does that mean?"

"It seems obvious," Emma said, as she plopped into the chair again.

"But how is she getting here?"

"I guess we'll find out soon," Emma said. "I'm just glad we're being rescued."

"Rescued? It's not like we're in a tomb."

Voices sounded down the hall, and within minutes, light bounced around as a flashlight shined into the room.

Piper stepped inside, dressed in a pair of unicorn pajamas with matching unicorn robe, followed by Cate, in a thick robe and pajamas, who held an electric hurricane lamp. She held the lantern up high and grinned, waving a paper clutched in her hand! "We found something!"

"You did?!" Maggie exclaimed.

Cate nodded. "Piper and I were going through some of Randolph's correspondence, and we came across a reference."

Maggie and Emma gathered around Cate as she set the lantern on the mantle of the fireplace and unfurled the paper.

"This letter is from Kendrick MacClyde. It says he enjoyed his recent visit to Dunhaven Castle and talks a bit about his family." Cate's finger traced down the paper. "But down here," she said as she searched for it, "he says…" She paused, still searching. "Here it is: *'I was very impressed by your placement of the key. I would very much like to work out something similar at Clydescolm, as it seems rather obvious to place it in a safe. But your hideaway is quite ingenious, though I have always been a fan of arcane puzzles. Obviously, your situation is rather different, given you built it in during construction, whereas mine will take some effort, but I believe it is still achievable. And, of course, hidden right behind you, as the keeper of the key and secret, is obvious yet obtuse enough to throw any curiosity-seekers off the scent'.*"

Maggie furrowed her brow. "So, he did hide the key here! But how does this help us find it?"

"Well," Cate said, as she pointed to a specific phrase, "he says he built it in during construction. The only construction Randolph oversaw was the addition of this wing. So, the key is somewhere in this wing."

Maggie's shoulder's slumped and Emma winced. "But the wing is huge."

"Yeah," Maggie agreed. "We've been wandering around here for over an hour and a half, and we've barely covered half of it."

Cate nodded. "I know, but it's a much smaller area to search than the entire castle."

"Yeah, boss lady, see the positive," Piper said. "Plus, there's more."

"Yes," Cate agreed, "here where he says, 'hidden right behind you.'"

"What does that mean?" Maggie asked.

"I think it refers to some likeness of Randolph, either a picture or a plaque. Maybe a bust? I'm not sure what's over here, but I think we're searching for some image of Randolph."

"Oh, I see, like a portrait of him, and the key's hidden behind it."

Cate nodded and pointed at Maggie.

"Exactly. The only problem is…" she said, squashing her brows together and placing her finger on her chin.

"What if they moved the portrait in the hundred or so odd years since Randolph built the wing?" Emma asked.

Cate nodded. "Yes," she answered with a wince. "What if the portrait hanging in the west wing with the dragon symbol originally hung in this wing?"

"Well, maybe they didn't move the one we're looking for."

"Or maybe we can find where it was hanging," Piper said with a shrug.

"It's worth a shot," Emma said. "Do you want to look now?"

"Heck yeah," Maggie said. "I'll never sleep now."

"I'll help," Cate agreed. "Let me see if I can find a breaker for this wing or at least some more flashlights."

"Okay," Maggie agreed. They filed from the room and wandered to a large hall. Floor-to-ceiling windows draped with dark velvety curtains lined the hallway, facing east. Paintings hung on the wall opposite them. Piper aimed her flashlight at them as they walked.

"No Randolph," Maggie lamented, as they approached the double doors leading to the main castle.

"None missing, either," Emma said.

Cate grasped the door handles and twisted, pulling them toward her. The doors didn't open. She set the lantern down and tried again. Cate leaned back and yanked. "Must be stuck," she grunted, as she jimmied the door back and forth.

She spun to face them, her face a mask of shock. "I think we're stuck."

"How could that be?" Piper asked. "We unlocked this!"

"And left it open," Cate said. "But it's closed now and apparently locked."

Cate turned and tried again. She banged against the door.

"Jack? Jack!" she called. "Molly! Mrs. Fraser! Mr. Fraser!" She turned and leaned against the door. "Nothing."

"We can always use the hidden passage to go back," Maggie said.

Cate offered an apologetic smile. "I don't know how to open it. I only know it existed. But I've never used it."

"We can call!" Maggie waved her cell phone in the air.

"Okay," Cate said. "Maybe Henry or Ollie?"

"Or Jack," Emma said.

"I keep Jack's number in my cell and…"

"You don't know it by heart," Emma finished.

Cate shook her head. "No."

"I'll try Henry," Maggie said. She tapped at the phone. After a moment she pulled it away from her ear and scrunched her nose at it. "That's weird." She tapped around again and held the phone to her ear. After a moment, she swiped at it and turned the display off. "I can't get a call out. It keeps saying the call cannot be completed."

"What?!" Cate exclaimed. "Do you have a signal?"

"It says I do. Three bars." Maggie flashed the screen at them.

Cate pulled a gold watch from under her robe and checked it. She blew out a long breath and nodded. "Well, someone should be up in a few hours."

"Someone will find us then," Piper said.

"I guess we have plenty of time to look around for Randolph until then," Maggie said.

"Yeah," Emma agreed. "We didn't see anything upstairs in the rooms we'd made it through. Though we could have missed something."

"Let's start with the rooms down here," Cate said.

"Should we split up?" Maggie said.

"I'm not sure that's a great idea," Cate said.

"I agree with Dr. Kensie," Emma said. "Splitting up is not the best idea. Especially with only two flashlights."

"And the crazy not-working cellphone and the weirdly locked door," Piper said.

They set off down the hall, exploring rooms as they went. They found no traces of any depictions of Randolph in the first hall.

They turned the corner and entered a large space through a set of double doors. The rectangular room featured a cathedral ceiling. Pillars rose to hold the ceiling at bay, and an archway led to another area in the room.

"Wow, this room must be as big as the entire hallway," Emma said.

"And it's a gallery," Cate said, holding her lantern up to light a landscape on the wall.

Piper swept the flashlight over several other paintings.

"Are any of Randolph?"

They searched both areas of the gallery, sweeping their lights over every painting.

"These are all landscapes," Emma shouted from the second space.

"Yeah," Piper answered, "no old-school dudes over here either."

Cate sighed. "I really thought this would be it."

"Me too," Maggie lamented.

Cate and Piper joined Maggie and Emma in the back room. "Should we move on?" Maggie asked.

Emma yawned. "Anyone mind if we take a break for a few minutes?"

Everyone agreed a rest was in order, and they slid to sitting against one of the walls.

"Sorry I got us stuck, ladies," Cate said, after a few moments of silence.

"It's okay," Maggie said. "Emma and I were stuck to begin with anyway. And at least it's in a swanky castle."

"Yeah, not the bowels of a tomb," Emma added.

"I can't believe you were trapped in there," Cate said.

"I can," Piper said. "I told them not to go in there. I've seen enough Indiana Jones movies to know that's what always happens."

The women chuckled over their circumstances.

"Mind if I borrow your flashlight?" Maggie asked Piper.

She handled the silver item over to Maggie, who clicked it on and pointed to a painting on the far wall.

"Okay, here's what I propose. We all take a minute and pretend we're at this place, wherever it may be. There's a nice soft breeze rustling those tree leaves. And the sun is shining down on us."

"Mmm, heavenly," Emma said. "It looks very beautiful."

Cate narrowed her eyes at the painting and tilted her head. "That's my loch," she said.

"Really?" Maggie inquired. "Wow, we'll have to check that out before we go. It's beautiful."

"Yes," Cate said. "I agree, but who painted the loch here? None of the other paintings were of Dunhaven's estate."

She climbed to her feet and approached it, toggling on her hurricane lamp. Her jaw fell open and she spun to face the others. "This was painted by Randolph MacKenzie!"

The remaining three women scrambled to their feet and hurried over. Cate held the lamp higher and studied the painting. "Could this be the painting holding the secret?"

"There!" Emma shouted. She pointed at the tree near the loch. Faintly painted into the weathered trunk was the symbol of the dragon.

"I see it!" Maggie exclaimed, bouncing on her toes. "This *has* to be it."

"But how do we open it?" Piper asked, peering behind the painting.

"Take the painting down?" Maggie suggested. "Help me."

She handed the flashlight off to Piper and grasped one corner. Emma grabbed the other. They tried to lift, but the painting didn't budge.

"Is it nailed to the wall?" Maggie said, annoyance filling her voice.

She grasped both corners and tugged. The painting's bottom gave way, tilting at a forty-five-degree angle. A scraping noise sounded and a whoosh of stale air gusted past them.

Cate swung the lantern in the direction of the wind. A hole gaped open where a panel had once stood.

CHAPTER 29

They all stared at the gaping hole now facing them.

"Whoa, dude, that's crazy," Piper said.

"It's amazing!" Maggie exclaimed. "Give me the light!" She swiped it from Piper's hands and shined it into the black space. "The key *has* to be in here."

"Do you see it?" Piper asked.

"No," Maggie answered. "It's a passageway."

"Another secret passage?" Emma asked.

"Yep."

"Do you know where this one leads?" Emma asked Cate.

"No," Cate said, with a shake of her head. "I didn't even know it was here."

"We should follow it." Maggie stepped toward the opening.

"I'm game," Cate said.

Emma shrugged. "Maybe we should wait for everyone else."

"Why?" Maggie moaned.

"Safety?"

"What could possibly happen?"

Emma opened her mouth to answer, when Maggie said, "Don't answer that. I'm going in, join me or not."

The remaining three women glanced at each other.

"Don't look at me," Piper said. "No way am I going into the creepy tunnel. I don't care how posh the castle is. There still could be a giant rolling ball ready to kill me in there."

Cate's expression turned pensive at the statement.

"All right, all right," Emma said, as she stepped in with Maggie. "I'll go."

"Are you okay staying here yourself?" Cate asked Piper.

"Yeah," Piper answered. "I'll be fine here. I'll let them know where to search for your bodies when I'm rescued," she shouted after Maggie.

"Okay," Maggie called back.

"Okay, I'm going with them. I'll leave the lantern with you." Cate swapped the flashlight for the lantern, before following Emma into the passage.

"Good luck," Piper called after them as they disappeared into the dark passage.

Maggie led the way, her cell phone shining a bright beam ahead but failing to penetrate the darkness fully. Cate swept her beam from side to side, searching for any sign of the key or a symbol pointing to it.

"Coming up to an endpoint," Maggie announced, a few steps ahead of both Cate and Emma.

"Any sign of the key?" Emma inquired.

"No," Maggie said. "Just a wall." She reached it and swung the beam around. "It continues to the right."

Emma and Cate hurried to catch up to Maggie as she rounded the corner. The tight corridor stretched long in front of them. Neither light beam reached the end.

They inched their way down the corridor. "This reminds me of something," Emma said.

"Yeah, the Library of Alexandria, but at least this time no

one is holding us at gunpoint."

Cate's eyes widened at the conversation, and she swallowed hard. "You ladies really know how to live," she whispered.

"We almost didn't," Emma answered.

Maggie squinted into the blackness ahead. "What is that? It looks like the passage disappears."

Ahead of them, the ceiling sloped downward toward the floor.

"Or ends," Emma said.

"But we haven't found the key yet!" Maggie exclaimed.

They approached the sloped ceiling and Maggie gulped. She shined her beam into the hole below. Stairs disappeared into the blackness.

"Wow, this must lead underground," Emma said.

"Yeah, that's not creepy at all," Maggie said.

"This was common. At least for the MacKenzies," Cate explained. "Douglas's lab was built underground, too. It makes sense his grandson would follow in his footsteps."

"Okay," Maggie said with a deep breath. "Down we go."

She stepped onto the first stone step. A few pieces of the block crumbled away, but the step held.

"Careful," Emma cautioned. "One at a time."

Maggie nodded and they proceeded single file down the hewn steps. Small pieces of stone skittered down in front of them, echoing in the tight chamber. Maggie reached the bottom and pulled her robe tighter around her.

"Why do we always end up in these filthy places in our pajamas?" Emma asked as she reached the bottom. "At this rate, you're going to owe me another robe before we leave Scotland."

"I should have a few extras if these need to be laundered," Cate said, stepping down from the final step and swinging her flashlight around.

"It's chilly down here," Maggie said, as they continued down the long corridor at the bottom of the stairs.

Within a few minutes, a wooden door appeared in the light beams. They hurried toward it. Maggie depressed the lever and pushed, but it didn't budge. She tried pulling to no avail.

"Stuck," she groaned.

"No," Emma countered, "locked."

She pointed toward a series of brass tumblers under the handle.

"Oh, no," Maggie groaned. "Not another word lock. We'll never open this."

"Another?" Cate inquired, as Maggie fiddled with the letters.

"We got locked in a secret passage at Clydescolm Castle. It had one of these, too. We still haven't figured it out," Emma explained.

"How did you get out?"

"We found a cave below," Maggie explained, as she spun the tumblers. "That's where the dragon symbol was. And there was an egress from it onto the property."

Maggie threw her hands in the air. "Nothing!"

"What did you try?" Emma asked.

"Enter and entry."

"Five letters," Cate murmured as she crinkled her brow. "Let me try."

She spun the cylinders starting with the second tumbler. When she finished, a clank sounded. Cate depressed the lever and swung the door open.

"Cate! You did it!" Maggie exclaimed. "What was the word?"

"Ethan."

Maggie scrunched her nose at the correct answer.

"Randolph's son's name," Cate explained.

Maggie and Emma nodded at the answer, as Cate led the way through the door. A large dark chamber lay beyond it. They swung their flashlight beams around. Maggie centered hers directly in front of them.

A large chest sat atop a pedestal. They approached it.

"Locked," Maggie said with a huff.

"Eight letters this time," Emma said. "So, it's not Ethan."

"Should we just take the chest and go?" Maggie suggested.

Emma shrugged. "What if it's not the key? It's also fairly large. I think it would take two of us to carry."

While Emma and Maggie discussed the possibilities, Cate approached the chest and studied the eight tumblers. She reached toward them and began spinning the letter-filled cylinders. When she reached the last one, the chest popped open.

"I got it!" Cate exclaimed in her soft voice.

Maggie's jaw dropped open. "How?"

"Victoria," Cate said. "His wife."

"Wow, he really was a family man," Emma said.

"Very much so, despite the rumors."

"What rumors?" Maggie questioned.

"That he was a womanizer who kept a girl locked in the tower room."

"What?" Maggie asked, her face a mask of surprised entertainment.

Cate shook her head. "All completely untrue, but they made for entertaining stories around the town."

"Well, you should do the honors and open it," Emma said to Cate. "He's your ancestor."

Cate nodded and lifted the chest's lid. A glint of metal caught the flashlight's beam. She swung the lid backward, revealing the contents. A gold coin sat nestled in velvet cloth, next to a large brass key with an ornate end.

"That's it!" Maggie exclaimed. "That's the second key!"

"We did it!" Emma said with a wide grin.

Maggie tapped around on her phone. "Selfie!" She held the phone out and snapped several pictures of them with the key.

"Let's grab it and get out of here. I can't wait to tell Piper!" Maggie exclaimed.

Cate lifted it and the coin from the dark green velvet lining and stowed them in her robe's square pocket. She closed the lid of the chest, as the room grew darker.

"Shoot, my phone died."

"You and your selfies," Emma said. "It's always draining the battery at the worst moment."

"It's important to have these images for posterity!" Maggie argued.

"Let's get out of here while we still have one working light," Emma said.

They retraced their steps after closing the door to the secret chamber. As they rounded the corner to the final passageway, light filtered in from the hurricane lamp Cate left with Piper. The light reflected off the wall before receding as it moved.

"Hey, Piper, guess what!" Maggie shouted.

She received no answer.

"Probably can't hear you yet," Emma said.

The trio hurried along the length of the corridor. Maggie emerged into the room first.

"We got it, Piper!" she announced, as the remaining two women spilled into the room. Her brow furrowed and she glanced around. "Piper?"

She put her hands on her hips. "Piper!" she shouted. "Where could she have gone?"

"She couldn't have gone too far," Emma said. "She left the lantern."

"Why is it toppled over?" Cate questioned.

Maggie bent down to the overturned lantern and grabbed it, holding it high and scanning the space.

She stepped toward the door and into the hall.

"Piper!" she shouted, her head swiveling in both directions. "This is ridiculous." She stepped back through the door. "Where is she?"

"I've got a bad feeling," Emma said.

"Don't be ridiculous. She has to be around here somewhere," Maggie said. "Come on, let's go look. She probably went out to look at something."

"What would she have gone to look at?" Emma inquired. "And why didn't she take the lantern?"

The ladies left the room and entered the hallway. They hurried up and down corridors of the east wing, peeking into rooms and calling for Piper. They found no trace of her. They climbed to the second floor. A search there also came up empty. Finally, they climbed to the turret room, but found nothing.

The three of them settled on the floor of the tower as the sky began to turn a deep shade of red.

"Where could she be?"

"Maybe she found her way back to the main castle," Emma conjectured.

"How? We can't find our way back," Maggie argued.

Cate checked the timepiece hanging around her neck. "Mrs. Fraser should be up. Once we fail to appear for breakfast, she'll send Jack on a search for us. We should be freed soon."

"And hopefully reunited with Piper," Emma said.

"Yeah, and then she can show us how she managed to get out of here."

They watched the sunrise over the moors, bathing the landscape in rich colors as the red sun peeked from behind the horizon.

Cate climbed to her feet as the fiery ball hung low in the morning sky. They descended to the main hallway leading to the castle. Cate jiggled the doors. "Still locked," she said with a sigh.

"So, Piper didn't get out that way," Maggie said.

Cate banged on the doors. "Jack! Molly! Mrs. Fraser! Anybody?"

A muffled noise sounded on the other side of the doors. Maggie's heart skipped a beat. "What was that?"

A faint voice reached her ears. "That's somebody!" Emma exclaimed.

Cate nodded enthusiastically. "Hello?! We're stuck in the east wing!" she shouted at the door.

"Cate?" Jack's voice answered, sounding dulled by the thick wooden door. They heard the jingling of keys. "Just a second."

The lock disengaged and the door swung open. Jack's shocked face peered in. "Cate, what happened? Are you ladies all right?"

Cate nodded. "We're okay. We were chasing down a lead, when we got stuck. I'm not sure how the door locked behind me. I left it open!"

"Didn't you have the key?" Jack asked.

"No, I left it in the lock. Is Piper with you?"

"Piper? The one with the bright hair? No."

Maggie bit her lower lip.

"Maybe she went back to her room," Emma said with a shrug.

"I'd like to be sure," Cate said. "I don't want her locked in the east wing for hours."

With everyone in agreement, they began the journey to Piper and Charlie's bedroom.

"So, did your lead pan out?" Jack inquired.

Cate's face lit up as she glanced at Jack. She pulled the key and coin from her pocket. "We found this!"

"Is that it? Is that the key?" Jack asked.

Maggie nodded. "Yes, it looks just like the other. Two down, two to go."

They climbed the stairs and navigated to the hallway containing their bedrooms. Henry stood leaning on the wall near Ollie's door.

"There you are," he said to Maggie. "I knocked and didn't get any response."

"I wasn't there. We were finding the second key."

"Really?" Henry said, as he straightened and approached them.

Cate handed Maggie the coin and key. "Here, you can handle it from here. You're the experts."

Ollie's door opened and he stepped into the hallway. "What's this? A plaid robe convention?" he said, as he eyed the three women in their tartan robes.

"Very funny, Uncle Ollie," Maggie said. "I think you'll be quite pleased though." Maggie waved the key at him. "We found the key!"

"Where?!" Ollie asked, as he carefully lifted it from Maggie's hand.

"In a hidden chamber under the east wing."

"Under it?" Jack asked.

"Yes," Cate explained. "We found a secret passage in the gallery there. It led to an underground chamber with the key."

"So, the old girl had another secret in her, huh?" Jack inquired.

"That she did."

"Speaking of girls," Maggie said. "We came up to see if Piper is up here. She was with us, but she chickened out of going into the secret passage. When we got back, she was gone."

Maggie crossed the hall, leaving Ollie studying the coin, and knocked on the newlyweds' door.

Charlie opened it a few moments later. "Now, now, chicky," he said, "I know how tempting this may be, but I'm a married man."

"Very funny, Charlie," Maggie said, crossing her arms over her chest. "Is your spouse in there?"

"No," Charlie said.

"What?" Maggie said, letting her arms fall to the side. She searched around Charlie as though he may have missed her. "Well, then, where is she?"

Charlie shrugged. "She hasn't been here all morning. Sadly, I woke up alone."

Maggie's eyes grew wide, and she glanced at the others in the group. "Where's Piper?"

"What do you mean, 'where's Piper?'" Charlie inquired, stepping into the hall with them. "Maybe she went to get breakfast, or went for a walk or something."

Maggie shook her head. "She was with us when we got the key."

"You found the key?" Charlie asked.

"Yes, in an underground chamber in the east wing. We went inside and she said she'd wait in the gallery. When we got back, she wasn't there. And we can't find her anywhere. We were locked in the east wing. We thought maybe she managed to find a way out, but then, where is she?"

"I've got a terrible feeling about this," Emma said.

"Me too," Maggie said, wrapping her arms around her abdomen. "She wouldn't just disappear like this. She wouldn't go for a walk and leave us in that passage alone."

"No, I don't think so either," Charlie said.

"Which means..." Maggie began.

"Nothing good," Henry finished.

"It means someone took Piper," Emma finished.

CHAPTER 30

"Let's not panic just yet," Ollie said. "Has anyone received a message from her?"

Charlie checked his phone. "Not me. Did she have her phone on her?"

"Not to my knowledge," Cate said.

"I'll check our room," Charlie announced. He returned moments later waving her bright pink cellphone at them. "The fair maiden does not have her phone."

"Which means if she's trapped somewhere, she can't let us know," Cate said.

"Okay, we need a plan. Let's change and give the castle a good going over and hope she turns up. If she doesn't, we'll have to reassess," Maggie said.

"Sounds like a plan," Ollie said.

With everyone in agreement, Maggie ducked into her room and pushed the door shut behind her. She leaned against it and blew out a long breath. Doubt filled her as she considered searching the property for Piper. She wouldn't disappear. Maggie worried something had happened to her.

She fought back her tears as she pushed herself to tear off

her pajamas and shimmy into a pair of athletic pants and a t-shirt. As she hung her robe on the back of the door, her pocket gaped open.

She grabbed the phone from inside and hurried across the room to plug it into the charger. As a red battery flashed on the screen, she darted across the room and out to meet everyone else.

"All right, we should go in pairs," Henry said, as Maggie emerged.

Emma said, "We'll take the west wing." She motioned to herself and Leo.

"Charlie and I will take the main castle," Ollie said.

"All right, Maggie and I will go to the east wing where she was last seen," Henry said.

Cate hurried down the hall with the other members of the household. Henry explained the plan to her. "Okay," she said with a nod.

"Molly, Mr. and Mrs. Fraser, can you look in the west wing, too? Jack and I will do a cursory search of the outside property, including any buildings where she may have become stuck."

"I've also called my Pap and he's going to take a stroll through town and check for any sign of her. I told him he can't miss her. She's got rainbow hair."

"All right," Henry said with a nod. "We meet back here in two hours, is that enough time?"

Everyone nodded. With a plan in place, they split up, each going to their respective locations to search. Maggie chewed on her lower lip as she and Henry hurried to the east wing.

They searched the location from top to bottom but found nothing. They tried doors leading to the outside, finding them all locked other than the turret's balcony doors. They called for Piper, but received no response.

With a frustrated huff, Maggie and Henry made their way

back to the main portion of the castle. They found most of the others gathered in the foyer.

"No sign," Molly said, a worried expression on her face.

"Us either," Maggie answered.

"We came up empty, too," Emma reported.

"Nothing," Ollie said.

Cate and Jack pushed through the main doors. Maggie searched behind them as her hope began to fade. Cate gave a small shake of her head, her face a mask of sadness. "We didn't find her."

"And Pap said there's no trace of her in town," Jack added.

Maggie's shoulders slumped.

"She couldn't just disappear!" Charlie shouted, his frustration apparent.

"I'll call the police," Jack said, grabbing his phone.

"No," Henry cautioned. "No police."

Cate and Jack stared at him with confused looks. "But surely..." Cate began.

"I'd agree with him," Ollie said. "It's most likely Piper has been taken by force. Calling the police will endanger her more than help her."

"Poor child," Mrs. Fraser said, with a shake of her head. "How could this happen in Dunhaven?!"

"If we can't call the police, then what do we do?" Molly inquired, her voice laced with panic.

"We track her down," Henry said.

"How?" Cate asked.

"Charlie..." Henry began.

"I'm already on it," he said, as he threaded past them and darted up the stairs.

Henry nodded. "We'll look at the most obvious suspects. The black car that's been chasing us and Sir William. We just stole a key from him that I'm sure he'd very much like returned."

"Has anyone received any messages to that effect?" Ollie asked.

Everyone checked their phones. "Oh, mine is upstairs. It was dead, I had to charge it," Maggie said. "I'll grab it."

"Stay here, I'll get it," Henry said, as he sprinted up the stairs.

"Poor Piper," Molly said, her arms wrapped around her midriff as she chewed her lower lip. Cate wrapped an arm around her shoulders. "She must be so scared." A sob escaped her.

"It's okay, Molly, Piper's strong," Maggie assured her.

"Still…" Her voice trailed off.

"Plus, it's not her first kidnapping."

"What?!" Molly inquired, snapping her head up to stare incredulously at Maggie.

"Yeah, we were held hostage last year, too." Before Maggie could explain any further, Henry and Charlie returned.

"If you don't mind, Lady Cate, I'll set up in the library." Charlie waved his laptop in the air. "Already searching networks for her likeness and that black car."

"No, go ahead," Cate said with a nod.

"And we've got contact," Henry said, waving Maggie's phone in the air.

"What?!" Maggie asked, snatching the phone from his hands and swiping at it. "What does it say?"

"Well?" Emma asked.

Maggie gripped the phone tightly as she read aloud. "We have Rainbow Brite. Find all four keys. Instructions for the swap will follow once you've secured all pieces."

Molly covered her face with her hands. Mr. Fraser slid his arm around Mrs. Fraser's shoulders as she wrung her hands. Cate swallowed hard, focusing on the floor. Jack sighed and shook his head.

"All right," Henry said, as though Maggie didn't just

THE LOST TREASURE OF DRAKON

announce one of their team had been kidnapped. "We need to work this from two angles."

"Yes, one team needs to locate the remaining keys. The other needs to work on tracking Piper," Ollie answered.

"Charlie's working on locating any traces of the black car, Sir William, or Piper. I'll stay with him in case we get a lead," Henry said. "Cate, do you have a car we could borrow?"

"Yes," Cate said. "We have an estate car. You're welcome to use it."

"And Jack," Henry continued, "I'm assuming you're familiar with the area. Would you be able to help us identify any locations we come across?"

Jack nodded. "Of course, whatever you need."

"Okay, that leaves the Navigator for you to find the rest of the keys," Henry said to Maggie.

Maggie nodded.

"I'll go with Maggie," Emma said.

"I'd like to go with you, too," Cate chimed in. "I feel terrible about what happened."

Maggie grasped her forearm. "It's not your fault, Cate. But we'll take all the help we can get in tracking these keys down."

Cate gave her an understanding smile.

Ollie offered to coordinate between the two teams, remaining at Dunhaven Castle in case another lead panned out. Leo suggested he stay with Henry and Charlie in case they needed extra help in a rescue effort.

Mrs. Fraser said she'd provide meals, promising food for those remaining at Dunhaven Castle and a hamper for those leaving, as well as dog care for Cate.

She gathered Molly to ready food for those preparing to leave.

"We should grab a few things," Maggie said.

"Phones, chargers, maybe a change of clothes," Emma

listed as they hurried up the stairs.

Cate swallowed hard and bit her lower lip as she nodded at the set of instructions.

"Cate, you don't have to go," Maggie said.

"Yeah," Emma agreed, "I'm sure this is very overwhelming to someone not involved in our usual undertakings."

Fear showed on Cate's features, but she shook her head. "No," she said emphatically, "I want to help." She punctuated the last statement with a curt nod.

"Okay, pack an overnight bag as quickly as you can and we'll meet downstairs," Maggie said.

Cate nodded and continued down the hallway to her room. Maggie and Emma entered their respective rooms.

Maggie hurried to her luggage, grabbing her spare duffel bag and filling it with a few essentials. As she grabbed her phone charger, her mind parsed through the message she'd received. They needed to come up with an answer. She'd discuss that with Henry and Ollie before they left.

Her mind ran over the message again, as she attempted to collect her thoughts and the rest of her items. Something about it bothered her, but she couldn't put her finger on what it was. She stared blankly into her pink bag for a moment as her mind attempted to piece together the clue.

After a moment, she shook her head. She didn't have time to waste. She zipped her bag shut and slung it over her shoulder, stalking into the hall. Emma emerged from her room seconds later.

"Maybe we should check on Cate," she said.

"Good idea," Maggie agreed. They started toward Cate's room. "Also, we need to think of a response to this message."

"Right," Emma agreed. "Perhaps something generic like 'we're working on it' or, 'we'll text when we have the keys.'"

Maggie nodded as they reached Cate's door. She knocked at it. A frazzled-looking Cate pulled open the double doors.

"I think I have everything," she murmured, out-of-breath. Two excited pups trailed behind her.

"Are you sure you want to go? This may be very dangerous," Maggie said.

"Of course," Cate said. "I want to help. And besides, you two are terrible with locks."

Maggie and Emma shared a glance before they chuckled. "Well, thank you for your help, and I'm glad you can keep your sense of humor."

"It helps," Emma assured her.

Cate offered a weak smile as they proceeded downstairs to the library. Charlie had two laptops set up. He pounded away on one while another blazed through images on the left side of the screen. The right showed a picture of Piper, smiling as she held up an iced coffee. The program attempted to match a picture of Piper with any cameras in the vicinity.

"We're ready," Maggie announced as she entered the room. "Anything yet?"

"Nothing yet," Henry answered. "Maggie, be careful. Don't take any unnecessary chances."

He removed a gun from his waistband and handed it over to her. She tucked it into her purse.

"We should answer the text before we go," Maggie said.

"You're right," Ollie answered. "Keep it generic. Tell them they will be the first to know when you have the keys and ask for proof of life."

Maggie nodded and typed into her phone. "Will let you know when we have the keys. I want to talk to Piper and make sure she is okay."

Molly and Mrs. Fraser entered the room. Molly carried a plate of cookies and a pot of coffee. Mrs. Fraser held a picnic basket.

"I packed this full of snacks, sandwiches and drinks," she said.

"Thank you, Mrs. Fraser," Cate said, relieving her of the item. She bent down and ruffled the fur on both dogs' heads. "Now, you boys behave for Mrs. Fraser and Molly. Promise?"

"Dinnae you worry, Lady Cate. The pups will be just fine here. You concentrate on finding those keys and helping that poor girl."

"We'll find her, Charlie," Maggie said, squeezing his shoulder.

He offered a weak smile and tapped Maggie's hand. "I know we will, chicky. No one nabs Charlie Rivers's wife and gets away with it."

Maggie returned his smile and gave him a nod.

Jack approached Cate. "Be careful, Lady Cate. I don't want to have to rescue you, too."

"I will be," she promised.

"Keep me updated. We'll take good care of Riley and Bailey."

"Thanks."

"Good luck, ladies," Ollie said. "I will be here to discuss anything if you come across any conundrums you may need help with."

They said their goodbyes and Maggie, Emma and Cate strolled into the bright sunshine outside. Maggie slid on her sunglasses. "All right, ladies, let's mount up."

"Ugh," Emma groaned, as Cate offered to take the backseat.

"What?" Maggie questioned, as she pulled open the driver's door.

"Will you stop saying things like that?" Emma said. "It sounds ridiculous."

"It doesn't," Maggie argued, sliding in behind the wheel.

"It does," Emma said, climbing into the car.

"You wouldn't say that if Henry said it."

"Henry doesn't sound ridiculous saying it."

"That's sexist."

"It's not."

"Ladies," Cate interrupted, "do we have a destination in mind?"

Emma tapped at the GPS. "We should start at Blackmoore Castle," she said.

"I agree," Maggie answered. "It's the closer of the two keys."

With the route programmed in, Maggie eased off the brake and swung toward Dunhaven.

"Remember to drive on the right side of the road," Emma said.

"Yes, I know," Maggie retorted.

They bounced down the driveway. Maggie furrowed her brow. "Wait, is it the right or left side?"

"The left!" Emma shouted.

"Are you sure? You just said right."

"It's the left," Cate agreed.

"I didn't say right."

"You did so," Maggie answered, as she approached the end of the drive.

"I did not."

"You said remember to drive on the right side of the road."

"I meant the correct side. Which is the left."

"But you said right, so that's why I was confused."

"It's left, left, just drive on the left and be quiet about it."

"All right, already. Just relax, Emma. Stop being a backseat driver."

Maggie swung out onto the road. She glanced in the rearview mirror. "Wishing you hadn't come yet?" she asked Cate.

Cate offered a weak chuckle.

"It only gets better," Emma promised.

CHAPTER 31

After twenty minutes of driving, Maggie pulled into a convenience store.

"I'm sorry, I need coffee."

They retrieved the warm beverages, with Cate opting for tea, added gas to the tank, and continued on their journey. Ten more minutes passed, before Maggie glanced in the rearview mirror.

"I hate to be a pain but," she said, eyeing Cate, "what snacks are in the picnic basket?"

Cate dug into the large wicker basket. "Mrs. Fraser packed a variety of cookies, sandwiches, bottled water, and several slices of pie."

"I'll take a few cookies," Maggie said.

"Okay, we've got lemon, shortbread, oatmeal raisin, oatmeal scotchies, or the old standby, chocolate chip."

"Ohh, umm," Maggie pondered aloud, "oatmeal scotchies. I missed breakfast."

"What's that got to do with anything?" Emma asked, as Cate unwrapped the cookie package.

"Well, it's oatmeal, which is a breakfast food, so it's a suitable replacement."

Cate handed her a cookie. Emma shrugged. "I'll take one, too, then. It's a decent enough logic."

They polished off the package of scotchies in short order. Cate crinkled the wrapper and tossed it into a bag. "We made short work of that dozen."

"We ate a dozen cookies?" Emma asked, as she popped the last bite into her mouth.

"Well, there's three of us, so we only ate like four each," Maggie said. "Plus, we missed breakfast. Besides, we're supposed to be on vacation."

"I'm so sorry this happened on your trip," Cate lamented. "First the weather issue, and now this."

"Keeps it interesting, I guess," Maggie said, as she turned onto another highway.

"How do you take it all in stride? My stomach is in knots. Although that could be the four cookies," Cate said.

"I'm focusing on what we need to do. Find the keys. We can't get distracted."

"Maggie's right. Plus, this isn't our first time in one of these situations. Panicking does us no good."

Cate bit her lower lip and nodded. "So, you've been to Blackmoore Castle before?"

"Yes," Emma answered. "We stopped here on our way to Inverness. It's a really interesting place."

"With quite a history," Maggie added.

"Oh?" Cate asked.

"It has some kind of weird black stuff on part of the stones. It looks like a network of black veins crawling across the castle," Maggie said.

"Which, of course, gives it the reputation of being haunted," Emma explained. "And then the duchess who speaks with the dead only added to that."

"The duchess who speaks with the dead?" Cate repeated.

Emma nodded. "Apparently the same Duke Blackmoore who was a member of the Brotherhood married a woman who claimed she could communicate with spirits. It was his second wife. She was an orphan. He married her and asked her to determine why his first wife killed herself."

"Wow, that's an interesting story."

Emma twisted in her seat and nodded. "It was, yes. Apparently, no one could ever disprove her ability and she often knew things no one but the dead could know."

"I may have to research that. It sounds really intriguing."

Emma returned her gaze forward. She spotted Maggie staring in the rearview mirror. "What?" she questioned.

Maggie's eyes narrowed. "I'm not sure. I thought I spotted a dark car behind us."

Emma spun to search the road. "I don't see anything."

"Must have just been a random traveler."

"Did the tour you took at the castle mention the Brotherhood?" Cate inquired.

"No, we stumbled on that by accident. Maggie insisted on taking a self-led "behind-the-scenes" tour." Emma rolled her eyes.

"But we learned something," Maggie contended. "So, it was worth…"

Her voice cut off.

"Worth what? Getting scolded by the current occupant? *After* you accused her of being a ghost?"

Maggie's gaze remained fixed in her rearview mirror.

"What is it?" Emma inquired, after a moment.

"That car," Maggie said. "I swear it's following us."

Emma craned her neck around and searched behind them. She swung around and faced front.

"I think you're right. I think it's our friend from our last visit."

Maggie glanced at the GPS. "Only thirty minutes left," she said. "Let's hope he doesn't try anything."

"Try anything?" Cate inquired.

"He's nearly run us off the road twice," Emma said. "There are plenty of other people around, maybe it'll deter him."

Cate's eyes went wide, and she glanced behind them before facing front again, a worried expression on her delicate porcelain features.

"Just make sure you've got your seatbelt on," Maggie said.

Cate snugged hers tighter across her lap and swallowed hard.

They drove for a nerve-wracking five minutes. Cars turned off at various areas. When the last car with them slowed and made a turn, they found themselves alone on the highway with only one other car.

"Great," Maggie muttered. "So much for other people being around." The black car behind them closed the gap. "Here he comes."

Cate spun to face the rear. The black sports car with its darkened windows rode almost on top of their bumper. In seconds, he shot into the opposite lane, pulling level with them. Maggie slowed. The black car matched her speed. "Damn it," she grumbled. "Hang on."

She punched the accelerator, smashing her occupants back into their seats. The Lincoln shot forward, passing the sports car. The solution was temporary, as the sports car sped up to keep pace.

Maggie stomped on the brake, sending everyone flying forward. Tires squealed and the brakes smoked. She swerved into the oncoming lane and tromped on the accelerator, flying up behind the other driver.

The car swerved into the appropriate driving lane. Maggie glanced out of her window at the other car. With her eyes narrowed, she said, "Well, come on."

"Don't tempt him," Emma said, pressing her arm against the ceiling to brace herself. "You're not that good of a driver."

"I'm an excellent driver," Maggie answered, as she pushed the car for more speed.

"Ah, excellent driver," Emma said, waving her hand at the windshield, "there's a car coming at us."

"I see it," Maggie said. She continued to barrel toward it as she inched back over into the correct lane.

"He's not going to let you in," Emma said.

Maggie tensed her jaw as she studied the road. The oncoming car sounded its horn. With a shake of her head, she slowed for a second before gunning it again.

"Maggie!" Emma shouted.

Maggie threaded her way between the oncoming car and their pursuer. The blaring horn blew by them as they swung back into their lane.

The black car inched around them. With the way clear, the driver whipped into the other lane.

"I've had enough of this," Maggie growled. She jerked the wheel, sending them careening toward the other car. With the nose of her car leading the sports car, Maggie wiggled the wheel again.

"What are you doing? Trying to wreck?" Emma shouted.

Maggie took an aggressive stance, her tires crossing into the opposite lane. The black car backed off as Maggie straddled both lanes.

"Yeah, that's what I thought," Maggie said.

The sports car dropped back and whipped to their opposite side, inching up again.

"Now what, genius?" Emma said.

Maggie scrunched her nose at the side mirror.

"Whatever you do," Emma said, "don't do the emergency brake thing."

"Emergency brake thing?" Cate exclaimed, her voice breathless with anxiety.

The black car pressed forward, inching up the driver's side.

"There's the road to Blackmoore!" Emma shouted, as she pointed forward at the pavement jutting off on their right.

"I see it," Maggie said as they barreled along.

Maggie pressed the accelerator to the floor and swung the car to the right. She pulled the emergency brake, causing the rear of their car to fishtail. They spun into the turn, before Maggie let go of the brake and raced onto the road.

Emma glanced behind them. Maggie's sudden move caused the black car to swerve to avoid a collision. With limited road available, it had crashed into the ditch running alongside the road. Steam rose from the crinkled hood.

"Ha!" Maggie said with a laugh. "I did it!"

Emma blew out a sigh of relief. "Beginner's luck."

"That's skill," Maggie argued.

Cate breathed a sigh of relief. "Let's just be glad we're okay."

Maggie glanced in the rearview mirror. "And it looks like our friend may be out of commission for a bit."

"Let's hope he stays that way," Emma quipped.

Maggie pointed upward. "There's the castle."

Cate leaned forward to glance at the castle on the moor. "Wow, that's an impressive castle."

"It's almost as big as yours, I think," Maggie answered.

They approached the parking area and Maggie swung the large SUV into the lot, easing it into a space.

They climbed from the car and stretched their legs. The three women stared up at the castle above them.

"Could be anywhere in that massive thing," Emma said.

Maggie narrowed her eyes and nodded. "I'm going to need a sandwich first. Maybe a cookie."

They returned to the car for a quick bite to eat while Maggie checked her messages. A text waited from Henry. Cate had received one from Jack and Emma had a message waiting from Leo. As they returned messages, Maggie's phone chimed. "It's a message from the kidnappers!"

Everyone leaned over Maggie's shoulder. "Send us a picture of the keys, and we'll send you proof of life."

Maggie grimaced at the phone. She pounded the virtual keyboard with her thumbs as she read her message aloud. "No dice, buddy. Proof of life now. Not doing your work for you without it."

"Maggie!" Emma shouted. "Do you think you should have sent that?"

"Why not? We have no idea if she's alive or not. And if she's not, I'm certainly not going to risk our lives for their gain!"

Cate sank back in her seat. "Do you really think she's..."

"No," Maggie answered before Cate finished. "But I want them to know they need to keep her alive."

Maggie's phone chimed again. She pulled up the message. A picture of Piper in her robe and pajamas filled the screen. She frowned at the camera.

Maggie studied the image. She shook her head and hit the call button. The line trilled as she placed it on speakerphone. It went to voicemail. Maggie hung up and tried again. The line rang before a voicemail robot answered.

"You're going to have to do better than that. I want real proof she's alive at this very moment." Maggie ended the call and bit a chunk off of her cookie.

Moments later her phone rang. "It's them," she announced as she answered it, toggling on the speakerphone.

"This had better be proof," Maggie said, in her toughest voice.

"Just find the keys, boss lady," Piper's voice said.

"Piper!" Maggie shouted. "Are you okay? Have they hurt you?"

A robotic voice sounded. "You have your proof. Now do what was asked." The line went dead.

Maggie sucked in a deep breath. "Okay," she said as she blew it out. "She's alive." She punched around on her phone and the line trilled again.

"You at Blackmoore yet, princess?" Henry asked after two rings.

"Piper's still alive. We just talked to her."

"You what? You talked to Piper?"

"Yes. I demanded proof of life. They sent a picture then called. I'm sending the picture to your phone now."

"I'll run it for any clues," Charlie said in the background.

"Anything on your end?" Maggie asked.

"Nothing yet," Henry said.

"Hey, that black car was back following us," Maggie said.

"What?" Henry exclaimed.

"I ran it off the road, so it should be out of commission for a while. But in case Charlie's searching for it, it's out here near Blackmoore."

"I'll let him know. Maggie, be careful."

"Will do. I'll let you know as soon as we find anything." They ended the call.

"All right, ladies," Maggie said, "we've got a job to do."

They climbed from the car for a second time and started their hike up to the castle.

"Wow, I bet these people were in shape if they walked this hill all the time," Cate gasped.

"It's a killer, right?" Emma said. She puffed out a breath as they climbed the steep hill.

They reached the top, all of them winded. Maggie pulled her phone from her purse and glanced at it while they caught their breath.

"Anything?" Emma asked.

"No, it's just…"

"What?" Emma inquired.

Maggie shook her head. "There's something about this first message. Something bothers me about it."

Maggie squashed her lips together and stared at her screen. Emma glanced over Maggie's shoulder at it.

"Can you zero in on what bothers you?" Cate questioned. "Which part of the message specifically?"

"The first part. Rainbow Brite," she repeated. Maggie's brow furrowed. "Why call her that?"

"I think that's kind of obvious, Maggie," Emma said. "Her hair is a rainbow."

"But that term specifically. When we were kidnapped and taken to Uncle Ollie's by James Michael Dean, he called her Rainbow Brite."

Emma's eyebrows shot skyward. "What are the chances someone else calls her that?"

"Exactly."

"But isn't James Michael Dean in jail?"

"Is he?" Maggie questioned. "Is Bryson? They had some powerful connections. I'm going to send this to Henry."

Maggie whipped off a text informing Henry of the theory and asking him to check into the whereabouts of James Michael Dean and one Mr. Brent Bryson.

With the text sent, Maggie heaved a sigh. "Okay, they're on it. Now, let's do our part."

CHAPTER 32

They strode in through the entrance of Blackmoore Castle. A woman stood behind a table selling tour tickets. Maggie recognized her as Melanie, their tour guide from their last visit.

She approached her with a broad smile. "Hi, remember us?"

Melanie narrowed her eyes at Maggie and Emma. "Yes, I do."

Oblivious, Maggie offered another smile. "I figured you might. Anyway, we need to speak with Lenora. Is she around?"

"Do you have an appointment?"

"No, but it's very important we speak with her. Could you give her a buzz and let her know Maggie Edwards is here?"

"No, I won't," Melanie answered.

Maggie's features formed a confused pout. Melanie continued, "The last time you were here, you two sneaked away from the tour group and harassed Ms. Fletcher. And I got in a heap of trouble for it."

"Oh, well we're really sorry about that, but it's really important that we see her this time so—"

"So, nothing," Melanie snapped. "Now turn around and get out of here before I call security."

"But—"

"No buts. I'm not getting in trouble again over the likes of you two."

Indignant, Maggie straightened her posture, raised her chin and her eyebrows. "Fine. I'd like to go on the tour." She dug in her purse and held out her credit card.

"No," Melanie said, crossing her arms.

"What do you mean no? I'm a paying customer."

"And I'm refusing your business. I don't want to have to keep track of you two and your new friend on the tour."

Maggie shoved her credit card back into her purse. "This is unbelievable. This is a matter of life and death!"

Melanie rolled her eyes. "I'm sure it is."

Maggie stamped her foot on the floor and issued a muffled shriek. Cate glanced at her before letting her gaze rest on Melanie. She plastered on a smile and said, "Hi. I think there's been some sort of misunderstanding. I'm Cate Kensie, Countess of Dunhavenshire. It is imperative that we speak with Ms. Fletcher. Could you please announce me?"

Maggie offered a coy smile at Cate's introduction and crossed her arms, fixing her stare on Melanie.

Melanie's eyes widened and her eyebrows shot up. "Countess of Dunhavenshire?"

"Yes," Cate said with a nod.

"Right. And I'm the Queen of England. Do you really believe I'd fall for that?"

"But…" Cate began.

The girl waved her hand at them. "Right. You're an American countess. Sure. I suppose you've got a bridge to sell me, too. Get out of here, the lot of you!"

Maggie huffed, but retreated with Emma and Cate.

"Unbelievable!" Maggie shrieked as they stepped into the sun outside.

"Nice going, Maggie," Emma snarked. "I told you roaming around the castle was a bad idea."

"How was I supposed to know we'd have to come back here to save Piper's life?"

"I can't believe she didn't believe I was a countess," Cate lamented.

"We'll just wait until she leads the next tour then sneak in," Maggie said. She checked her phone. "It leaves in 5 minutes."

They milled around outside until they saw the tour group forming inside. The group shuffled off after a few moments. "Okay, let's go," Maggie said.

Maggie, Emma and Cate reentered the castle. Maggie's jaw dropped open before she set her mouth in a firm line.

"Going somewhere, Ms. Edwards?" Melanie inquired.

"Restroom?" Maggie suggested.

Melanie twirled her finger in a circle and pointed outside, indicating Maggie and friends should turn around and leave.

"But I need to use the ladies' room!" Maggie whined.

"Find a bush."

Maggie offered an unimpressed stare before she flicked her hair and stormed out of the castle.

"Now what?" Emma inquired.

Maggie glanced around the area. "We'll have to find another way in. There's got to be a back door, right?"

With limited other options, they began a trek around the castle. They found several doors, all of which were locked.

Maggie sighed. "Are you kidding me? Not one of these is open?"

"Probably to keep people like you out," Emma said.

They finished their loop around the castle. Maggie

stopped before they rounded the corner to the front. She pressed her palm against her forehead.

Maggie put her hands on her hips. "We need a plan to get in."

Emma rolled her eyes. "No kidding."

"Pose as a cleaning crew?"

"In what outfits?" Emma said.

"Wait until after hours and break in?"

"So we're arrested? No thanks."

Maggie glanced skyward and let out a groan. Her hands balled into fists, and she stamped her feet on the ground.

"A famous Maggie Edwards meltdown isn't going to help," Emma said.

Maggie lowered her chin toward her chest. She caught sight of something on the horizon. Her head tilted as she focused on it. "What's that?"

Emma twisted and shielded her eyes. "Looks like someone riding a horse."

"Looks like Lenora riding a horse."

"What? How can you tell?"

"Who else would be riding a horse? Come on, let's go." Maggie trudged toward the rider. She spun to face them. "Looks like my tantrum did help." She twisted back and hurried away.

Cate and Emma followed her. They reached the stables.

"She's gone," Emma puffed, resting her hands on her thighs.

Maggie stared at the diminishing form of the horseback rider. She pressed her lips together and glanced inside the stables. "Not if I can help it."

"Maggie, what are you doing?"

Maggie tossed a saddle blanket over a dark bay-colored mare. "I'm going after her."

"We could wait for her to come back."

She pulled a saddle from the wall and tossed it over the horse's back, quickly fastening it. "That could be hours! And we may be arrested and tossed out by then. I'm going."

She tossed the reins over the horse's head and slipped her muzzle into the bridle.

"I'll be back!" she called, as she started the horse trotting and ran alongside, swinging herself into the saddle.

"Maggie!" Emma shouted behind her.

Maggie gripped the reins, squeezing the horse between her knees. She pressed herself against the horse, encouraging her to pick up speed. "Come on, girl, we've got a bit of catching up to do."

Maggie rocketed up the hill where she'd last seen the rider disappear over the hillside on horseback. She crested the hill and scanned the area.

She spotted the other rider in the distance. Maggie urged the horse forward toward her. She pushed the horse to a gallop. Hooves thundered against the ground as she pursued the other rider.

"Hey!" Maggie shouted as she approached. "Hey!"

The other rider spun her horse around, searching for the source of the shout. Even at a distance, Maggie recognized the piercing blue eyes of Lenora Fletcher beneath the riding helmet.

Maggie waved her arm as she continued to race toward her. The other horse danced in a circle. Maggie began to slow as she approached. Her brow furrowed as she noticed the other horse fight for control from its rider.

The snow-white horse's eyes bulged, and it offered a squeal in protest. The horse reared and let out a trumpeting roar. Lenora lost her grip on the reins, toppling backward as the horse kicked its front legs. Her flying feet got caught in the leather strap. The horse righted itself and took off, dragging Lenora behind it.

"Uh-oh," Maggie murmured, as she gave her horse the signal to follow. Maggie leaned close to the horse's neck, steadying herself in the saddle as the horse reached a full gallop. She steered it toward the side opposite the caught rider, now being dragged along by the frightened horse.

Maggie urged more speed from her horse as she tried to catch the other. Its frantic fugue made it difficult to predict its path, but eventually, Maggie's larger horse managed to catch up. Maggie rode alongside the white horse. With a hold of the bay's reins, she leapt from the saddle and onto the white horse. She flung her arm around the white mare's neck and took a tight hold of her reins.

"Whoa, girl, whoa," she said into its ear.

After a few moments of confused galloping, both horses slowed to a trot. Her former ride, the bay, offered a snort and a nicker as she breathed hard from the run. Maggie felt the heaving breaths of the white mare beneath her as she spun in the saddle.

"Are you alright?" she asked the fallen rider.

Lenora breathed hard and craned her neck to stare upward. She shielded her eyes from the bright sun. A look of shock crossed her face. "You!" she shouted, as she fought to free her twisted leg from the saddle mount.

"A thank you wouldn't be unwarranted," Maggie said, as she dismounted and helped free Lenora's ankle. She offered her hand. "Can you stand?"

Reluctantly, Lenora accepted and allowed Maggie to pull her to her feet. She hobbled around for a few moments. "I think it's fine, just twisted."

"What happened?" Maggie asked. "What spooked her?"

Lenora wiggled her eyebrows as she dusted her clothes. "I suppose your frantic shrieking did it. What are you doing here? And why are you gallivanting around on one of my horses?"

"No," Maggie said, with a shake of her head, "it wasn't me. She was frightened by something well after she spotted me."

"I don't know," Lenora said with a huff. "Does it matter? Why are you here?"

"We need your help," Maggie said.

"You must be joking."

Maggie shook her head. "I'm not. It's a matter of life and death."

"Are all Americans as dramatic as you?"

"I'm not being dramatic. This is serious. I can explain."

Lenora stared at her and motioned for her to proceed. "When I came to Scotland, it was supposed to be for a vacation. I was going to stay with a friend for two weeks. But then there was all the rain, and the roads were washed out and our flight was canceled—"

"Is there a point?" Lenora inquired, crossing her arms.

"Yes, sorry," Maggie said. "We ended up spending a weekend at Clydescolm Castle. And we found something there. A dragon symbol. I have a picture on my phone.

"Anyway, we found the symbol on two portraits in the castle. My uncle is an archeologist, and we started to search for some information on what it could mean. When we came here a few days ago, I saw the same symbol on a portrait here.

"Then we went to the Gordon Highlanders Museum, and we saw the symbol again, along with a key. The write-up at the museum said there were four keys made and the four keyholders formed something called the Brotherhood of the Dragon. And they hid and protected a cursed Viking treasure."

"So, you're a treasure hunter?"

"Yes. No. Not really. Just listen, I'm not finished."

Lenora sighed, but gave Maggie her attention.

"The key from the museum was stolen."

"Stolen? From a museum?"

"Yes, by some nasty people. But we stole it back. And then we went searching for the next key."

"And now I suppose you want to tear my castle apart to search for another and find the treasure?"

"No," Maggie said, with a shake of her head. "I mean, yes. We want to search the castle for your family's key. But not because we're treasure hunters."

"Then for what reason?"

Maggie inhaled deeply and pursed her lips before continuing. "While we were searching for the second key, someone kidnapped my friend. They're holding her hostage and will only trade her for all four keys. We need to find that key."

"All four? Didn't you say one was stolen?"

"Yes, but we stole it back. I told you that."

Lenora narrowed her eyes at Maggie. "Is this a joke?"

"No," Maggie insisted. "It very much isn't. Look, my friends, Emma and Cate, are waiting back at the stables. They can tell you the same thing. And I can show you my phone with the ransom demand."

"And why would I trust you or your friends?"

"For Piper. Please. I know we got off on the wrong foot, but her life is at stake. And I would do anything to save her." Maggie paused, her eyes pleading with the woman. "And if you say no, I'll just break into your castle and steal it from you. That's how important it is."

Lenora fluttered her eyelashes at the statement. She glanced to her side, before she blew out a breath and grabbed the reins of the white mare, still clutched in Maggie's hand. "I suppose, at least, you're honest." She began to lead the horse back toward the stables.

"So, you'll help us?" Maggie asked, following her and leading the bay.

"Well, I suppose you haven't left me much choice, have you, Ms. Edwards?"

"Not really, but still, it would be nice if we had your permission and didn't have to resort to using questionably legal methods."

"Theft is not questionable."

"Sometimes it is, depending on the circumstances. And if we're working together, you should call me Maggie."

Lenora didn't respond.

"How's your ankle?" Maggie asked after a moment.

"I'll live," Lenora said.

The stables came into view, and they ambled down the hill toward them. Emma and Cate milled around near the entrance. Emma spotted their approach. She flung her arms in the air. "Maggie!" she called.

"Good news!" Maggie shouted back. "She's going to help."

CHAPTER 33

*E*mma and Cate breathed a sigh of relief at the words. Maggie and Lenora closed the distance between them and led the horses into the stables.

A groom appeared, stunned at the presence of the other three women. "Never mind that, Roddy," Lenora said. "Just see that both horses are brushed and fed. They've both had a hard ride, and Snow was spooked by something. She's still quite a bit jumpy."

The man nodded as he led the horses into their stalls and began to remove their saddles. Maggie waited with Emma and Cate for Lenora.

As she approached, Maggie introduced the other women. "This is Emma, a colleague of mine and also an archeologist. And this is Lady Cate Kensie, a friend of ours."

Lenora furrowed her brow at Cate. "Lady Cate Kensie? The American countess from Dunhaven?"

"Yes," Cate said with a smile. "I tried to explain to your employee, but she didn't believe me."

"She must not read social announcements. Nevertheless, I

suppose we should proceed. Come along – we can discuss this at length in my office."

Lenora led them back to the castle.

"Why do you sound British and not Scottish?" Maggie asked as they walked.

"I went to a British boarding school at a young age. So did my parents. The accent stuck for all of us. I... why am I telling you this?"

Maggie shrugged. "I found it interesting," she answered, as they rounded to the front of the castle and strolled through the front door.

"Ms. Fletcher!" Melanie said, leaping from her stool behind the table. She stared wide-eyed at the other women and swallowed hard.

Lenora held up her hand. "It's all right, Melanie. They are my guests."

Melanie's eyes grew even wider at the statement, but she nodded and plastered on a shocked smile as Lenora led them up the main staircase. Maggie raised her eyebrows as she stepped on the first stair. She stuck her tongue out at the girl before darting up behind the rest of the group.

"Did you just stick your tongue out at her?" Emma asked.

"I did," Maggie admitted. "She was rude before."

"Classy, Maggie, really classy."

Lenora shook her head and heaved a sigh at the conversation, but said nothing. They wound through the halls. Cate studied the castle as they went.

"Your castle is really lovely," Cate said.

"Thank you. Though I imagine Dunhaven is quite nice, too," Lenora answered.

"It is," Cate agreed.

"I received an invitation to an event you hosted there, however, I was unable to attend."

"Maybe next time," Cate said. "I'd love for you to see it."

Lenora offered a fleeting smile but no verbal response. She led them into an office room and skirted around a large wooden desk, after dragging another chair toward it. Papers covered its top.

"Now," Lenora said, as she plopped into the chair and motioned for them to sit in the seats across from her, "what is this tale you babbled on about?"

Emma explained as Maggie pulled up pictures on her phone. "We're searching for a key like this one." She motioned to Maggie's phone. "There were four of them made. They supposedly open a vault containing Viking treasure. We have two in our possession. One from Sir Frederick MacKenna and one from Cate's ancestor, Randolph MacKenzie. We are searching for the other two. One of those keys belonged to your ancestor, Robert Fletcher, the seventh Duke of Blackmoore."

Maggie swiped at her phone and brought up the picture of the dragon on Robert's portrait. "Here, see," she said as she zoomed in. "We found this on a portrait of your ancestor."

"And the write-up at the museum confirmed he was a member of the Brotherhood of the Dragon," Emma said.

Lenora studied the images then shook her head. "I'm afraid I've never heard of this. And I have never seen a key like that anywhere here."

"Well," Maggie said, pausing for a moment, "could you ask?"

Lenora furrowed her brow. "Ask whom?"

Maggie tilted her head and narrowed her eyes at Lenora. "Robert."

"My great-great-great-grandfather? Oh yes, just allow me to phone him and ask."

"That's not what I meant."

"Then what did you mean, Ms. Edwards?"

"Maggie," Maggie reminded her. "And I meant just ask him. Don't you speak with the dead?"

"No," Lenora said in an aggravated tone.

Maggie scrunched up her face. "Are you sure? Have you tried?"

"Ms. Edwards, please."

"All right, all right, sorry. Well, we're going to have to do this the old-fashioned way."

"Are there any hiding places where this might be? You know the castle best, Ms. Fletcher," Emma said.

"There are plenty, though, as I said, I've never seen that key. So, if it is, indeed, here, it is not in any of the spots with which I am familiar."

"We're going to have to roll up our sleeves and do some searching," Maggie said.

"Perhaps it's like Randolph's and hidden behind a painting," Cate suggested.

Maggie snapped her fingers and pointed at her. "Yes. It's a good theory. We'll start there. Maybe it's behind this painting!" Maggie swiped to the portrait of Robert Fletcher in the upstairs sitting room. "Come on!" She leapt from her chair and darted from the room.

"Maggie, wait up!" Emma called.

"Is she always like that?" Lenora questioned, as they hurried down the hall after her.

"She's usually worse. This is mild for Maggie."

Maggie wound through the halls in search of the upstairs sitting room. As she rounded a corner, she narrowed her eyes and stared down the hall, before shaking her head and continuing past it to another hall.

She turned the next corner and raced to a set of double doors. She pushed through and grinned as she recognized the upstairs sitting room containing the portraits of Robert and Lenora Fletcher.

She approached the painting and studied it. Maggie toggled on her flashlight and glanced behind it.

The others caught up to her and filtered into the room. "Wow!" Cate exclaimed as she glanced up at the wall. "You really do look like her!"

"Yes, outside of a pesky mole on my cheek which I detest, we are quite close in appearance." Lenora rubbed at a large freckle on her cheek.

"Well, she's very pretty," Emma said, "so you're very lucky."

Lenora offered a polite smile as Maggie stared at the painting.

"Anything?" Emma inquired.

"I didn't see anything, but the painting at Dunhaven had to be tilted." Maggie tugged on the massive painting. It shimmied but did not trigger any panels or passages.

"Can we take it down?" Maggie asked.

"It's huge!" Emma countered.

"We have to check it!"

"I doubt the key's hidden in there. Even with that ornate frame. Let's move on to other options first."

"Okay, just hold this out a bit while I look behind it again," Maggie said.

"Fine," Emma agreed. She pulled the painting's bottom away from the wall while Maggie searched behind it with her flashlight.

"Nothing. Let's try the other portrait of him in the portrait gallery."

"Okay," Emma agreed. The quartet set off for the portrait gallery. With the tour finishing up inside, they had to wait before they could fully explore.

"Are there any other portraits of Robert Fletcher?" Maggie asked as they stood in the hallway outside.

"There is one other," Lenora said. "Downstairs."

Maggie nodded. "If this one doesn't pan out, we'll try there next."

"Then what?" Emma inquired.

"Are there any paintings by him?" Cate questioned. "The painting at Dunhaven was a landscape depicting the loch on the property and was signed with Randolph's name. It also had a faint replica of the dragon symbol."

Lenora chewed her lower lip as she mulled over the information. "I honestly cannot recall that symbol being on any paintings, though, again, I may have missed it. I did not realize it had any significance."

"Do you have any other paintings?" Maggie asked.

"Loads of them, yes. All over the castle."

"Okay, so after we check the paintings of Robert Fletcher, we'll do a tour and check the others for the dragon symbol."

The remaining tour participants filtered from the room and the women entered. Maggie went straight to the family portrait of Robert and Lenora Fletcher with their three children.

She studied it, searching for the dragon symbol.

"No dragon," Emma noted. Maggie nodded her head in agreement as she tilted the frame to glance behind it.

"Do you know which one of their children you're descended from?" Cate inquired.

Lenora pointed to the smallest child. "Robert," she said. "Their second son."

"How interesting," Cate said. "They named their second son after his father, instead of their first."

"The first was called Samuel, after Robert's father. Though I have only recently come to learn he was adopted by the couple."

"Really?" Cate asked.

"Yes, apparently his mother was a friend of the original

Lenora and died birthing him. My great-great-great-grandmother then took him into their home."

"Nothing here," Maggie announced.

"No," Emma agreed, "but we may as well check the rest of these paintings for the dragon symbol while we're here."

They made a search of the room, finding nothing. Lenora led them to the next painting. It, too, held no secrets. They finished their afternoon hours searching through the remaining artwork in the castle. None of them were marked with the dragon symbol.

"Great," Maggie said with a huff, flinging her arms in the air. "Nothing."

"No sign of the dragon symbol," Emma agreed. "At least not on any paintings."

"I tried to make a cursory search of the rooms for any sign of it," Cate said. "I didn't see anything."

"Neither did I," Emma admitted, "though my search was cursory, too."

Maggie slumped onto a chair in Lenora's office. "I'm starving."

"Maybe we should take a break and eat," Emma suggested.

"Sounds great," Maggie said, a frown on her face and her arms crossed tightly over her chest.

"Before you get too hangry."

"I'm not hangry," Maggie lamented, "I'm frustrated."

Emma asked Lenora, "Do you know of any pizza places that deliver?"

"Pizza?" Lenora inquired.

"Yeah, pizza," Maggie said, annoyance lacing her voice. "Quick, easy. I'm not about to cook."

"Here," Cate said, flashing her phone at them. "Here is a list of local pizzerias. We can try this one. It's the closest."

"Perfect," Emma said.

THE LOST TREASURE OF DRAKON

Cate stepped into the hallway to place the call. Maggie scrubbed her face with her hands and groaned.

"I guess we should be searching for a local hotel, too," Emma said. "Looks like this will be an overnight trip. Sorry." She flashed Lenora an apologetic expression.

Lenora stared at the doorway where Cate had disappeared moments earlier. Her eyes snapped to Emma when she realized Emma was staring at her.

"What? Oh, no trouble." She paused a moment, her eyes flitting back to the doorway. "And you can stay here for the night."

"Oh, we don't want to put you out," Emma began.

"You're not. There are over thirty bedrooms in this castle. I can spare three."

"Thank you," Maggie and Emma answered.

"Okay, ladies, pizza order is placed. They were a bit confused when I gave them the location."

Lenora flattened her lips into a thin line. "I don't order pizza very often. Will you ladies excuse me for a moment?"

"Sure," Maggie said.

Lenora darted from the room. Maggie sighed and sank her chin into her palm.

"That was nice of her to let us stay," Emma said.

"Yeah," Maggie murmured.

"We'll find it, Maggie. And we'll find Piper."

Maggie drew in a deep breath and nodded. "I know." Her eyes glistened as she fought back the tears stinging them. After a second, she glanced upward and batted her eyelashes. "I'm just hangry like you said."

Emma gave a weak chuckle. "Pizza will do you good."

"And maybe even Lenora, who apparently has never eaten pizza. How do you not order pizza?"

"Maybe she's a health nut."

Maggie shrugged.

"I ordered a mushroom one," Cate said. "I hope it passes muster."

"I'm going to check in with Henry." Maggie tapped her phone and the line trilled.

"Hey, princess, tell me you have that key," his voice answered.

"No," Maggie said, with a deflated sigh. "Not yet, but we haven't given up. We're just ordering some dinner, but we'll be staying at Blackmoore Castle for the night."

"Any leads?"

"Not a one. Tell me you found something on your end."

"We did."

Maggie sat straighter, her interest piqued. "You're not going to like it," Henry said.

CHAPTER 34

Maggie's shoulders slumped again at Henry's statement. "What is it?"

"Bryson and associates are all out of prison."

"Already?" Maggie asked.

"How can that be?" Emma added.

"He's got powerful connections," Henry said. "The good news is we're fairly certain they're involved, which will make tracking this easier. His last known whereabouts were Edinburgh. We're working on tracking him and anyone else involved in the Library of Alexandria search."

"Let me know what you find," Maggie said.

"Will do. Be safe, Maggie," Henry added.

"We will be."

"You're staying at the castle?" Henry asked.

"Yes. Lenora said we could stay here."

"Good. I'd prefer you not wandering around to a hotel."

"Thanks, Dad," Maggie said.

"Very funny, princess, very funny. With the number of castles you've stayed at, this trip should rate highly in your book."

"It will rate higher when we have Piper back, safe and sound."

"We'll get her."

"I know we will," Maggie said.

"Call if you find anything."

"You do the same."

They ended the call and Maggie suggested they run down to the car to get their overnight bags. Emma offered to help, and they hurried down the hill as the sun lowered in the sky. A chill had entered the evening air. Maggie zipped her hoodie up as she and Emma walked the steep grade to the parking lot.

With visiting hours over for the main castle, theirs was one of a handful of cars in the lot. The remaining few vehicles belonged to those guests who still meandered through the lower gardens, which remained open until dusk.

"It's pretty here," Maggie said.

"Yeah," Emma agreed as she stared out over the gardens, bathed in the deep red light of the setting sun.

Maggie swallowed hard. "If only we could enjoy it."

"We'll find her, Maggie," Emma said.

"Bryson isn't a nice guy. We know firsthand. And now he's got an axe to grind. I just don't want him to grind it against Piper."

Maggie opened the trunk and slung her bag over her shoulder. Emma placed a consoling hand on Maggie's back. Maggie's eyebrows crinkled. She squeezed her eyes shut as a tear rolled down her cheek.

"Oh, Maggie," Emma murmured, as she pulled her into a hug. Maggie clung to her as she sniffled. She pulled back a moment later.

"I'm okay," she said, as she wiped at her eyes. "I'm fine. I'm just hungry and tired."

Emma offered a lopsided smile. "Yeah, I'm sure that's all.

Cause you're the strongest woman I know, Maggie. So, I know you're going to come out on top."

Maggie hauled Cate's bag onto her shoulder as Emma lifted hers. "You're damn right I will." She slammed the trunk shut and they hiked back to the castle.

"Oh, perfect timing," Lenora called across the foyer as they entered. "I have rooms being prepared for you. You may leave your bags there for now. I had an idea about a place to search for information." She swallowed hard, avoiding eye contact with them. "The Robert Fletcher who first owned the key used a room on this floor as his office. There are still several items inside it. Perhaps we'll find a clue there."

Maggie dumped both bags on the floor near the staircase. "Great!"

Emma offloaded her bag next to the other two, as a knock sounded from the large lion's head brass door knocker.

"I'll get it!" Maggie swung the door open to find a winded and wide-eyed pizza delivery man on the opposite side.

"Pizza?" he squeaked, his features as questioning as his voice.

"Yep, perfect timing. Mmm, smells delicious. Thanks!" She accepted the two steaming boxes and Emma grabbed the two-liter of soda and a bag of plates, cups and napkins.

She swung the door shut with her foot as the boy called in, "Enjoy!"

"This way," Lenora said.

She led them through an archway branching off the rear of the foyer and down another hallway. Light streamed from an open doorway. They entered and found Cate standing over a box of papers.

"Thanks for grabbing my stuff," she said. "Mmm, that smells delicious."

"Do all Americans love pizza?" Lenora asked, as Maggie cleared a space on the desk for the food.

"Probably most," Maggie answered. "Pepperoni or mushroom?"

Lenora wrinkled her forehead and stared at the circular disks.

"Pepperoni," Cate answered.

Maggie pulled two pieces of the pepperoni pie onto a plate and offered it to Cate. Emma poured a cup of cold root beer.

"Emma?" Maggie asked.

"Mushroom, thanks."

Maggie nodded and plated the food, as Emma poured three more cups of root beer. She passed one over to Lenora.

Maggie glanced at Lenora. "Mushroom or pepperoni? If you don't pick, I'll pick for you."

"I will try one of each."

"A girl after my own heart. One of each coming up," Maggie said as she placed a slice of each pie on two plates, handing one off to Lenora before settling onto the floor next to Emma. "Mmmmm. Oh, this tastes so good!"

"It does," Emma agreed. "I was starving."

"I agree," Cate said.

"Enjoying it?" Maggie asked Lenora.

"Yes, it's very greasy, but rather good."

"You've really never had pizza before?" Emma asked.

"No," Lenora answered.

"You never had a pizza party with your friends?" Maggie asked.

"I don't have many friends," she admitted.

Maggie stared at her for a moment before offering her a smile. "Well, you do now."

She offered them a slight smile. "And now I've had a pizza party."

Maggie set her plate down next to her and wiped her

hands on her napkin. "I guess we should dig into this and see if we find anything."

Emma glanced at the stacks of boxes. "This could take all night."

Maggie pulled a box toward her and began to sort through it. "Do we know if these are all related to Robert's time or not?"

"No," Lenora said, as she grabbed another slice of the pepperoni.

"Mmm, me too, please," Maggie said.

"This room has become a catch-all of sorts. I'm sorry."

"So, we have our work cut out for us," Maggie said, shuffling through the papers.

Cate helped herself to another slice of pepperoni pizza before she pulled a box next to her and dove into it.

The women worked on their respective boxes as they finished their meal. Maggie reached the end of her box first. "Done! But I came up with nothing." She sighed. "I think I'll clean up here before I try another. Anyone want another slice? Going once, going twice?"

With head shakes all around the room, Maggie closed up the boxes and twisted the cap back on the soda bottle. "Okay, I suppose it's on to another box."

"Me too," Cate announced, as she turned her box upside and shook it. "I'm empty."

After returning the sorted materials to the box, she selected another and lifted the first item from the top when a loud crash sounded. Everyone jumped, startled by the noise. A box placed precariously on top of a stack slid to the floor, spilling its contents across the red area rug and hardwood peeking from beneath it.

The various papers and files formed an avalanche, ending near Cate. She winced and said, "Okay, I guess I'll work on this box next."

The comment elicited a chuckle from the others as Cate abandoned the previous box in favor of cleaning up the floor. She scooped up several papers and sorted through them, creating a neat stack next to her.

They worked for ten more minutes, before Cate paused in her search. She stared at a photograph, squinting at the black and white picture. Her brow furrowed and she bit her lower lip.

Maggie glanced up from her sorting, noticing the contemplative expression on Cate's face. "Did you find something, Cate?" she asked.

Cate shook her head. "No, but..."

"What is it?" Maggie asked, sidling up to her and glancing at the picture. The black and white photo showed a woman in a wedding dress. A man had his arm around her. Both grinned at the camera.

"Lenora," Cate said, "do you know who this man is?"

She spun the picture toward her. Lenora studied it. "Yes, that's my grandfather."

Cate turned the picture back toward her and Maggie. "With cousin Sophia," Maggie read aloud.

The crease between Cate's eyebrows deepened. "What is it, Cate?" Maggie asked again.

"This woman is my grandmother," she said.

Emma glanced up from her work. "Wait," she said, as she parsed through the information.

"If that's Lenora's grandfather," Maggie worked out aloud, "and this is his cousin, who is your grandmother then..."

"We're related," Cate said, flicking her gaze to Lenora.

Emma nodded. "Yes," she said, lifting her eyebrows and smiling. "You're third cousins to be exact. Assuming the caption on the photo refers to first cousins."

"Yes," Cate said.

"Oh my gosh!" Maggie gushed. "You're cousins! You're

family! We were meant to be here, see! This is the silver lining! You found your family!"

She beamed at the two women.

Cate offered a smile. "Well, I wish Piper didn't have to disappear in order to find this, but I'm thrilled to find more family. After my parents died, I thought I'd never have any."

The edges of Lenora's lips curled up into a slight smile. "Same," she said.

Cate reached out and grasped her hand.

"So, can we confirm they were first cousins?" Maggie asked.

"I'll certainly look into it after we find Piper. Unless you know offhand," Cate said.

Lenora crinkled her brow. "Just a minute," she said. She pulled herself to standing and hurried from the room, returning moments later with a large Bible. She flipped open the cover and traced her finger up the page.

The other women gathered around her, peering over her shoulder.

"Here's Daniel," she said, as she found him listed on the page. "He's my grandfather." She traced up the tree to Daniel's father. "His father was Robert Fletcher the third. Robert had a sister, Elizabeth. Elizabeth Fletcher married William Blackburn, producing one daughter, Sophia."

"So, they were first cousins!" Emma exclaimed.

"Yes," Cate said, "making your assessment correct! We are third cousins. Sophia Blackburn married Charles MacKenzie, later Charles Kensie, my grandfather."

"Wow!" Maggie said, placing her hands on her hips. "What a coincidence."

"What a small world!" Cate said.

"And you're both in Scotland. Not that far from each other!"

"And we never knew," Cate answered.

"Well, you do now!"

"And you both own castles. Luck must run in your family," Emma said.

Cate chuckled at the comment. "Let's hope our luck holds out to find a clue for this key."

"Yeah," Maggie said, staring at the remaining boxes. She blew out a long breath. "It's really too bad you can't talk to the dead, Lenora. You could have just asked your great-grandfather."

"Great-great-great-grandfather," Lenora corrected.

"Whatever," Maggie said. "I'm not good with ancestry."

"And it doesn't work that way."

Maggie glanced sharply at Lenora.

She lifted a shoulder. "At least that's my understanding of it."

"Right," Maggie said, narrowing her eyes at the girl. "Well, I guess back to it."

They settled in at their respective boxes and continued. Over the next several hours, they found nothing. Any excitement was limited to the occasional paper cut or tumbling of a stack of papers. They worked into the wee hours of the morning. With one stack of boxes to go, Maggie stretched.

"My eyes are glazing over," Maggie said.

"Mine too," Emma groaned, rubbing at them.

"Maybe we should take a break. Get some sleep," Maggie suggested.

"I agree," Emma said.

"As much as I hate to admit defeat, perhaps a few hours of sleep will bring a fresh perspective. I'm afraid I'll miss something crucial if I continue," Cate said.

"I had bedrooms made up," Lenora said.

"Thanks," Maggie said, as she climbed to her feet and stretched again.

They followed Lenora upstairs after retrieving their bags.

The large bedrooms sat in a row. Maggie slogged into hers and tossed her bag on the bed, before collapsing next to it. She checked her phone for the umpteenth time. No new messages awaited her.

Maggie reached out and ran her fingers along her duffel bag, intending to change. "I'll just close my eyes for a minute," she murmured.

CHAPTER 35

Maggie's head snapped up and she glanced around the dark room. She blinked her eyes several times, not recognizing her surroundings. After a moment, she groaned, letting her head collapse back to the bed below her. She recalled being in Blackmoore Castle. After a night of fruitless searching for clues to the third key, she'd fallen asleep in her clothes.

With a groan, Maggie rolled onto her back and rubbed her face. The reality of the situation set in, and she rose from the bed, intent on making progress. She checked her phone, finding nothing new, before she wandered into the en-suite bathroom. With a few splashes of cold water on her face, she found herself more awake.

She stalked into the bedroom and pulled on a change of clothes, leaving her current set draped over the armchair in an attempt to remove the wrinkles.

She emerged into the hall and knocked at Emma's door. A groggy Emma pulled the door open moments later, still in her nightclothes.

"Morning," she mumbled, as she wandered back into the room and pulled a set of clothes from her bag.

"Morning. I hope Lenora has coffee," Maggie said, as she perched on Emma's bed.

"You and me both," Emma groaned, stepping into the bathroom.

"At least you slept in your pajamas," Maggie called. "I fell asleep in my clothes. I don't think I moved all night."

"I wish I hadn't spent the extra time putting them on," Emma yelled. "I should have tried to go straight to sleep."

"Did donning your jammies wake you up?"

"Yes. And then all I could think about was the original Lenora roaming around the halls, seeing ghosts. Then I turned the light on and couldn't sleep because of that. But if I turned it off, I was too afraid to sleep."

Maggie began to chuckle. Her giggle turned into a full belly laugh as Emma slogged from the bathroom and flung her pajamas into her bag.

"It's not funny," Emma retorted. "You've got me all wound up with this ghosts and lore nonsense."

"Sorry," Maggie said, still laughing. "Out of the two of us, I can't believe you couldn't sleep because of ghosts. I have been so worried about ghosts, and it's you who had a sleepless night."

Emma joined in her chuckling. "I'm only laughing because I'm tired."

"Boy, I hope we find something today."

"Me too, otherwise we're going to have to give some serious thought to our next step."

Maggie nodded when a frantic knock sounded at the door. The noise startled both women. Emma hurried to the door, still shoving her foot in her shoe.

"Cate! Lenora! Is everything all right?"

Maggie raced over to join them.

Cate nodded and grinned, as Lenora said, "We found something!"

Maggie's pulse quickened and her eyes lit up. "Really?"

Emma motioned for them to enter the room. They gathered around Lenora, who held a stack of yellowed letters.

"Cate mentioned over breakfast that she found correspondence addressed to her ancestor, Randolph, as the clue that pointed to where the MacKenzie key was hidden. It struck me that there were several letters mixed in with my great-great-great-grandmother's things. Apparently, she, despite it being the so-called Brotherhood, was quite involved. It was her who corresponded with Randolph MacKenzie about creating a hiding spot for the Fletcher key."

"Really?" Emma inquired.

Cate nodded. "Apparently, she and Randolph were friends. She notes the MacKenzies of old were quite personable and very accepting of her, despite her humble beginnings."

"Yes, acceptance was something she struggled very much with," Lenora agreed. "Anyway, there are several letters here from Randolph, Lenora and even Robert. They were returned to us along with the stories she wrote about her life."

Lenora shuffled through the papers. "These all discuss hiding the keys. Randolph mentions building his hiding spot into a new wing. Obviously, Blackmoore Castle was not undergoing renovations at the time. So, instead, Robert and Lenora proposed building a hiding spot into the mausoleum Robert ordered built."

Maggie bit her lower lip as she grinned. "So, the key must be hidden there?"

"Yes, I would say so," Lenora said. "The crypt is located at the back of the property. It's not a far walk–"

"Let's go," Maggie said.

"Just let me put these letters back. I'll keep the sheet with the drawings, in case we need it to distinguish the compartment."

They followed Lenora to the foyer and waited while she disappeared down a hall. Maggie sent a text to Henry, informing him of their lead.

He filled her in on the progress they'd made in their search for Bryson and associates. They wished each other good luck as Lenora returned.

"Ready?" Maggie asked.

They ducked out the front door and Lenora led them around the side of the castle, continuing past the stables. A gray stone structure rose in the distance within a thicket of trees. They threaded through the gravestones poking from the ground in front of the structure at odd angles. The peaked roof stood over the arching entryway. The black hole yawned above them as they approached. Maggie swallowed hard.

"Why does it always have to involve a tomb?" she asked, as she craned her neck to stare at the two stone crosses rising from the roof at the back and front of the building.

Lenora eyed her sideways.

"We got stuck in one once before," she responded, motioning to herself and Emma.

"Well, this one does not have any doors," Lenora said. "So, we should be safe."

With an unconvinced glance, Maggie nodded and followed her into the crypt. The temperature dropped several degrees as they stepped inside. Maggie shivered and shrugged her hoodie tighter around her. Her nostrils flared as she scrunched her nose at the musty scent.

She studied the inside of the stone structure. Large blocks rose to the peaked ceiling. On each side of the rectangular space, two enormous stone coffins lay on raised platforms.

Maggie's eyes flitted between them, and her lips formed a frown. "You don't think it's in there with one of them, do you?"

"No," Lenora answered. "At least, not according to these schematics."

"Do you mind if I take a peek at those?" Emma inquired.

Lenora shook her head and handed the paper over to Emma. Cate peered over her shoulder. Sketches of various elements dotted the page. Notes were scrawled next to each.

Maggie glanced at the paper. "Well, this is very vague," she complained. "It doesn't show where any of these things are or anything!"

"There's the first one!" Cate exclaimed, pointing underneath the stained-glass window gracing the back wall. "A trinity cross."

Maggie hurried toward it. "What's the note say to do with it?"

"Umm," Emma said squinting at the scrawled script writing, "pull and turn three clicks."

"Three clicks?" Maggie questioned.

"That's what it says," Emma said with a shrug.

Maggie wiggled her eyebrows and grasped the square stone. Dust crumbled under her touch as she struggled to loosen it from its place in the wall.

"Were these people super strong?" she grunted, digging her fingertips into the stone's slim outline. With a bit more work, the stone tile popped loose. Maggie breathed a sigh of relief as she wiggled her fingers.

"Okay," she said, as she gripped it again. "Which way do I turn it?"

"Arrow shows clockwise," Emma reported.

Maggie twisted her wrist to the right. A click sounded as she spun the stone square. She continued turning slowly until she heard two more. The third click was followed by a sliding sound.

Maggie dusted her hands off. "One down, three things to go. What's next?"

"We're looking for a lion," Emma said, pointing to the next drawing. The picture showed a lion rearing on its hind legs, its mouth open in a roar.

Everyone studied the interior for the symbol.

"Here!" Cate announced. She squatted near the stone coffin on the right. "It's above Robert's name."

On the base of the coffin, the name and dates for Robert Fletcher appeared with a lion standing on its hind legs.

"Okay," Maggie said, as she squatted next to Cate. "What do we do with it?"

Emma squashed her lips together as she traced her finger on the paper. "I think depress the shaded regions. Its crown and claws."

She held the schematic out for Maggie to reference. Maggie pushed each of the shaded pieces. Another sliding noise echoed through the chamber.

"Sounds like success," Maggie said.

"All right, moving on," Emma said. "The next one is a unicorn."

"A unicorn?" Maggie questioned, giving Emma a double-take.

"It's the national animal," Lenora said.

"Really?" Maggie questioned. "Your national animal is fake?"

"Mythical," Emma corrected.

"Whatever," Maggie said, as her eyes searched the space. "Anybody see one in here?"

"Here," Lenora said. "It's above Lenora's name."

"Ah, that makes sense. A piece of the lock is on each of their tombs," Maggie said. "What do we do with it?"

"Umm," Emma said, her face a mask of confusion, "I can't tell."

"There's an arrow that looks like it's spiraling," Cate said.

Maggie tried to pull the unicorn from the stone coffin. "I can't get this out," she said.

"Maybe it's stuck like the other one," Emma suggested.

Maggie dug her fingers in around the unicorn's body. She shook her head. "Can't get it."

"Perhaps a tool or something?" Cate suggested.

"Yes," Emma agreed. "If it hasn't been used in centuries, it may be stuck."

Lenora pursed her lips and glanced sideways. She returned her gaze to the unicorn. She reached out and ran her fingers over the unicorn's horn.

"It's not indicating that we should rotate the horse," she said. "It's telling us to spin its horn." As she ran her fingers over the horn, it spun, revealing a gold spike in place of the stone one.

Another sliding noise reverberated. Maggie licked her lips as she stood. "One more."

"It's a coat of arms," Emma said.

"It's our family crest," Lenora said, pointing above the stained-glass window.

Maggie glanced up at the carved detail. A lion held one side of the shield with a unicorn on the other. The shield, split into four regions, showed another lion, unicorn and two patterns.

"Ugh," Maggie groaned. "How will we ever reach that?"

"Same way we reached that stupid hook in the tomb," Emma said. "Come on, climb on my shoulders." She squatted down.

"Yeah, and you complained I was too heavy. Come on, I'll lift you up."

"It's your funeral," Emma said, as Maggie lowered herself into a squat. Emma swung her legs over Maggie's shoulders.

"Ready?"

"Yep," Emma said.

Maggie groaned as she straightened. "Oh, stop," Emma said.

"Just hurry up," Maggie said through clenched teeth.

"Pull out, rotate and push in," Cate said, as she read the instructions.

Emma reached up toward the crest. As her fingers brushed the stone, something moved. A black bat flapped its wings, disturbed from its hiding spot by her presence. It flew blindly at her, striking her on the head, before seeking shelter in another dark corner.

Emma flailed her arms as she shrieked. Her wild motion caused Maggie to stumble back a few steps. The two toppled over in a heap, landing hard against the stone floor.

"Maggie! Emma! Are you okay?" Cate asked, kneeling next to them.

"Yeah," Emma answered as Maggie nodded her head. "It figures – the one time I do the cool job, a bat attacks me."

Emma stood up and brushed herself off before offering her hand to Maggie. "Want to switch?"

"No," Maggie said. "Come on, second time's the charm."

Emma climbed onto Maggie's shoulders again, and Maggie raised her up to the crest. Cate braced Maggie's posture as Emma worked to pull the crest out from the wall.

After a struggle, she managed to release it. The crest slid out several inches from the wall. "Does it say which way to rotate?"

"Clockwise," Lenora told her.

Emma grabbed the edges of the crest and rotated it into a complete circle before pressing it back toward the wall. A clank sounded. The floor shook and a boom echoed, rumbling through the air. A whoosh of musty air filled the crypt.

The sound of stone scraping on stone resounded in the chamber, coupled with a scream. Everyone twisted to face the entrance, realizing only three women now stood in the chamber.

CHAPTER 36

"Lenora?!" Cate shouted, hurrying around a large hole which had appeared in the floor of the crypt.

"Down here!" her voice answered faintly.

Cate stared into the pit. Maggie and Emma joined her after Emma scrambled off Maggie's shoulders. A set of stone stairs led down into blackness.

"Are you alright?" Cate called.

"Yes," Lenora answered.

Maggie toggled on her phone's flashlight. "We're coming down."

With cell phone flashlights on, the trio made their way down the stone steps.

"Careful in case of traps," Emma warned.

"It's not a tomb, Emma," Maggie said, as she navigated into the darkness.

"Technically, it is, Maggie," Emma snarked.

"Not that kind. You know what I mean!"

They reached the bottom. Lenora squinted against their flashlights.

"Are you okay? What happened?" Maggie asked.

"Yes, I'm fine. The floor slid away, and I lost my balance and toppled down the stairs," she said. "A few bumps and bruises, but I'm no worse for wear."

Emma ran her flashlight over the area. A tunnel was hewn into the earth. "Looks like this tunnel leads that way," Emma said, motioning behind Lenora.

"I guess we'll follow it," Maggie replied.

"Should one of us stay behind? In case the panel closes?" Cate asked.

"No," Maggie argued. "The last time we did that, Piper was kidnapped. We should stay together."

"Oh, that makes perfect sense," Lenora said. "That way if the panel closes, we can all die together."

"Let's hope it doesn't," Maggie answered, as she skirted around her to move down the passage.

The foursome followed the narrow passageway until they reached an opening. It led to a square chamber. A pedestal sat in the middle.

"Wow, this is just like the MacKenzie chamber," Maggie said. They approached the pedestal. A large wooden box rested on top. Maggie studied it. She frowned as she searched for the opening. She tried to grasp the lid and lift it. "How do you open this thing?"

"It's a puzzle box," Lenora said.

"Huh?" Maggie asked.

"A puzzle box. The first Lenora and Robert often gave each other unique gifts. He once gave her a singing box. It still sits in the tower she loved.

"He also gave her a puzzle box. Well, actually, the gift was a rather ostentatious emerald necklace, but before she could get to the gift, she had to solve the puzzle and open the box."

Maggie made a face. "If Henry made me solve a puzzle before the gift, I'd kill him. Though I wouldn't have turned down the emerald necklace."

"You ought to see the sapphires he bought her," Lenora said, as she circled the box, shining her light on various areas.

"Lucky girl," Maggie said. "So, how do we open the puzzle box? Do you know?"

"Yes," Lenora said. "Well, no. Yes and no."

Maggie tilted her head as she tried to discern the meaning of the contrary statement.

Lenora explained further, "I don't know how to open this box exactly, but I know how to open a similar puzzle box. I found the other as a child and played with the thing until I figured out how to open it."

"Do you think you can open this one?" Emma asked.

"Yes, though it may be easier to take it with us to the castle," Lenora answered. She grabbed each side of the box and tugged. It didn't budge. "Hmm, stuck."

"Let me try," Maggie said. She grasped hold of the box and pulled.

"It has to be opened here," Emma murmured, as it failed to budge even with Maggie straining against it.

"All right," Lenora said as she circled it. "I can do that."

Emma took her flashlight and held it aimed at the puzzle box. Lenora furrowed her brow as she tried sliding several pieces. After a few tries, a piece slid an inch, its edge sticking off the box.

Lenora studied it further, sliding another piece away. She then slid the entire side up an inch.

"How do you know which pieces slid?" Maggie asked.

"Trial and error," she answered, as she studied the patterns.

"How many pieces have to move to open it?" Maggie questioned.

"It could be anywhere from four to hundreds."

"Hundreds?" Maggie gasped.

"That's probably not the case here," Lenora assured her. She continued to search and slid pieces when she could.

Maggie chewed her lower lip, checking her phone every few minutes for the time. After over an hour of work and twenty-one slides, Lenora breathed a sigh of relief. She slid open the top, revealing the box's interior.

"You did it!" Maggie said, clapping her hands. "Now, let's get the key and get out of here."

Maggie raced forward and grasped hold of the brass key from within the box.

"Wait!" Emma shouted, a second too late. Maggie lifted the key from the box. A clanking sounded as she removed the key.

"What was that?" Maggie asked.

"Oh, no!" Emma shouted. She pointed toward the doorway where they'd entered.

They all spun to face the opening. A large stone slab slid down from the top, sealing off the tunnel. Maggie raced toward it, but it settled in a cloud of dust before she could get out.

"Oh, great!" she shouted, flinging her hands in the air. She banged against it and strained as she tried to shove it back up. "We're stuck."

"So much for no traps," Emma snarked.

"Sorry," Maggie said, with a wince.

"Try putting the key back," Emma said.

"Good idea," Maggie answered with a nod. She hastened back to the platform and dropped the key in the box. Nothing happened. She pressed the key down as she spun to face the doorway.

"Maybe we need to close the box," Cate said.

"Okay," Emma answered. "But if we close the box and that opens the door, we can't remove the key."

"Let's take the key then close the box," Maggie said.

"It's worth a shot," Emma agreed.

They removed the key and worked to slide the pieces back into place. As Maggie pushed the last piece back, she swiveled to face the door.

"Nothing," she said, stamping her foot.

"Maybe you were right, Cate," Emma said. "Maybe the key needs to be inside it."

"No, you made a good point. If the key needed to be inside it, it could never be removed. There must be another way."

"Maybe we needed to weight it, like on Indiana Jones," Maggie said.

"That's ridiculous," Emma said.

"Why? It worked for Indy."

"No, it didn't. He still triggered the trap."

"Oh, right. So, then we're just stuck, and no one can ever remove the key?"

"No," Emma said, with a shake of her head. "There has to be a way out. We're missing something."

"Okay, everyone spread out and look for something."

"What?" Lenora asked.

"Anything. A handle, or a lever, or anything."

They each started in an opposite corner and worked their way around the room.

"Here!" Cate shouted after forty minutes of searching. "There's something here!"

"What is it?" Maggie asked, as everyone hurried toward Cate. She pointed toward an area near the sealed-off tunnel.

"I'm not sure. Some sort of symbol."

"Press it!" Maggie shouted, as Emma said, "Don't press it!"

"What's it going to hurt?" Maggie questioned. "We're stuck."

"It may trigger another trap that kills us instead of just trapping us!"

Maggie made a face. She reached out and pressed it. "Didn't do anything anyway."

"It's not a button," Lenora said as she studied it. "It's a keyhole."

"Keyhole?" Maggie's heart sank. "Oh, great. We don't have a key."

"Actually," Emma said, snatching the brass key from Maggie's pocket and holding it high, "we do!"

Maggie's eyes lit up and she smiled and nodded at Emma. "Do it," she encouraged.

Emma blew on the symbol, sending a cloud of dust into the air. She lined the key up with the indentations and shoved. It slid into the wall.

She grinned at the others before she turned it. The panel closing their egress rumbled upward.

"Yay!" Maggie shouted. "Now, grab the key and let's get out of here."

"Wait, you three go out. I'll wait here and grab the key," Lenora said.

"But–" Maggie began.

Lenora shook her head. "If, when I remove the key, the door closes again, I'll toss the key out to you. Use it to find your friend."

"We're not leaving you," Cate said.

Lenora shook her head. "No, I hope you don't, but you need the key. Then one of you can get me out by whatever means it takes while the others continue to find your friend."

"She has a point," Emma said.

"All right," Maggie said. They stepped through the opening and into the tunnel. Maggie nodded to Lenora who returned the gesture.

Everyone held their breath as Lenora slid the key from the wall and handed it out the door to Emma. Nothing happened for a moment. They all blew out the air held in their lungs.

Then a clank sounded. Maggie's eyes widened as the stone slab began to lower. She reached through and pulled Lenora under it before it sealed shut again.

Lenora toppled to the ground from the force Maggie used to pull her forward. She pushed herself up on shaky hands. "Thanks," she said.

"Anytime. Now let's get out of here before something else closes."

Lenora nodded. They proceeded down the passageway and climbed the stairs, exiting into the mausoleum and then out into the sunshine beyond.

Maggie stared down at the key in her hand. "Three down. One to go."

They stood for a moment in silence before Maggie spoke again. "We should update Henry and Uncle Ollie."

"And get started on finding the last key," Emma said.

Maggie nodded. "I guess we should gather our things."

They headed back to the castle. On the walk, Cate said, "Lenora, part of this cache belongs to you. If you'd like to be there when it's opened, you could come with us."

Lenora glanced at her before returning her eyes to the castle. "No. I really don't want it. It's fine to continue on without me. I'm glad you found the key though, and I do hope your friend is okay."

Emma nodded. "It may be dangerous, so we certainly understand."

Lenora offered a weak smile before returning her gaze to the castle again. They pushed through the front door. Maggie swiped at her cell phone as they entered, tapping with her thumb to send a text.

"Okay, let's grab our stuff and head out. Next stop, Clydescolm Castle," Maggie said, as she shoved her phone into the pocket of her leggings.

Nods met her statement and they headed upstairs to collect their overnight bags. Maggie grabbed anything left out in her room and tossed it in the bag. She shouldered it and hurried into the hall. Finding herself alone, she wandered to the foyer to wait for everyone else.

As she stepped onto the marble floor, a voice floated into the room. Maggie furrowed her brow, wondering if she'd been the last one down. She followed the sound, finding Lenora alone in the office they'd searched yesterday.

"Did I hear you talking to someone?"

"No," Lenora said.

Maggie narrowed her eyes at the woman.

"I may have muttered something to myself," Lenora said, as Maggie stared at her.

"Ah," Maggie said with a nod, "I just wanted to make sure I wasn't the last one down here."

"No, I haven't seen the others."

"Well, thank you so much for your help. And sorry about the incident with the horse. I hope your ankle's okay."

"It seems fine."

Maggie heard Emma's voice calling her name.

"Good. Well, I guess we'll be heading out. Again, thank you. And I'm sure Piper will be grateful, too."

"You're welcome," Lenora said, with a curt smile and nod. "Oh, and please let me know when she's safe, if it's not too much trouble."

"It's no trouble at all. I'll definitely send you a message; just give me your number."

Maggie dug her phone from her pocket and prepared to input the number. After Lenora passed it along, she nodded and slipped the phone back into her pocket.

"Okay, I hope to have good news soon! I'll see myself out."

Maggie gave her a long stare and a smile before she ambled down the hall, her duffel bouncing off her hip, to meet the others.

"Ready?" she asked.

"Yeah," Emma said. "Have you seen Lenora? I wanted to thank her."

"I did," Maggie said.

"Oh, if we have a minute, I'd like to say goodbye," Cate added.

"Sure," Maggie said with a nod. "She's in the office room we searched last night."

"Thanks," Cate said, as she hurried down the hall toward the room.

"One more key to go," Emma said with a sigh. "Have you heard from Henry?"

"No," Maggie said. "I haven't heard a thing. I'll try calling him once we're in the car."

Emma nodded as Cate returned, and they stepped out into the late morning sunshine. After descending the steep hill to the car and tossing their luggage in the back, they climbed into the vehicle.

"Let me try calling Henry. I can't believe he hasn't answered my text."

"Jack isn't answering me either," Cate said.

"I hope everything's okay," Emma said.

The line trilled as Maggie set the phone on speaker and waited for an answer. "Maggie!" Henry answered.

"Henry! You didn't answer my text. I was worried."

"Sorry, we're on to something here."

"Really? Have you found Piper?"

"Not yet, but we've tracked Bryson to Edinburgh. We're about to head there now while we continue to track down leads. Have you made any progress on your end?"

"Yes. We have the third key," Maggie said, as she

processed the information. "We haven't heard anything else from Bryson."

"Are you heading to Clydescolm?"

"We were going to, but maybe we should come to Edinburgh."

"No, you need to search for the last key."

"But Henry–"

"We'll handle this on our end. Just get that key."

Maggie's shoulders slouched. "Okay, good luck."

"You too." The line clicked as Henry ended the call. Maggie drew her lips into a thin line as she tossed her phone into the cupholder.

"What are you thinking?" Emma said.

"That I don't like this plan at all," Maggie said.

"Me either," Emma agreed. "I don't like splitting the team when we're going after Bryson. And I don't like leaving us to search Clydescolm alone when the Edinburgh thing could be a decoy to draw half our team there, leaving us fair game."

"I agree," Maggie said.

"So, what do you want to do?"

"Go to Edinburgh," Maggie said. "You?"

"Same," Emma agreed. They both twisted in their seats to eye Cate.

She shrugged. "I have no objection. I'll go where you think it's best."

"Okay," Maggie said. "Edinburgh it is. I'm going to text Henry and tell him."

She quickly typed a message: *Coming to Edinburgh. Meet you there. Don't bother arguing, decision is made.*

After dumping her cell phone in the cupholder, she pressed the start button. Nothing happened.

CHAPTER 37

Maggie scrunched up her nose at the steering wheel. She pressed the start button again. "What the heck?" she mumbled.

Emma banged her head against the headrest behind her. "Did you run out of gas?"

"No!" Maggie said, incredulous. "I just put some in when we stopped for coffee."

"That was a million miles ago!" Emma exclaimed.

"It was not a *million* miles. I'm not out of gas."

"Are you sure?"

"Yes. Well, mostly."

"Ugh," Emma groaned, letting her head bang against the headrest again.

"Well, I can't see the gas gauge when the car is off!"

A shout sounded outside the car. Maggie, Emma and Cate glanced around, searching for the source. Maggie crinkled her brow as she spotted it.

"Is that..." Emma questioned.

"Lenora," Maggie answered.

Lenora hurried down the hill, shouting and waving her

arms. A bag bounced off her hip and she struggled to pull a sweater on over her top.

"Wait! Wait!" she shouted.

Maggie leapt from the car. "Lenora! Is everything okay?"

"Yes," she puffed, winded from the run. "I want to go."

Maggie's eyebrows shot skyward.

"I don't want to abandon my friends."

Maggie stood stunned for a moment, her mouth hanging open. After a second, she recovered and nodded. "Uh, yeah, sure."

She motioned toward the trunk as she ambled back to open it. "Toss your bag in here and climb in."

Maggie slid in behind the wheel as Lenora climbed into the captain's chair next to Cate. She sucked in a breath as she strapped on her seatbelt. She looked around at the others in the car.

"I'm glad you joined us," Cate said.

"We've had a change in plans, though," Emma explained. "We've got a lead on Piper in Edinburgh. We're heading there first instead of Clydescolm Castle. Sure you still want to go?"

Lenora nodded. "Yes. I'm certain."

"Well," Maggie chimed in, "we *will* be going to Edinburgh. As soon as we get the car started."

"Oh," Lenora said. "Sometimes cars are finicky here with the... uh... temperatures and so on. Maybe try again."

"Short of one of us climbing around under the hood, we don't have any other options," Maggie said.

She pressed her foot on the brake, closed her eyes and pressed the start button. The engine roared to life.

"Ha!" she shouted with a wide grin. "That did it!" She glanced over at Emma, offering her a wry glance. "I told you we weren't out of gas."

Emma shook her head at Maggie as she tapped at the GPS, setting a route for Edinburgh.

"Edinburgh, here we come," Maggie said, easing the car out of the parking space and onto the road.

After a brief stop for lunch and gas, at Emma's insistence, they continued on their three-hour drive to Edinburgh. Cate called Jack as they approached the city limits, inquiring as to their location.

After placing her phone on speaker, Henry talked Maggie through a series of turns, leading her to a nondescript set of row homes. Maggie circled the block before she found a parking space large enough to accommodate her vehicle in front of the row houses.

Henry and Jack approached the SUV as the women slid to the ground and stretched.

"Oh, Cate, thank goodness you're okay," Jack said to Cate.

"I told you not to come," Henry said to Maggie.

Maggie arched an eyebrow and crossed her arms. She pointed to Cate and Jack. "That's the greeting I expect."

Henry shook his head at her. "I'm glad you're okay, princess, but you shouldn't have come. You should have stayed as far from Bryson as possible."

"First of all, you don't get to tell me what to do."

"I know. I should have told you to come. Then you wouldn't have."

Maggie swung the trunk open as she rolled her eyes at him. "Second of all–" she began.

"We have no idea Bryson is here and not near Clydescolm," Emma interjected.

"Well–" Henry began.

"There's no sense in arguing," Maggie said, as she handed her bag off to Henry along with Emma's. "And besides, she's got a good point. The lead you're following may be a setup."

"We've got more. We can discuss it when you get inside." He stopped and stared at Lenora who stood apart from them, biting her lower lip as she studied the area. "Who's this?"

Cate looped her arm through Lenora's and led her closer to the group. "This is Lenora Fletcher. She owns Blackmoore Castle. And she's my cousin."

"Your cousin?" Jack asked.

"Yes," Cate said. "We didn't realize it until we were searching through some records for a clue to find the key. Instead, we found a picture of my grandmother with Lenora's grandfather. They were first cousins."

"Well, I suppose the trip was fruitful in more ways than one!" Jack said, then turned to Lenora. "Here, let me get that bag for you."

"Oh, I've got it, thanks," Lenora answered.

"Nonsense," Jack insisted. "Any cousin of Lady Cate's is a friend of mine."

After Lenora relinquished her bag, Henry led them into the safe house. Charlie sat at the dining room table, a pot of coffee next to him. Keys clacked as he pounded on his keyboard.

Leo leaned against the door jamb leading to the kitchen, sipping a coffee.

"Progress?" Henry asked.

"Nearly there, mate," Charlie answered, his eyes never leaving the screen.

Ollie studied the keys at the opposite end of the table, making notes and sketches in a brown journal.

"Maggie," he greeted her, "I'm so glad you're okay *and* that you got the third key! May I see it?"

"Of course," Maggie said, pulling it from her purse and handing it over.

He studied it, turning it over in his hands. "Fascinating," he murmured, as he returned to his seat and placed it with the other keys.

"What have you got on Piper?" Maggie asked, leaning over Charlie's shoulder at his screen.

"One second, chicky," Charlie said. "Coming online in three... two... and there she is." He grinned at his screen.

A grainy image of Piper wandering up a stairwell between two bulky men burst onto the screen. Maggie smiled.

"She looks unharmed," she noted, as Emma glanced over Charlie's other shoulder.

"And you know where this is?"

"I do, brainy," he answered. "We've found her. Now we just need to get her."

Henry pulled a gun from his waistband and checked the clip. "Not a problem, mate, I'll go in for her."

Maggie put her hand on her hip and stared at Henry with a confused expression on her face. "Henry, are you crazy?"

He glanced sideways at her. "No. I'll go in, grab Piper and get out. Simple."

"May I remind you of who we're dealing with?"

"No, I'm well aware of that."

"This is Bryson. The man who put a bullet in you once already, and nearly put one in me, too. You can't go into that building guns blazing and think you'll come out okay. Especially alone."

"You're not coming with me, princess."

"No, I'm not. Because this is the world's dumbest plan!"

"I don't see that we have another choice. They're not going to let her out of that apartment."

"It's a setup," Maggie said. "Do you really think Bryson didn't want you to find this footage?"

"No, I don't," Henry said. "I think he got sloppy. I think he thinks we don't even know who we're looking for and therefore, never identified him."

Maggie crossed her arms and offered an unimpressed stare.

"I'd agree with Maggie on this," Emma said.

"Well, that's a first," Henry said.

"Yeah, it is, and as such, you should pay attention. This is one of the few times Emma and I have ever agreed. That alone should stand for something."

"Look, I'll go in with him, chicky."

"Oh, well, now I feel so much better!"

"Joke all you want, but I know how to handle a weapon."

"Henry..."

"This isn't up for discussion, Maggie," Henry said.

"Fine, then I'll go with you," Maggie retorted.

"Like hell you will."

Maggie's jaw unhinged. She balled her hands into fists and stomped her foot on the floor. "You're being unreasonable."

"I'm not having you go into a firefight with Bryson."

"Oh, but you can go?"

"We're not having this argument," Henry said, as he pulled on a dark hoodie and zipped it up, shoving another gun into an arm holster and strapping it on.

He tossed a weapon to Charlie. "You sure?"

"She's my wife. You couldn't keep me away, mate."

"I'm in," Leo said.

"Oh, right," Maggie said, flailing her arms in the air. "Because you'll be so much help."

"I want to help. Piper and I dated."

Maggie shot him an incredulous look. "You went on one fake date. Are you serious? You don't even know how to shoot a gun."

"I do so," Leo contended. "I went on a hunting trip with my boss and his boss."

Maggie's shoulders slumped at the statement.

Jack stepped forward. "I'm not an expert, but I do know how to handle a weapon. I can help."

Henry gave him a nod and readied two pistols, handing one to each man.

"Jack!" Cate exclaimed.

"I'm not going to stand here and do nothing, Cate," Jack said as he accepted the gun from Henry.

"Maggie's right, this a foolish plan! Surely, this apartment is a stronghold for them."

"We'll be fine," Henry assured her.

Ollie and Lenora huddled at the table studying the keys as the argument ensued between the two groups, split by gender.

"And what if you're not?" Emma asked. "What then?"

"Then we'll re-evaluate. Look, ladies, I've been in tight spots before. I know what I'm doing," Henry said, with cool confidence.

Maggie closed her eyes in annoyance. "Fine," she gave in. "But give us two more guns. Just in case. You can't leave us here unprotected."

"Maggie!" Emma said. "This is ridiculous!"

"You can't talk them out of it, Emma. It's useless to try. So let the men go handle it."

Henry handed Maggie two handguns. "Safety's..."

"I know where it is," Maggie snapped, as she swiped the two weapons from him. She popped the clip, checking it before she slid it back into place.

Henry held his hands up in defeat. "I'll keep you updated. Be ready to move once we have Piper. Gentlemen, are we ready?"

"Bring it on," Leo said as Jack nodded.

Maggie rolled her eyes at the display of testosterone. Henry kissed her cheek and squeezed her arm. "We'll be back soon."

The four men stalked out the door into the waning light.

"I can't believe you're going to sit here and do nothing

while they rush into a building filled with Bryson and his bad guys!" Emma shouted as the door swung shut.

Maggie pulled her phone from her pocket and swiped at it. "Oh, I'm not."

"What are you doing?"

"Texting Bryson and setting up an exchange."

CHAPTER 38

"What?!" Emma exclaimed at Maggie's statement.

"Keys for Piper. Exchange at the Northside Vaults." She pressed a button, sending the message on its way.

"Am I the only one who thinks this is *also* a crazy plan?" Emma asked.

"It's less crazy than storming their proverbial castle," Maggie said. "We draw him out in the open. If it looks sketchy, we walk. We're also drawing him away from the four stallions who seem to think they are the only ones who can solve the problem."

Emma closed her eyes and shook her head. "Are you also forgetting one important detail?"

"What's that?"

"We only have three keys!"

"I have no intention of giving him those keys," Maggie said. "In fact, I don't plan on being anywhere near Bryson."

"What's your plan?" Cate inquired.

"I plan to play up to what exactly Bryson expects of me.

Someone stupid. He'll tell me to drop the keys somewhere and he'll release Piper after. I'll agree to that."

"And how do you plan to get Piper once Bryson realizes you haven't given him the keys?" Emma asked.

"I'll have Piper before he realizes that," Maggie said.

"Confident, aren't we?" Emma inquired. "Do you mind sharing how you plan to pull that off?"

"Simple. He'll come for the keys and bring most of his people with him, leaving Piper with a limited amount of guards. With our weapons, we can overpower them and take Piper back."

"This is never going to work."

"Too late for second-guessing," Maggie said as her phone chimed. "Leave the keys in the second stop on the tour leaving in one hour. Piper will be released once the keys are confirmed and in my possession at the corner of Cowgate and Blair Street."

"One hour?" Emma questioned.

"We need to check a map and get moving," Maggie said, as she slid in behind Charlie's closed laptop and popped it open.

"He's going to kill you," Emma said.

"Yeah, I know." She tapped around, pulling up a map of the area. She found the crossroad Bryson mentioned. They studied the area. "They'll wait in one of these locations." She pointed to a few areas where vehicles may wait near the drop-off point.

"This is assuming they're actually bringing her."

"Think positive. We'll need to keep an eye on these spots."

"You mean, I'll need to keep an eye on them," Emma said.

"I'll help," Lenora offered.

"No," Maggie said. "It's way too dangerous."

"I have experience with a firearm. I took several marksman courses during my boarding school days. And didn't you just scold your significant other for excluding you?"

Maggie sighed. "So I did. Fine. As long as you understand how dangerous this is."

"According to you, it's not dangerous at all," Lenora said.

"I'll help, too," Cate said. "I don't know much about guns, but I can drive. Wait with the car, maybe?"

"Perfect. One bag person, two sets of eyes in the field, one getaway driver."

Ollie raised his eyebrows. "I'll make the drop. Leave you ladies to the field, giving you three sets of eyes."

"Uncle Ollie," Maggie protested.

"Now, now, Maggie. I'll not be lectured to because I'm old. I'm perfectly capable of taking the tour, which I have been on once before. I can quickly navigate out to the waiting car and be ready with Cate to pick you up when you're ready."

"All right. Then we just need a few fake keys."

Maggie headed into the kitchen and grabbed a few large serving utensils, shoving them in an emptied backpack. She passed out earpieces from Charlie's stash to everyone along with the weapons. "And we're set."

As she reached to close the laptop, movement caught her eye. She grinned. "There they go."

Emma joined her, watching the screen as Piper was paraded down the stairwell with Bryson and three other men.

"Four of them," Maggie said. "That's what we're up against."

"Not great odds."

"Let's up our chances." Maggie dialed a number on her phone as they hurried out the door.

"Voicemail," Maggie groaned, as Henry's voice yammered on about leaving a message.

"Bryson's on the move," Maggie reported. "He's got Piper with him. He's going to the Vaults. He wants the keys in forty-five minutes. If you get this in time, meet us there."

She ended the call and climbed into the passenger's seat next to Cate. Ollie, Emma and Lenora piled into the backseats. Within fifteen minutes, they were approaching the Vaults. Cate pulled the car into a parking space marked "Permits Only," on a side street near the corner where Piper would be dropped off. She turned on her flashers.

"Everyone ready?" Maggie inquired. "Uncle Ollie, you'll do the drop. Let us know if you see any signs of Bryson or his people. The rest of us will spread out and search for them. If you see anything, radio the team of the location."

With nods all around, Maggie snapped open her door. "Let's go get Piper."

Cate remained in the car. "Good luck," she called as they left her behind, Ollie heading to the underground's entrance and the other women dispersing to monitor the streets.

"Heading in," Ollie said after ten minutes. "Will likely lose reception. Good luck. See you on the flip side."

"Thanks, Uncle Ollie," Maggie said, as she scanned the streets for any sign of her foe.

Five more tension-filled moments passed before Maggie announced, "I've got a white van parking in an alley."

"I saw that," Emma said. "Could be a delivery van."

A moment later, Maggie confirmed Emma's theory. "Yep, delivery van."

"Darn," Emma said.

"Lenora? You okay?" Maggie asked.

"All good," she responded.

"Got another white van," Maggie said two minutes later. "And I have eyes on Bryson."

"Where?" Emma asked.

Maggie rattled off the location a block away from the crossroads given as Piper's drop-off spot. "Bryson is exiting the vehicle with another man. No sign of Piper."

"She must be in the back," Emma answered.

"Yeah," Maggie agreed. "Uncle Ollie if you can hear this, Bryson is on his way to you."

Ollie didn't respond.

They waited a few moments. "Bryson has entered the underground," Lenora reported.

"I've got movement on the van," Maggie said. "Both men exiting; still no sign of Piper."

"Let's do this now," Emma answered. "We've got both of them out and Bryson looking for the keys. I'm on my way to you."

"I will hold my position and inform you if I see Bryson return," Lenora said.

"Okay, good thinking," Maggie answered.

Emma approached Maggie and they both drew their weapons discreetly, keeping them shielded from view as they approached the alley. A crackle sounded in Maggie's ear as they rounded the corner. She adjusted the earpiece, but heard nothing else.

"Hi there," Maggie said, as they approached the men. "We're lost, can you help us?"

Before either could answer, Maggie and Emma raised their weapons. "Actually, we're not. Hands up," Maggie said. The startled men raised their hands in the air. "We're looking for our friend. Now, slowly slide that door open and let her out."

"Look, lady," the man began.

"No!" Maggie shouted, shaking the gun at him and clicking off the safety. "Open that door now!"

The man reached one hand toward the door and slid it

open. Maggie spotted Piper's rainbow hair inside. She stepped out onto the cobblestone street.

"About time, boss lady," Piper said, as she inched away from the men.

"Now, we're going to back up. If you even flinch, we'll shoot."

Maggie took one step backward when she felt something cold and hard press into the back of her skull.

"You won't be going anywhere, Ms. Edwards," Bryson's crisp British accent said. "And I'd lower your weapon."

Maggie glanced sideways, noting the gun pressed against Emma's head. She squeezed her eyes shut as she held up her hands. Bryson ripped the gun from her fingers while his associate stripped Emma of hers.

"Where is your other half?" Bryson answered.

"Wouldn't you like to know?" Maggie said.

Bryson sneered at her. "At present, he doesn't seem to be near enough to help you, so I'd wager you're in a world of trouble."

His now-armed associates chuckled.

"I wouldn't be so certain about that," Lenora's voice said, as she stood with her gun aimed at Bryson's head.

"Oh, how charming," the man said, pulling Maggie toward him. He clutched his arm around her neck. "I'll bet you won't risk hitting your friend."

Lenora did not flinch. "In the first place, I wouldn't risk it if I were you. I am an expert markswoman, and I won't miss. And in the second, she is not my friend. You overestimate my concern for her."

Bryson's eyebrows raised. "Yet you are here, holding a gun aimed at me on her behalf."

"No," Lenora said. "On my behalf."

"Do tell."

"I couldn't care less about the illustrious Ms. Edwards,"

Lenora said. "She is a thorn in my side and has been since I met her. She pushes her way into people's lives with no regard for their feelings. Really, all I care about is finding the treasure. And, as it seems you will be the one to find it, I propose we make a deal."

CHAPTER 39

*B*ryson cocked his head at Lenora's proposal. "And what deal is that?" he questioned.

"I give you the keys, and we split the treasure fifty-fifty."

Bryson guffawed. "You must be joking. You hold no power here."

"I hold three keys, Mr. Bryson. You have none."

"Except you don't, Ms... What is your name?"

"Never mind. And I do. Well, I know where they are."

"Where?"

"Do we have a deal?"

"What of Ms. Edwards?"

"I do not care what you do with her. Do we have a deal?"

"Assuming you give me the three keys, yes. Why not?"

Lenora narrowed her eyes at Bryson. "Around the corner in a blue Navigator driven by one Lady Catherine Kensie."

"Who is likely driving away as we speak."

Lenora shook her head. "Not without this she won't." She held up a fuel pump fuse.

Bryson gave her a half-smile. "My, you are a clever girl, aren't you?"

Lenora wiggled her eyebrows and nodded at him. "Now, send your men to retrieve the keys and you'll see I am telling the truth."

"Marshall, Kelso, follow up on our mysterious friend's lead."

The men hurried down the alley, while Lenora continued to hold her gun aimed at Bryson.

"How could you?" Maggie shouted at her, hot tears stinging her eyes.

They waited for several painstaking moments. Bryson raised his eyebrows at Lenora.

"It seems you may not have been truthful."

"They'll find Lady Cate and the keys right where I said," she assured him.

Her statement was punctuated by the appearance of four individuals. Two dark figures crept down the alley hidden behind Cate and Ollie.

"Well," Bryson exclaimed, "it seems you were telling the truth after all! Do you have the keys?"

One man raised the duffel bag in response as they herded a frightened Cate and a stoic Ollie in front of them. Cate bit her lower lip, worry creasing her face.

"Sorry, Maggie," she whispered.

Maggie shook her head. "It's okay, Cate. It's not your fault."

The men circled around the van with their captives. Bryson said, "Well, I suppose after we take care of a bit of business, we'll be free to move on to the next location and retrieve the final key. Though I don't think we'll need you."

Bryson kept hold of Maggie, and shifted his gun to face Lenora. "I've got a clear shot, so I suppose this is goodbye."

"I don't think so, Bryson," Henry's voice said.

Bryson froze for a moment, confusion masking his features. Maggie used the opportunity to deliver a crushing blow to his instep and an elbow to his gut. Henry grasped the man as he doubled over and swung the butt of his gun toward him.

Bryson snapped out of his shock, spinning and landing a blow against Henry's abdomen. Henry swung at Bryson, who ducked out of the way.

"Go, Maggie," Henry yelled.

"Run, Cate!" Jack shouted, as he landed a blow against his opponent, raising his fists to block any incoming blows and ready for another strike.

Cate tore around the van with Ollie behind her. Maggie backed away from the scene as Charlie and Leo rounded the corner.

"My hero!" Piper shouted, as Charlie raced past her to help Henry in the fight. Leo followed close on his heels.

The women and Ollie hurried to the car. Two bound men lay hidden in front of the vehicle's bumper. Maggie leapt in behind the wheel. Emma joined her in the front, claiming the shotgun seat. Piper and Cate climbed in and crawled to the back as quickly as possible, leaving Lenora and Ollie with the middle seats. Maggie fired the engine as Ollie climbed into the car and slammed the door.

"Go, Maggie!" he shouted.

She nodded as she saw Leo and Charlie sprinting around the corner. Maggie's stomach dropped for a moment. They ran past them, diving into Cate's estate car and firing the engine. Maggie pulled from her parking space and floored it, making a hard turn onto the main road. Leo followed, screeching to a stop at the alley.

Maggie spotted both passenger doors fly open and two men dive in, as smoke poured from the tires and Leo sped toward them.

"Everybody all right in your car, princess?"

"Yeah," Maggie said. "We're all fine."

Maggie glanced in the rearview mirror at Lenora. She narrowed her eyes at the woman.

"Thank you for the save, Lenora," Cate said, as she leaned forward and rubbed the woman's arm.

"Save?" Maggie inquired. "She almost betrayed us!"

"I did not!" Lenora answered. "I stalled until your boyfriend could get there. I tried to warn you, but my earpiece cut out."

Maggie's brow crinkled as she continued down the highway. "Lenora spotted Bryson returning from the Underground," Cate explained. "She suggested the subterfuge as a stall tactic until backup could arrive."

"How did Henry get here?"

"I texted Jack when we left. He turned them around."

"Keep your foot planted on that gas, princess, we got company," Henry said.

"Seriously?" Emma questioned, glancing in the side mirror as she searched the streets behind them.

A white van weaved through traffic behind them. "You've got to be kidding," Maggie grumbled.

Leo closed the gap behind Maggie.

"Maggie," Henry said, "there's a crossroads coming up. You go left, we'll go right. He can't follow both of us. We'll draw him off."

"Got it," Maggie said. "Good luck."

They approached the crossroads at lightning speed. Maggie saw the turn and lifted her foot as she skidded into it, fishtailing onto the side street. She glanced in the rearview mirror, spotting Leo swerving in the opposite direction.

Traffic snarled behind them as other cars skidded to a halt, trying to avoid a collision. As Maggie glanced back again, a white van swung onto the road behind them. It jumped as the driver gunned the engine, fighting to catch up to them. It swerved around any cars between them, closing the distance quickly.

"Great," Emma groaned.

"Ugh," Maggie said with a sigh, "Henry, your great plan backfired. He followed us."

"Yeah, I see that. We're circling back to get to you. Try to hang on until we can get there."

"I'm doing my best," Maggie said, as she concentrated on the road ahead.

The van pushed at them. A car in front of Maggie slowed. Maggie swerved around it to avoid rear-ending the small vehicle.

The van followed with no trouble.

"Turn there!" Emma said, pointing to another street to the left. Emma gave the street name to Henry.

Maggie veered onto the street and flicked her gaze to the rearview mirror. "Still on us." She swerved onto another street on her right. The van followed.

They continued down the straightaway. Maggie ducked instinctively as bullets fired in their direction.

"Faster, boss lady, they're shooting at us."

"I see that," Maggie shouted, as she urged more speed in a desperate attempt to outrun the van.

Lenora glanced behind them. No cars rode between them and Bryson's white van. She glanced forward. "Stay on this road, do not turn," she said.

"What?!" Maggie said.

Lenora unbuckled her seatbelt and opened her window. Wind blasted the inside of the car, blowing everyone's hair wildly. Lenora stuck her head out the window. Another round of bullets whizzed past them. One ricocheted off their back window.

Lenora ducked back inside the car as the bullets whizzed past, before crawling out the window again. She aimed the handgun she carried at the van behind them. Maggie swerved as she squeezed off the first round. It went wide, missing its target.

"We're behind the van," Henry reported.

Lenora swore under her breath as she lined up her shot again. With narrowed eyes, she pulled the trigger a second time. The van behind them slowed and swerved back and forth.

Leo shot around it and pulled in behind Maggie, as the van slowed to a stop, inching to the side of the road.

"Seriously? Did she just shoot out his tire?" Henry questioned.

With a triumphant grin, Lenora slid back inside the car. "I told you I was an excellent markswoman. That wasn't a lie."

A cheer went up from the car's occupants.

"Oh my gosh, girl! You are amazing!" Maggie exclaimed. She offered her hand for a high-five, receiving one from Emma.

"Yeah, that was totally drip, sis," Piper said. "You're definitely the G.O.A.T."

"Great job, Lenora," Cate said.

"I hate to break up your celebration," Henry said, "but we should pull over and regroup."

"Okay, tell me where," Maggie said.

"Let's get out of the city limits. Slow up, we'll pass you."

Maggie allowed Leo to pull around her. They drove until the buildings thinned before pulling off at a gas station. Everyone climbed from the car. Piper raced to Charlie, flinging her arms around his neck. He scooped her up, lifting her off her feet in a bear hug.

Jack hurried to Cate. "Are you alright?"

She nodded up at him. "Yes, I'm fine. How did you fair?" She gazed at his bruised knuckles.

"You should see the other guy," he joked with a lopsided grin.

"Nice driving, Mario Andretti," Emma said to Leo.

He wiggled his eyebrows at her. "Didn't think I had it in me, huh?"

Emma lifted a shoulder. "I didn't say that."

"I'm full of surprises."

"Good work, princess," Henry said, as he looped his arms around Maggie's waist. "We really need to talk about communication, though."

Maggie raised her eyebrows and offered a coy smile. "First, we need to discuss your bullheadedness."

Henry chuckled at her. "Deal," he said. He spun to face Lenora, who stood by herself. His face formed an amused grin. "And you, that was some damn good shooting."

"Thank you," she answered.

"Where'd you learn to shoot like that?"

"Boarding school," she answered. "I took several courses in a variety of weapons. I have excellent aim."

"Seriously, double-oh-seven? They teach you to shoot like a secret agent in boarding school?" Charlie asked.

Lenora shrugged. "I didn't have many friends. I spent a lot of time practicing."

"I'm glad you did," Henry said.

"So am I," Maggie agreed. "You really saved us back there. Both times. Thank you."

Lenora smiled and nodded at them.

"All right," Henry said. "As much as I'd love to continue celebrating this victory…"

"We need to move on," Ollie finished for him.

"Right," Henry said. "Bryson won't be down for long."

"And we still have one more key to find," Maggie added.

"And I'd like to do it bad guy free," Emma said.

"You and me both, sis," Piper said.

"Are you okay, Piper?" Maggie asked. "Really?"

She nodded. "I'm fine. The worst they did was give me bad food. I don't like Pad Thai. By the way, thanks, everyone, for rescuing me."

"No team member left behind," Maggie said.

"So, should we go straight on to Clydescolm?" Leo asked.

"Wait," Maggie said, "is this Leo Hamilton I see who is super into tracking down the final clue?"

Leo offered her an unimpressed glance. "This whole adventure thing may be growing on me." He shot a glance at Emma.

"Okay, well, I guess we should get going then. Oh, unless Jack and Cate you prefer to go back to Dunhaven?" Maggie asked.

Jack glanced at Cate.

"No way! I didn't just almost get kidnapped to not see this through!" Cate exclaimed.

Jack shrugged. "Looks like we're in."

"Fair enough," Maggie said. "Let's get on the road then. Next stop Clydescolm Castle!"

CHAPTER 40

They split themselves between the cars, with Cate, Jack, Lenora and Ollie taking Cate's estate car, and the rest of the group piling into the Lincoln.

With several hours of driving ahead of them, a few passengers settled in for a nap. Maggie tapped around on her phone as she sat in the passenger's seat next to Henry.

"Please don't tell me you're going to take another selfie," Emma groaned from behind her.

"No," Maggie said. "I'm texting William."

"Who?" Leo inquired.

"William MacClyde," Maggie answered.

"You're texting him?" Emma asked.

"Yeah. I'm trying to explain the situation so he's ready for us when we get there."

"How do you have his number?" Emma asked.

Maggie shrugged. "He gave it to me after our stay. Said if we were ever coming back to text him. Now seemed an appropriate moment to text."

Emma scrunched up her nose. "Do men always give their numbers out to you?"

"No. We were guests there. It's just good business."

"He didn't give me his number."

Maggie rolled her eyes. "I guess you didn't seem interested. It's not a big deal. Anyway, I told him the situation. He said he'll wait up for us to get there. I told him we'd probably not arrive until close to midnight, but he said that didn't matter. Before we left, he told me about his financial troubles, so I imagine finding this may save his castle. He's fairly excited and more than willing to help us."

"Good enough," Henry said. "Looks like we're set."

* * *

Maggie shifted in her seat as the drive went into its second hour.

"Stiff?" Henry asked.

"Impatient," she answered.

"Sorry to say you've got over an hour left."

"I know. I'm using it to list the places this key may be based on where it was at the other two locations."

"I wonder if it's connected to that bookshelf," Emma said from the backseat.

"Oh, I didn't realize you were still awake," Maggie said.

"I'm the last man standing," Emma answered.

Maggie glanced backward. Piper and Charlie slept stretched across the third row of seats. Leo dozed, his head cradled in the seatbelt.

"Not tired?"

"Not in the slightest. I'm also trying to think of where this key may be."

"Okay, let's pool our efforts," Maggie suggested.

Together, they created a list of places to check. Without having explored the entire castle, they admitted the list was crude and likely lacking, but it would provide them with a starting point. They finished with forty-five minutes to spare on their ride.

Maggie sighed. Her eyelids grew heavy as the midnight hour approached. "I am in some serious need of coffee."

With one final stop for food and fuel, they made the last leg of their journey. Maggie ducked to stare up at the castle on the hill as they approached. With lights blazing from several windows, the castle welcomed them.

Maggie fidgeted in her seat as they made the drive up the hill. Her leg jiggled up and down as she waited for them to slow to a stop outside the entrance. She popped her door open before the car finished rolling.

"Maggie…" Henry called after her.

She used the ornate door knocker as Emma joined her. Piper and Charlie stretched and climbed from the car, still yawning, with Leo following them.

Cate, Jack, Ollie and Lenora climbed from the car behind them.

"Did you get any sleep?" Maggie asked as they joined her.

"Not a wink," Cate answered. "How could anyone sleep with all this excitement?"

"I did," Ollie said.

"Me too," Jack added.

Cate shook her head at him. "I certainly hope not! You were driving!"

"Aye, and you never knew I took a nap, did you, lassie?" he questioned with a grin.

The door to the castle popped open. A wide-eyed William MacClyde studied the group with a broad grin.

"Oh, brought the whole family this time, eh?" he asked with a chuckle. "Well, come in, come in."

They filed into the foyer and Maggie made introductions between William and the new arrivals.

"So," he said, rubbing his hands together, "where do we

start? I've poked around a few places since I got your message, but found nothing."

"Emma and I came up with a list of places to try on the drive, but this will really come down to searching for even the smallest clue. At Cate's, it was a landscape marked with the dragon symbol. At Lenora's, there was an elaborate system built into a crypt," Maggie answered.

"In either case, both were in hidden chambers underground," Emma said. "It could be similar here, or it could be entirely different."

William nodded emphatically. "Well, I'll help in any way I can."

"We've got a lot of ground to cover," Ollie said. "And we may not find this tonight."

William nodded.

"That being said," Ollie continued, "perhaps we should split up. Take the castle in sections, focusing on the spots Maggie and Emma identified and branching out from there."

"Good plan, Ollie," Henry said. "We all have our cell phones, right? Text if you find something. Do not, and I repeat, DO NOT enter any secret passages or chambers alone or without letting the rest of the group know. We know Bryson won't be far behind us. And we also don't want anyone becoming trapped accidentally."

Nods met the statement, and everyone paired off, receiving instructions from Maggie and Emma on where to search. Emma and Leo headed for the library with the secret passage. Charlie and Piper took the ground floor sitting room and library. Cate and Lenora would scour the upstairs hallways, while Jack and Ollie would search in the cave containing the dragon symbol. Maggie and Henry began with the portrait gallery.

"What should I do?" William asked.

"If there are any old papers, books or journals from your

ancestor, Kendrick, search them," Ollie said. "We found most of the clues to the other keys in correspondence or drawings of the plans to house it."

William nodded. "Okay, I have a few spots I can check."

Everyone dispersed, each heading to their location to search for clues. Maggie and Henry ambled down the hall, navigating to the portrait gallery.

"There are two portraits with the dragon symbol," Maggie said. "We'll start with those."

They arrived in the large rectangular room and Maggie headed straight for the portrait of Kendrick MacClyde. She toggled on her flashlight and peered behind the portrait.

Henry pulled the painting away from the wall. "Nothing," he murmured.

Maggie pushed against the wall, hoping a spring-loaded panel popped open. "Nothing. Let's try the other one."

They moved to the portrait of Kendrick's grandson, also marked with the symbol of the dragon. After a careful search, they came up empty there, too.

"Okay, we'll work through these systematically and hope we stumble upon something."

After forty minutes of work, they came up with nothing. Maggie checked her phone, finding no new messages.

"Now where?" she pondered aloud.

"There are probably a bunch of rooms we haven't even seen. Should we just start checking them all?"

Maggie nodded when her cell phone chimed. "Wait!" she called. "It's Cate." Her eyes widened as she read the message aloud. "They found something!"

"Where?" Henry inquired.

"Upstairs, take a right at the first hallway, left at the second."

"Let's go."

Maggie nodded. They hurried from the portrait gallery

and made their way to the foyer, taking the large staircase up a floor and following Cate's instructions.

As they rounded the corner, they spotted Cate, Lenora, Emma, Leo, Piper and Charlie grouped around a painting on the wall.

"What did you find?" Maggie asked.

"This painting," Cate said, pointing at it, "has the symbol."

Maggie studied it, squinting her eyes. A landscape showed rolling hills. Clydescolm Castle sat on top of one.

"Here," Lenora said. She pointed to a corner of the castle.

The symbol of the dragon was etched into a stone. Maggie grinned and bit her lower lip. "There it is."

"We haven't found anything else," Cate said.

"What have you tried?" Maggie asked. "And where is Uncle Ollie and Jack?"

"Reception in the cave is sketchy," Emma answered. "He may not have gotten the text."

"We'll go for him," Charlie said, motioning to encompass both him and Piper.

"Yeah, there's no way you're getting me into any creepy tunnels you find," Piper said.

"Thanks," Maggie said as she traced the edge of the frame and shined her flashlight behind it.

Emma tilted it from the wall. "Well, it's not triggered like Cate's was," she said.

"No." Maggie tried pressing the wall around and under the painting. She glanced up and down the hall.

"How are secret panels usually triggered in castles?" Leo questioned.

"Any number of ways," Henry answered.

"Such as?" Leo asked.

"One of the passages at Dunhaven is triggered by a wall sconce," Cate said.

"One of the Blackmoore passages is pressure-released," Lenora said.

"Another was triggered by a certain stone on the fireplace," Cate added.

"Yes, one of ours is triggered by rotating a stone, and another is hidden in the floor."

"So, basically anything can trigger a hidden passage," Leo said.

"Right," Cate answered.

"The trigger has to be close," Henry said, eyeing the hallway up and down.

"Okay, everyone spread out and search. Walls, paintings, sconces, anything," Maggie said.

They spent several minutes searching for the trigger. Emma pulled on the sconces, but they did not slide down the wall. She stared at them.

"What is it, Emma?" Maggie asked her, noticing her gaze.

"The sconce seems loose," she replied. "I thought sure this would be a trigger." She jiggled it on the wall.

Cate approached. "May I?" she asked, stepping toward the sconce. Emma nodded and released her grip on it.

Cate grabbed it with both hands and twisted. It tilted to the side. A hissing sounded, but nothing happened. Cate frowned at it. She jiggled the sconce again, trying to force it past its current angle. She returned it to its normal position and tried again. The hissing sounded a second time, but no panels slid open.

"Gosh, I really thought that would work," Cate said, as she scrunched her nose at the sconce.

Emma narrowed her eyes at it, then shifted her gaze to the next sconce. Mounted on the opposite side of the dragon-marked painting.

She reached out and grabbed the sconce, sliding it at an

angle toward the other. Another hissing noise sounded, followed by a scraping sound.

"Well, that did something," Maggie said.

"But what?" Emma inquired, as they scanned the immediate area and found nothing new.

Henry's head swiveled and he took a few steps down the hall, scanning the wall. "Nothing down here."

"Something opened," Maggie insisted.

"Well, it's nothing we can see," Leo answered.

"Maybe it's a hidden compartment behind the painting," Emma suggested.

"Maybe!" Maggie exclaimed.

Henry and Leo approached the wall and lifted the painting from its perch. As they pulled it away from its spot, Maggie's shoulders slumped.

"Nothing," she said with a frustrated sigh.

Emma's forehead wrinkled. "Then where…"

"Here!" Lenora's voice called, sounding muffled.

"Lenora?" Maggie glanced around, realizing the woman was missing. "Where are you?"

"In here!" she shouted again. "The bedroom behind the painting!"

Emma crossed to the open bedroom door and entered. The others followed behind her. Lenora stood facing the wall abutting the hallway.

"Here," she said, motioning in front of her.

A hole peeked from behind a large wardrobe. "This must be it!" Maggie exclaimed.

CHAPTER 41

Leo and Henry hurried over to move the massive wooden item away from the wall. With muscles flexed, they hauled the furniture piece away.

A dark hole yawned in the wall. Maggie toggled on her flashlight and shined it in the passage. A narrow corridor snaked past the confines of the room, disappearing around a corner. Maggie glanced at Emma. "You game?"

"I guess," Emma said.

"Someone should wait out here in case we get stuck," Maggie said.

Emma wiggled her eyebrows. "Who wants that short straw? The last time we left someone behind, they were kidnapped."

"Leo and I will stay," Henry said.

"Don't let Leo get kidnapped again," Maggie said. "We'll never hear the end of it."

"We'll be okay," Henry assured her.

"Anyone else venturing in?"

"I'll go," Lenora said.

"Me too," Cate replied.

"All right," Maggie said. "Let's get moving."

With cell phone flashlights lit, the foursome disappeared into the tiny passage. The narrowness of the space required them to march in a line single file.

Maggie led the group to the end where the passage disappeared around a corner. She peeked around the edge, shining her light down the dark corridor.

The passage continued past her flashlight's reach. "Looks like we're walking," she said over her shoulder.

"Can you see the end?" Emma inquired, rising to her toes to glance around Maggie.

"No," Maggie said.

"This is like walking around Noah's Ark," Cate said.

"What?" Maggie questioned, as she inched further down the corridor.

"Noah's Ark at Kennywood. It's like a funhouse-style amusement park ride. I'm not sure it's there anymore. My parents took me as a kid when we visited Pittsburgh once."

"Oh, sounds fun. Another twist up here," Maggie reported.

They turned to their left and continued walking.

"Where are we?" Emma asked.

"Winding around somewhere behind the bedrooms, I guess," Maggie said. "At least there's only one way forward."

"So far," Lenora added.

"If the passage splits, we're not splitting up," Emma warned.

"I'd prefer not to," Cate voiced.

"Me either, especially considering that Bryson fellow will likely not be too pleased with me," Lenora said.

"No, I can't imagine he will be," Emma answered.

"Welcome to the club. I'm pretty sure Henry and I are founding members," Maggie said.

The passage snaked around another corner. They

followed the length of the new corridor. It ended in a set of steep wooden stairs.

"Heading down. Careful, ladies, these stairs look steep!" Maggie warned.

She stepped on the first. It responded with a groan.

"Shouldn't have had those cheese curls at the rest stop," Emma said.

"Very funny, Emma. Just in case, maybe we should go one by one."

Maggie crept down the creaky stairs framed by walls pressing in on each side. She reached the bottom and breathed a sigh of relief. She spun to face the stairs and called up, "Made it!"

A groaning met her ears, indicating the next person descending the stairs. In a few moments, Emma joined her, shining her light around the small space after indicating her safe arrival on the floor below.

Within short order, both Lenora and Cate had made it down the rickety stairs safely.

"And we continue," Emma said, leading the way.

They ambled down another tight corridor. As they rounded the corner, Emma shrieked and stumbled backward, her arms flailing. She bumped into Maggie, who stepped on Lenora's foot and nearly collapsed into Cate.

"Ouch!" Lenora shouted.

"Sorry," Maggie said, "Emma ran into me."

Emma blew a raspberry as she swiped at her face. "Ugh. Why when I go first is there a spiderweb in the stupid hall?"

"That's payback for the trick you pulled on me on our last visit."

Emma wrinkled her nose.

"Let's just keep going. I'll go first," Maggie said.

They continued down the passage until they came to a thick metal door. Maggie studied it. "No keyhole."

"No lock of any kind," Emma added. "And also, no handle."

"There must be a trigger somewhere," Lenora answered, shining her flashlight on the walls nearby.

"Okay, everyone look for anything that might open this door," Maggie instructed.

With flashlights blazing, the women searched around the space.

"Here," Lenora said.

"What is it?" Maggie asked as she joined her.

A piece of the wall is missing," Lenora said, as she squatted to peer inside.

"Is there anything in there?" Emma asked.

"I'm not certain." Lenora squinted into the small opening. With a shake of her head, she reached blindly into the opening.

"There's something cold, metal," she reported. "I've almost got hold of it." She pressed her lips together and scrunched her eyebrows as she struggled with whatever lay behind the wall. "I can't budge it."

"Try twisting it," Emma suggested.

Lenora shook her head. "No, nothing."

"Pull it toward you," Maggie said.

Lenora strained with effort. "Nope."

"Slide it down or up," Cate suggested.

Lenora groaned and gasped out, "It's moving. I slid it down."

Maggie shined her light on the door. "Still closed."

"Maybe it's stuck," Emma said.

"Wait," Lenora answered. "Now I can turn the handle." She twisted her arm, jimmying the unseen object. "I can't turn it anymore."

"Still closed," Maggie reported.

"I'll try moving it again," Lenora said. She reached inside

and grasped hold of the metal handle. "It's sliding again, to the left."

A bead of sweat formed on her brow as she struggled to slide the ancient object away from the door. With the door still closed, she fiddled with it again. Finally, the door popped open.

"It's open!" Maggie said.

"I had to pull the handle toward me after all that," Lenora reported as she stood and dusted her hands off.

Maggie swung the door open and shined her light inside. A crumbling stone stairway led down another level.

"Ugh," Maggie groaned. "I thought this would be the chamber."

She stepped onto the first step. It gave way under her weight, and she plunged downward. Emma grabbed hold of her, dragging her back up to safety.

Maggie blew out a long breath. "Thanks. First step's a doozy."

"I'm not sure we should continue," Emma said.

"We have to," Maggie answered. "Maybe it was just the first step. I'll test the next one."

Maggie firmed her resolve, pushing her shoulders back and swallowing hard. She grasped the sides of the doorway and reached out with her foot for the second stair. She stepped on it, carefully shifting her weight onto it little by little. It held.

"So far, so good," Maggie said as she teetered on the second step. "I'm going to continue."

She carefully tested each step with one foot before placing all her weight on it. The remaining stones held. "I made it!" she shouted up.

"Okay, I'm coming down," Emma yelled.

A light bobbled at the top of the stairs before continuing

down. Emma reached hers moments later. Lenora and Cate followed, both reaching the ground safely.

"This is getting tedious," Maggie said, as they continued along in the underground chamber. "Couldn't they just have put it two halls ago?"

"I can't wait to find out what kind of security they've got on the box after all this," Emma said.

"There's the end!" Maggie exclaimed as her light hit a door. "Another door." She heaved a sigh.

"Wonder if this one needs a key, a code or a long list of intricate instructions with a hidden metal lever," Emma asked.

"I hope it's not a key," Cate said. "We may never find it."

"Perhaps we can pick the lock?" Lenora suggested.

"Did you study that in boarding school, too?" Maggie asked.

"I may have," she answered.

They approached the door. "There's a handle at least."

"And a code. Six letters," Maggie reported, fingering the cylinders under the handle.

"Great," Emma grumbled. "We'll never get this."

"We can figure it out," Cate said. "Let's think of some words that would be used. What was his father's name? Or his son's?"

"Or daughter's," Lenora added.

"Right."

"Uh," Maggie murmured, as she swiped through her pictures on her phone. "Let me see if I can read the names under the portraits."

She swiped back and forth for a moment before she said, "Okay, Kendrick's son was Andrew."

Emma counted on her fingers as she spelled. "That's six, let's try it." She spun the cylinders until they spelled "ANDREW" then pulled on the handle. "Nope."

"His father was Donald."

Emma keyed in the name and tried the handle again. "Not right, either."

"Okay, the other portrait with the dragon symbol belonged to Gordon."

"Gordon," Emma said as she spun the letter-filled wheels to spell it. She groaned as the door did not budge.

"I don't see any other names that are six letters," Maggie said.

"Though there could be other names. His wife, a daughter..."

"We're going to have to go back up and get more names," Maggie said with a sigh.

"Wait, let me try something," Lenora said.

Maggie motioned for her to try.

Lenora stepped forward and toggled in an answer. The door swung open on creaky hinges.

Maggie's eyes widened. "You did it! What was the answer?"

"Dragon," she said.

"Dragon? Seriously?" Maggie asked.

"Not very creative," Emma said.

"Apparently, Lord MacClyde was less clever than the others," Lenora said.

They entered the large underground chamber beyond the door. A few items littered the space.

"Looks like he stored a few things down here," Maggie said, as she swung her flashlight beam around.

A few paintings were covered with a cloth, and several trunks sat on the floor.

"Is it in one of these trunks?" Emma asked. "I don't see a pedestal with a box like the others."

Maggie pulled one trunk open and rummaged through it.

A few heavy golden candlesticks and a small box of jewelry lay inside. "Not in here," she reported.

They searched through the other chests but found no sign of the key.

"All right, everyone spread out and keep your eyes peeled. We must be overlooking something."

Cate scanned the walls with her flashlight. "What's this?" she asked, as she focused her light on a brass lever.

Maggie rose to stand and approached it, narrowing her eyes at it. "Hmm," she murmured.

Emma spun to face them. "Whatever it is, don't…" she began, when Maggie wrapped her fingers around it and shoved it upward toward the ceiling.

A clanking sounded followed by a bang. The metal door to the corridor slammed shut. A crash sounded and a whirring began. The ceiling began a slow creep toward the floor.

CHAPTER 42

"...Touch it," Emma finished her previous statement with a groan.

"Sorry!" Maggie said. "I thought it would open a secret panel with the key!"

"Well, instead, it's entombed us inside here *and* set off a trap!"

"I know!" Maggie shouted.

"We must find a way to stop it," Lenora said.

"Try moving the lever again," Cate shouted over the groaning noise of the ceiling.

Maggie nodded and slid the lever down. It did nothing to stop the progress of the encroaching ceiling.

"Nope, not that," Maggie said. She slid the handle up and down several times.

"There must be a mechanism to stop this," Lenora said. "Quickly, search for it."

They spread out in the boxy room as the ceiling crept ever closer toward them.

"You've got to be kidding," Emma said, as she swished the

flashlight around in a frantic search. "I can't believe you set off a trap. Again."

"How was I supposed to know? It's not like we're in a tomb. I had no idea there would be one in a hidden room under a castle!"

"So much for the least clever member of the Brotherhood," Emma said.

"Look!" Lenora shouted, her flashlight beam aimed at the ceiling.

All eyes turned to follow her light. A box was mounted to the ceiling.

"Maybe it wasn't a trap!" Maggie exclaimed. "Maybe it was a trigger to lower the key to us!"

"How do you open it?" Emma inquired.

Maggie reached for the box, still above her head, but creeping ever closer. Her fingers searched for a way to open it. She felt a groove in the wood and hooked her finger in it. With a shove, the side of the box slid open. The key lay inside.

"The key!" Cate said.

Maggie retrieved it with a grin. "We did it!"

A cheer went up within the chamber.

After a moment, Emma said, "I hate to be a party pooper, but the ceiling hasn't stopped trying to crush us."

"And the door hasn't opened either," Cate added.

"Uh," Maggie said, as she shoved the key into her pocket. "Okay, keep looking for something to shut it off and get us out of here."

They continued their search, triumphant but trapped.

"Here!" Emma said. "Another lever, hanging from the ceiling!"

"Use it!" Maggie said.

Emma grabbed hold of the brass lever and tried to push it. "It's stuck!" she yelled.

Lenora, closest to her, pocketed her cell phone, and grabbed hold of the lever with both hands. Her feet slipped on the dirt floor as she and Emma struggled to push the bar. Cate joined them and Maggie hurried to help.

The four of them tugged at the rusted mechanism, trying to break it free. With the added force, the lever swung loose, rust showering down on them and sending them sprawling as it swung from one side to the other.

The ceiling continued marching toward them for a moment, before it shuddered and bounced to a stop. With a screeching, it began to retreat upward.

"Ugh," Maggie said, letting her head fall to the ground below her. "Thank goodness."

"Yeah, now we're only just trapped, instead of almost flattened," Emma said. She pointed her flashlight at the still-closed door.

"One thing at a time," Maggie said, climbing to her feet.

"Don't touch anything else until we've determined if it's safe," Emma said.

"How was I supposed to know it would do that?" Maggie asked.

"Just spread out and let's find a way out of here."

Maggie and the others returned to scanning the space for any sign of a way out. After several more minutes of searching, Maggie found another set of six alphabet-coded dials. "I got something!" she shouted from near the door.

"What is it? Don't touch it!" Emma warned.

"It's another set of dials," Maggie said. "And I'm touching it."

She spun the dials around, setting the letters. As she finished the last letter, she glanced at the door. Her brow furrowed as it remained shut. She jiggled it, trying to shove it open.

"What the heck?" she exclaimed, as she pounded against the door.

"What did you put in?" Cate inquired.

"Dragon," Maggie said.

"So, entry code isn't the same as exit code."

Maggie spun the dials again. "What are you trying now?"

"Dragon backward," Maggie said.

"Seriously?" Emma asked, when the so-called word failed to produce anything.

"It was worth a shot," Maggie said with a shrug.

They tried the names of both Kendrick's father, son and progeny marked with the dragon symbol. None of them worked.

"Great," Maggie said, scuffing her foot against the ground.

"Someone will come looking for us eventually," Emma said, as she slumped to sitting. "And then we can tell them how to open the door from the other side."

Maggie crossed her arms over her chest. "But how long will that take?"

"I don't know," Emma said.

"Well, I don't want to wait!" Maggie said. "The last time we waited, our friends were kidnapped and weren't able to rescue us."

"Unless you can think of any other words to try or find another exit, we're stuck."

Cate's brow furrowed at the comment. "Maybe that's it!" Cate exclaimed.

"What?" Maggie inquired.

Cate reached to the dials and spun them. The door popped open as she spun the last dial into place. "Ha!" she exclaimed.

Emma leapt to her feet and Maggie clapped her hands. "You did it!"

Lenora ducked through the door. "I'll celebrate out here in case it closes again."

"Good point," Maggie said, as they all hurried through the door. "Let's get out of here."

They continued down the hall and Emma asked, "So, what was the word?"

"Exitus."

"Exitus? Like a made-up word?" Maggie said.

"No, the Latin word for exit," Cate said. "They often used Latin for things like this. Just a lucky guess after Emma said exit."

"Good thing," Maggie said. "I had no desire to be the damsel-in-distress waiting for a rescue."

Cate chuckled at her comment as they reached the first set of stairs. They proceeded up one at a time and continued after everyone reached the top. After snaking through the corridors and climbing another set of stairs, they spotted light streaming from the bedroom.

Maggie sped up to close the distance, bursting from the passage and into the bedroom.

"Henry, we found it–" Her voice trailed off as she spun in a circle, searching the room. Her lips formed a frown as the others emerged from the passage.

"No one's here," Maggie said.

"I have a bad feeling about this," Emma said, as Maggie's phone chimed.

"It's from Uncle Ollie to the group." The others' phones chimed as Maggie swiped hers open. "Found something, meet us in the cave. Ah, that explains it. Everyone must have gone down there!"

Emma narrowed her eyes at the message. "Really? Henry would have left with us still in the passage?"

"Well, he knows how to open it and where we are, so maybe," Maggie said with a shrug. "Either way, we need to head down there with the last key and find out if it will open anything."

"All right," Emma said, as Maggie texted to tell them they were on their way.

"Is William there?" Cate asked as they left the room.

"He doesn't say," Maggie answered.

"He should be there when we use the keys. I'll see if I can find him," Cate replied.

"I'll go with you, cousin," Lenora said.

"Be careful," Maggie said as they parted ways.

"You too," Cate answered.

Maggie and Emma continued down the hall. "Should we use the library entrance?"

"It's probably easier," Emma said. "It's hard to find that cave entrance."

Maggie nodded. They threaded through the halls and to the small library. Maggie triggered the bookcase, and it swung open. They entered the passage and descended the stairs. Voice floated up as they neared the bottom.

"–don't have the fourth key!" Ollie shouted.

"You'd better hope the lovely Ms. Edwards finds it soon for your sakes," a British voice growled.

Maggie and Emma slowed as they neared the end of the passage. They retreated back a few steps as the situation became clear.

Maggie stumbled as she tried to inch up the stairs. Her shoe scuffed against the stone and a scraping noise echoed throughout the chamber.

"Ah, Ms. Edwards. Leaving so soon?" Bryson asked, as he leveled his weapon in their direction.

"Run, Emma!" Maggie shouted, stepping in front of her.

"I wouldn't if I were you, Ms. Fielding," Bryson warned. "The bullet can go through you both."

Emma froze one step above Maggie. She turned and

raised her hands. Maggie surveyed the scene. Her team, outside of Ollie, sat against one of the stone walls, their hands bound behind their backs.

Maggie pursed her lips as she stepped into the cavern, hands held high. "And do you have the key?" Bryson inquired.

Maggie nodded and reached toward her pocket.

"Uh-uh, keep your hands up." He waved the gun at her to signal her arms remain up. Bryson approached her, standing inches from her as he slid his hand into her pocket.

She glared at him. He freed the key from the fabric compartment.

"Excellent work, Ms. Edwards. It really is a shame you and I aren't on the same side. We could make a great team."

Maggie shook her head in silent response as she grimaced at him.

"Oh, please," Emma murmured. "You've got to be kidding me."

"Marshall, tie up Ms. Fielding. And duct tape her mouth."

"Hey!" Emma shouted, as one of Bryson's four goons holstered his weapon and roughly grasped Emma's arm.

"Leave her alone."

"You're in no position to make demands, Ms. Edwards." Bryson delivered the key to Ollie. "Get to work, doctor. I have a treasure to collect."

Ollie grasped the key and studied it.

"Stop stalling!" Bryson said, leveling his weapon at Maggie's head.

"I'm not stalling, but I'm certain this will take some finesse. I could use Maggie's help."

"I'll bet," Bryson said.

"There are four keys," Maggie said. "That's a lot for one person to handle."

"Marshall, get over there and help."

THE LOST TREASURE OF DRAKON

The man started across the room, when Maggie said, "Sure, if he's cool risking his life."

The man hesitated. "She's bluffing," Bryson said.

"I'm not," Maggie retorted.

"Ms. Edwards, don't make me duct tape that lovely mouth shut."

Maggie shrugged as Marshall took another step.

"We literally just got stuck in a room with a collapsing ceiling and nearly didn't make it out alive, but yeah, go ahead, Marshall."

Marshall's eyes grew wide, and he glanced between Maggie and Bryson.

"Unbelievable," Bryson hissed. "Fine, get over there with your uncle. But I swear, if you try anything, I'll kill your friends, starting with the colorful one and ending with Taylor."

Maggie held her hands up to indicate defeat as she crossed to Ollie and knelt down near the carving.

"I've removed most of the dirt," Ollie said. "What I don't know is the order the keys go in."

"Have you tried any?" Maggie inquired.

"Not yet." Ollie studied each key. "It appears these decorative ends match the carving."

"Oh, yeah!" Maggie agreed. "This one looks like the dragon's head." She frowned as she lined it up. "But it's sideways. The prongs don't line up with any of the center holes or runes."

Ollie spun the key and inserted it. "My hypothesis is that they will line up once we turn them."

Maggie nodded. They sorted through the remaining three keys and placed the other dragon's head key. The final two formed the Celtic knot.

"Okay," Ollie said, blowing out a long breath. "Now, is there any order to turning them?"

"Left to right?" Maggie suggested. She twisted the first key. It turned to form the head of the first dragon. A loud clanking sounded.

"So far, so good," she said as she moved to the next key. She twisted it but it did not budge. "Nope."

"Try the opposite way," Ollie suggested.

Maggie nodded and twisted to the left. "Nope. How about the other dragon's head?"

Ollie twisted the key to form the dragon's head. "Yep, that's it," he said, as another click echoed in the cave.

"Now which one?" Maggie asked, as she studied the last two keys. With a shrug, Maggie reached for the one she'd already tried and turned it. It spun easily.

"One to go!" she exclaimed. "You do the honors."

Ollie spun the final key. A loud bang resounded, and a scraping noise reverberated.

"Over here!" one of Bryson's men yelled.

Maggie whipped her head in his direction. A hole gaped in the side of the cave.

"That must be it! The treasure must be in there!" Maggie said, climbing to her feet.

"Easy, Ms. Edwards," Bryson cautioned. "Marshall, check it out."

"Uh," the man said, his eyes darting around the space searching for a reason to disobey the order.

"What's the problem? Go!"

"What if there's a trap or something? Like she said." He waved a finger at Maggie.

"She was bluffing."

"I wasn't," Maggie assured him.

"We should proceed with caution," Ollie said. "We do not know if there are any traps or not."

Bryson sighed and shook his head. "Fine. The illustrious Ms. Edwards and her crafty uncle can go in first."

"Thank you," Maggie said with a smile. "We are the ones who did the work for it, after all."

"Don't be too giddy. I'll be right behind you."

"We shouldn't–" Ollie began.

"Pipe down, professor, and get moving," Bryson said.

Ollie sighed and proceeded over to the hole. "Flashlight?" Ollie asked of Bryson's men.

Two flashlights were passed over to Ollie and Maggie. Ollie flicked his on and studied the opening. He shined the light inside.

Maggie toggled on her flashlight and joined him.

"What?!" she gasped.

Ollie's brow furrowed as he stepped inside the chamber.

"Well?" Bryson asked as Maggie followed.

"There's nothing here!" Maggie shouted. "It's empty!"

"What?!" Bryson shouted, rushing into the chamber.

"No, wait!" Ollie called.

As Bryson hurried into the chamber, the opening slid shut. The chamber plunged into darkness but for the light of their flashlights.

CHAPTER 43

"What happened? And why is there no treasure?" Bryson asked.

"I'm not certain, but I believe there's a pressure plate near the entrance," Ollie said. "I felt a shift when Maggie stepped inside. The weight of three people must have proved too much."

"Marshall!" Bryson shouted through the cave. "Can you hear me?"

"I hear you! What happened?"

"Try to open the door with the keys!"

"It's stuck!" Marshall answered a moment later. "We can't move it."

"Bloody wonderful! How do we get out?"

"I'm not certain," Ollie admitted. "And as far as the treasure goes…" He shrugged as he glanced around the empty chamber. "Perhaps it was raided years ago. Or maybe it was moved."

"How could it have been moved when the keys were still locked up?"

"Perhaps the four members of the Brotherhood got together and moved it."

"Or perhaps you're lying, professor."

Ollie thrust his hands out at his sides. "Do you see the treasure?"

"I hate to say this, but I agree with Bryson. There has to be something we're missing," Maggie said.

"Well, either way, we need to find a way out of here, since it does not appear that your men can help us."

Bryson slid his gun into his waistband and pulled a flashlight from it. He toggled it on and joined the search. Uncle Ollie squatted down near the back of the chamber.

"What is it?" Maggie inquired as she joined him.

"A small box," Ollie answered. The hinges squealed in protest as he flipped open the lid.

"What did you find?" Bryson asked, approaching and leaning over them.

A folded paper sat inside the metal box. Ollie unfolded it and Maggie aimed her flashlight at it. In neat and precise handwriting, eight lines were written in black ink.

You've come this far
But there's more to go
To find the treasure
There are more tests to undergo

Search the back of the chamber
To find what you seek
Be mindful of where you step
To be safe, your steps should be meek

"What does that mean?" Maggie asked.

Ollie turned it over. "It's signed by Gordon MacClyde," Ollie said, as he spotted the signature on the back.

"Gordon MacClyde? That's the name on the other portrait that had the dragon symbol," Maggie said.

"It appears he's left us some clues on how to proceed. He must have been the one who added the lights to the cave."

"But what does it mean?" Maggie asked.

"It says to search the back of the chamber," Bryson said. "So, let's get to it."

"You could help, you know," Maggie said, as she stood and made her way to the back wall.

"I prefer to leave the hard work to the experts," Bryson said.

Maggie shook her head as she swung her beam over the wall.

"Here," Ollie said, as he focused his beam on a brass handle.

"Pull it," Bryson said.

"Will you stop ordering us around?" Maggie said. "What do you want to do, Uncle Ollie?"

"This time, I agree with Bryson," Ollie said with a chuckle. "I'll pull it." He grasped the handle and tugged. The handled unhinged toward them and a whooshing sound filled the chamber.

"There!" Bryson said, training his beam on a new opening leading them further into the cave system.

Maggie shined her light inside and started to take a step in.

"Wait!" Ollie shouted.

Maggie stopped and spun to face him. "What is it?"

"This clue. Your steps should be meek. Be mindful of where you step," Ollie said, motioning toward the paper he pulled from his pocket.

"What does that mean?" Maggie asked.

THE LOST TREASURE OF DRAKON

"I'm not certain," Ollie answered. He shined his light into the chamber and studied the floor. "No obvious markings." He flipped the light up to the ceiling. "Nothing above."

His face scrunched into a pensive expression as he gazed at the floor.

"We have to try something," Maggie said.

"I agree," Bryson said. "And I believe Ms. Edwards is the best person to try." He shoved her forward into the chamber. She teetered on her feet before stumbling forward several steps into the chamber. The ground below her broke away. Maggie shrieked as she began falling through the jagged hole in the stone floor.

Bryson dove forward and grasped her. She dangled from his grip and Ollie knelt down at the edge of the hole. He grasped Maggie's hand and tugged. Together, the two men hauled her up onto the solid ground.

Maggie gulped in air. "Are you okay, Maggie?" Ollie asked.

"Yeah," she said with a nod. "Yeah, just a few scrapes." Her eyes flicked to Bryson. "Thanks."

"Oh, I wasn't about to let you die, Ms. Edwards. I still need you. Now, if you've recovered, let's press on, shall we?"

Maggie groaned as she climbed to her feet. "Charming," she mumbled, dusting off her clothes. "Well, I guess we know the meaning of 'step carefully.'"

"Yes," Ollie said as he studied the craggy hole. He shined his light down it. It revealed a deep pit.

"But how can we step meekly? Tiptoe?"

Ollie shook his head, pulling his mouth back into a half-frown. "No, but–" He glanced around behind him. "This part held. And it's near the wall. I believe 'meekly' means to hug the wall."

Ollie crept to the wall and used it to circle the chamber,

ending on the opposite side where another metal box and lever awaited them.

"Good thinking, Uncle Ollie!" Maggie exclaimed.

"Careful," Ollie warned. "One at a time."

Maggie nodded and inched along the wall toward Ollie. Bryson followed as Ollie opened the box. Another piece of paper lay inside. Ollie unfurled it and read aloud.

> *You've passed the first test*
> *Congratulations to you*
> *You've proven your worth*
> *And are one step closer to your due*
>
> *Move to the next chamber*
> *By pulling the lever*
> *To defeat my next trap*
> *You must be clever*
>
> *In the correct order*
> *Press the tiles*
> *Think of the Brotherhood of the Dragon*
> *To complete the next two trials*

"Wow," Maggie murmured. "This guy was a real prankster with the rhymes, huh?"

"And not much more information," Ollie said.

With a shrug, Ollie pulled the lever and opened the next chamber. They wandered into the dark room, careful to keep to the edges in the event this chamber had a similar trap as the last one.

Ollie crept to the back wall. "Wow," he breathed.

Maggie joined him, sweeping her beam over the wall. Her eyebrows shot skyward as she studied the hundreds of tiles making up the back wall. Each of them contained a carving. Some were of dragons, others of partial Celtic knots.

"There are hundreds of these!" Maggie said. "And they all look alike!"

"How will we know which ones to press?" Bryson asked as he reached them.

"They are similar," Ollie said, as he studied them closely, "but they all have slight variations."

"I see it!" Maggie exclaimed. "Some are slightly different than the others."

"Yes. I'm betting we need to press the tiles that represent the symbol of the Brotherhood of the Dragon." Ollie shook his head. "These are so very similar. I'm uncertain as to which are exact matches."

"Wait, I have this," Maggie said, as she pulled her phone from her pocket. She opened her photo gallery and swiped to her image of the dragon symbol. Ollie studied it then returned to the symbols.

"We should work left to right, top to bottom," he said.

Maggie nodded in agreement. They studied each symbol, selecting the ones that matched a piece of the Brotherhood dragon. The painstaking work went slowly.

Working from the tiles previously selected, Maggie pocketed her phone and concentrated on the stones.

"How many do you think there are?" she questioned, as they scanned the carvings.

"I'm not sure," Ollie answered. "But I'm betting it's a multiple of four. It takes four tiles to complete each dragon."

"Just like the four members of the Brotherhood," Maggie answered. "So maybe there are four sets?"

"Possibly," Ollie answered. "So far, we've found two complete sets and one tile on the third."

Maggie huffed as she snaked her flashlight along another row. "Here," she said, pressing a tile.

"No!" Ollie shouted a second too late.

"Shoot!" Maggie cursed. A clanking sounded. She winced. "I wonder how many incorrect answers we get before something goes haywire?"

"Let's try not to find out," Ollie said.

Maggie nodded and wiped a bead of sweat from her brow. They continued through the remaining tiles, pushing those that matched. As they pushed the final tile, Maggie shined her flashlight around, expecting a door to open.

She scratched her head. "What went wrong?" She swept her beam over the wall and counted. "We have sixteen tiles pressed."

"We should have seventeen. You pressed an incorrect one."

"Oh, right," Maggie said with a groan.

They studied the tiles again until they found the missing symbol. Ollie pressed it and a door next to him slid open.

"Yay!" Maggie exclaimed as they approached the door.

"Oh, no!" Ollie gasped, as he hurried through the opening.

"What?" Maggie questioned.

A wall faced them with cylinders containing letters. Next to it, a recess in the stone held an hourglass. Grains of sand sped through the opening into the bottom chamber.

Ollie swallowed hard. "I think this trial is timed."

"Oh, great!" Maggie hissed, studying the cylinders. "I'm terrible at these."

"Okay, let's try to think through this. This has nine letters."

"Nine?!" Maggie exclaimed, pressing her palm against her forehead. "Ummm."

The grains continued to tumble through the hourglass which was already half empty.

"What are some nine-letter words?" Maggie said, waving her hands to fan her face.

"Wait, the clue said we needed to think about the Brotherhood of the Dragon for both of the trials," Ollie said.

"Yes!" Maggie's eyes grew wide. "Dragon is too short."

"Brotherhood is too long."

"Names?" Maggie inquired.

She swiped through her phone again. "The brotherhood was made up of Robert Blackmoore. Neither of those work. Randolph MacKenzie. Oh, try MacKenzie."

Ollie spun the cylinders to spell "MacKenzie." He shook his head when nothing happened.

"Uh, Kendrick MacClyde. No. Frederick MacKenna. Frederick! Try Frederick!"

Ollie nodded and adjusted the brass cylinders. A hissing noise sounded, and the wall retracted.

Behind the stone, another wall stood with another set of cylinders. A new hourglass counted down their time, this one moving faster than the last.

"Eight letters," Ollie reported.

"Randolph or Kendrick."

Ollie input Kendrick first. It did not work. As the grains dwindled, he quickly adjusted it to read "Randolph."

With a hiss, the wall slid away, revealing the next challenge. They stepped forward to the new wall.

"Six letters - Robert," Maggie said. With shaky hands, she input the name, as the hourglass emptied at lightning speed.

She breathed a sigh of relief as the door slid away.

"This must be Kendrick," she said, as she hurried to the cylinders embedded in the wall. "There's eight." She keyed it in as the minimally filled hourglass emptied.

She breathed a sigh of relief as the doorway slid open.

"WHAT?!" she shouted, as they were met with another set of six cylinders and an already almost-empty hourglass. "There wasn't a fifth member."

Her eyes widened as she spun to face Ollie. Ollie shook his head. "We're not going to make it," he said.

"We have to. I don't want to find out what happens if we don't. Who else was in the Brotherhood? Blackmoore is too long, MacKenna is too long, MacKenzie, MacClyde. Ummm." Maggie bit her lower lip. Ollie pulled the clue from his pocket and studied it. He turned the paper over and stared at it.

"Nothing outside of what we already read, and the signature."

The grains dwindled, with only a handful left.

"Wait!" Maggie shouted. "That's it! Gordon! He's the last member!"

She spun the cylinders as quickly as possible. As the final few grains fell to the bottom chamber, Maggie reached the "n." She held her breath as she spun to the last letter. The final grain of sand fell, before a hissing sounded and the door released.

Maggie collapsed against the wall with a sigh of relief. She squeezed her eyes shut, thanking a higher power for the breakthrough.

"Oh, Maggie!" Ollie said, his voice filled with awe.

"What? What is it?" Maggie gasped, her eyes shooting open as her heart skipped a beat, assuming another trial awaited them.

She shone her flashlight into the open space. Objects glittered under the beam.

"Oh," she murmured, awestruck. The corners of her mouth turned up into a slight grin. "Wow."

Maggie swept her flashlight beam across the piled objects, some in chests, some loose. Gold coins glittered in the bright light. Gems sparkled from ostentatious jewelry pieces. A massive golden dragon stood prominently in the center of the space.

"Drakon's treasure," Maggie said in an excited squeal, "we found it!"

She squeezed Ollie's forearm as she grinned at him.

"So you have, Ms. Edwards," Bryson said. "And now it's mine for the taking."

CHAPTER 44

Maggie turned to find a weapon leveled at her. Her expression soured as she stared down the barrel of his gun.

"Couldn't even give us a minute to celebrate, could you?" she snapped.

"I don't see the point," he replied. "It's not yours."

"It's not yours either."

"Ah, but soon enough it will be," Bryson said as he shooed her away from the entrance and back into the corridor.

Ollie bent over a metal box. "What are you doing, Professor?"

"There's another note," he reported. He unfolded the paper and read it aloud.

> *You've reached the end*
> *And solved all the clues*
> *You've passed all my trials*
> *And did not lose*
>
> *The way back is now open*

You'll find no restraint
You can now leave
Without a complaint

"So, we can get out?!" Maggie said.

"That seems to be the case," Ollie answered with a nod.

"Excellent," Bryson said. "That will save me the trouble of dragging your bodies back through all the chambers."

"Oh, like you'd do it," Maggie snarked. "You'd just get one of your goons to instead."

"Quiet, Ms. Edwards," Bryson said, as he herded them out of the treasure chamber. "I will still kill you here if I am so inclined."

Maggie rolled her eyes, but began to march back down the passageway and into the previous chamber. Her mind darted in a thousand directions as she attempted to come up with a solution to their imminent demise.

"You know," she said as they arrived in the chamber filled with tiles, "you had a point before."

"Oh?" Bryson inquired. "Not that I care, but I suppose that won't stop you from voicing it."

"We do make a good team. This is, what, the second treasure we've found together?"

An amused expression darted across Bryson's face. He raised his eyebrows at her. "What an interesting theory."

"Well, it was your theory, not mine," Maggie said, offering him a coy half-smile. "Maybe I'm wasting my time with Henry." She side-eyed Bryson, letting her eyes travel up and down his body.

Bryson arched an eyebrow at her. "How amusing. Do you really expect me to fall for this?"

"Fall for what?" Maggie asked, playing innocent.

"Flattery will get you nowhere, Ms. Edwards," Bryson said, as they entered the first chamber.

"And neither will that gun," Henry answered.

Bryson's amused expression turned serious as a half dozen weapons were aimed at him. Outside the first chamber, his men, bound and gagged, sat propped against the wall. Maggie noted the appearance of Tarik, standing next to Henry.

"Lower your weapon, Bryson," Henry said.

"I don't think so," he said, grasping hold of Maggie and tugging her backward.

Maggie clutched his arm around her throat.

"Now, lower your weapons, or the lovely Ms. Edwards will never make it out of this chamber alive."

"Let her go, Bryson," Henry growled.

"Not a chance."

Henry pointed his gun upward and raised both hands as he slowly lowered himself to the ground and set his weapon down. The remaining members of the group continued to point their weapons at Bryson.

"Okay," Henry said. "Let her go and take me as your hostage."

"Mmm, I think not, Taylor. You're far less pretty. And when I said lower your weapons, I meant everyone, including your Egyptian friend. A little far from home, aren't we?"

The others relinquished their weapons, laying them on the ground. "Excellent," Bryson said, as he kept a firm hold of Maggie. He swung her around as he waved everyone to one side of the chamber, clearing a path for him to back toward the opening.

"And now, Ms. Edwards and I will bid you adieu."

Maggie stumbled as Bryson dragged her backward. "Remember what I said about you and me joining forces?" she choked out.

"Yes," Bryson answered.

"I changed my mind," Maggie spat. She slid her chin down and bit down hard on his arm. Bryson howled in pain.

A gunshot blasted within the chamber, deafening those around them. The force against her throat went slack, and Maggie felt herself begin to fall. She collapsed to the ground as blood splattered onto the dirt below.

"Maggie!" Henry cried, racing toward her. She fell in a heap onto the dirt.

Maggie glanced down at her body, expecting to find a bullet hole. She spotted the spattering of blood in the dirt.

"I'm okay," she murmured. She glanced up at Bryson, who hurried from the chamber, clutching his arm.

Maggie spun to glance behind her, finding Lenora with her weapon still raised. Tarik scooped his gun off the ground and pursued the fleeing Bryson with Lenora, as Henry scooped Maggie into his arms.

"Are you sure?"

Maggie nodded. "Yeah," she said, as she sat back from him. "I'm fine. How did you–"

"I called Tarik at the first sign of trouble. He showed up just in the nick of time. When Cate and Lenora couldn't find William, they started to worry something had happened. With Tarik's help, they managed to overtake Bryson's men and free us."

"Lucky break," Maggie said, climbing to her feet.

Tarik and Lenora returned to the chamber a few moments later.

"He's gone," Tarik reported.

"Figures," Henry said.

William MacClyde approached them. "Are you alright?" he questioned, his eyes wide.

Maggie smiled at him. "Yeah, I'm fine."

"I'm so sorry about this," he said. "I suppose it'll be

curtains for Clydescolm Castle once word gets out that someone was held at gunpoint here."

"Not necessarily," Maggie said. She smiled at him again. "There's something you should see."

* * *

Maggie walked out of the cave and into the cool Scottish air. A storm was blowing in from the west. Ominous black clouds filled the sky as they pushed up the coast. Emma, Ollie, and William were busy assessing the fortune they'd just found.

With the amount of riches in the chamber, Clydescolm Castle would be maintained by the MacClydes for generations to come. Cate relinquished her share, stating her estate to be healthy and not in need of the funds it would bring. Lenora offered a similar sentiment before ambling from the chamber.

Piper and Charlie wandered around the cave's exterior in search of a particular item.

"Here it is," Charlie shouted. Piper sauntered over and glanced at it then fired off a text to Leo.

Moments later, bagpipes filled the air. "Hidden speaker, huh?" Maggie asked.

"That it is, chicky," Charlie said.

"Turns out the lights aren't the only thing that handle controls. When Gordon MacClyde added the lights, he also added a mechanism to play bagpipes over a set of speakers. Thus, creating fodder for the legend of the Phantom Bagpiper," Piper explained.

"He was a clever man," Maggie said. "Almost too clever."

"At least you outsmarted him, boss lady. I'm glad."

"Aww, thanks, Piper," Maggie said, with a genuine grin.

Piper nodded. "I don't want to have to find another job. My hours are sweet."

Maggie shook her head at the girl. "Have you seen Lenora? I haven't seen her since we showed everyone the treasure."

Piper pointed toward the cliff. Lenora stood on the edge, her arms wrapped around her midriff as she stared out at the turbulent water. Her dark hair blew in the wind.

Maggie shoved her hands in her pockets and climbed up toward her. "Hey, thanks for the save," she said.

Lenora offered a fleeting smile. "You seemed capable of handling the situation."

Maggie shrugged as she turned her gaze to the water. "A bullet never hurts."

"Glad I could help."

They stood for a few moments in silence, before Maggie turned toward the woman. "You can really talk to the dead, can't you?"

Lenora shot her a sideways glance. She began to shake her head when Maggie said, "Come on."

Lenora shut her eyes a moment, before opening them and staring out over the choppy water. "I don't advertise it. It generally doesn't go over very well. Though I suppose the entire world will know now."

Maggie offered her a tight-lipped smile. She drew her finger and thumb across her lips, turned an invisible lock and tossed away an imaginary key.

"Your secret's safe with me," Maggie assured her.

Lenora's lips curled at the corners. "Thank you. But how did you know?"

"Ah, a few things. First, your focus is sometimes odd. You stare at blank places before you respond to people in the room. And when you said talking to the dead didn't work that way. And then in the tomb, when you figured out what to do with the unicorn. I pieced it together and figured out that you could speak with the dead. That's who you're always looking at, a ghost."

Lenora offered her a slight chuckle as she bit her lower lip.

"So, what are you going to do now?"

"I suppose I'll head back to Blackmoore. Or maybe to Dunhaven to visit Cate. We'll see."

"Well, if you're ever in Rosemont, look me up. I'll give you the grand tour!"

Lenora smiled at her and she lifted her eyebrows and shook her head. "What?" Maggie asked.

"My great-great-great-grandmother was right. She told me I'd find acceptance in the oddest of places. And I certainly never expected it to be with you, Maggie Edwards."

"She was right," Maggie answered. "You saved my life, so that makes us BFFs."

"I wouldn't go that far – but friends, yes."

"Okay," Maggie said with a nod.

Henry and Tarik wandered up the hill toward the two women.

"Well, Maggie Edwards does it again," Henry said.

Maggie struck a pose before she wrapped an arm around Tarik's waist. "Hey, stranger, great to see you!"

"It's good to be here. But I missed most of the fun."

"Will we get to see you much before you head back to Egypt?"

Tarik nodded. "Yes. I am not going back to Egypt."

"Going to take a vacation in the Scottish countryside?" Maggie asked.

"No," Tarik answered. "I'm going to go to Rosemont with you when you return."

Maggie's eyebrows shot up. "Really?"

"It seems you cannot stay out of trouble, Maggie. You may need my help again."

"I'm sure we will," Maggie said.

"With Maggie, you can bet your bottom dollar trouble is only a heartbeat away."

Maggie nodded. "I'm sure I'll stumble onto another adventure soon enough," she said with a wink.

The End

Look for Book 4 coming in 2023! Until then, check out my other adventure series, Clif & Ri on the Sea. Book 1, *Rise of a Pirate*, is filled with swashbuckling adventure!

A NOTE FROM THE AUTHOR

Dear Reader,

If you'd like to stay up to date with all my news, be the first to find out about new releases first, sales and get free offers, join the Nellie H. Steele's Mystery Readers' Group! Or sign up for my newsletter now!

All the best, Nellie

OTHER SERIES BY NELLIE H. STEELE

Cozy Mystery Series

Cate Kensie Mysteries
Lily & Cassie by the Sea Mysteries
Pearl Party Mysteries
Middle Age is Murder Cozy Mysteries

Supernatural Suspense/Urban Fantasy

Shadow Slayers Stories
Duchess of Blackmoore Mysteries

Adventure

Maggie Edwards Adventures
Clif & Ri on the Sea

Made in the USA
Las Vegas, NV
21 September 2022